D1808158

Sniffing Papa

Praise for SNIFFING PAPA

"Where every writer, every person, must begin...Inderjit Badhwar raises a free voice in his first book."

—India Abroad

"An evocative cocktail of shikar, sex and metaphysics. The main strength of this first novel by Inderjit Badhwar is its originality, of both theme and style of writing. A welcome addition to the growing body of Indian contributions to English literature."

—Khushwant Singh

"The book spanning four generations tackles the very pertinent question about the true identity of a person..."

—HINDUSTAN TIMES

"The mother's *puja* room, father's shikari heritage and (the author's) intellectual growth during the anti-Vietnam protests and the music of Bob Dylan and Doors provide the architectural framework for this novel."

—TEHELKA

"An amazing piece of work on may levels. The prose is shimmering, the observations unique and rich, the cultural context is brilliantly done...It's like Naipaul without the unbridled anger and with love. Badhwar has taken the expatriate experience, re-invented it, and turned a Third World novel into a whole world novel. It's very brave. It's wise..."

—LAURENCE LEAMER

"Along with his wealth of experience, Badhwar has drawn consciously upon his exceptionally powerful imagination and sub-consciously upon his breadth of reading."

—THE ASIAN AGE

"Twenty-three years of journalistic experience has helped load the novel with information, insight and vision..."

—THE PIONEER

Sniffing
Papa

Inderjit Badhwar

TARA
press
mass market division

India Research Press
new delhi

Published by

Tara Press
Mass Market Division
India Research Press
B-4/22, Safdarjung Enclave, New Delhi – 110 029.
Ph.: 4694610; Fax : 4618637
e-mail : bahrisons@vsnl.com
2002

ISBN : 81-87943- 33-5

Work of Fictional Writing

Cataloging in Publication Data
INDERJIT BADHWAR
Sniffing Papa
by   Inderjit Badhwar

Includes bibliographical references and index.
1. Fiction - Indian. 2. Novel – Shikar / Hunting. 3. Title.
Inderjit Badhwar

Printed in India by Focus Impressions, New Delhi – 110 003.

India Research Press
B-4/22, Safdarjung Enclave, New Delhi – 110 029
Ph.: 4694610 Fax : 4618637 www.indiaresarchpress.com

Preface

This book is not about people you recognize. It is about those who resemble them. They are, therefore, unknowable. The only reality is the forest which, even after its disappearance, still remains mirrored in the sky.

Part One

Part One

Chapter I

1

Papa, he smelled so good. Outside, in June, the molten winds swirled and the sand dunes swirled with them, rose into baking heavens and descended in yellow palls of dust which flowed into the rooms of our house from the spaces under the solid sheesham wood doors and choked our nostrils. Indoors, we breathed dust and dungmud. Occasionally, when the water coolers which thudded with the rotation of the giant fan blades which threw in cool air that first passed through screens padded with straw or wood-shavings dampened by a circulating water system that poured droplets into the screens, we inhaled the goodly smell of rain on dry ground.

But electric power in Raipur, Uttar Pradesh, was at best a blessing. It was doled out to us at the whims of State Electricity Boards – those state monopolies – and their sadistic, whimsical officials who would switch the power supply off when they ate lunch, slept, played cards, made love or went on wildcat strikes.

Our rooms would hum with heat. The smell of dust – the sky was made of dust, the leaves on our mango trees, caked with it, looked like clods of earth on their branches, the tree trunks and their barks took on shapes of dinosaur scales molded by clay – was everywhere.

In our home – a disorganized four-bedroom rambler with ceilings so high that they could accommodate a studio crane-shoot, a banquet-sized dining room with chandeliers that hung 20 feet above eye level – we had a haven. Papa's room. It was recessed in a corner of the house and played host to almirahs with glass doors, a dressing table with a square mirrors with swivels at both ends enabling the mirror to change angles. Papa's inventions. But his greatest invention which he regarded with special pride was his false ceiling. It was made of quilts stitched end to end and hammered to the roof on all four corners. That it sagged in the middle and might, one day, like Chicken Licken's sky, smother its inventor within its generous folds as he slept on his wooden bed with planks at dead center of the room, mattered not a whit to Papa.

Papa's family rarely questioned this autocrat or his wisdom. But nobody, nobody criticized Papa's inventions – the swimming "tank" which he designed by cutting the earth in the middle of a mango and neem grove into progressively deepening steps, cementing it, and constructing four holding walls around; the leather and canvas shoes of which he lopped off the front ends to give his knotty toes additional wiggling room; the Grundig radio and radio player console – 'radiogram' we called that contraption in the 1950s – that rose majestically to a height of three feet, a strange round box with lids that opened side by side to display a turntable and a radio dial with wooden knobs, which he later converted into a bar; the old pieces of elastic with which he used to encircle the waistbands of his pyjamas to avoid the bother of undoing tangled drawstrings.

Papa the inventor belonged in that crazy room of his. It was our home's sanctum sanctorum. We entered in his absence at our own peril. And we outfoxed Papa in our desire to do so. Large double doors opened into his room from the commodious, oval-shaped drawing room that was home to the radiogram-turned-bar. This was another crazy room with a green and buff nine-by twelve Aubusson rug, high-backed Edwardian chairs, rosewood tables, family photographs of ancestors wearing white gloves and spats. Everything distant from the other. The paintings – two Sudhir Khastagir originals, a half-clad Bengali woman with her Rapunzelesque tresses caught in a westerly breeze, an army of turban-clad tribal drummers – were hung on two opposite walls so near the ceiling that you saw them at the grave risk of getting an attack of spondylitis. Alcoves with Ming vases and fake Edwardian fruitbowls.

A green Edwardian love-seat stood three feet away from the double doors which were the entrance to Papa's false-ceilinged boudoir. The doors had four glass panes at slightly above eye level. But a seizure of privacy had driven Papa one day to paint them black to defy the eyes of prying offspring. Cleverly, though, he had scratched off a little of the black on one of them leaving a peephole about an inch in circumference. Through this, a fatherly eye – or so we imagined – surveyed his creations and inventions in the drawing room from behind a fortress of privacy.

This little peephole was also our bridgehead. Since Papa could leave his room through two other doors that led into office and workshop the peephole door remained closed unless he wished to enter the drawing room or stalk other areas of the house. The only way we could determine whether he was in or out was to use our side of the peephole on the drawing room side. If our surveillance disclosed his absence we barged in. For some reason, he never kept those doors locked.

Later, I was to discover that all five of his offspring – this unbeknownst to one another – were in the habit of making this illegal pilgrimage. Especially on those hot, dusty summer afternoons. Papa's room was a haven from dust and choked nostrils. It was more than that. If we breathed deep enough we smelled Papa. Not Papa, really, but what we thought wafted from some chemical, perhaps, even spiritual pact he had made with the cosmos. Did souls have smells? Soul to us then was nothing but a word uttered by pundits over loudspeakers or at pujas – Atman, Brahman, Triyambakam. But even as novitiate Hindus who imbibed their religious traditions not at any pulpit but through the fractured and hopelessly mismatched vocal chords of Mama on those festivals when she mispronounced and with tuneless determination intoned the *Om Jai Jagdish Hare* invocation to the ONE on Diwali and Dussehra and Janmashtami, her reedy and compassionate voice had the power to distract even Lord Krishna during a bellicose *updesh* to Arjuna, we sensed soul.

2

It emanated from Papa's presence. On Diwali evenings, before the firecrackers were lit, Mama's cracked little vocal chords vibrated and hummed in dissonance. Her family had gathered for the Diwali puja. Wealth Goddess Laxmi was the reigning deity for that pecuniary ritual. It would establish for the family a fiduciary pact with the *devi*. The supplicants, five children, an aunt, and Papa stand hands folded in prayer before the family safe, the interior of which had lost most of its valuables to jewelers whose purchase of the family valuables increased in direct proportion to Papa's steadily declining coffers even as he struggled to keep aristocratic values alive.

So we stand reverently in front of this iron safe which hides within its confines the secret of the vanished wealth of the family that once lorded over factories and laborers and peons dressed in turbans sporting fake silver emblems and khaki pants with latticed cuffs. Mama leads the chant. Seema, 18, high cheek-boned like Papa, her mother's glistening dark eyes, Seema who did not menstruate until her late teens and did not even wear a practice bra until she was 16, giggles. Tips, 16, who looks like Seema except that he has an outsized Adam's Apple and a crew cut, as he lights the wicker lamps and with sadistic impishness flicks hot wax drippings on me, whose arrival in the household, two years after him, was a source of rejoicing in Raipur because two sons had arrived in succession. Then came a third, Tally, again, two years after me, followed by Sara nine years later. Curly-haired, beak-nosed, wild-eyed and with a milky-white skin, Sara could well have fit a description of a Jewish girl right out a Singer novel. Naipaul was dead right. Midnight's Children were given fashionable Westernized names. Horoscopes were prepared for all of them by the family pundits at birth in which their Zodiac signs determined the consonants and vowels with which their names would begin. The family name, at least in the north, remained the same for all successive generations but the first names were horoscopic. If the horoscope decreed that, say, a newborn's first name should begin with a "cha" a boy would be named Chaman, or Chetan. "Sha" for a boy would produce names like Shyam or Shailendra, while a girl would be named Shalini or Sheena. And, so on. Most names came from ancient epics like the *Ramayana* and *Mahabharata* and the *Vedas* – names like Savitri, Usha, Sita, Rama, Shatrughan, Sridevi, Mandakini, Arjun, Malika, Prahlad, Indra, Indrajit.

But Midnight's Children, especially those exposed to Western education, no matter how deeply their families were steeped in traditional rituals and religious beliefs and a faith unbroken for 3,000 years, sported names like Tony, Bobby, Tippy, Sammy, Dennis, Bunny, Bunty. Not all, but many of them. But when Midnight's baby boomers spawned their own children, they reversed the trend and scanned the ancient texts and Hindu versions of the Gemara for names that would be rarer than others – Meenakshi, Vandana, Rahil, Shruti, Meghna, Prerna, Rashib. Papa's children came in all colors – brown-skinned, wheaten, fair, depending on which Indo-European sperm won the race at the moment of conception. I am as dark as Sara is fair.

On this Diwali night, Mama sings. I step on Tally's toe. Tally pinches Sara's bottom. She is oblivious to the undercurrent of the irreverence of her young on this day of Diwali, all celebrating creation with lights and hymns in defiance of atheism. Mama too, seems to burst with light, her witchy voice celebrating these celestial orgies.

Om Jai Jagdish Hare...The children pretend to get serious and lip-read their mother under the stern atheistic gaze of Papa who sports a vermilion *tikka* on his forehead – smudged into shape by Mama who cowers under husbandly machismo for most of the year but rises like a Phoenix from the ashes of wifely docility on Diwali, to put her own badge of courage on the wrinkled and questioning brow of her brow-beating husband.

Pa looks devilishly religious with his smeared forehead and splendidly starched white kurta pyjama suit. The last stanza of the *aarti* and we all sing together... *"Kripa karo deva, Om Jai..."*

3

If you get the idea that there was rootlessness in our family, a sense of anomie, a nagging feeling that we were hung between a world of tradition and a world of rapidly changing technologies, then I've given you the wrong impression. True we were Midnight's Children. True we learned and spoke English better than the King himself. True we were the inheritors of educational, bureaucratic, cultural legacies of the Raj. We inherited snobbery, elitism. We realized we all lived in India in tribes of cultures. We were born in an India of 400 million people, one fifth of mankind, a population that was to double within 40 years. Poverty, mostly poverty of a kind, of urban ghettos, of rural privation, perhaps never witnessed in Europe or America or even Tolstoy's Russia. But there was no guilt. We did not dangle between reason and revolution. We were not agonized by existential dilemmas like the Jews of the pre-World War II diaspora – whether to migrate to the Holy Land under the Palestine Mandate and take up Hebrew, whether to join the Bolsheviks in Russia to create the permanent revolution, whether to remain cloistered in Yiddish speaking pockets in New York, or whether to assimilate with the Gentiles. No, we were not afflicted by the dilemma of the Fabians either, whether to sit in libraries and continue to make the Revolution an esoteric exercise and indulge in theories of Sovereignty from Hobbes to Bentham and Laski or cut the bullshit and get on the right sides of the barricades with the masses. Nor did we torment ourselves like European intellectuals about which side to join during the Spanish Civil War.

I mean, social historians may legitimately ask, weren't you torn between two cultures, several languages, the need to emulate Gandhian renunciation and bourgeois acquisitiveness and conspicuous consumption, to become the vanguard for the workers and peasants to reorder the political structure that was a British hand-me-down of constitutional legalisms? There was no dilemma either invented or promulgated by the dictators of social conscience anywhere in the world that did not stare us in the face and threaten to drive us crazy. We were Veblen's Leisure Class. We were the Marxist-Leninist historical garbage that belongs in history's dustbins. We were the Indian Left's lickspittle of neocolonialism and neo-imperialism. To India's populists and ultra nationalists we were the exponents of a corrupt Urban Culture who scoffed at their own roots.

We stood guilty as charged. At least Papa did. And frankly, he didn't give a damned rat's ass. He had read Spinoza when young. He had armed himself with Churchill's volumes on the Second Great War. Trevelyan's *Social History* lay dog-eared on his bookshelf from the very first page on the analysis of Chaucer's age and the influence of the French on Anglo Saxon culture.

The feast of green coriander and bitter gourds and *moong dal* and mustard greens with dollops of white home-churned butter served at the table over which he presided in formal coat and tie would at his command the next day turn into a banquet of partridge cooked in sherry, garlic and Worcestershire sauce. Cauliflower with white gravy, fricasseed chicken served with roasted potatoes and carrots topped with parsley, French onion soup, steak and onions, baked fish, deviled eggs, Russian salad with home-made mayonnaise, caramel custard, fudge brownies. These table habits have become part of family memory, along with Papa's letters of admonishment and advice to his family –stand straight, develop character, tolerate others, learn not to hate, be compassionate, respect precision in language, be charitable, do what is just, respect knowledge, adore books, respect eclecticism, believe in the rule of law, get married and bolster your husband's career, learn how to wield a rifle and shotgun. Don't shoot at a sitting duck or partridge. If you cannot allow yourself not to believe in, then at least doubt God.

Chapter II

1

Godless Papa did not inherit his atheism from Marxist literature. He considered Communists boorish. He lumped them with soothsayers, mendicants, fortune tellers, wandering sadhus, fake holy men and the assorted conmen and mahatmas who promised redemption, religious nirvana, a better tomorrow in the name of Hinduism, fooled women into accepting gurus. His concerns were more erudite. In those rare moments when he would care to explain himself he would tell his friends that he admired those aristocratic Gentiles in Arthur Miller's *Incident at Vichy* who had the courage to surrender themselves to the Nazis in order to protect Jews. We were later to learn that during India's post-partition riots in which Hindus and Muslims slaughtered each other in their hundreds of thousands over the creation of the separate countries of India and Pakistan, Papa who detested religious states and Jinnah's vision of Pakistan as much as he distrusted Hindu rituals, for more than a month hid a Muslim friend, a Razakar (Muslims involved in planting bombs and blowing up trains in India for the Pakistani cause) in his private bathroom. Later, when people asked Papa repeatedly why he had taken the risk, Papa's only reply was: "He was a friend." The friend ultimately chose to remain in India with 50 million other Muslims who, 50 years later, doubled in size making India a country with the second largest Muslim population in the world.

In school, the siblings, at whatever age, learned the sentimental, humanistic songs of Tagore, of Nanak, of Kabir. I fell in love with Siya Ram Sharan Gupt's *Ek Phool Ki Chhah*. The story of an untouchable lower caste Hindu, set in verse, whose little daughter lies on her deathbed. Her dying wish is that her father bring her a rose offered to a goddess in a temple. The father rushes there oblivious that he is an untouchable and will be denied entry by the Brahmins. He disguises himself. Wears a caste mark *tilak* on his forehead – just like Papa on those Diwali pujas at home – wears starched white clothes and rushes to the temple to pick up a rose. He is recognized by the head priest. Thrashed soundly for breaking the caste barrier. Half-conscious as he is evicted from the premise, he hangs on to a single rose petal. When he regains consciousness he remembers his mission. Rushes home to find his child had waited, died, and had been taken to the cremation ground. There she lies, the flames engulfing her, her father in breathless agony reaches the pyre and just before she turns to cinders throws the petal on to her ash-turning little body. *Ek Phool Ki Chhah*. We read others. Subadhra Kumari Chauhan, *Thukra Do Ya Pyar Karo* – Love me or Leave me – never knowing whether it was addressed to God or her Lover; Mahadevi Verma,

14

Nirala and his brilliant descriptions of working women breaking stones for building material in 110 degree Fahrenheit temperatures, Maithili Sharan Gupt who brought small portions of the Ramayana, especially Rama's exile to poetic life perhaps even more evocatively than the original Sanskrit authors.

And dammit there was the most wondrous sound of all. Indian film music. Which child, growing up in the fifties did not know how to hum Sehgal's *Kya Maine Kiya Hai*, Atma's *Priyatam Aan Milo*, the love songs of Raj Kapoor's *Awara* and *Chori Chori* which became hits in the Soviet Union and the Middle East.They were not oldies then. They were live. They were happening. Even today's children hum these Bombay melodies and can recall them more readily than what was on yesterday's V-Channel pop charts. We mixed everything. Metaphors, philosophies, music, nursery rhymes, Victor Sylvester and his ballroom orchestra (Papa loved to fox-trot and tango and often dragged a petrified Mama onto the dance floor, once even with a rose stem clenched in his teeth), Fred Astaire and Ginger Rogers, Benny Goodman Stompin' at the Savoy, Sachmo and Ella, Bhim Sen Joshi and Bismillah Khan. Nothing was incongruous.

2

Sexually, during the years at college in the United States and the U.K. where many of my friends and I journeyed for Masters degrees in the sixties, these admixtures proved to be the most powerful politically correct formulas for seduction. First, we were Hindus, already sexually and erotically exotic thanks to translations of the *Kama Sutra* and power given our sensual prowess by E.M. Forster. Second, we were THIRD WORLD. Thanks to Allen Ginzberg, Jerry Rubin, Abbie Hoffman, Danny the Red, James Reston, Third World was *in*, even for Indians of feudal origin studying abroad, especially in the Vietnam protest era. From India's engineering colleges and institutions of the liberal arts, they had fanned out into Oxbridge, the London School of Economics, Ivy League schools in the U.S. I was a Leftist then. A Trotskyite who later ditched him for Karl Kautsky and Rosa Luxemburg. So were many of my Indian friends. For an Indian who could recite Dylan Thomas's *Under Milk Wood* with the same ease that he could sing Bob Dylan and Mississipi John Hurt, while explaining the war maneuvers of General Giapp and the French debacle at Dien Ben Phu, while boasting of personal letters we had received from fellow Third-Worlders Fidel and Che, was sexually irresistible to blonde WASP maidens who found in our simultaneous boasting of our knowledge of ancient Indian rope tricks, fantasies of Oriental tumescent longevity before which male Boston Brahmins paled in flaccid comparison. We Hindu lovers of these Eastern shore beauties were politically correct on another ground: as true Brahmins we regarded the workers of America as redneck reactionaries who should be given courses in Joan Baez in order to wean them away from Loretta Lynn. When we took them out to pizza parlors we decried American consumption with every delicious mouthful of Mozzarella, and when we went shopping in the arcades we bought out entire counters of after-shave lotions while denouncing American decadence at the pay counters. For this they loved us even more. Many of us were later to take back these values to Indian schools like Delhi's Jawaharlal Nehru University and teach post-Marxism Indian students the values of denouncing progressive decadence.

That we often failed to live up to the promises of rope trick intercourse did not matter. Premature ejaculation was attributed to the mental distraction caused by a sudden sequel that we had thought of – during the love-making – to add to the works of Herbert Marcuse. In England we charmed the maidens with our Oxford accents. But that was nothing compared to the sexual hunger we aroused in them when punting on the Thames we burst into, *I'll Sing You One Ho, Green Grow the Rushes Ho*; or *Where Are you Going to My Pretty Maid*; or *On Richmond Hill There Lives A Lass*; or *Row my Nutbrown Maiden*; or *A Partidge in a Pear Tree*. English, even Scottish folk songs and ditties we were taught in Indian prep schools at age five. We hated learning them then. But little did we know that music teacher Ms Cox was preparing us for seductions 20 years later in her own home country. Our nutbrown maidens and English prettymaids were bowled over by these Olde English serenades by youths from a bygone colonial era. "You are the truest Englishman of all," she remarked as she fell swooning on to my Hindu bosom.

17

But these are memories of the future. That Diwali night, as Papa looked devilish in his starched kurta pyjama suit we finished the last stanza of the *aarti* with seriousness. "*Kripa Karo Deva...*" The crackers burst outside. Rama is returning to his lost kingdom after 14 years in exile with his beloved wife Sita recently rescued from Ravana, King of Sri Lanka, the world's most powerful and relentless kidnapper whose empire has been reduced to ashes by fires set by Rama's brigade of monkey warriors led by Hanuman the Hindu deity of faithfulness and fearlessness in whose name the Hanuman Chalisa – a poem which, if repeated daily, vanquishes all fear from within the heart of individuals – we still recite at condolence ceremonies for the families of the dead.

The crackers burst in the air, on the ground in multiples of explosions, the *anaars* whoosh into the sky in myriads of gushing, fiery colors, and Papa, the prayers over, wants to head for the booze cabinet so he can watch the sky with a little Scotch or Vodka behind his eyeballs. I remain glued to the candles. In the melting wax I smell Papa. Today, he is wearing Old Spice, that old after-shave cologne that college kids from St Stephen's College established by the Cambridge Mission in Old Delhi in the 19th Century, bought in the early sixties from smugglers' markets in Kamlanagar, the neighborhood university bazaar.

Papa was made of perfumes. Part of me wanted to go outdoors and inhale the sulphur and the acrid fumes, the pungent smell of Diwali. The throat-choking, eye-piercing clouds of fireworks smog. This was October. The end of summerdust. That dust and haze that clogged our lungs and drove us from afternoon summer smells into Papa's crazy room. Diwali, you went out and sneezed and lit crackers while Papa sat on a wicker chair and nursed his drink, now that the prayer ceremony was over and Mama had mischievously surrendered her power over him to the deity who would reinvest it in her when the next religious festival arrived.

Mama was enveloped in the aromas of the ritual incense. Seema, Tips, Tally and Sara smelled of firecrackers as they pranced under the night skies in the front lawn. Papa, he smelled so good. Old Spice? Heck. Seize the moment No more looking through the peephole in the glass pane of his door to his boudoir. March right in. Into the land of the perfumes of Arabia. Diwali nights were special to me. Because under the ruse of doing an additional puja in Mama's little puja room where Jesus and Krishna and Nanak smiled with benedictory beneficence from framed portraits balanced against the walls surrounding three sides of a raised wooden platform – Mama's altar – I would sneak, unmolested by the eldest boy of the brood into the chamber of perfumes.

The same room that defied the malodorous days of the shit-carrying winds which picked up the putrefying stench of India's clogged, open sewers, also barricaded itself from the intrusion of the acrid, semi-toxic smoke of

Diwali fireworks. Olfactory privacy. What joy. What wanton sensuality. A beloved perversion for which El Sigmundo had no imagination or clinical experience to invent a psychosis, a neurosis. A fetish without an adjective. Later, I would give it a name: Nasal Compulsive.

How long I had done this I cannot remember. Even as a six-year-old, well before little Sara was born, I had sneaked into Papa's fragrant space. If I could have bottled that air with some sleight of alchemy, I would ruminate later, surely I could have offered little whiffs of it as an antidote to Nazi gas chambers. Eat Shit, Hitler! Turn on your damned taps of venomous vapors. Because your victims have already sniffed from little bottles of Papa's elixir. They'll breathe deeply of your noxious fumes, then march out and step all over those heel-clicking, goose-stepping goons. But in Papa's room, you really did not need to sniff or inhale. The fragrance entered us through osmosis, as if through the pores, nostrils, hair. In fact, sometimes you had to stop breathing in order to savor the fragrance, just like you have to keep absolutely still to hear a sound. The senses perceive. The ear does not listen. The nose does not smell. The fragrance simply wafts. Perhaps in that room there were silent tornadoes and twisters of aromas. How do you describe a fragrance. Well, Papa used Yardleys, Cuticura powder with lavender. There was Silkvikrin hair dressing. The combs, the brushes – ellipsoidal or oblong structures without handles, about the size of my palms whose bristles smelled of Brylcream and perfumed Vaseline hair tonic. But here, there was no hint of the odors of a perfumed dandy. No these were manly smells. The after-shaves and body colognes depended on what world manufacturers were producing or what was new at Marks and Spencers.

Papa's inventive table was adorned at various times with bottles of Evening in Paris, Aqua Velva (I once pronounced it "vulva" as a joke and was immediately admonished by Papa who did not believe in lewd liberties from his children) with its lemony appeal, Versace Pour Hommes, Harvard for Men, objets de parfum from everywhere. The chest of drawers had the mysteries of Listerine and Dettol and Vitalis hair conditioner into all of which had insinuated itself the odors of grease with which he rubbed his .38 Smith and Wesson revolver, cleaning fluids for guns, Three-in-One oil for his gadgetry, mosquito-repelling smoke-throwers, the lingering smell of hair-oil on pith helmets or solar *topees* –those jungle-proof, wide-brimmed, low-domed hats worn by Hollywood heroes on safaris for warding off tree monsters from attacking Deborah Kerr. I wondered, once when watching *African Queen*, whether the pith helmets on the heads of Hollywood heroes smelled like Papa's.

I was six, seven, eight, nine. Dammit, would it be the same when I got into my fifties? Papa's brushes. Grease. Jungle hats. Semi-soaked false ceiling in the Monsoons. Black and White Scotch, Dewars, Haig, Bombay gin. An assortment of liqueurs locked in a bottom cupboard. Booze, grease, compressed gas from the Frigidaire air conditioner. Arabian perfumes. The steely smell of rusty keys to closets that never shut. No one dared fart in that room.

21

Chapter III

1

I was to discover, later, in my forties, that I was not the only one to sneak into that room. Seema, Tips, Tally, Sara and, much later, even grandchildren also undertook that pilgrimage. I overheard a conversation between my son, Godot, and his cousins. This was some years before Papa prostrated his body before the God he never believed in and simply refused to live. He had gone hunting that day, aquiline-nosed, eagle-eyed and armed with a Holland & Holland .12 gauge shotgun. The Shikari who believed in conservation but not conservationists because he felt conservationists killed their meat the easy way in slaughterhouses with electric prods and throat-slitting knives, and boiling water into which they dunked living foul.

The conversation between the grandchildren (ages 7 to 12 years):

Akhila: Dada's room smells of partridge feathers. I hate hunters.

23

Godot: But I want to shoot just like him.

Meghna: Killers all of you. How would you like it if you were a quail and flew out a bush and a hundred pellets hit your tail and you had eggs inside you?

Godot: I'd love it if they hit my neck.

Sumita: Just sadists. Just like Dada.

Neha: Wait, here's an empty shell. Smell it. Smells good.

Meghna: It smells of Diwali. Probably the one Pa fired yesterday.

Godot: Yeah, and you ate what it killed.

Meghna: Shut up, asshole.

Sumita: Hey look, the dressing table. Let's smell all.

The third generation also had this olfactory infatuation. The pacifists, shikaris, would-be poets attacked Papa's dressing table. They sniffed within the drawers, uncapped cans of Dreamflower talcum powder, uncapped and re-capped after-shave lotions. I came in just then.

"What are you doing in here?"

"Just playing hide-and-seek."

"We lost our way."

"Tell me the truth."

24

"We tried to smell him, to find him."

"But he's not here."

"We tried."

"Through his talcs and after-shaves?"

"But they're not like every other ones. They're the best."

"Did you (wink wink) look at his *Playboy* magazines?"

"Nooooo."

I had to try that line. For long ago I thought I'd figured out, or so I thought, that the blackened windows on Papa's doors were to discourage his brood from discovering he had a clandestine admiration for Hugh Heffner's Bunnies. Perhaps. Or perhaps he performed secret rituals of aromatic alchemy that he wanted to keep as private as possible.

"Out kids, out."

"Yeah but Dada's room doesn't smell like it really smells when he's here or nearby."

"Who told you my Papa smells?"

"We smell him on you, on *chacha*, on *taya*, on *bua*, on *chachi*, on *massi*."

"What?"

25

"You told us."

"What?"

"Monsoon, dust, incense, joss sticks, saffron, curry powder, turmeric, coriander, dill."

"Sure. Parsley, Sage, Rosemary and Thyme."

"Children of hell," I said. "Go. King Solomon carries his mines within his heart not in his dresser. I know this is a terribly mixed metaphor, but nothing cogent comes to mind except unsolved mysteries and contradictions. But it well may be that Papa is not the product of manufactured perfumes. He is the manufacturer himself."

2

Who understood? Not even I. The words made no sense. Only music. On that same February evening the great Shikari of the scrub forest, hunter of black partridge, teal, widgeon, pintail, grouse, fan-tailed snipe, gadwall ducks, greylag and pinkfoot geese walked in to see two generations he had spawned cowering in his false-ceilinged hunter's cave.

He had hunted nothing. The geese had begun to honk a mile before they smelled his presence. The teal had taken flight way out of shotgun range. In the afternoon, the snipe from the harvested paddy fields still knee deep with the previous year's Monsoon water, had zigzagged away a hundred feet before his approach. And even the imperial sandgrouse, it seemed, had risen and slipped into the slipstream of the miles-high circling vultures.

Papa entered dressed in khaki fatigues, his Australian jungle hat perched at the back of his bead, his Hunter shoes unlaced. Dried salt of sweat caked his brow. A filth-bedraggled wretch of a shikari, smelling of ditches putrid with stale moss, green stink-bugs stuck to his waistband, his breath full of stale, cold tea. The smell of a defeated shikari. He wanted to undo his boots. When he sat down on his bed and began to loosen them it was it was the signal for us to get out.

We left him alone for a while because we knew that he would sit under that sagging quilted ceiling and make up the most wondrous stories about "the one that got away." That idiot of a bird-picker who had refused to see that brilliant left-and-right shot with Number Four shells. But right now, for that Shikari who at this moment of writing is probably tip-toeing after buxom angels in the sky or, God forbid, stalking the Almighty Himself, with a John Wayne Special – a 32/40 hunting rifle – the post-shikar bath was as important as the shikar itself.

No one, but no one dared enter his chambers during this moment of ablution. His bathtub overflowed with scalding water. Pears soap. Yardleys. Scented suds. Bathroom slippers powdered to dry his toes instantly. The steam from the bath rising like vapors from mountain valleys. The mirror over the sink clouding over, wiped with a towel to ensure that Papa's acquiline nose still held its unique distinctiveness.

Trumpets should have flourished when post-bath Papa in his pyjama suit and smoking jacket entered his quilted bedroom. We knew it. It was as if a gong had sounded. And the family, on these occasions found the door to his room open. The doors ajar, the music from the radiogram (before it became a bar in the early sixties), blared. Radio Ceylon (now Sri Lanka) commercial service. The Binaca toothpaste hit parade of Hindi film songs and American pop. Lata Mangeshkar and Pat Boone. Geeta Dutt and the Shirelles. Mohammed Rafi and Frankie Avalon. And the family was allowed in.

Papa, or whoever or whatever it was that smelled, never smelled better. Music was in the air. Good Scotch. And Papa smoothens his Valentino hairwaves and blows smoke rings from Three Castle, and 999 cigarettes drawn from within monogrammed silver cigarette cases, into the mirror with an eyebrow raised in disbelief at his own image, while the wife and brood – no grandchildren yet – sit and joke until the yogurt-marinated *masala* lamb chops and fried okra are announced by the pot-bellied chef who always cooks while naked to the waist with pearl drops of perspiration collecting into his bomb-crater of a belly-button. In these moments and the moments which preceded these moments we all breathed ourselves. Aromatic meditation. Papa had turned the magic on. We all smelled of Papa who smelled so good.

Like all of us reading the same book in absolute silence. Papa the narcissist had surrendered his image to the waters and the water rippled into waves of sharing, enveloping all who dared look into them, not suffocating but enveloping, caressing.

Was I six, seven, eleven, fifteen? And we carried the perfumes out with us and on to the dining table where they mixed with the warm wheat steam odors of puffed *chapattis*, peppered slices of tomatoes sprinkled with the fresh juice of lemons, lemon-topped cucumbers, lentil soup sizzling with whole cumin seeds fried in butter, sauted cauliflower, yogurt sauce sprinkled with freshly ground cumin powder. It all tasted just fresh and fine while Papa munched and crunched the fresh cucumbers with an audible movement of his jaws. When he left the table, rudely, suddenly, driven by a desire to shit, or read, or sleep, the food still tasted good, but those special odors were gone. He took them away. And when he slept in his room, the devil, he kept them stashed away, like a genie in a bottle. Perhaps secretly and selectively to be opened only for Mama and their love-making when on days they designated by sign language known only to them she would sneak into his false-ceilinged boudoir from her own in a distant corner of the house while the rest of the household slumbered.

Chapter IV

1

Outside was the world of Raipur. Main Street. Housing facades. Pedestrians in dhotis and pyjamas and jeans and sneakers and leather sandals, armed with wooden staves. Bullock carts, earlier with wooden wheels but in the late seventies with tyres (the carts were accordingly renamed 'Dunlops'), black Hercules bicycles, Lambretta and Bajaj scooters, pavements and sand and melting tar with the drains, the ubiquitous, stinking open, clogged drains on all sides in which huge mosquitoes laid huge eggs. They multiplied, it seems, without any controlling life cycle to limit their growth. They penetrated mosquito nets and even blue jeans and attacked Papa's children and grandchildren in their cradles.

Papa's home was like a fortress that kept most of Raipur out of its confines. We allowed the residents free access into the compound but kept the city or town or pseudo town out. Our rambler was fortified on three acres of land by a nine-foot tall encircling wall topped with shrapnels of glass wedged in cement to keep Rhesus monkeys at bay. Later the fortification – when crime increased – would act as a deterrent to criminals.

The town outside was a congeries of narrow lanes, bylanes, alleys housing a 20,000 strong population. *Halwais*, moneylenders, cloth merchants, roadside kebab vendors, cyclerickshaw pullers, roadside barbers with rusty instruments, cotton candy sellers, pantomime artists, hermaphrodites, flies, cockroaches, dragonflies in summer, giant moths and winged ants in the Monsoon when lizards appeared from hibernation in every household and scurried about catching their prey upside down on the ceilings of every house and hovel. Yellow wasps hovering over snowhite mounds of *bataashas* – little sugar puffs – and never stinging. Pot-bellied Punjabi refugees from post-Partition Lahore and Multan and Gujranwala who had fled these cities of their ancestors when they became part of Pakistan in 1947 carrying their babies on their backs and their belongings in little sacks. Here they had settled to begin life anew and had within a decade transformed themselves into local moneylenders and cloth merchants, set up temples to Vishnu and Shiva and Ganesha. Sattan Mian, who had never made up his mind between migrating to Pakistan as a true believer in Jinnah's Two-Nation theory or Nehru's Secularist ideals, but had chosen, nonetheless, along with thousands of other Muslims to remain in Raipur once ruled by Muslim dynasties. Sattan, the proud owner of two brick kilns whose short and stout chimneys spat out black coal and wood smoke onto the golden mustard and wheat fields.

He would recite freely from Iqbal and Ghalib and the Holy Qoran. But despite the fiercely egalitarian philosophy of the Holy Book, Sattan, like many of his peers had Indianized his social beliefs. He too, espoused views of caste divisions ostensibly the preserve of Hinduism. He liked it to be known that he was a high-caste Syyed Muslim as were the Pathans. The lower castes were the Julahas, a weaving community; Quereshis, the butcher trade, who were also expert horticulturists and made a living on the side by taking mango orchards on hire; Gaddis, the cattle herders. And they rarely intermarried. Marriages, as among the Hindus, were still mostly arranged. In fact, if a bride or groom of a suitable caste could not be found in Raipur or for that matter, India, matchmakers would travel to Pakistan to arrange the *rishta*. Sattan's friend Yamin the kitemaker selling his pre-monsoon wizardry which took to the skies like giant multi-colored bats out of hell just before the hot westerlies changed into humid eastern winds after the breezes that had sipped generously from the Arabian Sea traveled across the Indian peninsula, drank again from the Bay of Bengal and bounced around until they found their way into the skies of Raipur.

Beneath were the cemented sidewalks, alleys so narrow that a single buffalo could block a 1948 model Super Eight Buick (in the fifties there were still a couple of these sedans in town) an Ambassador, a Fiat and in the eighties even the small Suzukis that began plying the streets. Drains clogged with mulch and shit and cowdung, the powerful sulphuric acid and ammonia-like stench of the bodies of unwashed human weight-carriers. Lice-infested Raipur where, at 5 a.m. winter or summer, the residents sauntered out into the streets in their lungis sucking and chewing on neem twigs to disinfect their gums and teeth in which stuck particles of lentils, leavened bread, spiced potatoes, raw onions, of their standard dinner. Kids shitting on the sides of the streets because the bath-houses built by Indian ruling dynasties in Delhi and Agra and Mysore and Jaipur and Gwalior were alien to the culture of Raipur.

On Saturdays, Raipur's population swelled to 25,000. The extra 5,000 came from the villages, hundreds of which surrounded Raipur. For outside the circumference of Raipur were umbras and penumbras of sandy-yellow brown and green prairieland. Wheat and carpets of saffron, and gold mustard, and sugarcane forests in winter, paddy and pulses and bajra in summer. Their cultivators were tribes of Muraos, and Jatavas and Lodhas, as ancient as India herself, not described in any anthropological details in the scriptures, vocational hierarchies of castes and tribes, inbreeding, distrustful of other castes, uniting during state and general elections into familiar groups to back candidates of their own castes against competing castes for political power and patronage. Living in mud huts barely rising above the ground, electricity — in my youth and middle age still a distant dream — their fields, their mass toilets. Not even hygienic ditches for fecal ablution established in Mao's China in the fifties. Beatific drudgery beginning at sunrise and not ending at sunset when the heat and mosquitoes invaded

34

their leathery brown bodies and winter pierced their soles and souls. The only warmth, the only solace in these winters and summers of stoic discontent were the herds of buffaloes. Their tails swatted flies in the summers and their impregnated girths radiated warmth in the winters when they slept inside the huts and hovels. All year round their dung – dung is never shit because it is nothing but a mass of compressed grass and fodder – provided fuel for cooking, for warmth, for fire for the raw tobacco in the hookah bowls.

2

The rural sweat, the sight of stoic eyes, the smell of labor came to Raipur on Saturdays when its population swelled by 5,000. Market days, when the peasants walked as many as 15 miles with their earthgoods to the city. City? Heck, Raipur was a city only in the sense that it was atmospherically walled off from the tribulations of the surrounding villages in the same way that Papa's chamber cloistered us from invasions of relativity and reality.

On market days – bazaar – the villagers, vests, dhotis, dirty pyjamas, giant mufflers in winters, wicker baskets, rotting teeth, putrid genitals, tired bullocks pulling creaky carts, kestrels and kites swooping down on little silver fish trapped in makeshift nets in fetid swamps, villagers squatting alongside brick-coated streets screaming their prices down down down until dusk and dust and the thought of a homeward journey in the darkness killed their competitive and commercial resolve and they parted with the last turnip for anything a buyer would offer. Now the kerosene lanterns glowed everywhere. When these lamps did not light in their thousands in the dusk outside it signaled the arrival of the Monsoon.

Monsoon nimbus formations tell the summer skies their days are over. It's all thunder. Boom. Boom. Boom. Shalambang. Crakthatthat. Raindrops like curtains of dew. Dewdrops like sprinkles of a bath showerhead. Then raindrops like snowless snowdrops, sheets of mist hardening like spikes when they pierce the earth which seems to bubble like oil in a hot frying pan. A tumult of earth and sky.

Mad Monsoon used to drive Papa crazier than a loon. He welcomed this perspiration of the sky as a grand relief from the incessant body perspiration that preceded the Monsoon cloudbursts for six weeks making us into a mass of walking, sleeping steambaths. He raised a nasty eyebrow at anybody who dared to mistake the pre-Monsoon showers of May for the real thing. And when the real thing came, recognized by the horizon-to-horizon blue-black ink cloud formations, and the croaking of bullfrogs, the birth of millions of winged ants, he would run out to the front lawn in his shorts and invite us to suck on mangoes while the rain drenched us as we stood in ankle-deep rainwater and we would pile into an open jeep in the rain and drive into the scrub forests and listen to it patter on the broad *dhak* leaves and on the sturdy jamun trees. Hunting, he forbade. This was the breeding and laying season. Partridges, lapwings, weaver birds, the crow-pheasants, grey hornbills, stone curlews, mynahs, doves, bulbuls had mated and were with eggs. The nests were ready. The crows would lay eggs of bluish hues spotted with black, little pearl white doves eggs, Easter-egg sized white vulture eggs, curlew eggs with their buff and black camouflage because they were laid on the ground in areas near railroad tracks surrounded by coal ash dropped by steam engines.

With each successive Monsoon the memory of the past one usually receded – when did it rain? Was the Monsoon late last year? Is it more comfortable during the Monsoon than during the dry hot summer? When did the heaviest showers come? Did the season last the full three or four months? Which parts of the country did it hit first? Was July drier than August, than June? Were the meteorological projections carried in the papers with headlines like, "Monsoon Plays Truant," or "Met Predicts Late Onset, Paddy Crop to be Hurt," accurate? We debated endlessly and nobody won because there was no real record anywhere. That a solution lay to this dilemma of Monsoon memory – at least in 1995 – in Papa's diary I was to chance upon some years later. I discovered that Papa had kept what he called a "Rain Diary" in which he kept track of the Monsoon from June till September 1995. He had done some traveling then in and around Punjab, Delhi, the Himalayan foothills in the old Amdassador car of his:

"June 7-29th – rained heavily in Dehra Dun and Mussoorie. June 15-29: Monsoon hits Kasauli in the Simla hills, Chandigarh on 26th, Delhi had first real cloudburst on June 26. July 1-7: Hot, muggy, not a drop of rain. Clouds up every night some drizzles. July 7: Cloudburst in Delhi 3-6p.m. flooding entire city, cars stranded all over. July 7-22: Cloudy all day, intermittent showers, with two all- night showers. July 22-August 5: Monsoon recedes. Blue sky. The most uncomfortable part of the year. Unbelievable humidity and depression. August 12 –16: Clear, hot sky, no sign of clouds. August 16 evening: high hazy Stratus skies, pressure and humidity building up again. August 21: after several days of clear blue hot skies again, Cumulus, white fluffs build up around noon. August 28-30: fishbone Cirrus clouds all over the sky. Shows impending weather change. September 2-4: Real banks of Monsoon clouds. September 4-10: Rain, rain rain. All day. Three hours. All night. Thunder. Continuous moderate drizzles, cool breezes, azure skies…"

When not on the road, Papa watched the Monsoon quietly from his office window. It was the thrill of God for him, and during those months he would rarely use the chamber of perfumes. It was then ours. Because I had no idea until I was in my mid-twenties when most of his children had moved out of Raipur but would visit regularly – that my brothers and sisters thought it was theirs, too. Exclusively.

Dilemma. We had learned to love the Monsoon and its fickle behavior. Giver of life in an India on which crops and farming – the livelihood of 80 per cent of her people depended on the rain. Soul of the paddy crop. Lentils. Reliever of infernal heat. Re-charger of underground water. God giving us back our Ganges in sprinkles. The miracle of wetness descending on us from 10,000 feet above. Even from these divine manifestations we still had the compulsion of retreating into Papa's chamber.

While Papa watched the Gods create son et lumiere in the sky, just as he used to the Diwali fireworks, I would sneak back into his chamber. Now there was nothing to run away from. The Monsoon smelled of the skies. The mango trees were bursting with green, having recently shed most of their pear-shaped fruit-scented Dussheris, tangy Langras, sweet, sour, honey-flavored, jasmine-scented local varieties. You don't run away from this for a whiff of Harvard for Men or a Fa underarm smell. The reason for this retreat, it would somehow flash upon some inward eye was the bliss of breathing in EVERYTHING in solitude. Nice, convenient intellectual reasoning I suppose. But what really mattered was that I was there, emptied of mind, emptied of waves of thought, emptied of having to think.

Chapter V

1

Our fortress within a fortress has now been around for 70 years. Papa and Papa's smells had been born here. The family's recent history was rooted in Punjab, the fabled battleground where Alexander's cavalry had outmaneuvered King Porus' elephant divisions in 327 B.C. Where Huns, Scythians, Parthians, Macedonian Greeks settled, intermarried and produced generations of fair-complexioned, beak-nosed Punjabis. Papa's nose, even though described as semetically splendid had its origin not in Jacob but in the procreative powers of some Alexandrian general.

Here the ancestors had settled, fought wars, fornicated and spoken in tongues of Sanskrit-Indo-European grammar and vocabulary, sprinkled all of it with local dialects and patois. And they had produced the Punjabi language rich with onomatopoeic words derived from the sounds of herding cattle, calling out to lost cows, threshing wheat, listening to whooshing Monsoon sounds, the clashing of swords, and wrestling bodies.

This language gradually armed itself with harsh pejoratives and violently pronounced obscenities which even to a foreign, uncomprehending ear conveyed nearly the exact meaning of the spiteful utterances. As effective a verbal truncheon as can be imagined. They are still in use and in fact have become the *lingua franca* of Indian oral chastisement. A country with more than a dozen distinct languages and a thousand dialects has Punjabi to thank for its unity in scatology. Over the years Punjabi invective has been honed, sharpened and coarsened.

Sonofabitch and motherfucker, well, these are Mills & Boon stuff compared to Punjabi invective which is spat out through clenched teeth, tightly compressed lips in which the P's, M's and B's sound like bursts of Uzi fire. These cusswords endow their victims' mothers and sisters with male genitalia – the specific name given to the genital drawn from a lexicon of genital christenings depending on the mood of the verbal attacker; put hexes on the privates of mothers and sisters; condemn female relatives to incest and animal coitus. The predicate in these abusive orgies, true to universal male prerogative, is always the female.

It was in 1898, to a torrent of such abuse that the white Cockney factory inspector fell prey on a freezing morning in Ferozepur, Punjab. By then Papa's grandparents had switched from the more manly pursuits of agriculture, to running factories. Their livelihood had become part of the cycle of what anti-imperialist historians called the Economic Drain. Pre-World War I India was still the jewel in the British Crown. Her Maharajas who had signed treaties with the British, and feudal landowners on whom the British had endowed satrapies of land that produced Crown revenues, rolled in sumptuous jewels, while recent millocrats, like Papa's grandparents ran cotton ginning and spinning and weaving mills which produced raw material at slave rates for the mighty manufacturing towns of Lancashire and Manchester.

The Brits, egalitarian to a fault, insisted that India share equally in their vast treasure of bureaucracy and corruption. The Factory Acts which applied in Britain to British industry also applied to the colonies. The acts required that factories comply with requisite labor laws, safety standards and so on. Armies of inspectors were created to ensure compliance. Defaulting factories were "failed" by these inspectors and shut down until regulatory satisfaction was guaranteed.

It was in the pursuit of this humanitarian chore that the Cockney gentleman – a man named Smithers – had sailed from London to the port of Bombay and journeyed on India's vast steam-driven railroad system to Punjab. "Passing" a factory in India was not just a question of worker wages having been paid on time, or the engine room not emitting noxious fumes. Those were minor details. The real test was what the industry called the "weight factor."

When the inspector arrived at a factory – "mills" we called them – he made a bee-line for the *khajanchi's* (accountant) office and hung his overcoat with outsized

43

pockets on a strategically-positioned wooden coat rack, usually opposite the money vault. While the inspector did his rounds, the *khajanchi* would quietly open the safe, withdraw from it fistfuls of silver rupee coins and stuff the pockets of the hanging overcoat. Small wonder that winter inspections were *de rigeur*. Back from his travails in the mill compound, the inspector would head for his overcoat, weigh it with both hands holding it by the scruff of the collar, and if the value-addition to the weight, measured by the new loot in the pockets satisfied him, he would smile and put on his coat. That was the signal that he had "passed" the factory. A downward movement of the inspector's lips was a signal that a few more coins needed to be added to the deepening pockets. In his absence, of course. So he would stroll out for a while, giving the *khajanchi* a little more time to dip into the till.

But on that fateful Ferozepur winter morning Grandpa happened to be in the *khajanchi's* office. He hated inspectors, not only because they were troublesome petty bureaucrats and jingled his coins in their pockets, but also because he hated Cockneys who wore their racism on their sleeves. Perhaps a more compelling source of this aversion was Grandpa's own prejudices. Being a chaste Punjabi upper caste Hindu, he considered Cockneys lower caste Englishmen to be treated with appropriate casteist disdain.

As a millocrat Grandpa milled with British aristocrats at their soirees and and "at homes" where even to his Punjabi ear "propah" sounded like a "propah" upper

44

caste utterance. To this discerning ear "okhai mayet" which, according to his aural training sounded nothing like "okay mate," reverberated like the cheeky and indecorous prattle of a lower-caste Limey hick. In addition to his Hindi and Punjabi, Grandpa spoke a smooth English. Simple. Direct. With few conjunctions and clauses or sub clauses. Lots of active verbs. Universally comprehensible to the world.

2

Papa had inherited his father's biases for sound. For him the music and intonation and cadence of dialects were only of academic interest. During his sojourn in England where he was called to the Bar at the Inns of Court and practiced law in London in his twenties, he had honed the art of never putting the emphasis on the wrong syllable. It was he, and not the Anglo-Indian prep and boarding schools we attended and learned formal English, who was a stickler for pronunciation. To pronounce "measure," as *"maiyyur,"* as the Punjabis did when they burst forth into the King's tongue, was to invite his wrath. To say *"ijj,"* instead of "is," as the Biharis did, invited a lecture on the differences between j's and z's. To pronounce "window," as *"vindow,"* – as was wont in Uttar Pradesh English – meant learning the difference between pouting in a whistle and placing the front teeth over the lower lip before uttering the word. The teaching of the pronunciation of "the" as "the" instead of the universally Indian "*tha*" or "*da,*" he undertook as a constant pedantic endeavor. And he warned us that it was at our peril that we should ever pronounce – as the Tamils of the South often did – "It was yellow," as "*Yit vaas ellow.*" Ts, Ps and Bs in English – unlike Punjabi cussword – he reminded us, were always aspirated.

In the fifties, he would enjoy, with bemused indifference, the sounds of Doris Day, and Connie Francis, the Platters, and even learned to jive to Bill Haley's *Rock Around the Clock,* to Elvis's *Hound Dog,* and his eyes would go misty with *Are You Lonesome Tonight,* and *Cry Me a River,* as they filled our rooms from 33-1/2 LPs. His Benny Goodmans and Saigals, and Sylvesters were on stacks of 78s. He found the new technology astounding not only in the sturdiness of the hardware but also in the quality of sound. American accents in American pop music were sheer entertainment not to be taken seriously.

But things changed when the Beatles arrived. He liked the music. But for English aristrocrats to be taken in by long-haired young men singing in Liverpool accents to him was blasphemy. Not that he ever forbade us from listening to *I Wanna Hold Your Hand,* or *I Saw Her Standing There* or *Lucy in The Sky With Diamonds.* It was just that he wanted no part of it. And to drown out our Beatle Sounds on our record players, he would retire to his drawing room and play a ghazal from Shamshad Begum or even the pop hit *Lal Lal Gaal* – the Mohammed Rafi Hindi film hit, a shameless copy of Rock-around-the-clock – which he found more dignified than the maniacal sounds of Liverpool. "Pop music," he once said, "should have stayed in America with the Americans." God spared him the indignity of being alive when Doctor Dray hit the Indian charts, or when Indi-pop, Bhangra Pop, Daler Mehndi, and Apache Indian were coming to robust age in the 1990s and attending his grandchildren's wedding celebrations and watching his offspring dance to these disc jockey selections on the dance floors of posh hotels – where he had once done the fox-trot with ladies from foreign embassies – his children and grandchildren mixing festive Indian folk dance movements with M-Channel and V-Channel gyrations to braying, thudding rhythms, a cacophony of East and West. Sounds which when they first began to blare on our radios, he kept out of his reach in the late eighties and nineties by gluing himself, along with Mama, to the TV on which he watched the latest offerings from cable and satellite TV – *The Bold and the Beautiful, Picket Fences, The Flinstones.* And there must have been something of the flower child of the sixties in him, for even though he had never been a part of the anti-Vietnam War generation, his favorites were re-runs of *MASH*. Somehow he seemed to have sensed a kinship between Alan Alda and *Catch-22*'s Yossarian.

3

Yes, about the Cockney Smithers (was this the genesis of Papa's anti-Beatle bias?). Perhaps out of a surge of casteist propriety, perhaps out of a sudden concern for his *khajanchi*'s money vault, Grandfather, to the utter horror of his office babus, put his foot down. All size Nine of it. Not a paisa, he thundered, would be put into the pockets of the Cockney, whose coat hung in splendid isolation on the coat-rack while he was away on his rounds. And to add sartorial injury to insult, Grandpa, out of sheer cussedness, even snipped two brass buttons off its front.

When the inspector returned, he was not amused. The coat, instead of increasing in weight, had actually shed an ounce or so with the loss of the two buttons. The Cockney fumed. But all his fuming was nothing compared to the Punjabi Ps and Bs and Ms – some say that Grandpa even went a step further and threw in some choice Ks and Zs for good measure – that erupted from the clenched teeth and compressed lips of Grandpa.

The denouement came rapidly. The inspector retreated to the safety of the Inspection Bungalow but not before he had "failed" the mill in which Grandpa and his two older brothers were shareholders. Reports that Grandpa had manhandled the inspector (nothing was said of the coat or the pockets) reached the British Governor of the Punjab. (Punjab was always called "the" Punjab by the Brits before Independence when Prime Minister Nehru decided in a tribute to the King's English that articles were ungrammatical in an independent confederation.) The governor threatened to "fail" all of Grandpa's family's 10 mills in retaliation. The Raj was ruthless in its treatment of obscenities which accused its officials' mothers of sporting penises.

Grandpa's brothers apologized profusely. But the governor relented only when the brothers reached a compromise to save their mills from closure – Grandpa would be banished from Punjab, the land of his ancestors. They gave him his shares in cash along with several bullock-drawn covered-wagons, and Grandpa and Grandma, still childless, journeyed eastward through the plains of Punjab for 30 days and 30 nights until they crossed over into Uttar Pradesh (then called the United Provinces) and pitched tents in Raipur. This was at least 60 years before the Green Revolution turned this part dustbowl into waving fields of paddy, and wheat and cane. Then, the peasants who lived in scattered villages which still survive, grew only coarse millets like bajra and pulses which could withstand errant Monsoons.

Raipur and its environs, though, had a special attraction. Under the right climatic conditions, it was a good cotton-growing area for Grandpa. It was perfect place to begin life again. He was then in his twenties.

Chapter VI

1

True to Punjabi fashion he hit the ground running. He had carried money with him and labor was cheap. And the peasants of Raipur who had lived around there probably since time began were hungry for jobs because sustenance farming no longer really sustained the growing population. This Punjabi pilgrim set about acquiring land. And his and his teenage wife who grew into a formidable crusader for women's rights even as she kept up old traditions was the real social power to reckon with in the area. As Grandpa set about building two of the greatest cotton and ginning mills, Grandma organized a tented colony for her family. In the privacy of her tent she gave birth to Papa and two of his brothers and a sister. Papa arrived in 1912. Spindles were already bobbing on the latest machines imported from England in the two mills which now gave employment to 500 workers. The town now had a municipal committee of which Grandpa was the first chairman. A new railroad station. A paved Main

Street. British lords and ladies came to high teas and dinners after the Raipur household was completed – the one with Papa's chamber of perfumes. And Grandma turned out be a great farmer herself, and experimented with new strains of seeds and grew hybrid mango trees and over the years she greened the household campus. And when cars arrived Grandpa bought himself an Austin.

In the thickness of the scrub forests that stretched endlessly then, and in the wilderness of marshes Grandpa taught Papa to hunt and trap. And Papa turned into an intrepid explorer, staying away for nights at a time, discovering, on foot or on elephant-back or horse-back, villages and streams and lakes and *jheels* which were on nobody's map, and he learned the ways of the villagers, and they learned from him. He too, attended boarding school in the Himalayas. And Grandpa had then sent him off to London at the age of 16 where he became a barrister, and practiced several years until he was summoned back for marriage and to help out in the family business which had flourished, with ups and downs and because Grandpa's health had been failing. (He died of a stroke at age 55 before I was born.) For his bride, Grandma had picked a shy, wavy-haired princess from a royal family in the south. Mama was 16 and Papa 23 when they married. And Seema was born when Mama was 17, and Grandma delivered her in Mama's bed, as she was to deliver the rest of Mama's children. And she was a friend to Mama and taught her to sew and write Hindi, and to bathe and potty-train Mama's babies.

Papa was not unduly worried about the slowly deteriorating cotton business. It had provided the family wealth and earned them respect as honorable men of commerce. Besides, Papa kept himself busy in the wilds and since he was also an honorary magistrate he dispensed justice swiftly and fairly and with compassion. And the people learned to trust him. Villagers still do not readily trust people from outside their communities. Also, he had then, great personal wealth having come into a handsome dowry from Mama's side, and he spent like a king, once even taking a brief trip to France – after his return from England – to polish up his French and to buy original editions of rare books which still adorn his study next to his chamber of perfumes. He would speak to Mama in both Hindi as well as English to help her keep up with the language of the Raj, and he even subscribed, for Mama's reading, to an Urdu daily because Mama's father, a Hindu Maharaja with many wives, Hindus and Muslims – a poet with Sufi leanings who corresponded with Tagore – had insisted that his children learn Arabic and Persian in order to read the Qoran.

After Partition in 1947, hundreds of families of Punjabi Hindu refugees who had honored and done good business with Grandpa, who had died a few years earlier, flocked to Raipur to seek the help of his family to resettle themselves, having lost everything. And Papa worked tirelessly helping them acquire land and open small trading businesses and shops and, most of all, helped them gain acceptance from the local and rural inhabitants of Raipur and its surrounding villages. And the new

Punjabi community multiplied. Their businesses thrived and even when Papa's wealth had begun to decline and the money and wealth was in the hands of enterprising refugees, they still called Papa their king.

And until his last days, Papa was proudest of all of what he considered Grandpa's greatest architectural achievement that symbolized the family's grandeur – the two 150-feet tall factory chimneys visible from miles away, later jotted down on local maps as critical landmarks which would also serve as navigational aids to pilots later on. Every morning, before the factories opened, sharp at six a.m., the sound of the factory siren, louder than a ship's fog-horn would emit its deafening wake-up call heard as many as 10 miles away and village dogs would turn their heads to the sky and emit howls like wolves emit in Bram Stoker's Transylvania.

Chapter VII

1

As he lay dying in the eighth decade of his life, on his bed of wooden planks beneath the sagging quilted ceiling, his voice no more than a gurgle of phlegm as pneumonia and congestive heart failure progressively weakened his body, his children and grandchildren who had been summoned from different parts of the land – at his request – to witness the grand finale, took turns in bringing him his meals, mostly soup because he was too tired even to put on his dentures to chew on anything solid. Even then, we would first peep through the little clearing in the painted panes to ensure he was awake. He liked to be left alone when he was sleeping. And when we entered he would prop himself up and smile a smile indicating that the knowledge of the existence of the peephole was the best kept open secret of the family.

We sniffed. Kept absolutely still as he slurped soup. The room was bereft of Papa's perfumes. The genie was resting in its bottle. We smelled, instead, the flavorless odors of dried mushroom soup flakes in boiling water. Perspiration. The steam mixed with camphor from the hissing humidifier. There were the smells of the indignities of old age. Papa fought incontinence as bravely as he could but not always and the bedsheets would have to be changed often. But even a year before he began his final rage against the dying of the light, Papa's bathroom where scented steams had risen like mists from mountain valleys was witness to the first signals of his decay. He no longer powdered his slippers, and soft canvas shoes with their front ends lopped off for they were usually moist now. His prostate had enlarged and weakened and instead of a trajectory in which a powerful stream was aimed at and hit dead center of the toilet bowl, it now dribbled onto his footwear. He sometimes joked about this, comparing the phenomenon to that of a rifle that had lost its grooving.

Barely a week before, for a magical hour, the aromas had wafted in that perfumed chamber. Had sat in his chair in the evening and invited the grandchildren now well into their teens and earlier twenties inside. His eyes for nearly six months had become too tired to do any reading. But he remembered phrases and passages from books he loved. And that day he had this TV generation listen transfixed as he told them about Poe's *Mask of the Red Death*. Later he had babbled endlessly until a grandson asked him why he didn't ever write a book about shikar.

"It's over," he said. "You have to live the experience

not write it. Shotgun shells are now beyond reach. The marshes have been drained. The scrub forests have all but disappeared. And in any case, I was an outlaw. You know, hunting even migratory birds has been forbidden by law. But we had our own laws. Never shoot for the numbers. Shoot for the table. Mine was a generation haunted by forests."

"But didn't the villagers in whose fields you trekked with your guns, object?"

"Sometimes. But they enjoyed watching the sport of zigzagging game birds falling out of the sky. Most of them are poor and are the hunted themselves, fair game to predator officials and bureaucrats and scavenging politicians. They often thought of me as their protector. In exchange for letting us hunt in their fields," he smiled. "They expected me to hunt their tormentors, catch people asking for bribes, go after local policemen extorting money and grain, write complaints against officials delaying their pensions."

2

He was summing up his life for his grandchildren. And without any appropriate transition he embarked on his last sermon: "With a rifle, it's simpler. Of course it has to be kept greased, its barrel cleaned regularly. The main thing is sighting. With a U-sight make sure the bead at the end is in the dead center of where the u curves. Hold still while aiming. In fact hold you breath. Sometimes the barrel will move with your heartbeat. Remember a centimeter of movement may mean being off your target by six inches to a foot at 50 yards. Stop the heartbeat if you can. While aligning sights barrel and target don't wait too long or your hands will start shaking. There is a psychological moment when you will know when to fire. Let that instinct guide you. If you lose that moment you miss, and like you have one life, you have one shot with a single-shot rifle. Don't pull the trigger. Squeeze it. Like a knife going through butter. And believe me shooting a running partridge or hare with a .22 rifle is more difficult than doing a double-loop in a stunt plane. With a V sight it's the same. Only thing is you align the bead at the end exactly flush with the two arms of the V." And he held up the index and middle fingers of his right hand and inserted between them the index finger of his left hand as a demonstration. The grandchildren followed suit.

He continued: "With a double-barreled shotgun, no matter what anybody else might tell you, it's the swing that counts. Go in for a Geoffreys, a Purdy, Holland & Holland, Lyons, Webley & Scott, Westley Richards. All finer makes. I wouldn't recommend a Mantons. Too heavy. Or the Indian makes. Like wielding an axe. For game a 32-inch barrel is perfect. Preferably with a double choke. This sends the pellets in a concentrated pattern. Remember to swing. Hold the butt tight against your shoulder and jaw. Point at the flying bird as if your gun is an extension of your out-stretched arm and pointed finger. Watch the bird. You must pull the trigger while the gun is in motion and it must still be in motion – left to right or right to left – after you've fired. Here too, there's a psychological mo-ment. If it's gone, it's gone. Most shikaris get trigger-freeze. They wait too long or something inside them prevents them from pulling thé trigger at the right moment and they make the excuse that the bird was out of range. When you hit, it's like fishing. Just like the pole and line and underwater fish feel connected to your body the moment the fish takes the hook, an accurate shot connects you, your gun, the flying pel-lets and the bird. A good shikari doesn't have to see the bird fall to know he's hit it. He can feel it. While swinging keep both eyes on the bird. Your eye gives the lead. Remember if you're firing at the bird with-out swinging, a fast flying partridge or teal is already 20 to 50 feet ahead of the shot. When a bird is flying away from you, shoot at it, keeping a straight line just as fast bowlers in cricket do. If he's rising shoot above his head. If the bird is dipping fast, just pray to God and shoot.

"But never shoot out of range. An Alphamax or Eley Number Four shot is an all-rounder for duck and partridge. For greylag and pinkfoot geese a Number One is just fine and knocks them over at up to 60 yards. A Number Four is very effective at about 30-40 yards.

How do you know when they're out of range? Well for ducks you should be able to see their feet when they fly over you. Other game birds usually fly out from close to you and it's your quickness that counts before they go out of range. You don't shoot out of range because you will probably wing them or a few pellets will lodge in their bodies and they will die a slow death many days later or be unable to escape predators like jackals and falcons. The same with ducks. If a large flight comes over you, don't get excited and shoot blindly in the middle. Again you risk simply winging some of them and wounding others or even hitting a duck like a shoveller that's not for your table. Choose just one. Follow it, swing and bang just at the moment your gun is swinging past the bird.

"When you're shooting in a group, don't shoot at a bird crossing the shikari on your left or right. This is etiquette. Never, never point a gun at anyone even if you know it's not loaded, and no matter how tempting a shot, never shoot under a 45 degree angle. This is safety. And be generous enough to give the kill to the person who nicked the bird first even if it was your own last shot that finally brought it down. Shoot for the table and know when enough is enough. Take care of your gun when you go home. Dis-assemble it. Clean out its barrels with soft steel brushes if it is pitted, and then with gauze soaked in oil and then with flannel with a proper cleaning rod."

3

Papa sounded like a wheezing instruction manual that day. But his body had come alive. Because it was mid-March and a month earlier the swamps and *jheels* had been teeming with ducks and snipe. Snipe, our favorite table bird, roasted in brandy and sherry. Usually reserved for the youngest of the offspring because they were so hard to shoot. You needed a larger spread for them so you used Number Eights – large spread but small range – about 15 to 20 yards. With their six-inch long beaks they would dart out of old paddy fields and zig-zag with the speed of rockets high into the sky. Even half a dozen of them in a day's shoot was considered a prize bag. And each bird provided no more than a mouthful of chewing, bones, head, neck, legs.

"Snipe spook from a distance," Papa went on. "That is why we stalk them at noon when the sun is high and they are sluggish. More importantly, our shadows are not long and snipe take off from a distance when a lengthening shadow falls on them." The marshes and swamps had yielded their secrets to the Shikari. And even their smells. That is why he forbade all hunting after February, especially duck. These winter visitors were now resting in large lakes and adding on fat that would fuel their migration back to Central Asia and even Siberia until their return the following November. They should be allowed their rest. Besides to eat them then was to savor the fish-like, gamy smell of their added fat.

That winter-end, as he lectured his grandchildren, his body had come alive. Then he wanted to rest. The dining table that should have been producing aromas of roast teal, and browned potatoes, or pochard kebabs or curried goose, was devoid of this winter fare. The Shikari had been on an enforced diet. Part of sniffing Papa was sniffing the dining room just when the food was served. But for a year these smells had disappeared from the household. A heart specialist who had examined him, had put him on a low-cholesterol diet that would, he believed, let Papa live to be a hundred. Papa distrusted doctors. He feared medicine. But he went along with the dietary advice, perhaps, in the hope, that his health would return and maybe he would be able to drive his open jeep and hunt the marshes again. But the outlaw, who was haunted by forests, did not, while he lived, see them again.

The table was now devoid of meats. Boiled cabbage, gourds, *dal* without the fried cumin, soups, Vitamin E capsules, Waterbury's Compound, and a variety of elixirs were his diet. And whenever we ate with him we made sure that we ate like him so as not to remind him of the flavors which had once blessed this table. Gone, too, was the sound of his crunching while he ate. His cheeks sank, his eyes which had blazed like meteors began to dim, his shikari legs became spindly. Eating, for him, was a dreary, studious exercise in mastication without joy. Just as living had become an academic exercise in breathing, during that last winter of his illness as he sat in his chair talking to his grandchildren.

As his talk sputtered to an end the perfumes, too evanesced. It was the last time that his grandchildren would imbibe them during his lifetime. In his presence they were obedient, fastidiously traditional. They knew him as playful and adventurous, not overly demonstrative about affection, not mushy. But he knew little of their lives or the India they were growing up in. When they talked about WINDOWS '95 he would go into a trance. Rap, he knew not what it meant even though his grandchildren had a sharp ear for every consonant and syllable and mispronounced vowel from the streets of the Bronx, Watts, Harlem, Chicago and Haight Ashbury. Just as he knew, and they didn't, who Lee Iacocca was, they knew and didn't who Bill Gates was. Keyboard, Server, Icons, Format, Tools, Table, Window, meant to him piano, liveried waiter, religious symbol, a place for family meals, the layout of a novel, a wooden frame with a glass pane. GREs and G-MATs, CBSE, and ICSE, the new math. He could share none of these with his grandchildren.

Since he was rarely in the habit of prying, asking inquisitive questions, or taking a salacious interest in people's private lives including those of his children and grandchildren, he did not know them or even want to know them beyond what was necessary. He knew their characters, whims, temperaments, tempers, but not their habits or lifestyles outside Raipur and his fortress, in the same way that he knew with precision the different sounds made by a teal or mallard when they landed in a marsh in his hunting grounds but was oblivious to what they did when they migrated back to Siberia or Ladakh or Central Asia.

4

In Raipur the generations, when they conversed in Hindi – up or down the family hierarchy – they still greeted one another with the formal *"aap"* instead of the informal *"tu"* or *"tum."* When male strangers came visiting, the women left the room for their own chambers. Attendance at family meals together, starting with breakfast, was enforced with the strictness of a Cromwellian edict. Women, even though they were encouraged to hunt, to drive jeeps and explore the wilds, rarely went shopping in the bazaar by themselves. Wares were brought to the house by shopkeepers or servants. And if they did venture out, they slipped out of their blue jeans and loose tops, changed into formal wear like salwar kameezes or saris, and covered their heads with *chunnis*.

When the grandchildren migrated out of Raipur to their parents' or husbands' homes in Delhi or Calcutta and Bombay and Bangalore the metropolises gobbled them up. Their lifestyles were as alien to me as they would have been repugnant to Papa. Their bookshelves were lined with Archie comics. They surfed the Net for porn and exchanged pornographic missives with Net-pals on laptop Toshibas hooked to superfast modems moving information at 50 kilo bits per second. Skin-tight jeans and skimpy halters and above-the-navel tops. Black lipstick and Escape perfume. Smirnoff Vodka and Peach Schnapps. Parties that began at 11 p.m. and ended at 5 a.m. Sprawling farmhouses in the middle of urban macadam. New vehicles on the road, Korean Cielos, Suzukis, Ford Escorts, Fiat Unos in which they drove like madmen – through pot-holed and dimly-lit streets, sidewalks and road-dividers occupied by homeless refugees who had fled their villages in search of jobs – and often killed themselves. Some even committed suicide by hanging from bedsheets tied to ceiling fans. And the funerals the next day in which my friends and I would tearfully shake our heads and say, we have nobody to blame but ourselves. We gave them, too much, too soon. This was a constant refrain.

5

Two years before he died, it was a day when the aromas hovered around him like a tenacious, perfumed aura, he and I were discussing what was in the day's newspapers. He was asking me to explain what network marketing and Amway and Tupperware were all about. I explained as best as I could and added:

"Looks like we're doing things differently on all fronts. Exporting onions and potatoes. Importing dinner plates. I believe Amway has created 60,000 new jobs, just for women in the past eight months. That's not really bad is it?" The rhetorical question was intended to provoke the 84-year-old Shikari to share some of his political or economic wisdom with me. Maybe even give me a few new lines I could use in a debate. It was rare that he would be provoked into an argument or discourse at the prodding of others. Personal advice, freely. But political philosophy he preferred, most of the time to keep bottled up within himself. He chose to digress:

"There's something about Mahatma Gandhi that always struck me as interesting," he said. "Even though he was a vegetarian I liked him because he stressed hygiene and plain, simple, civility and the cleaning up of villages. Whenever I think of him I think how rude India has been to him. Somehow the most indelible image of India that sticks in my mind is the suffocation of our cities. The worst image that comes to mind is that of our garbage vans. They ply through the streets picking up garbage. But on their way to the garbage dumps these open vans bounce up and down on our awful roads and spill the garbage back on to the streets and when they reach the dumps they are empty and our streets are dirtier." He laughed. "And the garbage pickers in our neighborhoods! They pick up garbage in wheelbarrows as they go from house to house and keep dropping the overflowing stuff on the sidewalks as they head for the next house, and by the time their wheelbarrows reach the garbage trucks they've already spilled most of the filth in the neighborhoods they are supposed to be cleaning. Everybody knows this and yet we don't lift a finger to right this terrible wrong."

Chapter VIII

1

Papa's silence, when he rested with his eyes closed, during his last days, was strong. The hunter was invaded by organisms blasting his lungs, his throat, his larynx, and he lay wheezing under the quilted ceiling looking at the world through stale eyes and exhaling stale breath as the humidifier hissed. As I sat by his side I saw him walking through the scrub forest as he had done for 70 years. He had seen the wilderness change. The *dhak* leaves on which the July rain had fallen like the brushes of a jazz drummer had refused to return having withered several years ago under the onslaught of lantana bushes. They had withered because the land had been drained and the forest had been mercilessly uprooted by illegal fellers under the patronage of forest officials who spent their fat bribe money on dowries for their daughters.

Along with the forest, the Shikari's body, too, had withered. It had weakened progressively with each leaf that fell from the forest. Each strike of the feller's axe was a simultaneous body blow on the Shikari. As he lay dying, Papa's shins looked liked the dehydrated, sap-starved, discolored, knotty, axe-marked tree trunks, spindles of their former muscular girths of pulp and greenwood and sinew. The stubble on the Shikari's face seemed to move like the bracken in what had once been the forest, as he lay dying.

"No amount of rain," Papa had once said, "will ever revive that forest. The Monsoon is now useless to it. It has no more use for fertilizer. The killers have killed it. They have killed the forest and the hunter. Days were when you could smell that forest 50 miles away. You could smell the *bers* ripening on their spiny twigs and you could see its colors reflected in the sky. The clouds would mirror its landscape, each cloud like a floating, billowing mirror in which you could see the forest. And when it rained, the forest floated into the clouds and the skies and leaves and brambles and streams and chess-board mud-scape were all one and we all breathed together."

The hunter had outlived the death of his forest for several years but he knew that the cells of decay were already in him. He remained for several years the only memory of that forest. In him, still, were its smells and fragrances. For those who are haunted by forests, forests walk with them. The woods are always in motion. The trees do not pass by. They walk with you. The leaves move with you, the grasses and thorns waft like vapors.

He had been walking through the brambles for two

hours. Even in late January when the cold wave is in retreat, the sun can roast the nape of your neck. He had worn a French Foreign Legion cap for protection. Hunter shoes. The twin barrels of his 12 gauge Geoffrey's shotgun held at 45 degrees from the waist and hip. The Shikari and his team of hired beaters had poked and thrashed the clumps and bristles and bushes covering low ridges in vast expanses of sand. They had followed the call of the Brown. The birds had been calling incessantly since 3.30 p.m. That left an hour and a half of light in which to shoot. The beaters thrashed the bushes with wooden staves and sturdy stalks of sugarcane to flush out the birds. But they had remained stuck deep within the roots, refusing to fly out.

The Shikari knew why. A strong breeze had risen from the west and the partridge would rather stay cloistered in the deep safety of bushes rather than flying into the breeze and failing to attain maximum speed or risk navigational failure by flying with it. The birds did not fear the ground as much as they did the air when the Shikari was on the prowl, for it was in the air that the Shikari would be waiting for them. The hunter suddenly changed tactics. "Too thick in here," he said, and after scanning what seemed to be the horizon to his left and right, he began to stride briskly to the east. Here the ground dipped and then flattened out into small fields of mustard glowing gold. On the ridge, from where the land dipped and flattened out into small fields of mustard glowing gold, rose clumps of *jhoor* bushes with their razor sharp edges, in contours and zigzags encircling the low-

69

lying area of mustard fields over which the wind seemed
to have died down somewhat.

He ordered the men to take the *jhoor* clumps 100
yards at a time, north to south. The beaters walked to the
bushes on the ridge. We walked alongside. The Shikari
moved way ahead and took the forward eastern end of
the mustard fields.

"Move!" he yelled. "All together, all in a line.
Remember, they can fly out at any time, and most likely
they'll fly towards the fields. Don't shoot low or out of
range. Use Sixes or Fours."

Was I 10 then, 15, 18, 35, 45? Everytime this
happened, it was like a first beginning, a first experience,
a *déjà vu* that never staled. The world was in slow motion.
My feet moved. A sickening, bitter, bile arose in my throat,
even as my stomach knotted and fluttered in anticipation.
The seaforest forestsea was about to yield its fruit. The
fishermanhunter hunterfisherman was suddenly
thousands of years old and I saw him bearded to the knee
with a wooden staff shimmering in the winter heat. I
remember in my childhood being mesmerized by a
Rajasthani wandering shepherd in a red turban and silver
anklets and a white moustache and no teeth leading a
thousand sheep to greener pastures, something he had
done for a thousand years, and he whistled at his sheep,
and he had no teeth, only wrinkles from brow to chin
and the wildest young eyes I had ever seen in my life,
and I had sat on the ground as those sheep passed by me
in their hundreds, and the thousand-year-old shepherd,

whistling his commands at them, had passed me by and stopped and stroked my head, and said he would return with those sheep a year later, after he was sure they had been fed, and mated on their way, and he had a staff which was crooked where he held it, and his eyes were all smiles and the wrinkles disappeared, and he gave life to a thousand more sheep, and his children and grandchildren still walk the children and grandchildren of the sheep I saw with that old man many, many years ago, and I still dream of those smiling eyes and his wrinkles which started from the ground and reached the sky, and his whistle and his non-dead eyes.

2

During that particular hunt (was I 15? 18?) I was ankle-deep in sand, the gun seemed to gain in weight. Its barrel growing longer. "Mooove!" a command came from somewhere. It was the voice of toothless Gafoor, the guide instructing his team of beaters. On the ridge the staves prodded the bushes. Hurr. Hurr, Grrraa... The scrub moved and grew until the brushes poked holes into the sky creating concentric ripples in the blue while the sun gained weight and dipped into the horizon and then reappeared mid-sky and the kikkar thorns snapped under my feet, and then, another sound, like a roar from the bushes, like an electric lawnmower being suddenly turned on between my feet, but actually the winged flutter of two partridges shooting out of the bushes and into the sky, and I'm looking in wonderment at where the roar came from, while the birds speed over my head, and they're saying, "Over you! Over you! Shoot, shoot, you idiot!" and I pivot and press the front trigger to shoot from the right barrel and the butt kicks my shoulder as the blast deafens me, and then the back trigger to activate the left barrel for the concentrated choke pattern for the pellets, and because I'm holding the gun loose, the trigger guard bruises the outer portion of my index finger, and nothing drops from the sky, as more birds roar into the air, and phut, phut, over the Shikari, they begin falling from the sky. The man in the great beard motions a halt. Papa comes into focus. He has dropped four. He has swung at one in an arc, then turned from waist upwards, his body, gun, hands moving in unison in the opposite direction and dropped another. He reloaded and in a blur, arched backwards, obtuse angle from the ground gun and body in one line, and then pivoted 180 degrees again, and while you could hear no sound, birds fall again, as if he was using a fishing pole, not a gun.

And he motions to us to walk to the fields. "Don't enter yet. Make a line on the other side. Stay in line. When I say move, start walking through the fields in a row. This should yield at least 10. I know this patch of cultivation. Haven't shot here for three years and they've multiplied through three mating seasons. They usually lay four eggs a female. Okay, start walking, and remember they're not likely to fly out of the middle as they did from the bushes on the ridges. These birds will run swiftly along the ground, one or two feet ahead of you and they'll fly only if they see their cover running out, right at the end of the field. If you break your line they'll simply run backwards in the field through gaps you leave."

We walk about 10 feet apart, the field is 100 feet broad and 100 yards long, five- feet high mustard stalks, so dense that my feet are caught as if in the weeds of a riverbed. It's also like wading through chest-high water, guns held at 45 degrees. Don't break the line, don't break the line, and we smell the still ripening mustard and the winter heat is turning into the winter cold, and why is the Shikari standing at the far outside edge of the field? For he knows the flight path, he knows the birds will not fly in any other direction except over him because behind him are the outer ridges of the scrub forest and the birds will fly in the direction of scrub shelter rather than into the open areas, and they fly as he expects, and he dances and brings them down, and says, Enough!

The bag is 6 Black, and two Brown from that patch and the Shikari has notched up a score of 6 by himself. Not one miss. And a fellow hunter says, one last beat, please, I just saw three of them, really fat Blacks, fly from this field, and they landed on that ridge and ran into that bush there. I'll go after them, and the Shikari laughs and says Enough! Besides, he laughs, these birds never stay where they seem to land. After they land they put their heads down and sprint like hell along the ground for another 50 yards, zigzagging all the time. Besides, the Shikari says, it's about a half-hour to sundown and we still have duck to do.

The wind is dying down and the winter heat is now winter chill again with a Milky Way mist encircling the horizon. The *jheel*, 15 minutes away is a small one, overgrown with slimy, thistly weeds, a shady Mango orchard on one side, small sugarcane fields which draw water from this jheel, and a village a half mile to the north, whose mudhuts are now barely visible in the smoke from evening dungfires which mingles with thin films of waking mists from the ground and they rise together, mist and smoke and suddenly stop to form a canopy of haze over the village.

The Shikari has chosen this *jheel* because it is remote and totally in the environment of the scrub. It is a "feeding *jheel*" where geese and duck will arrive at sundown to feed through the night. It is inaccessible to most men except the local villagers who do not hunt. It is wild. It is haunted by wilderness. And it has always always haunted us and haunted Papa. And we know why we're trudging to this *jheel*, because tonight's moonlight and we'll play in the moonbeams, waist-deep in water holding on to our guns. And the Shikari will do what he has done forever when he reaches the *jheel* as the sun turns cold and orange and magenta and pink and starts settling into the Mango grove and flutters like a ball of mirages as the village smoke rises above it sending out smells of baking wheat and dung and buffalo piss, while the waters of the *jheel* remain undisturbed except for ripples made by a pair of brahmany ducks who yodel like cattle herders. A dozen cormorants and a black ibis-like snakebird swim to the shore and watch us while we lie spreadeagled on the earth, squares of dry and moist clay beneath our shoulders, buttocks, thighs, calves, heels, we gaze at the sky, prop ourselves up on elbows and drink tea from porcelain cups, hot sweet tea whitened with powdered milk out of an Eagle thermos flask, while the Shikari bites into a Cadbury's bar, and we smell the smell of seaweed, rotting clam shells, musky odors of black slush mixed with duck feathers, as swallows and green bea-eaters and fruit bats dip in and out of sight from the graying sky and lapwings cry out hysterically. The sound of silence, the Shikari once told us, is not no sound. It is this – the sound of the *jheel* and the scrub forest.

4

There is a psychological moment, known only to the Shikari, when he knows it is time to prepare. Night is upon us and we know how to move. We have done this forever. And the Shikari reminds us – remember, this is a feeding *jheel*, the birds will start coming in shortly. But don't shoot until the geese come in. If they fly in, they'll do so in the next half hour and they'll come in over that Mango grove in the direction of the Ganges where they've been snoozing all day out of harm's way in and around a sand blank in the middle of the river. They'll be rested and may come in flying relatively fast. Shoot only when they come low and are circling before settling. If they don't come in within the next half hour, they won't at all. By then you'll have moonlight for the other ducks. And hide well.

And we hid well in clumps of reeds in waist-deep water, without waders, the waterproof apparel which the Shikari often derided as "stuff for sissy Americans," ankle- deep in slush, in previously agreed upon positions. The Shikari had moved to the farthest spot, away from the direction of the orchard, so that I could have the first shot, for to bag a pinkfoot, or greylag, or barhead was a big prize (my first success several years ago had brought me a Peter Scot book of illustrations as an award from Papa), and even though I had stood hidden in the rushes, with a BB shell in the right chamber and a number one in the left of my Savage (which the Shikari had once scornfully described as an American blunderbuss), the flight of 50 barheads had circled so low over the Shikari that he had brought down two of them with Number Sixes because he was preparing only for ducks. And the first two shots had echoed across the waters as if the *jheel* had concrete corners as in a squash court and the sound had bounced off from every direction and frogs had suddenly begun to croak, the bugs to scream, the sarus cranes to sound their sirens, those ear-piercing screams – *kurrrrrrrs* – of sentinel alarm sounds so different from the same sarus *kurs* that herald the evening or sunrise as this great bird, the size of a small Ostrich, floats in, always in pairs, the wings of the two in perfect synchronousness, out-

76

stretched like human arms with the hands flapping from the wrist joints in jerky upward movements. And the moon had risen without light and then lighted the sky as we stood in the water in the slush and flights of teal and pintail, and widgeon whistling like the whistles of men teasing women, had come come in from the Ganges and we had shot at swift black shadows, like aiming and shooting at moving holes in the sky and we knew we had hit when the bird thudded into the water, not splashed but thudded, because live ducks splash when they land but dead ducks thud. And in the moonlight the Shikari had already retrieved his birds from the water and on dry ground he lifted his feet and soaked trousers into a crackling fire of thorns and dry weeds and we shivered and lit Gold Flake cigarettes and put our trousered legs into the flames of the red and orange crackling fire whose smoke rose into the moon, and we identified our ducks and we had enough for the pot. Overhead the ducks were still flighting in, big black holes with wings, arrghing, hissing, swishing sounds and we knew by their sounds what kind they were though they never quacked. We shivered and wrapped our home-knitted green and black mufflers around our necks and walked through the scrub forest to the Willys jeep parked five miles away, through the scrub forest which was black and silent beneath but shook its fingertips at the moonlight and we said nothing as we listened to the crunch of our footsteps and breathed in the smell of the lantana and the dew as it fell and moistened the white mud. We walked with the forest and the forest walked with us.

5

The hunt amused the Shikari for another reason. It caused him enormous satisfaction that just as he was able to learn the ways of the hunted and characterize species – he called shovellers lower caste ducks because they collected garbage from the bottom of ponds; he called the brahmany an idiot duck because of its refusal to take flight from afar – so too he would learn the ways of his friends and offspring.

He believed shikar unmasks people, and the observations he would make and characterizations he would give would remain unchanged in his mind, as if etched in a tablet of God. He who hankered after wild game for his table but was a reluctant participant in the hunt or shikar drill was a slovenly freeloader and sluggard. Stalking game on your own, as part of the loneliness of the long distance hunter, was the highest of all the calling, but if you were part of a shikar party yet broke away from the hunt and went off on your own track, you were, crafty, cunning and selfish. If you brought off a fine shot and screamed for attention (did you see that great shot?) – an opportunist and exhibitionist. If you refused to partake of the common pool of tea and sandwiches but kept hidden your own special food in your shikar bag you were pathologically greedy and crafty. Poaching across your line of fire into someone else's shot or claiming another's kill as your own earned you the distinction of going down in Papa's book of judgements, as utterly lacking in character.

CHAPTER IX

1

As Papa's body wasted along with the scrub forest, his eyes too began to dry like the waters of the *jheel* of the mallard and the geese. News about the health of the ponds and *jheels* and scrub forests was delivered regularly to Papa by two of his most trusted friends, Gafoor and Khalifa. Both lived in villages cut off from Raipur by forbidding terrain and approachable only by jeep. To reach their villages, about 20 miles out of Raipur, you had to drive for two hours or more through endless craters and ditches, and often through the edges of ploughed fields and through groves of mango trees. They were about Papa's age. Gafoor was a Muslim tenant farmer, toothless and lean with yellow eyes and thin legs with calf muscles that seemed to be made of rock. Khalifa (a nick name loosely meaning chief) was a *mallah*, a fisherman, a man of the water who stood six-feet tall, had the shoulders of a bull, a large nose in the middle of a full-moon face with nostrils like those of a race horse, spoke in a baritone and when he laughed after drinking, or so the legend went, trees would start to sway and the thatch from village huts would start to scatter as if hit by a tornado.

Gafoor lived in a village built on the edges of an enormous *jheel* that was home to snipe, geese, and the largest variety of migratory ducks in the entire territory in which the Shikari and his entourage hunted. And surrounding it was scrub country where black buck once roamed in magnificent herds and where blue bulls with their goatee beards still gallop across peanut and sugarcane fields with thunder in their hooves, and sand grouse and partridge and quail were among the most abundant in the land. Khalifa's land was river country. He lived in a three-room shack in the flood area of the Ganges. And he moved his shack according to the moods of the river. Moving in when the river became tame starting in October, and moving away nearer to civilization when the Ganges was beginning to swell and threaten the very shape of the landscape in unpredictable meanders starting mid-June. In his life, Khalifa had seen entire villages swept away. He had seen hundreds of buffalo carcasses bobbing up and down like gigantic black corks as they floated downstream. And he had heard the call of the wild – of the *kurr*ing of flocks of demoiselle cranes as they came to settle along the endless length of swamp and brush and reed forests and sand-flats the river left behind after it receded in November, of the first sounds of barhead geese as they came in to settle in the river or feed on sweet potatoes.

And miles away Gafoor would also be listening. And when he was sure of the sounds and convinced that the *jheels* and ponds had begun to seethe with life and that the partridge had begun to feed in areas where they could be hunted he would journey on foot – about six hours – to Raipur where he knew the Shikari would eagerly be awaiting his news. The two guides would often arrive at the same time and they would compete for attention while the Shikari listened attentively. While they distrusted all outsiders and would even chase them out of their villages, it was an honor for them to have the Shikari and his entourage hunt near their villages. Of course, at the end of the hunt, they and their teams of bird-pickers and bird-flushers would be rewarded handsomely. And this income, even if meagre, would see them through the winter season. But more than that they considered the Shikari's visit an act of love. The spirit and the camaraderie of the hunt was, for them too, an intoxicant. It also gave them power, the power of patronage to select people from their villages to join the hunting party as trackers and pickers. And at night when they went back to their villages they would hold court late into the night regaling audiences of villagers with tales about their exploits. How I had retrieved a diving mallard duck from submerged reeds by catching its neck between my toes. How I got caught in a mighty whirlpool in the middle of the river into which a prize-sized goose had fallen. How I jumped between the Shikari and an elephant-sized blue bull that suddenly came charging out of a cane field we were beating to flush black partridge, and saved his life.

81

When Gafoor competed with Khalifa for the Shikari to come to his area first he argued robustly and with passion:

"If you clap your hands the teal rise from the reeds like flies. But the west wind has started to blow and they may leave for another area soon. And the geese are still staying all day instead of taking off for the Ganges. We can definitely bag a dozen geese. And I've never seen so many pintail. And I've seen a special place where I can guarantee at least 30 male black partridge..."

Khalifa was not one to be left behind:

"I walked all night through the sweet potato fields. The cranes were flying so low I could have dropped a few with stones. They're still there. It must be a record of sorts. And can you believe it, they're feeding alongside the geese right now. There are no geese in Gafoor's area right now. How can there be when they're all flying into the banks of the Ganges where I've just seen them? And you never know, the winter Monsoon may arrive soon this year, and if the river changes course..."

The Shikari would listen with amusement. He had known the two rivals since when he was in his late twenties. They were both congenital braggarts. And Papa knew that ultimately, no matter in whose area he decided to hunt for the day, he would have to use his own instinct for the land and for the wilderness to guide his entourage into a successful day's shoot. An instinct which finally overawed all the villagers – including Gafoor and Khalifa

– the two expert guides, who came in contact with the Shikari. They saw in this part of his nature a vibrant and comforting presence of their own soil. And they saw in his marksmanship flashes of drama that brought entertainment, amusement and wonderment into their lives.

The Shikari would make up his mind about where to go based on his own feeling of which landscape would be more bewitching or haunting on that particular day based on the color of the sky, the smell of the earth, the direction of the breeze, and always, always, the feel of the light. On a whim he might choose an area he had discovered all by himself, an area to which Gafoor and Khalifa were strangers. But if Gafoor won the day, Khalifa would be asked to accompany us to Gafoor's area. The same the other way around. And if, after a hard day's hunt, Gafoor's area did not turn out to be the promised land Gafoor had sold with such brilliance, Khalifa would take the lead in heaping on him the choicest abuses:

"Where were those geese Gafoor?" he would taunt. "Did they fly away and sit on trees? Ah yes, those partridges which were supposed to buzz and swarm like flies? Did they all fly into your asshole?"

And the Shikari, in the rare moments when he would throw linguistic circumspection to the winds, would take Khalifa's cue, and say: "Maybe I should fire a shot into his asshole." And Khalifa would laugh that drunken laugh and the trees would shiver. But at the end of the day both braggarts, no matter how much their credibility had suffered on the ground, would be handsomely rewarded. And the Shikari would say:

"Come back next week. And if you lie again, don't show your faces here." They exaggerated, they lied, but they always came back and were never turned away. And whenever I saw Gafoor or Khalifa enter our house's compound on a winter morning my heart leaped with excitement. Even when I think of them now my pulse quickens and the staleness of everyday living is transformed into mystery.

2

On a cold January afternoon, when Papa was in his late twenties, he had decided to go tracking demoiselle cranes which were reported to be flighting along the banks of the Ganges. This crane is a slender bird of a pale, bluish-gray colour with long pectoral plumes drooping over the breast, about three-feet tall, slow flying, and it floats in circles, carefully reconnoitering the area, before landing. While the flock feeds, appointed sentinels keep a vigil on the area. And the birds will take off from more than a 100 yards – well out of gunshot range – at the approach of a hunter. You can chase them all day in a jeep in the scrubby wilderness of the banks of the Ganges and never even get to fire a shot. They simply take off and land 200 yards away as you approach them and the chase is endless and calls for some of the best jeep-driving with four-by-four gears constantly engaged as you manipulate your way across sand, loam, shallow sandy canyons, thickets of reeds and shrubs, and countless ponds left behind by the river when it recedes for the winter and exposes this vast expanse of wild, sandy jungle.

Driving through this terrain and tracking wild game is really for the bravehearts. For one, you can get lost easily. Because once you are the middle of these sand flats there are no discernible landmarks, and the fixed horizon seems to change with each contour of land carved by the meanderings of the mighty river. If you get stuck, there's no help for miles around and chances are that if you run out of gas and get lost while trying to walk back you could spend a couple of days in this maze of sand and water and shrubs. The region was, and still is, a safe haven for gangs of brigands.

The trick is to get out well before sundown. And during the hunt and chase, the technique the Shikari used was to drive undetected as close to the flock as possible, and then crawl on his belly, holding his gun at a right angle and propelling himself on his elbows to within shooting distance. If he could get to within 20 yards of them, both the barrels of his gun loaded with Number One Alpahamax shells, he would jump to his feet and charge headlong into the flock, barrels blazing. And usually, even as the flock took off, he would have time to reload and fire again. If roasted right, the birds were a table delicacy. And their gizzards usually contained small multi-colored stones which looked beautiful in any collection.

That sparkling January afternoon had proved fruitless. The Shikari had ventured out on his own without any hunting companion. And he was keen to get out before evening fell. He thought he was crossing a shallow pond through which the jeep usually made it with ease with some careful driving. When he was about six feet across he felt the wheels – all four of them – turning in place. He tried to reverse. The wheels simply kicked up watery black slush. And the jeep seemed to sink a little. The Shikari knew he had landed in a huge patch of quicksand which he usually knew how to avoid. He clambered onto the back benchseat and took a huge leap backwards and landed on firmer ground. The jeep sank and stopped and sank and stopped until the slime had reached the jeep's hood.

The Shikari knew the situation to be hopeless and made a quick decision to start walking back the six miles or so to the nearest village. He would come back the next day in another jeep and try and tow the marooned vehicle unless it had sunk completely by then.

As he began to trudge back, five men, naked to the waist, carrying spears and fishing nets blocked his path. Their leader had the shoulders of a bull. The Shikari steadied his gun and pointed it in the direction of the bull. He knew this was brigand or "dacoit" country. The man, undeterred, walked to within a foot of the Shikari, grabbed his gun by the barrel and yanked it out of his hands. He was stinking of country liquor. He opened his mouth as wide as he could and he began to laugh and the Shikari thought he heard thunder in the sky and the languid flow of the Ganges had suddenly begun to ripple.

The man asked: "Are you from the police?"

And Papa replied: "No. No policeman would dare come here alone. Not even a posse. I am a shikari. I've been chasing *kulang*. My jeep seems to be sinking in quicksand. I'm walking back home."

"He's walking back home! He's walking back home!" the man teased. And roared out another laugh and his companions laughed with him. "Where's your home?"

"Raipur."

"And you think you'll find your way out of here?"

"I always find my way. I belong here."

"In this wilderness?"

"This wilderness is my home. Perhaps I can even guide you."

The man laughed. Even louder. And he threw the Shikari's gun to the ground. He asked:

"You'll squeal on us when you get back?"

"I don't squeal on people who have done nothing to me."

87

"You're not afraid of us?"

"No you're fishermen, you're shikaris. Shikaris don't fear other shikaris. You're wearing nothing. Aren't you cold?"

The man guffawed: "Shikaris don't feel cold. What would you do if we killed you?"

"I don't think you would. And if you did, I'd be dead and wouldn't be able to do anything, anyway. I could have shot you before you touched my gun."

"Why didn't you?"

"I spared your life."

"You know what else we do, don't you? When the fishing is bad, when there's drought...?"

"Yes, you rob rich farmers' villages. You even kill them with spears and country-made pistols."

"What is your name?"

Papa told the man his name.

And the man said: "I've heard of you. You're the Shikari. Show us. Show us how you shoot." And he handed Papa back his gun. Papa said:

"Take one of those small stones with which you anchor your nets in the river. And fling it as far as you can. High up. Use all the strength you've got."

The man did as Papa had asked, and Papa fired at

the rock as it sailed through the air and he hit it with such accuracy that it shattered into smithereens.

The man laughed. His men clapped. "More!" they shouted. "More!" And they flung rocks in the air, dozens of them, and the Shikari kept blowing them to bits and the fragments came back to earth like small meteorite showers.

And Papa said enough was enough and he asked the bull-shouldered man his name and the man replied:

"They call me Khalifa. I rule this wilderness. I am the strongest swimmer the river has ever seen. My whole family perished in a flood when I was eight years old. The men and women were strong swimmers but they were swept away with the children. I was the only one able to swim to safety on a dark night when the Ganges had reached 20 feet above danger level during the Monsoon of 1920."

The Shikari said: "I've heard of you, too, Khalifa."

Khalifa asked Papa where his jeep was stuck. Papa said there was nothing anybody could do and that he would bring help the next day. And Khalifa laughed again and said:

"Watch what we can do."

Papa led the men to the jeep. It had not sunk any farther. Khalifa and his men tested the edge of the quicksand pit for firmness. Then they placed themselves in a ring around it and began moving clockwise in a continuous circle stomping the ground as hard as they could with their bare feet. For about five minutes they continued this exercise, and suddenly water began to trickle down the edges of the pit. The tyres of the jeep became visible, and within a few more minutes, the pit had been drained. The men jumped in and scooped the slush out with their hands. With the water having drained out, the slush had also begun to harden into clay, and the jeep was soon standing on relatively hard ground at the bottom. Its tyres could now grip. And Khalifa and his men, with a few hard pushes, managed to free the vehicle.

Papa cheered and clapped. And Khalifa told him this was a technique they often used to free up their bullock carts or even cattle which had sunk too deep. The jeep would not start because the spark plugs needed to dry. And evening was floating across the Ganges a little distance away. And Khalifa asked the Shikari to accompany him and his men to the river and to spend the night with them and to watch them fish and to drink and eat with them. Papa watched them wade naked into the cold January river and then swim into it holding their nets and then diving to secure them. There were boundary nets to prevent fish – mahaseer, carp, sole – from disappearing into some other part of the river. There were casting nets to trap the fish. And through the night the men waded and dived to adjust the nets. He watched them cast in the moonlight and retrieve netfuls of fish they would store in baskets. And he watched Khalifa drink and laugh and he laughed with him and he drank with him. And the men gave the Shikari lessons in casting nets on that moonlit night and they laughed when he entangled himself repeatedly and Khalifa would lift him off the ground as he struggled to disentangle himself and say:

"This is the biggest catch of all. This one I'll take home and skin myself. This one is for Khalifa." And then he would lower the entangled Shikari to the ground and dance and pirouette around him and then stand still on wobbly legs his arms outstretched as if the earth had turned into a small globe underneath his feet and he was balancing himself so as not to lose his balance and float away into space.

All night the men played in the river, plunging in and out, shivering, working for the fish, lighting small fires when they needed warmth and the liquor had run out. And at dawn, they lay exhausted on the sand, bare-bodied while the Shikari covered himself with his windcheater.

The dawn came pink and magenta and gold and the river was silent. And even as the Shikari rested he suddenly felt the blood rushing to his head. He sat up and listened attentively and his gaze was fixed about 30 feet high above the opposite bank of the river. The sound was unmistakable. And then a grayish line began to emerge from the sky. And the honking was now a distinct gaggle. A flight of 20 greylags was moving slowly across the river in the direction of the Shikari. He shook Khalifa and whispered:

"My gun's next to you. Give it to me quick. And don't make a sound. Tell your men to lie flat and not move."

The Shikari knew that before the geese came within firing range they would sense danger and veer away from the men. By their formation it was apparent that they would peel off to their right – to the Shikari's left. Bending low, the Shikari, almost in a crouch ran to his left along the bank. The geese were going to cross the river exactly where he had expected them to. The explosion from the barrels of his gun sounded as if a peel of thunder had emanated from the river. Khalifa and the men watched as they lay on their bellies. And two large birds which had been hit changed direction and plunged into the river closer to where the men were.

The Shikari shouted: "Did you see where they fell?"

Khalifa said: "They're floating down the river, almost near the middle."

"I guess we've lost them," the Shikari said. "I should have waited till they had crossed but they were already changing direction when I fired."

Khalifa and his entire crew had begun wading into the river and when they reached the main current they began to swim in the direction of the floating birds. They swam soundlessly. The Shikari could see them gaining on the floating birds. And then the swimmers disappeared behind a deep bend in the river. The Shikari waited in silence. And to his left he heard that familiar sound again. The laugh that made the waters ripple. And from a distance he could see Khalifa trudging through the sand like a drum major holding a goose in each hand by the neck. His men were marching proudly behind him.

"Khalifa, you're a genius," the Shikari exclaimed.

He replied: "No I'm a *mallah*."

3

How often I was to see this scene repeated when I was old enough to accompany Papa on shoots on the banks of the Ganges. But on that day, when Khalifa retrieved those two greylags, he and his men became an inseparable part of the Shikari's entourage. And Papa and Khalifa would regale us for years with tales built around their first encounter which began near the jeep bogged down in quicksand.

I remember Khalifa's shoulders. Papa, who was constantly admonishing him to stay out of trouble, suggested that Khalifa should go into business. Papa advised him, that in addition to the small fishing boats he and his men used when they wanted to go miles downstream, Khalifa should build a sturdy ferry boat in which he could transport cattle, people and even bullock carts to the other shore. Because in the Monsoon months when the Ganges turned a greenish yellow, swelled to several times its size, the entire region on this side of the river was cut off from the rest of the country. To cross the river, people had to travel 50 miles in one or the other direction along the course of the river in order to make use of two train bridges built by the British. Cars, of course, could not cross until early October.

Papa agreed to finance the scheme and Khalifa even worked out nominal rates he would charge as fare. The project took six months to complete and Khalifa and his men began the construction in a secluded area on the bank of the river. To ward off the evil eye only the builders and a few of Khalifa's closest associates were allowed to visit the site of creation. He even asked Papa to keep away. He wanted to surprise him. When it was built Khalifa came to Raipur to invite Papa to see it. The structure was standing on the bank near where Khalifa had taken Papa fishing the first day they met. And Papa couldn't believe his eyes.

It was huge. Shaped like a barge on top with a platform area more than 25 feet by 25 feet with wooden railings along the edges for safety, and rounded at the bottom with a regular bow and stern and rudder. Papa said:

"Khalifa, but this is wonderful. But why so big? You could cross an ocean with this."

Khalifa said: "To ferry your car across so you can drive to Delhi. Of course I'll charge you double. A man has to make a living."

"But how will I get the car on to this thing. I can't reach this part of the river in my big car as I can in a jeep."

"You won´t have to come this side anyway. We've worked things out. We'll show you when the river swells." This was around May. In late July when the river had risen and was flowing fast and furious and when its waters stretched to more than a mile from shore to shore at their closest points, Khalifa asked Papa to bring one of his cars, a Humber, to a point where a motorable bank, just off the main road, sloped gently into the shallows of the river. The boat was bobbing in the water. A sturdy bed of wooden planks joined expertly together – six feet wide and 15 feet long – propped up so they sloped at a gentle angle, formed a bridge over which the car could drive on to the carriage area of the boat.

The Shikari stared in wonderment: "Are you sure it's strong enough? I hope the planks don't crumble underneath the weight of the car."

Khalifa laughed and the boat bobbed a little harder as a result: "No, we've tested it with an elephant."

The planks never crumbled and the boat never lost direction or suffered defeat at the hands of the Ganges in any way while crossing it even when the river was at its angriest. I remember Khalifa's shoulders because I was about four years old when I got to cross in his boat, a journey I made several times for more than a decade until the first motorable bridge was completed in the area. I remember Khalifa's shoulders because until I was six or seven years old he would pick me up and seat me on one shoulder and my brother Tips on the other and charge up that wooden ramp to the boat's commodious platform, and then turn around and guide Papa's car on to the boat much the same way as a ground crew guides a modern passenger airplane into its parking bay. Khalifa's men would untie the boat, clamber aboard, pull in the portable bed of planks, and guide the contraption along the currents to the other shore steadily with a combination of oars, and sturdy, long wooden staves which were built to touch the bottom. At the other end, the men would jump off, position the bed of planks and Papa would drive his car off the boat. Khalifa seemed to guide the boat with movements of his shoulders. Throughout the crossing the breeze was strong, and a spray soaked our faces and we closed our eyes and breathed deeply. Khalifa's shoulders moved like a rudder.

Part Two

Part Two

Chapter X

1

His fragrances had evanesced as he lay dying – the overpowering hiss of the humidifier, the smell of disinfectants and antiseptics trapped underneath the quilted false ceiling. But there were other times, when he was younger and utterly robust, when Papa's aura of fragrances turned into hellish no-smells: when his temper flared. When his anger began to erupt, first his front teeth would clench tight, his chin thrust forward by a movement of his lower jaw would force the center of his lower lip to jam against the center of the upper lip and in this compression of angry lip against lip, the corners of his mouth would droop in a fierce semi-circle, his nostrils would flare outwards and upwards and become so tight that you would, it seemed, need a pair of pliers to press them back to normal, and his bushy eyebrows would knit and hold the upper ridge of his nose in a vice-like grip, creating on his forehead two vertical furrows, and his eyes would narrow and spit out black sunbursts. The howl that he would emit would start as a rumbling in his stomach and by the time it reached his throat it would animalize his vocal chords and develop into a sound that alternated between the baying and braying of creatures who were fed on sandpaper as a staple diet. The family shook and trembled before these hellish tantrums, especially when they occurred at the dining table when, this man, a prisoner of fastidious cuisine, sensed that the *moong daal* was cold, the meat was not properly trimmed of its muscle and fat, or that a dish – no matter how much of a delicacy – had made an uninvited appearance at the table.

Mama was usually the target of these tyrannical onslaughts. An unwanted dish would make a surreptitious appearance on the table usually through an error of omission by the servant. There were days when Mama, not always able to live up to the culinary *entente* of the dining table – unilaterally dictated by her husband – would tell the cook to rustle up a special dish for her. Usually, this special dish would arrive at the table only after Papa had finished his dessert of caramel custard, or mangoes and cream, or jelly with custard, or rice *kheer*, or stewed prunes or stewed guavas, and risen from the table to retire to his chambers of perfumes. But once in a while Mama's special dish, was served with the other dishes.

It was a mystery what made the Shikari explode when this happened. Perhaps it was as if he had sighted a non gamebird smack bang in the middle of a morning flight of wild geese. Mama never fought back tears. He seemed to derive not just satisfaction but also energy from his hysteria.

These shameless outbursts of sultanism before which the perfumes retreated faster than Napoleon's bedraggled army under the counter-attack from Mother Russia's patriots often had gastronomical origins. The Dance of the Toast and the Egg, as we were later to dub the breakfast soap opera in Mussoorie was inspired by Chivers Marmalade.

A dozen years after the Brits had vacated the subcontinent its educated subculture was still plussing and minusing the effects of 300 years of the Raj. The bastards ruined our native cottage industries. Well, they gave us the first symbols of unity – railroads, the telegraph, modern management methods. Bullshit, that was just to facilitate their penetration of India's deeper markets. They gave us a language that made us competitive world citizens. Crap, the language was simply an instrument to enslave us within mindless bureaucratic jobs. Hindu nationalists were not moved by nuances and gray areas. For them the British were simply a white curse, a pollution best confined within the boundaries of the nook-shotten isle of Albion. And for a large number of peasants and residents of rural India some of whom may even have participated in Gandhi's marches – and Papa earned universal hostility when he brazenly articulated this sentiment on behalf of the peasants he knew, for which proud post-independence Indian, no matter what he believed in his heart, would articulate this? — there was relatively less corruption, speedier justice, exemplary public works such as roads and bridges, worthy of emulation under the Raj. Even today, villages in India carry hand-me-down memories, even a strange nostalgia about caring and compassion in local Brit officialdom.

Papa was well aware of the Cockney Smithers whose empty overcoat pockets had determined the destiny of his family. But he was loath to condemn all of Britishdom, especially the upper classes, for why, had they not given the Shikari his Holland & Holland, his Westley Richards? And only a highly civilized race was capable of producing Worcestershire Sauce, and Chivers Marmalade. And the perfect fried egg, soft in the yellow, never jagged around the white edges, only to be enjoyed to the full when eaten at an 8 a.m. breakfast on a misty morning in a spacious dining room in a British-style hotel in a Himalayan hillstation following a warm bath and a shave using a Gillette blade – another fine legacy from the Brits.

When Papa showered praise on the Brits he often mentioned Chivers and Gillette and hill stations. For when our rooms would hum with heat and the dust would seep into our rooms in Raipur from under the wooden sheesham doors, Papa's chamber of perfumes would sometimes be converted into an Operations Room where plans would be made to make a strategic retreat into what he considered to be among the Brits' greatest gift to Indian humankind: hill stations. In the north, they still dot the lower and middle ranges of the Himalayas.

Kasauli. Mussourie. Dalhousie. Darjeeling. Ranikhet. Gulmarg. Simla. Meticulously planned and ingeniously built towns 6,000, 7,000, even 10,000 feet high, approach roads snaking around ridges and spurs, chateaux, villas, Elizabethan and Edwardian mansions, groves of deodar and chir pines, plum trees, apples, peaches, pomegranates, Himalayan oak, bungalows and cobbled streets, clubs and skating rinks, cinema halls, Rialto and Odeon and Picture Palace, horsetrails and picnic baskets, male beauty contests and wooden dance floors and Goan bands playing fox-trot numbers and sambas, burnished leather chairs in libraries, and smoking areas with Rattan cane, Sobranie cigarettes and the coolth of the morning mists where you wore sweaters while the plains baked and baked, where the high Dhauladhar ranges and the peaks of Everest and Nanga Parbat and Nanda Devi remained behind veils of cumulus and nimbus and mammatus clouds often spreading like flames across the sky and where a peak sighting whenever the clouds lifted was a cause for celebration with tankards of Becks beer in an afternoon lawn party under multi-colored parasoles, and black partridge teet-teeter-teeteree'd in meadows which had once reminded the Brits of Scotland and the gentleness of their own countryside, and in these hill stations they had recreated moors and valleys and dales with mules and mule tracks and coolies and handpulled rickshaws, and palanquins for the higher slopes, unique drainage systems in the mountains in the Himalayas in the skies amid pine leaves and pinewinds and warblers and bulbuls and paradise flycatchers and magpies, and ravens which did not caw but kahaa'ed and cackow'ed, and it was this phenomenon that held Papa in awe.

2

On the eve for a retreat to Mussoorie in the Doon Himalayas Papa was in a high state of loquacity. We were to drive through the night and stay at the Shropshire Gardens, a hotel built among deodar pines and redolent with evening breezes of jasmine and pinecones which wafted into the wood-paneled rooms from across the fine tennis courts built in the middle of a grove and the verandah outside the front office displayed large movie posters of Laurel and Hardy and W.C. Fields and the Three Stooges and Bogart and Victor Mature and Raj Kapoor and Madhubala. Papa was persuading a friend, Monty Singh, a slim, greasy-haired, mustachioed scion of a former Rajput princely family to stay at the Shropshire with us instead of at the Tukesbury Inn where Monty had made a booking.

"Monty," Papa said, "Shropshire rooms have fine tin roofs and you have to lie still and listen to the rain as it hits the surface at night, starting at first like audible dewdrops and climaxing in a fortissimo clash of cymbals. And there's always perfect breakfast weather there. The fried eggs are perfection. Cooked over a slow fire in butter in a flat pan. The chef takes care with them. He does not break the eggs directly into the pan but first breaks them into a saucer and then pours them from the saucer gently into the pan so they maintain their shapes. And just before they're done, he covers the pan for a brief few seconds before serving. The toast is served perfect. Not so hot that it absorbs the butter – which is cut in small squares and placed in crushed ice in the butter dish – and gets soggy, and not so cold that it hardens completely and crumbles beneath the butter knife. Now some may think of this as gross, but I consider it to be the ultimate in civilized eating. After you butter your toast, and lay it on thick, top it with Chivers marmalade. Then place your fried egg on top of the buttered, marmaladed toast and add salt and pepper. As you bite and chew, look out through the bay windows. And now you know why you should go with us to the Shropshire."

We journeyed through the heat that night, because the night was cooler for travel and arrived at the Shropshire at midnight and it was drizzling and we used blankets at night. Eight a.m. was breakfast in the hall and the mist scented with hill grasses was blowing in the wind. Papa and Monty wore Harris tweed coats, Monty a striped tie and gray flannels, Papa a colorful scarf and corduroy pants. We wore white ducks and blazers, the girls formal dresses and Mama a blue sari with a white shawl. Papa sat at the head table, lifted the cone-shaped white table napkin from the embroidered table cloth, unfurled it with a flourish and spread it on his lap. We tucked ours into our shirt collars. We had all ordered fried eggs. The Chivers and butter were already in place, the marmalade in two cutglass bowls. Waiters in blue serving jackets, cummerbunds, starched white trousers with vertical bands running from hip to ankle brought in toasts in two toast-racks each holding four and laid one in front of Papa and the other near Monty.

That this scene of peace beneath the Christmas tree was undergoing a rapid transition was noticeable to none of us until Seema happened to glance casually at Mama. For a moment it left Seema transfixed until she shook herself out of it, kicked me under the table and nodded in Mama's direction. Mama through sheer instinct could perceive impending changes in Papa's moods, especially the prelude to a bout of uncontrollable sultanism. And we could see this in Mama's expression. Her face was flushed with the anticipation of an incipient embarrassment. There were specks of fear in her eyes which darted from her husband to her lap with her head slightly bowed. We looked sideways at Papa and sure enough, the teeth had begun to clench, the corners of his mouth to drop, the nostrils to flare, the brows to knit. God! Had Mama sneaked one of her special dishes into the dining hall, and that too for breakfast? Would he bray or bay? I for one was ready to whisk Mama away to safety as soon as the eruption came. But what Papa did, stunned even the person who knew him best – Mama. He picked a piece of toast and slammed it to the ground where it lay sad and shattered. He repeated this strange ritual with yet another piece of toast, which to my horrified amusement actually took one bounce on the parquet floor before it died. Then Papa folded his arms before his chest and looked at all of us not in triumph or in defiance but rather tauntingly, as if to elicit a query about this dastardly attack on two pieces of toast. We avoided his gaze. Monty was, simply, paralyzed.

The waiter came in with the fried eggs in silver dishes and laid them on the table. Papa spoke in a low bellow from behind clenched teeth:

"What do I eat them with?"

"With your toast, Sir," the waiter said.

Papa pointed to the floor where lay the toast carcasses.

"Oh, you dropped them. I'll get you new ones and send someone to clean the floor, Sir."

"No," Papa thundered. "I threw the bloody things myself. One was so hard it cracked when I tried to butter it. One was so hot and soft it turned into a sponge when I tried to butter it."

"Sorry, Sir."

"No sorry," Papa said. "Call Miss Hanklin. Now." Even though the British had left nearly a dozen years ago, the hotel, like many others, was under British management, and Betty Hanklin had remained behind as a manager. A lissome, 45-year old brunette with a boy's crop, silver-capped teeth, who wore long floral dresses.

Apprised by the waiters of the developments in the dining hall, Miss Hanklin strutted in well-prepared. She walked to our table, looked with raised eyebrows at the floor and spoke directly to Papa:

"We don't throw things on the floor in this dining room."

Papa did not even hesitate to clear his throat before responding.

"*We* don't," he growled, "but *I* do."

Miss Hanklin, whose father had been a grenadier in the light infantry and had seen action in Afghanistan, did not budge. "Well," she said, "this is most uncivilized, and it will be reported."

Papa retorted: "Go report it to your ruddy Queen. You took back recipes of chutneys and curries from us Indians and we gave them to you graciously. And now you can't even serve us a decent toast you bloody racists. We developed the perfect toast and fried egg breakfast here. Back home you Brits probably don't even know what a decent toast is. Uncouth, uncivilized race. Disgrace to your own hill stations. In fact, the Crown should apologize for this."

And suddenly filled with the desire to add further indignation to righteousness, Papa selected a fried egg, hooked it with a fork and hurled it onto the floor where the second toast had taken a bounce and where the egg, too, now that it had hardened as it lay unattended on the silver dish, took a small bounce and lay bleeding.

Miss Hanklin screamed, then fled.

"The Brits every now and then need a kick in the pants to keep them in their place," Papa said to us. "My father's sister, my *bua*," he said, his voice calm with a new memory in it, "was a tough woman. While visiting Raipur in 1914, she was waiting for a change of trains at the Bareilly railway platform. She could read or speak no English. By mistake she sat down on a bench which was reserved only for the whites. There were many places where the Brits practiced racial segregation. A white policeman asked her to vacate. She did not understand but found the tone of his voice so provocative that she took off her slipper and beat him ferociously around the head until some others came to his rescue. In her own defense she argued before the gathering of spectators that the policeman had been the aggressor – that he had tried to pat her in some unmentionable part of her body. She was so convincing that the white Station Master had to offer her a personal apology along with a promise that he would recommend to the appropriate authorities that the erring policeman be confined to his barracks pending an investigation. But that was not the end of the episode. In beating the policeman my aunt had made contact with a race she considered impure and a blight on her religion. In fact, she was so fastidious that when Brits came to her house for dinner – and despite segregation and racism they would socialize with their subjects – they were fed from a separate pantry and separate dishes. After beating up the policeman, my aunt made a special trip to the Holy city of Haridwar in order to bathe in the Ganges and purify herself."

Monty wanted to leave but Papa would have none of it. He suddenly turned towards Mama and asked her, straight-faced, if she had any leftovers from the previous night or any special dish of hers in the kitchenette in our suite of rooms in the hotel. We all looked at Papa dumbfounded. Then Mama answered:

"Yes, there's a little spicy *moong dal* I brought along with me and some rice sauteed in cumin and some sour mango pickle."

Papa summoned a waiter and instructed him to accompany me to our rooms, to heat the *dal* and rice and bring it to our table in the dining room. He tipped him in advance.

That day, for breakfast in the Shropshire dining hall we partook of Mama's *dal* and rice – items usually served for lunch or dinner. It was on this day, probably at this moment that Elizabeth Seymour fell in love with Papa.

3

The hotel, in summer, was packed with foreign guests. Many of them senior members of embassies, many of them Europeans and Brits who had served or grown up in India during the Raj and had returned yearly on sentimental journeys. That morning after Papa created the brouhaha, most of them had left their tables in a hurry.

But Elizabeth Seymour had remained seated watching and hearing everything from an adjoining table. She was tall. She wore her hair in a blonde bun. She wore high heels. Two-piece woolen suits. Smelled of Ma Griffe perfume. Wore no lipstick. Was married to the British Army attache in New Delhi. She had ancestral homes in Devon, Hertfordshire, Harrow on the Hill, Hampstead Heath. Prep school. Cambridge. She looked like Grace Kelly.

She floated towards our table, her hand held out to Papa, her eyes smiling. And she said: "I'm Elizabeth Seymour. May I join you for some of your *dal*?"

Papa shook her hand firmly. Offered her a plate and a bowl. Mama looked the other way. She was uncomfortable. She had sensed that Papa was about to fall in love.

Chapter XI

1

That summer of 1959, 12 years after the British had left India Papa did the fox-trot with British ladies. The first ritual dance was always with Mama to the piano of the Goan 'Dad' d'Noronha who, Papa said, was a mean match for Ellington and Basie. Within the first year of their marriage, when Mama was 17, and Papa, 28, he had engaged a private dance instructor who taught Mama the steps. He would count out the rhythms while Mama practiced using a light chair as partner, holding on to its arms at both ends and sliding along the floor. She spoke little English but understood enough of the language to flavor Garbo and Valentino, and Tyrone Power, and Gable, and read the script in silent Buster Keaton and Harold Lloyd movies.

She danced stiffly, somewhat comically, like the scarecrow in the Wizard of Oz, looking straight across Papa's shoulder, never into his eyes, while Papa positively floated. But she enjoyed dancing. And after having spent a spell on the floor with him, you could see in her face a gentle sensuous glow of wanting Papa. But that summer of '59 Mama was pensive. There was a quiet brooding in her eyes when Papa, after a couple of dances with her, would ask the foreign ladies to the floor. Not that Mama was jealous of Papa's other worldly contacts. For her, marriage was an indestructible contract that even the Gods could not rent asunder. Being bonded to a man was life. Being bonded to a good man was living. Being bonded to a man you loved was life ever after. And she had loved Papa, shyly, quietly. It was not Papa on the floor with the other ladies which made her brood. It was Papa with Elizabeth Seymour.

When Papa danced, he would usually fix his gaze on the nape of the neck of his partner. But with Elizabeth Seymour, he would draw himself back just a little and look into her eyes. And what annoyed Mama was that he would dance with Elizabeth Seymour only once or twice the entire evening. This was Papa's way of throwing people off the scent. Attempting to show people, by dancing fewer times with Elizabeth Seymour than he did with the others, that he cared little for her. Pretending to be casual and nonchalant with someone special so as to keep your feelings undetected by other people. He may have fooled Elizabeth Seymour's husband, or maybe Mr Seymour was a cuckold. But the Shikari's wife wasn't fooled. Mama knew.

And we knew, because she had rummaged through Papa's things – at the Shropshire, there were no forbidden perfumed chambers – and come across letters "she" had written within two weeks of having made his acquaintance. Mama did not understand them all. But she knew enough about Gable and Kelly to realize that she was wife to a moonstruck Shikari. Papa, too, had composed missives to Elizabeth Seymour.

Mama never fussed loudly about Elizabeth Seymour. She raised the subject with Papa, very quietly, very privately. Papa remained impassive. Sometimes Mama wept, softly. She said silent prayers. But she did not sulk. She was always by Papa's-side at the dances and picnics. Many, many years later, 20 years later, when most of her children were married, Mama and Seema were talking about the summer of 1959. It was a good summer, they said, and Mama said she felt sorry for Elizabeth Seymour. Mama was by Papa's side when Elizabeth Seymour came to say goodbye to our family before we departed from the Shropshire for the plains. Mama recalled that Elizabeth Seymour was fighting back tears, her lower lip was fluttering like a moth out of control when she held her hand out to Papa to say goodbye, and Mama was so moved by pity and affection for Elizabeth Seymour that she too began to cry.

Mama said to Seema: "I still have that one letter your father wrote. I pinched it before it was delivered. I still feel guilty that Elizabeth Seymour did not see it. It belongs to her. But I want you to read it. And never tell your father."

Seema read the letter by herself. And then read it to me. It was in the handwriting so familiar to all of us:

June 29, 1959

"We willed our dream. You willed a canvas and breathed life into it. You painted love. I was a smudge, and then a color, and then a fused form, a blob of unconscious awakening wanting to be caressed from afar, admired from afar and yet ever yearning to feel of the creator's brush. Losing color when untouched, sinking into the comfortable repose of the half-life, resplendent and iridescent when touched.

"Filling empty paper with teardrops of ink I grieve for my loneliness, jealous of your freedom, clipping your wings when you want to soar as mine were clipped in a cathedral of traditional love. I escape and want you in fetters. Handcuffed to the devil. Seared in hellish flames. The acrid pungency of your flaming being, your soul in flames is an intoxication. My mind reels. A drunk mind. An ego inebriated with the burningness of forgiveness. The lifetime that cannot last. The seed that must germinate. The infant that must but grow. The youth that must bear the insults of adulthood. The adult who must suffer the indignities of age. But you soothe the wrinkles. You brush them away and leave scars of your own. Scars that will outlive the corpse. Be the one that gave me birth so when you give birth you shall be a bloodmother and a bloodlover. One your child from your own world. One your child from the world you inherited. You didn't ask to be born, but only to live. For to be born is mortal and terrifying.

"Plunging, plunging from infancy, wedded to be gallows, for the trapdoor opens at birth, the noose irrevocably tightening. You are the reprieve. A fleeting sense of eternity which loosens the noose. To live is never to have existed before, without form, without obeisance, without doubt, beyond sorrow, beyond hurt. Floating forever with an unfucked mind. Beyond the sordid and the shitless.

"I seek reassurance in experience. Experience in reassurance. With feet of clay and jellied mind I suckle at your being and mix your nectar with my poison. They effervesce in sulphurous fumes. Blurring visages. Phantasmal musings. And all that's real is holding your hand over a breakfast toast. A weakening clasp, a grip of trembling strength, the power you created in teenage laughter. If love can be scripted, then is there not cause for rejoicing? For surely then we can script joy as surely as we can script tragedy."

Seema and I were left speechless. This flashback was a rare moment in which we were able to see a dimension of rhapsodic sentimentality the Shikari had never shared with us and nor would he ever until his end. We realized, too, that he had left the final script open and that neither he nor Elizabeth Seymour would write its completion. That task, we did not know then, was left to us. And unwittingly we took on the challenge.

During that period, Papa seemed to have changed. He smelled no longer like Papa. For dance nights and clandestine trysts with Elizabeth Seymour, Papa had equipped himself with a new array of colognes and perfumes. He would splash them on liberally, under his armpits, on his face, behind his neck. Papa adorned himself with polka-dotted scarves. He even bought himself a pair of riding boots and a slim cane with a gold-plated knob. Papa now smelled like a dandy. He smelled of commercial products.

And he had extended our vacation into late July to coincide with the stay of Elizabeth Seymour. This would be the first time Papa would miss the onset of the Monsoon in Raipur. The mists were getting thicker everyday in Mussourie. The dance bands played. Occasionally bagpipers played martial tunes at the bandstand. And we children grew sick with sorrow. Not so much because Mama had stopped laughing and had been brooding about "her". But because we were repelled by Papa's dandy smells and because we longed for the Monsoon in Raipur. We sulked. We refused to go horseback riding. We refused to accompany Papa to the ice cream stands. We lingered about in our rooms and littered the place with Dell comics, something Papa hated.

On the last day of June he summoned us to his chamber.

"You don't seem to be too happy," he said.

"We want to go home," Tips said.

"But it's boiling out there in the plains," Papa said.

I said: "But Papa, the Monsoon is setting in, everything's going to change. We *have* to be there, the new mangoes…"

Papa fell silent, blinked, knitted his brows, then raised them and looked out of the window. The script had begun to unfold in all our minds. In Raipur the easterlies had begun to blow and true to Papa's rain diary, the pre-monsoon showers would be making way for the real thing. Heavens cut to shreds by forks of golden light as tree-pies and koels barked and the partridge would be getting ready to lay. As life greened each year as the dust and mud and dinosaur bark on the mango trees absorbed more rain and more rain and the hot winds were chased back across the western deserts, a family had frolicked in the early July wetness, barechested in jeeprides through waterfalls of rain, now trudging through scrub forest slush to see where the partridges had made their nests, driving to the *jheels* and watching them fill up again, from dustbowls into lakes and ponds again, burgeoning with froglife and hovering kingfishers, getting ready for the migratory flights which would start coming in by the end of October.

And from the memories of thunder, the Shikari drove back into the plains the next day, into the thunder itself and it was humid and hot and the clouds were billowing above us like blue and black and white and gray sails catching the wind for us as we sailed with the Shikari deep into the rain and its goodly smell on dry ground, and the Shikari's smells all around us, sucking on mangoes in the rain, past the scrub forest on this Monsoon journey, deep, deep into the mists and shadows and caverns of the Monsoon, we float like paper boats amidst the laughter of the haunted and the forests walk with us scripting the joy in which God and atheist have no say.

Many more Monsoons were to sail in and out of Raipur. And many of them were to stretch the Shikari's spirit to a breaking point of exhaustion and no smells before revivifying him with aromatic fury. For a delay in the Monsoon was nothing less than the short-circuiting of the cycle of rebirth. And when this happened the Shikari wilted and to be near him as he lay tortured and looked with tortured eyes at the heavens was to wilt yourself. Like giant sunflowers bending from the middle of their stalks we drooped from the waist downwards. This was when July was well into its second week. And we had been sweating for three weeks. We showered with water heated around the clock by the sun on overhead tanks, and toweled ourselves dry thrice a day and we were never dry because the sweat poured out like droplets of white blood within seconds from wherever we dried ourselves and we stood underneath the direct blasts of ceiling fans and the sweat, instead of evaporating, simply slithered off our bodies under the onslaught of the gushes of air like water off the rain-drenched windshield of a speeding car, and puddled on the floor and even the bare soles of our feet which had burned all summer long were not free of sweat, the bedsheets always soggy with the nightlong perspiration which spread across our beds as nightlong we turned and twisted and our arms and legs flayed about to throw off wave upon wave of damp heat we saw in our dreams as water-saturated woolen blankets sown together with warm flames of water, and with dehydrated brains we dreamed we were drinking pitcher after pitcher of water and with each swallow the thirst increased and increased until the dream, the sentinel of reality, nudged us awake, awoke us to the reality of our thirst, and we groped in the dark for our bed-stands, encircled our fingers over the water jugs, and still lying on our backs poured the water, stiff-armed from above, from open spouts, in a thick stream into our open mouths, on our night faces, on our chests, warm water, for there had been no power in the towns since electricity was being diverted to the rural areas to keep the fields of transplanted paddy alive, and the refrigerator had made no ice cubes, and to buy ice in the markets was a folly because it came from factories that used contaminated water from morgues or funeral vehicles after cadavers had been dispatched to their cremation grounds. And no human eyebrow was bushy enough or strong enough to provide a frontline barrier against the sweat that poured from our foreheads and into our eyes where the stupid defense of blinking hard would simply force the salt into the entire circumference of the cornea and we would use the bony outer joints of our fingers to rub our eyes and

121

the salt went in deeper and burned and we sweated from our eyeballs.

"The idiots," Papa would say – a reference to Western civilizations – "they actually pay for this. They call it sauna bathing. The idiots actually pay for lotions and lie under the scorching sun to turn the color of their skins brown. Our natural color. And then they have the gall to look down on brown people." Perhaps because his offspring came in several Eurasian tints Papa was never really color-conscious as so many North Indians. But he, too, must have suffered from some Aryan hangover because he was never a dissenting voice in the constant household refrain from the family elders – common to so many Indian households – cautioning children, especially girls, to stay out of the summer sun, not because of the fear of heatstroke, which was real, but as a precaution against getting an even darker complexion. Personally, for the Shikari, the browner the better. Pigmentation was a tactical imperative. It was a better camouflage, a more natural order of things among weeds and reeds and brown and green water mosses and lichen in a jheel against a flight of ducks than an upturned white and red face yo-yoing above the lily pads.

The admonition against the tanning effect of the summer sun did not, however, apply to the July skies. In this grand Monsoon month the skies were awash in thick, billowing paints. And our sauna sufferings and burning eyeballs were an essential process of a cosmic metamorphosis in which summer would give birth to rain and we would revivify with aromatic fury. We were a part of the churning of the seasons. Our torture was not a test of endurance but the hideously painful celebration of the anticipated. With each weak-kneed convulsion as the damp heat tore into our bodies we gave birth to a newer and more menacing cloud in the sky, hastened the pace of the Monsoon currents, provided the electrical charge that ignited the firmament and squeezed the water out of the skies. The greater our suffering, the greater the joy of anticipation. For this debilitating physical trauma actually kindled the spirit. We knew that in its absence, that without the asphyxiating perspiration, if the temperatures were cooler, if our bodies relaxed in temperate bliss, there would be no rain. The greater our discomfiture the closer the rains. For we were actually in labor, giving birth to a new season.

The Shikari stuffed endless handkerchiefs under his chin, between his vest and chest, under his armpits to soak up the sweat during these weeks of labor, and strutted to and from the verandah like an expectant father, scanning the skies for telltale cloud formations. When he actually wilted, and we wilted with him, it was not for lack of endurance but because the hour had gone. When the Monsoon was delayed. When the body labored on but the skies registered nothing but a white haze, when the westerlies refused to let the east winds blow, when the puffs of clouds remained disjointed and refused to billow into black-based floating cauliflowers taking turns to cover the sun and casting deep shadows in which the brown grass looked green, and when winged ants and giant moths refused to rise from the ground and knock themselves out against light bulbs in sounds of grains of sand, and lapwings and white-breasted kingfishers, and mynahs refused to shut their beaks even when in repose. A Monsoon without rain was like endless labor without childbirth.

This did not happen often, but when it did, the Shikari betrayed his world. He would talk about moving to the hills and simply dumping Raipur. He was angry with God for not believing in him. Our chamber of perfumes would, like Atlantis, simply sink beneath the sea.

"But Papa," I said, "Soon there will be October, and Diwali, and your evening drink after Mama's puja when we light the firecrackers. Two months on there will be winter. You'll be cleaning out your gun, and the *jheels* will be teeming with duck."

He replied: "God has crippled the year." For him everything went together. The scrub forest, teeming *jheels*, the Monsoon, the dust storms. Nothing was complete without the other. Even the brilliance of a sparkling winter and white roses and blooming bougainvillea met with disdainful disapproval – or simply a lack of acknowledgement –unless it had followed, in orderly seasonal succession, a good Monsoon and Diwali season. And to show his contempt for this celestial aberration, the Shikari would pick out a bone-chilling January morning and appear at the breakfast table dressed in a light cotton T-shirt. When a solicitous Mama asked him to wear woolens he replied:

"But what makes you think this is winter?"

Mama was confused. "But last year we had a warm winter. And yet you wore your woolens."

"That was a proper winter," he replied. "You remember the Monsoon that year? In one spell it rained eight days without a break. Just like it used to. And I taught the servants' children how to make paper boats and sail them in our flooded lawn, just as we used to when I was a child and Monsoon was real. This year we did not even have earthworms seeking shelter in our verandahs. And no rain insects sticking in our hair at nights. In fact the rain insects have disappeared. It takes a scorching summer to bring in a Monsoon. One must follow the other. This summer we suffered but we had a piss of a Monsoon. If such an excuse for a Monsoon followed that summer, virtually no rain, then everything is wrong, and this winter has no business being here."

Quietly, Mama draped a woolen shawl across his shoulders, and said: "But the ducks are here already. Or are they not ducks?" Papa studied his toast, silently, and then took a big crunch out of it.

Chapter XII

1

In one occasional delirium during the last lap when the Shikari was making a rapid and dignified dash towards the finishing line under the quilted false ceiling and his lungs no longer expanded like the bellows they had been but sound like the last gasps of a squeezed accordion he hears the humidifier hissing and with half-eyes he sees the vapor fogging up the mirror dangling in between its swivels on the sides on top of the dresser while Mama keeps a meditative vigil from a straight-backed chair, slouched, her left hand clasping her left knee, her right elbow resting on her right thigh, her chin hooked between her forefinger extended along the ridge of her nose and her thumb balled up with the rest of her fingers under her chin. "Mussoorie?" he asks. And Mama sees the vapors and the mist and in barely a whisper she says, No, you're dreaming. And she shivers and draws her shawl tightly around her.

No, Mama never resented her husband for not loving God. She joined with him freely, in fact in a pagan ceremony, at the dinner table. Why, goddamit, when he picked out the wishbone from the roast partridge, well, hello, she looked up from the mashed potatoes and gravy, and actually joined the Shikari, finger-and-thumb, in a ritual to break the wishbone apart. And the dinner table children clapped. What had she wished for? That one day she should join him in reading Spinoza's *Ethics*, or Hemingway, or Dostoievsky, or Loyd C. Douglas, or his tomes on Roman jurisprudence? Or that she would make a temple-fearing believer out of him? Why, she forgave as naturally and as effortlessly as children forgive God in their innocent prayers before they realize what a devil He is.

Mama did not drive men to madness and distraction. Her power came from a perennial suspension of judgement. And her unabashed shyness. In Mussoorie, Mama had displayed her bashfulness to me, once. When Papa was out on a ride with Elizabeth Seymour, Mama had her period. We did not know this then. But she was out of Tampax. Tampax came to India before Coke and Pepsi. Perhaps even before Fridge. And Papa was the only one privileged to go shopping for menstruating Ma. I do not know what came over her. From the mists, from the pines and pony rides, Mama summoned me to the cottage outside the parquet-floored dining hall where the egg had danced with the toast and I'd never seen Mama looking so stern. Her *bindi* rotated in incandescent heat in the middle of her forehead like in Indian movies, a sequence in which a third eye shimmers on the head of a deity (against an offending male) before a religiously beseeching Meena Kumari.

Mama handed me two rupees. "Ask the shopkeeper to give you a box of santowels," she said. She gave me the name of a shop. She pronounced it "saintoles." And she warned: "Have it packed in brown wrapper. And don't look into it." I trudged to the mall, paid for the saintoles. I thought there might be candy. So I opened one from its wrapper. A piece of fluffy cotton in the shape of a feathery dog turd. Stuffed it back and delivered the contraband to Mama who took possession without a word of thanks or acknowledgement.

I asked Tips about it and he said: "Just some shit that women stuff up their cunts when they bleed each month." I was too horrified even to let the thought sink in that Mama even ever touched that part of her body. In my world where below the waist was dirty, sisters may have cunts and brothers and friends may have dicks but mothers and fathers and people you respected were, simply, clean. I drew reproductive organs with clarity in biology class, dissected frogs, learned about spermatozoa and ova but I was damned if I was going to believe that Papa actually mounted Mama, that Shikari would actually move his butt up and down in between the thighs which had been my lap when she stroked my head, no sir, your parents may do that all, but I believed in binary fission, and even when the age of sexual reason dawned on me, I searched fervently for scientific evidence of parthenogenesis, and even late in my years I could feel a warm glow flow like a sap of vindication through my body when, in George Lucas's *Phantom Menace*, Anakin Skywalker's mother says that the young Jedi was conceived without a father.

Part Three

CHAPTER XIII

1

In the late 1960s Tips and Mama and the rest were writing letters to me which flew across the Atlantic. I had left Raipur for New York, to write and to study. I had promised Papa, who was nearing his late fifties then, that I'd be back. And he had told me: "At least come back when I'm still in my seventies! My eyesight will still be good, and I hope there will still be *jheels* and forests around. I'll keep your gun greased. And when I'm ready to make my final journey, I want you and your children, if you have any, to be by my side."

Those were the early feminist years in the U.S. We marched down Manhattan's Fifth Avenue, when Betty Friedan and Gloria Steinem were trying to knock our balls into sensitivity. We carried placards, "Liberation *oui*, Castration *non!*" a slogan composed by a Polish Jew, heading a publishing firm I worked for, a bushy-haired Manhattan patrician, whose t's were the soft t's of Brooklyn, with the tongue flattened out where the palate meets the front teeth, whose father and brother had had their genitals crushed by a Nazi guard in Treblinka. While composing the slogan, he, Mort Tussand, (his name had been Marck Tussanovic) told us that if we didn't march with Leftist and liberal causes we were all doomed, but he had also scribbled another slogan at which he winked, before he threw it into the garbage can, that read: "The vagina is the unkindest cut of all."

And we streaked naked in Woodstock and alternative lifestyle festivals in Goddard College, Vermont. Joplin and Baez and Dylan are singing, and Ginzberg is chanting a Vedic prayer and several LSD'd kids look into the burning sun above and start chorusing I AM THE RESURRECTION, and they fall flat on their backs with purple blind eyes, aah, aaah, aaah, aaah, and there were no ambulances or Blue Cross or eye drops, only acid-freaked junkheads, and a belief in the curative power of the Hindu. And two blacks, naked waist upwards, Afros tied in ribbons, with loin cloths to hide their Masai-painted dicks, huge dongs and schlongs kept in harness because their sisters had told them that they'd dipped enough in white pussy to last them a lifetime, and they led me – the Hindu – to the near blind acid-freaked kids from Minnesota and Dubuque and Sioux Falls, eyes rolling with the pain of the Easter proclamation that never came, and the black dudes say, Hey Hindu do your stuff, Hey fuck you says the Hindu, treat me nice, your motherfucking W.D Fard and Malcolm, they came from my part of the world and taught you how to deal with Honky, Don't say motherfucking the big dude says, and I say, Okay, okay, and then I recognize him and says to me, Asshole, I know you, I've been to your apartment in Manhattan, man, we drunk that Indian beer together and we got high on Muscatel, now I want to do these white brothers a favor, coz they're alright! And I ask Why, and he says, Remember, you told me that your old man – Papa – had read you a book in which it said that there's a Mamba snake in Kenya that spits poison into the eyes of people, dead set on target?

The Shikari reads to his children all the time. And he tells us about the Mamba. A Cobra-like beast that spits poison into the cornea and aims it well. And the only cure is urine. Human urine. Piss immediately into the victim's eye. And I told this story to the this black dude in my Manhattan apartment and now he reminds me of Papa's cure and says, Hey man, let's help these honky cocksuckers.

And I say, How, and he says, Dammit, you nail-bed-sleeping-ropetrick-Taj-Mahal turd, piss into their eyes! But, they've looked into the sun, I say, they might need balm or eyedrops. Piss into their eyes, you sonofabitch, the dude says, and he's got, like two quarts of rum in him, and he's smoked a dozen joints, Or I'll drop some of that same acid shit, look into the sun, blind myself and ask you to piss in mine! Besides, he says, your Papa, the guy seems cool, man, a great black dude, do it for his memory, man, if not for me. But what if it doesn't work, brother, I say, I mean, this shit has no FDA approval. This is too much for the dude. Pull down your pants asshole, he says. And I say, no, I'm shy. I'm shy because I remember Mama wouldn't even say santowels in front of me, and I still was convinced in my spiritual self that Mama did not have anything but gods and angels below her waist.

"I'm shy man," I say. And he says: "Fuck you. You're doing this to help the honky liberals who are going to be the shitguard of the Black Revolution. The more you keep alive, the larger our shitguard. This is only our training ground. Do it man. For my sake." Do you know that this doped out black dude is really in tears? He's a huge guy, like about six-feet-eight. A basketball player who got admission to Brown on a scholarship, almost got invited to the Harlem Globetrotters, but blew it because after he dunked a fantastic net, instead of giving a high five he took off his shorts and laid a large lonely turd right under the net. The cops rushed to pick up Jim Stacey, a bunch of long-hairs said Long Live the Revolution, rushed to his rescue, re-named him Turdy Dribble and sneaked him off to Cuba to do the cane fields until he called one of Castro's supervisors a half-nigger and then escaped on a refugee boat to Miami and convinced the CIA that he was an agent provocateur, and while they were checking him out he went to Chicago, attended Malcolm's gatherings and was re-christened Ahmad Jamal Hussain Farid Ali Khan. And when he met me first, not too long ago in Manhattan, he said, Hi Hindu you must be Singh, I'm Khan, let's get this India-Pakistan shit over with and I'll get you some of the warmest black pussy if you can arrange for some Hindu tight shit. And I told Khan seriously, Hindu women don't fuck, they mastermind, or they're clean below the waist. And Khan tells me, I'll come to India, man, we'll live in Goa, it's cheap out there, I'll write a book, maybe even teach the kids how to play basketball. Just because you can get inside the pants of a Hindu woman? I say. And he kind of sulks and says, nah man, it's kind of spiritual; you know, like all that Rajneesh funk, I kinda missed out on that, and that Maharishi shit, well maybe I can get all that directly. And I say, Listen Man, this Third World shit is a lot of crap. The Chinks massacre the Japs and the Mongolians, and the Arabs are at each others' throats and African tribes take human trophies from other tribes, like your Injuns who fight not just Bill Cody and Custer but massacre each other, and in my country they kill little brown babies for religion, and let me tell you, you're going to have it tough there. They're going to call you hubshee and little brown kids are going to chase you and ask you if you live on trees. And Khan says, Whazzat mean? And I say it means, n-i-g-g-e-r, and he says, But we're brothers, we Afro-Asians, I mean, look at what all these dudes here are saying that America's liberation will be inspired by the Third World and Vietnam is proof of it. Hubshee means nigger, I repeat, and I tell Khan, we Indians are racist, my old man's a racist, half of our people are blacker than shit man but I doubt whether they'll give their girls in marriage to a nigger. Khan looks sort of sad and handsome. And I look at big dude Khan and wink and say, Where you from, boy? And he says Larkin, Mississippi, where my old man grew corn and caught carp and hunted Turkey, and snared rabbits, and stalked deer, and made decoys for mallards. Mallards! I said. Mallards? Ducks?? And Khan says, Yeah. Did you ever, I ask, shoot them flying, from a marsh, in waist deep water, in the cold, in the evening when the smoke rose from the villages and there was a canopy of haze and the evening flights whistled in? Khan was saying something.

And I had a vision of Papa in the marsh. The moonlight flights were swarming in and we were swinging at them. Thuck. Flop. Splash. In the water. And the Shikari began wading out. A last gaggle of geese went above him. He had a Number Four in his choke barrel. He could hardly see them. He heard their gaggling. We were not watching. We had learned enough from the Shikari. We didn't have to watch him either for technique or for pleasure. That he was with us was simply joy. And then, lonely for appreciation, the Shikari swung his Holland & Holland, Number Four in choke barrel. High into the evening sky and he aimed it, eyes closed, about 30 feet ahead of the leader of the flock. He watched in amusement. Too far to hear the thrrrup of the pellets strike. But he watched with evening eyes in the evening after-sun sky streaked with high cirrus fishbone vapors. And she shouted: "It's peeling off!" The ninth bird in the V-formation had been hit. When it peels away from the flight it either goes 10 miles into the Ganges to heal and rest its wounds or it flies a mile and simply gives up, says its last prayer and plummets to the ground to be eaten by jackals or retrieved, rarely, by a dogged shikari. Twilight time. Papa knows he's going to retrieve it. Get into the jeep, he cries. Six of us. We know the Shikari is going to pick up the felled greylag. Out of the darkness, almost with the slowness of a moth, and then with a speed of a zigzagging bat, a feathered creature rises, rises and dips at terrific speed, camouflaged with the scrubby ground. In a less than a second, there's a deafening blast, the down-spiralling bird hits ground with a thud, rolls over and is still. We think Papa has killed a bat in the dark. He walks to it. Picks it up and throws it into the jeep. It's a fine brown partridge, shot in the dark. A brilliant forward shot. I ask: "How did you do it?" The Shikari answers: "Wait." And as night fell, the Shikari, after what seemed like endless meandering in the scrub forest, motions the jeep to halt. We thought he had wanted to take a piss. He smiled at us, pulled his zipper down, went behind a lantana bush and came back holding the felled greylag by the neck. We never asked him how he tracked it down, how he found it. You never did. That was bad manners. You either had it or you didn't.

2

And here was Khan, reminding me of stories Papa had read to us, and prodding me to take a piss in the doped-out eyes of resurrection freaks at this convention of New Leftist Americans when bombs were dropping in faraway Hanoi and the convention kids here were beating bongo drums and cymbals and bass drums. And not out of any subconscious fear about what Mama would

139

have thought about this, but for other compelling reasons, I desisted. "But Khan, I said, "I'm a Hindu. I'm an Austro-Dravidian-Indo-Sanskrit Aryan from south of the Hindukush, and we're told that our special mark of Cain is that no matter how black or wheaten or fair our faces, we're ethnically stamped by our black dicks. That I don't mind, man, but what bugs me is that I'm circumcised. It's embarrassing and at one time it was historically dangerous. In 1947 when my country was partitioned into India and Pakistan, when the circumcised Muslims opted for Pakistan and there were riots, the fanatical Hindus would pull people's pants down to see if their foreskins were cut off and if that were so they'd chop their heads off. Luckily, I was a kid then, and no Partition mania happened in Raipur. But I've still got that fear."

And Khan said: "Woo woo. So was Moses. Maybe so were Martin and Elridge. And most of these freaks to whom you'll deliver a stream of Amrit are Jewish, so go to it man." And Khan shook his Afro like a buffalo shaking flies off its hide, pulled down my jeans and led me around by the belt, and I aimed straight as a Mamba, pissing into their eyes and saying You're bit by the Mamba snake, Awake to the Revolutionary sun, for I am King of Kings, Ozymandias may have been trunkless but not dick-less, urine is all it takes, and the acid freaks saying, aaah, aaah, and waiting for the Communists of America to redeem them with memories of Gus Hall and Charlene Mitchell and telling them of the Vanguard and of Infantile Leftism of the Hip Capitalists and chanting Che, Che, Che, Fidel, fiddle, guitar, Fidel, Fidel, Fidelity, the hi-fis blaring the guitar, Doors, and the Mothers of Invention, and the Incredible String Band Quartet, and WHO while the Voice and the East Village Other and the men from Time n'Newsweek sat with Brothers typewriters in their motel and said the American Left is alive even as Nixon led the Liberal State into more and more Welfare spending and the children of Moynihan's benign neglect fucked on the rooftops with malignant dildos and the softer mamas offered their nipples to bearded impotents and suckled hardened revolutionaries into slumber. And as I suckled white flat-breasted, erect-nippled Mother Mimi who, in between, cradling my head to her ribbed tit, and flapping her thighs like an egret getting dry, would cry death to male pigs, and feeding her orgasm into my mouth through her tits and with every come she'd cry that the milk of feminist kindness is flowing into the poisons and diluting the blood of chauvinist venom.

Ah Mimi, that I had your lactose in my veins when Mama sent me out for those damned santoles. I would have told Mama just as the Offourbacks ladies were burning bras, so what? Remember? Don't shave armpits. Let the tits smell of sweat. So let the pubic juices flow – and why bother about santoles? So I pissed into blind eyes which refused to blaze like meteors and be gay. And the Mambas danced in the Kenyan forests. And Mama would never know, for if she had the slightest inkling that I had bared my genitals to piss into the eyes of half-crazed, dope-dazed innocents she would have banished me from her puja room forever, prayed for my soul, held *havans*, and, very quietly, very, very quietly, in her sleep and in her dreams, remonstrated with Papa for having fathered such a beast. But mostly, and what I said earlier in this paragraph is my fantasy of Mama as the conservative, she would neither have judged nor been angry. She had been frightened to death about me during Partition, had warned me never to take a piss in the open for fear of being detected, and when she was ribbed by relatives and aunts who had seen my wee-wee in my infancy about her having given me an unsheathed, un-Hindu Muslim-Jewish knob, she would whisper expert medical explanations to prove that her son had to forego a centimeter of his foreskin a day or two after birth just because the piss had collected there in a bubble. And now that the bubble was no longer there, her son was streaming in wide arcs of resplendent yellow and orange, computer-generated colors, into the eyeballs of salvation-seeking freaks without FDA approval, and Khan is cheering him on, saying, Hey man, when that bladder's empty, I got lots more, but maan, it ain't worth a shit coz it aint your old man's piss, what'dya call him Sheekari? And I say offmyback, Nigger, I'm almost as black as your ass, motherfucker, and I read James Baldwin before you. Now listen sweetass, before you get all sassy white and talk about my country like those motherfucking Wasps, you know, Nehroooo, Gaaandayee, Mahaaarreeeshheee, Mahaaaraajaas, well, sonofabitch, coz I bared my black circumcised dick in front of you so you could revive those white folk, hell, Khan, go to Inja, get a taste of that dirt man, then you'll get a smell of my Papa. Maybe he's not all you ever imagined. But man, he's for real. And if he's for real, then, man, you're for real. Not coz of me or him or you, but coz, we've gotta FEEL, like in Cat On A Hot Tin Roof. Tennessee's people, hell they were stinkeroos, but you could feel them. And that Shikari...mmmmmm...uuuhhmmmm...mmmm...you can smell that shit so good it smells like a forest of flowers... ummmm... hmmmm.mmm! Khan you sonofabitch.

Chapter XIV

1

Intimacy in the Raipur family was smelling sherry and partridge, of the shared cleaning of the inside of pock- marked gun-barrels after a shoot, or the lachrymose – mostly melodramatically invented but dramaturgically imperfect – tale of the shot that missed, or the sinful felling of female bird while the male got away. Sex was the lusty call of the black partridge, the snorting of a wild boar in search of yams or sweet-potatoes, the bellowing of a blue bull standing in an open field, fully bearded and defying the hunter. But never the mating of the human male and female. Human sex and human sexual relationships were completely private, to be respected like undiscovered galaxies, or hunting preserves which may open up some day to human incursion.

The Shikari was always a model of circumspection except for occasional orgies of ill-tempered abuse directed against sadhus and mendicants and gurus and

145

cumbersome wedding ceremonies. On sexual matters, he too, kept a distance. He, the Shikari, who could copy the roar of a sex-starved lion to such perfection that even Mama would forget herself and blink in sensual anticipation. Papa's children, however, lacked linguistic reserve. As did nephews and friends of nephews. They discussed sexual escapades in vocabulary that would exceed the sailor slang at a Legionnnaires get-together. And teen-age or about-to-be-married family members received adult ribbings about their fiancees' adroitness at blow jobs, tit-sucking and bum-fucks. The Shikari would immediately have expelled from the hunt any member of his troupe overheard using such language in front of the younger generation. Choice Punjabi abuse, while appropriate for British factory inspectors and truckers who would not give way for passing cars, had no place in family lexicon. For the Shikari believed in selective purdah. Masks and shields were important. They kept up the mystique of nobility. Purdah came instinctively. There were parts of yourself and your routine that were kept hidden. A psychic strength of silence that added stature to personality. Like knowing in front of whom to drink. Before whom to let down the defenses of language. Papa's Sunday pre-lunch beer sessions were a cat and mouse game. He watched attentively from the verandah for visitors. For some, the privilege of watching the Shikari quaff beer was pre-ordained. For others, who never even saw the bottle hidden upon their arrival underneath the chair, it was guesswork about whether the Shikari ever drank or not.

Mama, too, as well as Seema and Sara suffered the fate of the beer bottle. Seated in full view before certain visitors or packed off to their boudoirs before the lesser privileged.

2

Throwing linguistic reserve to the winds, and with it the purdah, was sheer rebellion on the part of the next generation. Little Woodstocks of tradition-bashing in a country whose om and sitar and gurus had become the very symbol of rebellion and tradition-bashing in Woodstock. Om and Ravi Shankar and the gurus would have been nauseated at Tips's language at home and yet they gave benevolent benediction to their incantations at Woodstock which at one time was even given historical respectability as a 'nation' in an instant book. And this was the whole debate that ensued after arcs of piss had found themselves into the eyeballs of dope-dazed resurrectionists who awoke after the Mamba cure and Khan pressed my hand in delight. And they rubbed their eyes in wonderment and a Leftist intellectual in a bow-tie and horn-rimmed glasses, Irv Silven who wrote for the Marxist paper, the Guardian and was a pal of Izzy Stone, and claimed he had helped "I.F", as he called him, with a few chapters of "In a Time of Torment." And Silven tells one of the piss-awakened long-hairs, Cruise Gartland, a Harvard dropout whose father owned a chain of hardware stores across the Eastern Seaboard:

"Well, what are you guys trying to accomplish?"

And Gartland still wiping Hindu piss from his eyes, says: "It's here, man. We've arrived. The revolution doesn't happen unless it's happened. And it's happened man. It's right here. We've corn-holed our parents. This IS the revolution. We've buggered American capitalism and Johnson's war through the ying-yang. This is Ho Chi Minh country fella, look around ya."

And Silven says: "This is a historical incongruity. A perversion of the dialectical idiom. Blue collar workers are not with you. The American Left needs to radicalize the workers like the Wobblies did and where Norman Thomas left off. We don't even have a silver-tongued orator. You guys can't man the barricades. All you can do is go to Canada to dodge the draft and hold acid-rock meets like this where the record companies make free recordings and make profits."

Gartland, who'd been speaking with straight New England A's and syllabic pauses decides to go into a revolutionary drawl: "Who dis, Thomas, man? Dontcha see that it's already happened. My old man's ready to kick my butt. Look around you. Mexican dudes. Puerto Ricans. We and not Amerikka have won Viet Nam."

Silven shakes his head and the dots on his bow-tie shimmer and dance: "But you guys can't fight the American army on the streets. You don't know history. Those GIs are taught all about San Juan Hill and Iwo Jima. You don't even know that Stalin buried a hatchet into

Trotsky's head or how even to preserve the gains of the Revolution. Or read Edgar Snow's *The Other Side of the River, Red China Today.*"

Gartland, pug-nosed, wide-eyed, high cheek bones and Desperate Dan jaw says: "One free man is the revolution. And here you see thousands. Which equals one thousand revolutions. So who cares about the Russkis or Mexican hatchets? These guys need us to run GM and IBM and Coke and Pepsico and ATT and Grumman and Rothschilds and we just aint gonna do that shit, man, so let them get those motherfucking hardhats to be the managers and its gonna land them in shit."

And Silven says: "So you think lowly of the proletariat? You think they can't run America. So you're really feudal and capitalists and prejudiced. How can you call yourself revolutionaries? You're supposed to lead and impart radical education, but all you're doing is opting out. I mean, you guys don't even know the letters between Engels and Marx."

And Gartland says: "Fuck the Angels and fuck Mark Rudd."

"Christ", says Silben, "You neither know the history of the revolution you're trying to create and even if you're breaking away from traditional revolution you don't even know that tradition."

And little did Gartland and Silven know then, that the bytes were already working their way into the millennium, that the new bandits of wealth would be the cyberfreaks, that Bill Gates would replace Marx and Abbie Hoffan and Rajneesh would give Billy Graham a run for his evangelist money. For Hinduism somehow transcended incipient megabytes and neo-Christian evangelism.

3

Khan had listened to all this with delight. He dipped into his loin-cloth and produced a circular which read: "Tonite, 10 p.m. onwards, bring your own dope, but not your babe. Fuck-in at the Pond. Antibiotic shots available at the condom counter." He showed Silven the invitation. Silven read it, scowled and moved away saying he had to write a gravitational analysis of how a generation gap had poked a hole in *Das Kapital* and how there was an urgent need for American Correctionism that Reason and Revolution had not been able to provide.

Khan guffawed. "All these Mamas," he said. "When we got our screwing gig together, there were 300 signatures, and we put it up on the noticeboard, and that Mimi chic that let you suck her titty, man, she was mad, and she says this is an insult to female revolutionaries, and she tore it off the bulletin board and I snatched it from her before she could shove it up her snatch and now I'm showing it privately, of course to all the chics and dudes who wanna participate and except for that Marxist junkie with that crazy bow-tie, they all want a piece of the action."

I told Khan to back off. I was still fresh from the Manhattan marches and the Steinem placards, and I told Khan: "Listen guy, these "fuck-ins" hurt the dignity of women. They treat women like objects. We're into a new age now. We're not beasts beating females into submission."

Khan takes off, verbally, like a bat out of hell. Khan's soliloquy:

"It's like 'his bro," he says, putting his arms around me. "This is a Nigger rapping with a Hindu coz once you told me your old man liked Paul Robeson. Where he heard him, I don't give a shit about. And I know you like Streisand and Menachem Begin and say your mama looks like Golda Meier. I don't know how much each of them fucked including your old man, the Sheekari. But I know this much so long as it comes to men and women. See, I like the feminists coz they say women must have power and maybe go to abortionists and all that. But why should they object to a fuck-in at the pond man? After all their feminist gurus, I don't read them, but there's a lot of rap about that shit in the poolrooms, their feminist gurus say that women are conditioned. That they are conditioned not to enjoy sex or play a passive role and dump on Henry Miller. So they are told by their gurus to discover their clit orgasms. And to be sexually aggressive. Well, you see, I get a kick out of X-rated movies. Great stuff, man.

151

And the main theme is sexually aggressive mamas, black and white sex, black dicks stroking white cunts, black mamas whipping the shit out of white asses until they turn crimson or purple like the eyes you pissed on. That's sexual liberation, man, just what the sexual ideologues want. Female sexual aggression. No role models. Male fantasies made multisexual or even desexualized. Females riding males like Fellini's 8 1/2. That's what porn's full of, man. Woman sexually over man. And yet the feminists picket the adult halls saying that porn degrades women. Are they for Erica Jong or Frances Willard and her Women's Christian Temperance Union or your Gandhi?

"Take them at home, man. Now my old man, he beat the shit out of mama and I could beat his dick for that. And I had this small education in Virginia Beach and I said, shit, that aint no deal so I became sensitive. I even stopped saying bitch. So I get married even though I don't believe in marriage, coz I owe this chic an emotional deal, and, man, I get whupped. Right in the brain. She's preaching this feminist crap to me all the time, and I'm guilty as shit, even afraid to have my own orgasm, while she holds her back until she can consult some white guru, and I'm working like a pig hacking cabs in Detroit and Michigan and New York, and coming back to her, and she's mad all the time because I don't call her from a pay phone all day, and she's mad coz I haven't done the groceries, or forgotten a condom, and she hates my family and cusses me out for meeting them coz she's scared that if I do someone may ask a question that may expose her, or that I may get too close to a brother or sister again and seek refuge from her, coz she's not sure of my love and wants me to disengage from everybody but her, and she's got the education, but takes no initiative, either to buy the groceries, or learn to drive a car, or face the bill-collectors, coz she says that's my job, talks about independence but takes no step to be independent, not only of me, but her own chores, and I bring in the money and when I budget it, she screams she's been shortchanged, my liberated, feminist black-assed chic, who screams liberation but won't do a tit-ass job to prove it, and I'm stuck in that shitfaced ideology, with a conservative conscience that can't leave a helpless woman to fend for herself, a helpless woman, who hides behind Freidan and Steinem, and butt-fucks her husband's brain, earns only to go to the beauty parlor to compete against other feminists and their eyeliners and mascaras and hair-dye, and hates social gatherings and cusses me out for avoiding them, and then appears on Donahue and Oprah as is if she was the subject of Franz Fanon's *Wretched of the Earth*, and the audience claps in sympathy for this black beauty while her husband hacks and hacks and fights for tips and hands her the grocery money just so he can have peace at home, because she has learned through his adulterous escapades, orchestrated to warn her of the male's forgotten independence, that he will retire hurt, home, and that the paramour will never be promised marriage, because he is too conservative, and steeped, not in Woodstock but in conservative Harlem values, like Hindu catechism, that the destruction of the peace of mind, when a woman learns it is her most

153

powerful weapon. I love feminism. A woman to share my burdens. To have equal orgasms. To earn as much as me. To share in my bank account. To stand up to my old man. To learn karate and give me a whack across the windpipe when I get too sassy or violent. But for feminism to be used as a subtle ideology to continue to perpetrate the dependence of the female on the man but yet to dominate him politically through a ruse that can blackmail him because he is intellectual and sensitive, and can be blackmailed into feminist memory because he marched with Steinem in Manhattan well, man, that's mean. The only way out is radical homosexuality; you lose the cunt, but at least you don't lose your mind."

Khan went on and on. Family politics. How a much better way of a woman to dominate her man was through family politics. Poison him against the brother. Poison him against a beloved sister. Against parents, playing on sibling rivalry and exaggerating its importance. Gifts that We gave and THEY didn't give us. Phone calls not returned. A brother visiting another brother more than he visits YOU. A family clique secretly in the making that excludes YOU. And you, the hippie, ignore it for a while, but the woman, the idle woman, the idle woman, soaking in feminist rhetoric, who refuses to work a day, but snatches your purse, and when you run, run, run, she goes to court and the courts catch you on the catch-a-daddy program and handcuff you, and you can't explain why you ran away, coz the statistics are against you – Man Deserting Pregnant Wife, Man Beating Up Woman and Absconding With Mistress etc etc – and you a sensitive feminist approach a sister feminist and she says, Fuck You, Asshole, You Deserved It. And neither women get justice, nor do men. And as Khan carried on, I said, I guess this is so because ideology replaces relationships and we all play the game of articulating slogans rather than emotion and speech.

And Mama had once asked: "What is feminism all about?" in a letter to me in America from India.

I wrote back: "Mama, the empowerment of women so they don't have to depend on males for their livelihood. (Of course I said nothing, I dared not, about sexual liberation or the independence of the clitoral orgasm) The right of women to perform traditional male tasks like constructing buildings and wearing hard hats. For Blacks and Women to have equal rights."

Mama wrote back in Hindi: "Son, I was interested in what you wrote. But doesn't everyone depend on everyone for a livelihood, sometimes the male is sick and sometimes the woman is. And construction jobs? About 80 per cent of all the bricklaying and hard labor jobs in Raipur are done by women. Unfortunately they don't have hard hats. What are those? So we are ahead of your country. Even our Prime Minister is a woman. How about that, in a country that used to promote sati, burning of widows on the husband's funeral pyre, not everywhere, but in a few places, every now and then. And how can you say "Blacks and Women" in the same breath? Son, I saw *Gone with the Wind* with Papa. And it was obvious that white women enslaved and ran the lives of both black men and black women. So if white women were slavemasters of black men and women with the connivance of their white men, how can you club white women with blacks? It makes no sense. In parts of our country, in the South, the women do all the work in the fields, and their husbands stay home and drink. Physically, women are battered but emotionally and economically they're stronger in our lower classes. It's only you upper classes who think that you have more wisdom just because you learned a lot of English. The drunken peasants may beat up their women for a night but the women can leave and find young lovers anytime they want. So who is stronger?"

Chapter XV

1

I had no real answer for Mama. She had obviously received her answers in the puja room. We never found out what she prayed about, whether she sought answers or whether simply solace. Only that when her visits to the puja room increased in frequency or lasted longer than usual it was a sign that she was battling with some private crisis. Like when Seema had wanted a bedroom of her own and Mama had resisted.

Seema was only 17 and the siblings slept together where Mama could oversee them in their pre-sleep prayer. Tips would sit up in bed, endlessly, it would seem to me as I watched him eyes half-closed before sleep caught up, hands folded lips moving praying, he later told me, when he had stopped praying and before he resumed prayer but this time as an adult with his very own Guru to guide him in Vedic mantras and lucky stones, in turn to Hanuman, Shiva, Brahma and Vishnu and sometimes to Guru Nanak whose portrait, yellow turban and flowing beard, seemed to dominate the statuettes of the religious pantheon in Mama's puja room.

Seema had taken to teenage Christianity, wore a silver crucifix around her neck, kept a picture of the Virgin Mary by her bedside before which she would dutifully kneel every night and make the sign of the Cross. The Virgin Mary, after Seema got married would be replaced as she progressed through life in an ever-changing Top Ten of spiritual guides and masters. The bushy-haired Sai Baba held pride of place for several years. Then reigned a Sikh spiritual master from whom Seema learned to speak in tongues. For a year there was the rule of terror of a fierce hermit from the holy city of Haridwar. More benevolent icons included a flowing-haired "mother" from Varanasi, and a smiling, cherubic old swami from Mathura all honored with aromatic incense and petals of marigold and cassettes belting out sing-along religious hymns. Then came the Ganeshas, in whose endlessly flowing benevolent trunks Seema found security and total peace and religious salvation as she had found with the previous icons. In this saga of pious promiscuity each episode of religious infidelity redeemed her and during every episodic redemption Seema fulminated with evangelical verve before which the heathens could only moo guffishly in return.

Seema's Christian chapter had everything to with her schooling. At the age of nine she had been packed off to a missionary boarding school in, well, Mussoorie, run by American Methodists, and within eight years she was thumping the Bible like a Salvation Army drummer. In Raipur, she would line up little village kids and administer the Holy Communion and the hungry little brats were only too happy to line up for the home-baked fudge she would substitute for bread. And whether or not she had been tutored in ecclesiastical history in her school is anybody's guess because regardless of the traditions and teachings of Zwingli, Luther, Calvin or St Thomas Aquinas, St Francis, Seema on two Christmases held compulsory Midnight Mass near a Muslim graveyard and instructed her flock that regardless of any ability to comprehend they must, even if by rote, start mastering the catechism in Latin. Her brothers were forced to attend. Not because of any sanctimonious persuasion about the core belief in the Original Sin, Guilt, Sacrifice, Redemption and Resurrection but out of a huge sense of fascination with the trimmings that came with Seema's peculiar brand of proselytism.

See, we kind of found Christianity fun. It was the medium through which Seema the messenger brought America into the Raipur household. She would bring home chestfuls of treasures from her school church sales, made in America. Things that no shopper in India could then lay his hands on except through embassy garage sales. Santa brought us stockings – no matter that we had no fireplace (Seema told us he slid down one of the enormous mill smoke stacks, warmed his frozen hands in the enormous boiler room and slipped into our compound in the guise of a needy sadhu) – full of Mars Bars and Fleers Double Bubble Gum (Seema taught us to blow bubbles the size of balloons) and Levis jeans and packets of marshmallows and Daffy Duck comics and Charles Atlas muscle books and baseball bats and baseball caps that read YANKEES and ORIOLES and DODGERS and 45 rpm gramophone records with Doris Day and the Platters and Frankie Avalon and Connie Francis and James Darren, and Tweedly Tweedly Dee, and Walkin' My Baby Back Home, and posters of Jimmy Dean and maple syrup and we cooked fudge with real vanilla essence and chased after crooks in our PFs in the lawn and Seema taught us to sing *Rudolf the Red-nosed Reindeer* and I would choke with tears at the part Rudolf wasn't allowed to play in any reindeer games, and we'd roll Easter eggs on the lawn and even Mama would join us, having learned the words, of *0 Come All Ye Faithful, and Good King Wenceslas* and *Silent Night*, Seema leading the chorus, just as Mama led the Chorus when we sang *Om Jai Jagdish Hare* on Diwali nights, Papa ever the atheist and the children belting out the hymns not from any idealistic feeling for ecumenism or secular humanism, but simply to compete for the best stuffed stocking, the special one with the peanut butter cookies, and mostly because Christianity and America were a whole lot of fun. Especially when Seema taught us cheerleader jingles for our fiercely competitives cricket matches, like:

Felix the Cat, the Cat, the Cat

Wants to know,

Whose gonna win,

They? No.

We? Sure !!!!!!!

2

From Seema we learned to say wanna and gonna. For she was fast unlearning Hindi and picking up American in school, middle-American, teenage patois. And one day, at the breakfast table, when she was home for her three-month winter holiday from school, she said:

"Ma, I want my own room. I want to sleep in my own private room." Ma looked up disapprovingly. So did the male siblings. Disapprovingly. Seema was forcing the first major watershed in the household's family life. So far the children had all slept together, dorm-style, in the same bedroom, respected one another's privacy in the changing rooms and bathrooms but there was no question, especially in Mama's mind, that the house should one day be partitioned. American independence and individuality had their place, but were strictly to be kept out of the bedroom. Perhaps there was a larger concern. Why should Seema grow up? Was there any reason to? And any reason for her to demand special privacy away from her brothers? Their shared privacy had been their bonding, tickling one another's backs, toe and foot massages, the affectionate stroking of faces. A very special physical kinship of blood. Besides, Seema, too had been a shikari. She had waded into chilly waters of *jheels* without waders. She had faced hot winds and wind-chill factors in an open jeep with the windshield pinned down to the hood. She had wielded a shotgun. And as a shikari she had also played a unique role. When the hunters brought back with them wounded ducks, only slightly winged, she would play nurse to the birds, treating their wounds with turmeric and warm mustard oil, after which the birds were put into the swimming tank which served as a sheltered pond for recuperating ducks during winter and Seema would feed them grain and little fish and many of the birds, when healed would wait for overhead migratory flights in March and shoot out like rockets from the pond to catch up with the V-formations in the skies heading back, over the Himalayas, for Siberia or Canada. She was a shikari, blue blood. And shikaris flock together. They are not supposed to grow up and demand independence.

Besides, Seema's first foray into independence had caused a spat between Mama and Papa. About a year ago, Seema had had her first period. She had menstruated late and discovered her cramps while climbing a tree in the mango orchard. By the time she descended, it was quite heavy. Mama was knitting a sweater in the verandah, and Seema said:

"Ma, I need some Tampax."

Then, too, as Mama did at the breakfast table, when Seema demanded her own room, she looked at her disapprovingly. Mama was probably disconcerted and upset. Usually, the tradition was for grandmothers to teach and counsel their grandchildren in such matters. Not that Seema needed any such counseling considering that most of her friends were already of age in school. But both grandmas were dead. And Mama, who had a horror of discussing matters of such privacy and delicacy with her children was probably struck with a bolt of guilt at not having discussed and explained these matters to Seema earlier. In front of Mama now stood a daughter who had suddenly grown up without her counseling or her permission. Her guilt – and the premonition of bereavement – found expression in irritation.

Mama said: "I was going to explain all this to you, but you let it happen without discussing it with me. You see, when a girl starts maturing, changes take place within her body…"

"But Mama," said Seema, miffed: "I know all about that, believe me. It's no surprise. And you don't have to feel bad. But it's quite heavy, Ma, and I need some Tampax."

Mama said: "What Tampax? Get yourself some fresh cotton from the closet. And remember when you're in that condition, you're not allowed to go inside the puja room or enter a temple or even visit a holy shrine. This is a religious proscription."

Seema knew this religious bit. Aunts and older cousins in the family had stayed away from religious functions when they were down. And only recently, when Seema had taken a group of Christians from Raipur to a church meeting nearby, a few of the women had on their own refused to enter the Church for this reason. But that was not Seema's immediate problem.

Seema said: "Ma, that cotton is for emergencies. I need proper Tampax. Ma let me use yours in your closet."

Mama said: "There is not any in the house." With her strange puritanical streak, Mama would be damned if she would admit, to her child, that she used these things or that she was a captive of biology. And with her stubborn streak she continued to refuse to confess to existence of any stock of Tampax in her closet and Seema had to shield the first signs of entry into womanhood with surgical cotton. No wonder, when the years went by, the two women would smile at each other everytime a Whisper or Stayfree maxipad commercial came on the TV screen.

But at that time, about 15 years before television came to India, it was no smiling matter. For Seema went straight to Papa and asked that he drive to a large town nearby and get her the pads. When he asked, obliquely, why she did not use some from those available in the house Seema told him that Mama said she didn't keep any. Papa must have remonstrated with Mama later because she was in a sulk for a few days and although she was affectionate as always towards Seema, she was still trying to sort out her own guilt.

And now that Seema had demanded her own room in a no-nonsense rite of passage assertion, Mama, even though she saw a crisis coming if she did not go with the tide, refused to give in even though she saw defeat staring her in the face. She said:

"No. Why? Are you *pagal*? (meshugga) You have a nice room with your brothers. Besides, you're in school nine months of the year. I don't understand this privacy nonsense. And your brothers don't agree either."

"You're right, Ma," Tips chimed in, his oversized Adam's Apple looking like it was smiling. Seema's getting too Americanized. Besides, we'll have no extra playroom for carom."

Seema got her way because Papa intervened. There were no arguments or family pow-wows. From his chamber of perfumes he decreed that Seema was to have the front room whose three screened bay-windows overlooked the front lawn where we burst firecrackers on Diwali.

"You must realize that Seema's a young lady now. And she needs her space. She needs to be by herself when she wants. She has moved from a dormitory to her own room in school. And she's doing the same here. And I don't believe in the oppressive norms and rules of joint families."

Although when Seema had moved from Junior High to Senior School Papa had not been overly happy with American individualism. The school had sent all parents circulars about the move and they had to tick parental consent against different questions on a special form among two dozen questions, like, should your child be allowed to go to the market on certain days, could she be served beef, compulsory church attendance etcetera, and one question asked if Seema should be allowed to go on single dates.

"Dates?" asked Mama, having heard for the first time that American slang. "What does that mean?"

Tips volunteered: "It means going out alone with boys to movies and picnics and dances." He knew already that Seema had dated off and on, and while we all slept in the same room at home I would often hear Tips and Seema talking softly late into the night and Tips wanted to know if she had even kissed a guy, because Tips had never been alone with a girl in his life at the time, and Seema would tell him about necking and petting, words I learned for the first time.

As Papa went through the school form, Mama repeated:

"Dates? How can she? She's getting her own room, isn't that enough? Dates! When we arrange her marriage, what are we going to tell the boy's parents? That Seema was allowed to go out with boys on her own? If the people of Raipur found out, they would be horrified."

Papa did not take much time to decide. "Beef, yes, it comes frozen from America. No dates," he said firmly. That was it. Mama, a radical non-beef-eating Hindu raised her eyebrows only a little at the beef part, but smiled at her victory over the dates business.

When Seema moved into her own room, Mama helped decorate it with fluffy pillows and stuffed toys, the Virgin Mary, Jimmy Dean posters and even framed photographs of two of her school heart-throbs. Mama raised no further questions. Mama had not tasted defeat. She had simply asserted the sense of herself and her own world had begun to co-exist under the roof of her home. Sometimes you can never explain these phenomenal graces of the human soul. The rebellion, in fact, came from Tips who, one day, entered Seema's room and with an airgun shot the eyes out of the framed photographs of Seema's American boyfriends. No matter how Mama may have felt, to her this was a transgression of human decency. She reported the matter to Papa. Papa summoned Tips and called him a name which he considered the most powerful in his lexicon of pejoratives: "Bloody loafer."

Even though Papa had interceded with Mama on behalf of Seema's interests, he had not been in the habit of doing so. He abhorred the idea of parents using their children as political weapons and for taking sides for selfish long-term convenience. It is the habit of parents to instigate the other to discipline or remonstrate with a child but then to take up immediately for the child thus piling up a debt of gratitude from the child as his protector. They probably do this because they want to compete for special attention from the child during old age or because during a serious parental quarrel which the two cannot settle amongst themselves they seek intervention from friends or family. The protected child comes in as a handy ally to tilt the emotional balance in favor of one of the parents. Blissfully, the Raipur household was mostly free from this.

Chapter XVI

1

During Seema's graduation year, Papa had made several trips to Delhi. Mama and he seemed to share a secret. Generally given to communicating through body language most of the day – conversation time between Mama and Papa was mostly a dining-table mealtime affair – there now seemed to be one of those periodic exceptions when Mama would go into Papa's study for talks and repeat none of what happened behind closed doors to her children. The two were planning Seema's marriage.

And one day, when Seema was in school, and the other children were on a break at home, we were summoned to the chamber of perfumes for the grand announcement. Papa first looked in the direction of Mama and then at us, a warm smile lit up his face:

"We have chosen a boy for Seema. He is a Punjabi, fair, twenty-eight years old which is the right age for Seema. We all believe that the girl should be at least eight or nine years younger. Because as the couple gets older the wife still remains relatively young and attractive to the husband. Because if you close the gap, the woman may start looking older because women age sooner. I have met the young man. And I am taking your mother to see him soon. He will then come to Raipur with his parents who have already met Seema at a friend's house and are keen on having her as a daughter-in-law. I have a picture of the young man." He passed around a large black and white photograph. A man with large eyes, a straight nose, a little pointed at the end, arched eyebrows, very long curled eyelashes that gave him a dreamy appearance, a fleshy bow-shaped lower-lip and sidelocks up to his jaw. He was a successful lawyer. And Papa and his circle of friends had checked out his antecedents, blood line, the kind of rituals his family practiced, uncle's history, schooling etcetera – in an investigation so thorough that even the CIA, which was said to have established new records in the art of snooping when the agency was able to procure Nikita Khruschev's turds when the Soviet leader first visited the United Nations in New York, and submit them to a clinical analysis to discover the eating habits of the Communist species, could take a lesson out of the Hindu book of a pre-nuptial probe during the course of arranging a marriage.

The surprise announcement did not surprise us. You grow to a marriageable age, and well, you get married. Period. And it was rare for a marriage not to be arranged. Once parents and families agreed, the boy and the girl seeing each other was only a formality. In the villages the brides and grooms still saw each other only at the *mandap* or altar – a blind date that was followed with sex with a stranger to whom you had tied the knot for life. Tally asked Papa:

"But can our brother-in-law shoot? Will he go hunting with us?"

Papa paused for a while and said: "I don't know, but he has to be made to fit into the family and you and Seema will have to teach him." We all wrote letters to Seema in school, congratulating her, ribbing her, and when she received the official word from Papa she called her American friends to a special treat to spread the news of her impending betrothal. Her friends, of course, were horrified. They had known, they had studied that arranged marriages happened in India, that there were dowry demands, and movies had been made on girls being forced into marriages, but that happened out there somewhere, out there somewhere in India, and not to their high school pal who was the most popular girl at the recent square dance. And would probably have hogged the limelight at the Prom with her raven black page-boy, eyes in which pools eddied into pools, high cheekbones, a short slightly hooked nose with gentle nostrils and a pouty overbite that gave her upper lip a hint of a perpetually mischievous smile.

She wrote to Papa: "Thanks for finding me what seems to be a real nice guy. I respect the advice you gave me in your letter about being a supporting wife. But Pa, please send me his photograph. My pals here are dying to see what he looks like." Her next letter: "Pa, he looks real swell. Wow, I'm dying to meet him. Can I write to him? I showed his photo to my friends, and guess what, they think he's a loveable dreamboat and they all have crushes on him. Can you arrange marriages for my best friends Carol and Yvonne? Hee hee. Luv Ya, your favoritest child."

Papa's family was not entirely subservient to the archconservative Hindu marriage scene where the couple met at the *mandap*. In our scheme of things we had "liberal" arranged marriages – before, within a decade, educated upper class families began allowing their children to marry for love – in which, after the boy and girl met, mostly chaperoned by a trusted relative, and sometimes not, if either had a strenuous objection, supported either by reason or non-stop hysterical tantrums, the marriage would be called off and another match tried. If the to-be-weds took to each other after the first few meetings, there would be a quick engagement, presents exchanged, rings exchanged, and the couple would be allowed an occasional date and the parents, while hoping that heavy sexual encounters did not occur during this pre-mating interregnum, would ask no questions either, unless the girl decided on her own to confide in her mother.

We kind of suspected that Seema was petting heavily with Dreamboat (now nick-named 'Dee') before marriage but that was of no consequence to us. The union had the Shikari's blessing and Mama would not dare broach the subject with her. We were more excited about the wedding. For Hindu weddings, like Christianity, were kind of fun. There were no sleighs or Christmas stockings but there were huge tents and music and relatives in resplendent saris and a fire around which the couple went round and round, and scrumptious food and *shehnai* music and horses and dancing and traditional rituals, and Vedic chanting and Papa had invested his dwindling money to create a tented city for the guests and relatives as if he was about to receive the Shah of Iran. And Seema was in a gold brocade sari. And in traditional Hindu bride tradition her eyes were cast downwards, never to look into the eyes of guests or relatives in order to avoid the evil eye and also never lock eyes with her parents and brothers in order to give away any hint of sadness that may bring home the reality that she is leaving home.

And when we carried her off in her covered palanquin, the *doli*, her brothers bearing the weight, to the car in which Dreambat was waiting to whisk her away to the honeymoon, Mama followed for a while choking with sobs, inconsolable, and Papa tried to hide his tears with dark glasses except that his tears would form a reverse delta uniting into single streams just below the hollow of the cheekbones flowing down his cheeks and jaws from behind the nimbus clouds of his sun shades to form horizontal pools of moisture on his collar bones.

Mama didn't recover for a week. And after she did, I asked her:

"Mama, why were you hysterical? Before the

wedding you were like a little girl with a new toy. So excited and then greeting the guests and all and ordering the jewelry and the saris and the wedding clothes for the servants and organizing the menu and then you just broke down."

Mama said: "Who knows? The man may be a *badmaash*, a rogue. Maybe he'll beat her and submit her to all kinds of things. And sometimes those males turn their wives against their parents and their families. And what if she's not happy? What if she wants to come back to us? Will I take her back? Because we Hindus believe that once our girls are given away in front of the fire, they lose their parents' home and if you take them back it's sinful." On that last score Mama didn't need to worry at all because a month after her honeymoon, Seema invited Papa and Mama to her home and she made sure that every time she invited them, with ma-in-law joke cards, Dreamboat would make them feel more at home than they felt in their own. Seema had tried to create another Raipur in her wedded domicile.

Sara grew up into a Barbara Streisand look-alike. She couldn't sing like her but she made sure she'd do a whole lot of Jewish numbers on her husband. Her first introduction to feminism – after she was married – was to be able to dare to cuss at the Raipur dining table (of course when Papa was out of earshot). And she made her first break with family tradition and thought she'd get off her back when she called her husband a Bastard. This was *de rigeur*. Call your husband a Bastard and you were on the right feminist track no matter how you did everything to depend on his slave-earnings at sweatshops and publishing houses and incipient multinationals. The language, as it had freed Tips and the Woodstock freaks from familial and social servitude would also, Sara and her ilk believed, free them from domestic enslavement.

As Sara grew older and she and I could talk, I asked her:

"So what happened? How come Seema got forced into that arranged marriage? I know it was okay for us, we were kids, and okay for Dreamboat, but what about Pa? And her?"

Sara said: "You know, I had this weird conversation with Papa. And this is the first time I am talking about it. I asked him the same question, what with Seema's education and all that, why did you rush her into this marriage, and you know what Papa said? He said: 'You know, I really don't believe in marriage. I detest those pundits and all their Sanskrit garbage. I hate inviting loafers and relatives to feast on money that I could have given my daughter for a higher education. Most of those silly relatives come and give us presents and each time they dip into their pockets they curse that they have to go to a wedding they would rather not attend. I don't want a marriage and neither do they. And each of their gifts are tainted with the curses of the money they either did not have and had to borrow or had and did not have to spend. Just like me.

" 'And I hate most of those idiots I know I'll never see them again, and I don't want to because people carried tales to us about how they hugged me and hugged Seema and her husband and went back and said the *dal* was too cold or the Scotch was not real, these bastards, why did I spend money on them so that I could have saved for my old age or really given it you or Tips or Seema when they really wanted it, or spent it on Mom if she ever got breast cancer? What do I do now if she gets breast cancer? Go to the Hindu Vedas and do a *mantra* for the money to drop on my head?'"

Sara looked up and sighed, while relating this to me.

Sara resumed her conversation with me. Papa had told her another story. He was once in charge of the engagement of a cousin, PJ, whose parents had long died. PJ was to get married to Divya. The engagement was to take place in Divya's home and her parents had requested a small affair and so Papa won Mama's reluctant consent to invite only a handful of direct family members for the ceremony. Divya's parents did the same. After the engagement all hell broke loose. Papa's relatives, many of whom he hadn't seen for years, who had been left out of the engagement, actually returned the gifts and *shagun* they were sent by Divya's parents through Papa. This was tantamount to putting a social and religious curse on the marriage. Papa stayed firm in the sense that he maintained a strong silence and cut himself loose from any social contact with those petty-bourgoise cousins. Yet, when the time for PJ's wedding arrived a few months later those same cousins and relatives who had not been invited to the engagement – and some of them were a part of the Shikari's troupe – received Papa's invitation for the wedding, where Papa served them roast partridge and drinks he would like to have thrown in their faces. "'But Papa, you had the will, why did you do it?" Sara asked.

"And Papa said: 'I don't believe in marriage, in birthdays, in death anniversaries, postcards, and maybe even death. Maybe we're just spooked into believing about them by religion and ceremonies. And maybe I defied all of them by following their rituals with my fingers crossed behind my back because maybe that's the only passport to salvation. Do it all, but way back in your mind, keep that little napsack on your back, a few clean undies, a light pillow, a blanket, a small water canteen with potassium permanganate crystals, a gun, canvas shoes, books like *Travels With Charlie* and go where the forces take you. Of course this is not to say that I don't love the family, I love you dearly, but maybe, if there's a next life, we'll all be together as a family again but follow my prescription. I may have had to invite those people to the wedding, he said, but I never again invited them to go hunting with me. They were not shikaris anymore.'"

" 'But Papa," I said, 'You're like Walter Mitty.' And he said: 'Look at the reality. Maybe the Shikari has blessed adventure and cursed tradition, and tradition has turned into adventure.'"

I asked Sara: "Do you see this?"

And Sara said: "Well look at Seema. Her marriage lasted through at least eight lovers for 15 years during which she bore two beautiful daughters and coached them in traditions that would make a conservative Hindu go berserk with envy. Even Mama is astonished at the way they go to the puja room and do *aarti* and sing hymns and *bhajans*. And all this while Seema was once going around with a teenager and Dreamboat suspected it and she convinced him that husbands shouldn't interfere with what she cleverly disguised as intellectual liaisons. She busted loose like a Number One shot from a choke barrel. She burst forth from that Hindu Christmas stocking like a whooshing firecracker, became a publishing executive with her high school education, left her husband and his home with a couple of suitcases to take on the males who had banished her into teenage marriage from Raipur, settled in her own room, defied Papa's wisdom by entering politics, then wormed her way back into his affectionate smile and won thumping victories in assembly elections, delivered thumping perorations in chaste Hindi, and donned the Shikari's social mantle even as he was waning. Her life with Dee seemed something like out of another existence."

CHAPTER XVII

1

Dee, when he first came into our lives, was not exactly without a reputation. The lawyer, in his circles, was known to be a bit of a sexual swashbuckler. A ladies' man with a pathological proclivity for other men's ladies – girlfriends as well as wives. He had scars on his knees, and a slash-mark below his right ear – he described them as "war medals" – as proofs of battles he had been in with the men who had discovered in him the proof of the infidelity of their women. In Raipur, Dee had taken to the hunt after rigorous practice with Papa's Holland & Holland double-barreled shotgun. His tenacity had impressed the entire Raipur household and we had little doubt that he would soon become an integral part of the Shikari's entourage. At first he couldn't hit a floating crow 30 feet up in the air with a Number Eight. But he had remained in dogged pursuit. On one of his visits during the period of his engagement to Seema, Dee stood in the front lawn of the house – starting after breakfast until sundown –

with an arsenal of 500 shells and shot at anything that moved – bats, moths, sparrows, stray locusts, mynah birds, parakeets, and pigeons.

He missed most of the time, and each time he missed Tips would make a loud farting sound with his mouth. And Dee would sulk at the dinner table. His mood would be sullen. Papa would give him oral instructions on how to swing his gun, how to use his eyes to give the bird a lead, but nothing would make Dee's frown disappear. He seemed to relax only when Seema would put her arm around him and tell us that he would soon outgun the whole lot of us.

"Of course that doesn't mean you, Papa," she said, when the Shikari raised his eyebrow. And Papa said:

"He's got to learn to love the forests first. That's more important than hitting targets. He's got to learn to recognize the difference between a sand grouse and a dove. Let him walk with us. Let him enter gently into the experience instead of trying to possess it."

On the third day, Dee began to hit his targets. He left the crows alone. He went for the fast flying pigeons and they began falling out of the sky. And that night at dinner Dee was boasting of his skills as if he had been born with them. He said:

"I guess I was just a little bit rusty."

Tips said: "But you've never really held a gun before!"

180

Dee replied: "I think I simply have the natural instinct for it. Did you see how I hit that one that was flying with the wind? And the one before that? He was actually coming at me and that's the most difficult shot." And when Tips simulated a farting sound again, Papa gave him a stern look and asked him to leave the table.

In the months that followed, Dee became a hunter. He had bought himself a used Czechoslovakian gun. He brought off some dazzling shots which even the Shikari, at times, could scarce forbear to cheer. But, too often, in the manner that he liked to chase other men's women, he shot at birds which had already received a first hit by another hunter or one which was rightfully – according to shikar etiquette – not his to shoot at.

"Stop poaching, Dee!" the Shikari would yell.

And Dee would respond: "Nobody else even nicked it. Look at the speed he was flying at. I think you're picking on me because I have the biggest bag so far."

And Tips said: "Yeah, of other people's birds."

And during one partridge shoot at the end of a similar conversation, Dee suddenly swung his body from left to right, his gun flashing as the evening sun hit its barrel, and he fired both barrels in quick succession and hit two birds with such perfection that they dropped like stones to the ground. He ejected the shells, and the smoke curled out of the breech, and he smiled proudly in the direction of the Shikari in the manner of a gunslinger looking for approval as he blows the smoke off the tip of his six-shooter after a duel. And Dreamboat said:

"Well, Pa, don't tell me those two birds belonged to someone else, or that they had already been nicked."

And Papa replied: "None of us would even have aimed at those birds. One is a lapwing and the other is a cattle egret. Now maybe you'll cook them for yourself when we get home."

And Tips made that farting sound again. And Dee remained dejected for the rest of the shoot not even attempting a shot even when it was clearly his. And he kept muttering:

"Gosh, but they flew just like partridge. I mean I really thought they were partridge."

Before dinner it was routine for the family to sit in Papa's chamber of perfumes and mull over the day's shoot. The bag. The mistakes made. The health of the forest. After dinner we would huddle together with Dee in his room to hear stories about his girlfriends.

Seema, perhaps because of her virtual pre-marital sexual innocence, found Dee's tales about his promiscuity attractive. She actually appeared to admire him for his boasting. She believed he had lived his life with danger all around. In his bachelor life, in his pursuit of his quarry, Dee had lived on the edge of wilderness. In his professional life he had to deal with criminals and bandits and powerful politicians. With one of them, a prominent Supreme Court lawyer, Dee had actually fought a gun duel in the middle of the nation's capital. There was a crude and rugged quality about him that transfixed Seema in admiration. She confided in me:

"He's got *experience*. If he wanted a woman to chase him, she'd be running after him like she was doing a steeplechase. All the married women wanted to leave their husbands and marry him. Do you know how many hearts he's broken now that he's with me? He had a party for me in Delhi and a few of his ex's were there and he would whisper to me and point them out, and some of them are really beautiful."

I asked: "And you didn't get jealous?"

"Why should I? After all the freedom he had, he got into an arranged marriage agreement with me. And I could see them looking at me with such envy. Actually several women came up to me and said I must have something in me to be able to hook him. You must ask him about the wife of the Supreme Court lawyer when you get a chance."

And on one of those evenings in Raipur when Tips and I would gather inside Dreamboat's room for bedtime stories about his girlfriends, Seema asked him to tell us about the Supreme Court lawyer's wife. Dreamboat first shut the doors and then looked around the room to make sure nobody else was present. He had this peculiar habit – a preliminary ritual that preceded his narration of a private story. As if he was safeguarding the privacy of the protagonists of his tale while simultaneously ensuring that no adult in the family was listening to his admission of his social blasphemies. This was one aspect of his studiously-maintained conservative posture. Family adults and all others outside the circle of those on whom he bestowed the honor of confidant were never to be given even a glimpse of his private side. The lawyer, Dreamboat revealed, was actually his mentor. And his wife, whom Dreamboat, for the purposes of this story, nicknamed Rini, was of Central Asian stock – gushing light brown hair, pale flawless skin, large, misty brown eyes, a Rita Hayworth mouth dripping passion. She stood six-feet tall without heels. Her husband whom, for some reason she called "Dusky" was two inches taller than her. And Rini and Dusky entertained lavishly in their bungalow in Civil Lines in New Delhi. There was dancing at all their parties and they always invited Dee who stood apart from the rest of the crowd on the dance floor because he would fox-trot with his partner to any number. Whether it was a cha-cha-cha, a samba, a bee-bop jive beat, it made no difference to Dreamboat. He would insist on doing the fox-trot or simply refuse to dance.

Rini and Dusky could do just about anything on the floor – from a tango to the Lambeth Walk. And occasionally, they would even persuade their guests – Delhi's most sought-after rich and famous – to form a line to do the Bunny-hop. Characteristically, Dee would refuse to join.

"Why this hang-up, Dee?" I asked, breaking into his narration.

And Dee replied: "Those dances are for sissies. Where's the point in dancing when you can't even hold your woman close and..." he paused and looked around the room to make sure nobody else was around except Seema and Tips, lowered his voice to a barely audible whisper, and continued, "...you can't even feel your woman's breasts against your chest, or feel her pelvic movements against your groin, or even smell that special odor from the nape of her neck. Hell, those other dances are effeminate."

Dee was a cave man. It was on the dance floor that he made his moves on his women. Not for him the secret notes and letters and flowers furtively delivered to some woman he was wooing; or the innocent-sounding invitation to lunch, or regular double-dates with the woman and her husband to movies and dinners as preludes to clinching a sexual relationship.

"Hell, all that stuff takes too long, and that's probably okay for you teenagers," Dee would say. So, what was his approach? Tips and I asked that evening when we had gathered in his room to learn about his conquest of Rini. And Dreamboat looked at Seema with a rakish smile and asked:

"Shall I tell them? Well I'm their brother-in-law and I suppose I ought to share the secrets of life with them."

And Seema said: "Go ahead, they're grown up now. And Tips and I share secrets all the time."

Dee looked around the room furtively to make sure there were no unwelcome guests, and he said in a lowered voice: "I've never had to wait more than a day for any woman I've wanted. The dance floor is where I first seduce them. Nowhere else. If I'm attracted to a woman I get a hard-on the moment I bring her close to me on the floor. In the course of a slow dance I manage to brush her hand against my groin, first making it look accidental, and if the woman doesn't stiffen up – and most of them don't – I repeat this several times. And after a few dances she's playing, and I know she's game. I make an appointment for the next day. Almost always at her own home. If she's married, and they usually are, she'll know when her husband is away and she'll know how to get rid of the children and the maid for an hour. Her own home is the best place. She's more relaxed, and her sense of danger – doing it on her husband's own bed – really arouses her. The next best place is in a car, a short drive into the countryside. But in this case I always carry my revolver with me in case some hooligans come around."

Seema had a broad grin on her face. She said: "Quite a ladies' man."

Tips said: "Seema, what if he had met you for the first time, and asked you to dance with him and guided your hand to his parts."

Seema replied: "I'd probably puke, Yukk. I'd probably slap him right in front of everybody."

I said: "But that's crazy. You enjoy listening to his

stories. You even admire his exploits. They even attract you to him."

Seema said: "But I'm not those other women. I'm me. And Dee is so manly. And he's so protective."

Dreamboat said: "That's right. Seema is not those other women. She is going to be my wife. And I'm not going to go to bed with her before we are married. She's from a good family. And I have the deepest respect for your parents. "

Tips said: "You mean with all these women you seduced on the dance floor by guiding their hands, you mean, no one actually ever slapped you?"

Before he could answer, Seema said: "I know about that! One of them did slap him, and you know what, he slapped her right back. And then her husband fisted him one, and Dee got involved in a brawl with her husband and threw him out of the door, and then he went after him again and knocked him out. Don't forget, Dee was also a boxing champion in school. And then he got all drunk and sentimental and begged that woman for forgiveness in front of the whole crowd at the club. But he refused to apologize to her husband."

I asked: "Is that true, Dee?"

And Dee said: "That guy started it."

Seema said: "Go ahead with your story. About Rini. Tell them what happened."

Dreamboat first went into a detailed description of Rini. He had known her casually before she married Dusky. She was the hottest property in town. The only daughter of a mega-industrialist. Filmstars and young politicians and London-returned chartered accountants competed for her attention. Some of the men were as tall as her. The real short ones did not dare approach her. And those of medium height – as was Dreamboat –did not consider themselves as looking silly even when she towered over them on the dance floor. Dusky, for reasons Dreamboat didn't elucidate, scored over all other suitors.

Dreamboat said: "Of course, I was the only person who hardly even looked at her. Never even asked her to dance. She would often ask me, even after she married Dusky, why I never took her to the floor, and whether I had ever thought of dating her when she was unmarried."

In any case, Dreamboat would sit out all the dances unless they were slow fox-trots, and Rini loved to cha-cha. And soon, there was a wager. Dreamboat's social circle would buy a case of champagne for any woman who could persuade him to do the cha-cha with her at a party.

Dreamboat recalled: "You know, it became like real challenge for them. It was not a matter of a case of champagne. The bigger thing was the challenge. And believe you me, there were some women who even offered to sleep with me if I would oblige them. But I stuck to my principles. I never wanted to look like a fool on the floor."

He did compromise, some months later. And Rini made him do so. The "Dee-cup challenge" was really hotting up in Delhi circles. And more than anybody else, Rini wanted to win it. She had bent men all her life. And she was determined to bend Dreamboat on the dance floor. She chose her husband to soften her target.

Rini told Dusky: "Dee's your associate. You virtually trained him in his job. Besides, he's your friend. I really want this, Dusky. It'll be great fun. A great party where we'll see Dee cha-cha for the first time. You've got to convince him – for my sake. I'm sure he'll listen to you."

It took a little persuasion, but Dusky was able to get Dreamboat to agree.

I asked Dreamboat: "What argument did he use? I thought you had a principle on that point."

Dreamboat said: "Well, he told me it was not for her that he was asking me to do this, but for him. As a friend. That it would strengthen their marriage because she would look on him as a man who, for her sake, had convinced a man to break his principles. He kept telling me: 'For my sake, Dee, for my sake, just do it. Just only once. We're going to throw a special party for the event, and we'll go through the drama of Rini asking you, and you can play rigid for a little while, and then she can lead you triumphantly to the dance floor in the grand finale, and we'll play the *Isle of Capri* cha-cha number. Look, it will be a lot of fun. A lark. And we'll pop the champagne.'"

Dreamboat told Dusky: "But I don't know how to do that wretched cha-cha."

And Dusky said: "That's the point. She'll take you to the floor, and she'll teach you while everybody claps. It'll be the biggest social event in Delhi."

Dreamboat dropped his principle, and agreed. "It was a matter of honor between two men," he told us.

The script unfolded in front of some 200 guests. They cheered. They popped balloons. Champagne corks hit the angles of the walls. As a 33 ½ rpm disc belted out *Isle of Capri* Dreamboat and Rini danced alone on the floor. Well, they kind of danced. Because Rini was teaching him aloud: "One, two, cha-cha-cha... step, step, step-step-step..." and Dreamboat looked like a flat-footed web-toed greylag goose treading water and flapping its wings before taking to the air.

After the applause had abated and more and different music was in the air, Dreamboat led Rini to a dark corner of the room and said:

"You bitch, you don't get this for free."

"What do you want?" Rini asked.

"You," Dreamboat said. "In your house. Tomorrow. I know when Dusky goes to court. I'll be there. Get rid of anybody else. I agreed to drop my principles just this one time. Now you drop your pants, just for one time."

Dreamboat's self-inflicted sense of circumspection

did not allow him to describe the love-making – and he probably would not have, anyway, within earshot of Seema – except for a brief reference to Rini's "satin skin," but he did grin with narrowed eyes.

He continued: "We were still in the bedroom and I felt Rini stiffen. 'What is it?' I asked. 'It's Dusky, he's here! He'll be in the house any minute,' she said. I asked: 'What do you mean?' She whispered: 'Didn't you hear the car? That's his car. And the dog always barks like that when he's here.' I asked: 'Does he suspect something?' And Rini said, no, that it must be that he forgot something, and that he would recognize my car outside their gate. Then she said: 'But that's it! That's okay! I told him last night that I had called you over to the house to take cha-cha lessons any time you wanted to. Quick! Here, put on your clothes. I'm running to the living room,' she said struggling to put on her top and jeans, 'and I'm going to turn the record player on real loud. Hurry in and pretend you're taking a lesson.' I said: 'Let's just tell him, no matter what happens. It's the honorable thing to do,' and she said: 'Just do as I say. For my sake. Please! Don't you honor women?' "

Rini disappeared in a jiffy, and Dreamboat followed her. The player was blasting *Isle of Capri* and Rini was chanting "one, two, cha-cha-cha," and Dreamboat was jumping up and down like he was bouncing on a trampoline, when Dusky entered the room. Rini feigned nonchalance.

"Hi, Dusky," she said. "God, look how sweaty I am.

He agreed to come for his dance lesson. But he's impossible to teach. He'll get better. Here, why don't you try teaching him. I'm going to take a shower and relax."

Dusky watched Dreamboat and Rini cha-cha-cha-ing and he turned purple. And he screamed:

"You bastard! You sonofabitch! What the hell do you think you're doing with my wife?"

Dreamboat turned towards Dusky and said: "Nothing. You asked me to learn this stupid dance. I sort of like it. She's teaching me, Dusky, she's a great teacher."

Dusky screamed: "You bastard! You take dancing lessons with your pants off?! Where did you leave your pants? In the bedroom?"

Dreamboat looked down below his stomach. Underneath his shirt there was no belt buckle, no belt, no underwear, and certainly, no trousers. All he could see was his pubic hair – in his own sentimental phraseology – "standing out like a smoking gun".

He did not bother to go and fetch his trousers from the bedroom. He looked Dusky straight in the eyes and said: "Okay. You want to know? I just fucked your wife. I did not rape *her*. She raped *me* on the dance floor last night. Against my will. You have honor? Let's have a shootout. Let's get guns." Dusky, enraged, said he had a pair of revolvers and that he would shoot Dreamboat's balls off. He fetched them – two .38 Smith & Wessons. They loaded. They went into the garden. And Dreamboat said:

"If you kill me, you don't say a word to Rini. No resentment, no chastisement. It's like a new wedding for you. You tell the world it's a suicide. If I kill you, I'll marry her. I'll tell the world it's a suicide. I'm a man of honor."

They went into the back garden. Dreamboat was still nude underneath his shirt. The rivals faced off. They aimed. Dusky aimed at Dreamboat's balls. Dreamboat aimed at the center of Dusky's head. Dreamboat counted, one-two-three, and they both fired. Dusky's barrel jumped so high that his bullet nicked Dreamboat just below his ear. Dreamboat missed completely. He was yet to meet Papa and become a shikari. And Rini came running out in her nightgown and threw herself on Dusky screaming unintelligibly.

Dreamboat said: "You keep her."

When Dreamboat ended his story, I asked him: "But Dee, these other peoples' wives and all that. What about Seema? You're going to chase women all the time. And what if Seema gets involved?"

Dreamboat said: "It's a matter of honor. It's all over. No more playing around for me, after we're married. I will not look at another woman. She is going to be the center of all my life. The president of my home. A mother for as many children as I want to have. She will perform all the prayers and rituals. That's a real marriage."

I asked: "And what if there's another man in her life?"

Dreamboat said: "I'll kill him. I'll slaughter anybody that tries to make a pass at her. There are too many bastards around. She has to be protected. I'll guard her. I'll guard your entire family."

And Seema had a beatific look on her face, and she said: "I feel so secure with him. He's a real man."

2

After their honeymoon we wanted to know how Dreamboat had behaved on the first night. Was he gentle? Was he really all that he was made out to be? And Seema would blush and stare into space and say: "Well, he's really rugged, you know. He sure knows a lot of tricks."

Her babies came quickly. Two girls in three years. And she took to mothering them naturally, without fuss, without ado, without complaining about keeping awake nights for breastfeeding. She was protective and proud. Like a dog who takes to her first litter. Dreamboat remained a fair-weather daddy. Nuzzling them and playing with his children when they were in good humor, and keeping out of the way when they had the gripes or threw up their milk. Those first three years, when Seema was busy converting her new home into her own version of Raipur, appeared to be relatively uneventful so far as the marriage was concerned. But at the end of that period Seema was beginning to show signs of restlessness.

194

During her visits to Raipur she no longer spoke about Dreamboat with the same animation she had displayed during their engagement and first few years of marriage. Often, when we asked about his welfare she shrugged off the question with a "oh-he's-okay" answer.

As a child I was always the most sensitive to Seema's moods, aside from Papa, that is. We had a routine. Before I went to bed for the night I would always knock on Seema's door, sit by her bedside, or lie down by her side and chat until she was very sleepy. And she always spoke with her eyes closed. We continued this practice even after we got along in years. And one night, when Seema was in Raipur by herself, lying in bed, her children fast asleep on a separate bed, I asked her:

"How come you never talk about your hero any more."

She asked, perplexed: "Which hero?"

"Why, Dee, of course," I said.

She remained silent for a while, and then replied:

"Well, you know, Dee doesn't read at all. He's not like us. I can't even discuss a book with him. He thinks it's boring to go out and get soaking wet in the monsoon rain. In fact, he's so conservative that he once said people would think of me as a tart if I got all my clothes wet and sticking to me. He's so worried about what other people think all the time. I feel suffocated. And he's always nagging me about how I pay more attention to my brothers and my family rather than his. But they're really a bunch of stuffy middle-class robots always doing what is 'proper'. And Dee keeps using this horrible word 'proper' all the time. When I tell him that Raipur and my family are in my blood he says it's not 'proper' for a married woman to feel that way because after the wedding the wife belongs to the husband's family and should feel like a guest in her own parents' home. He seems to resent those parts of my life that were or never will be a part of his own life. I think he is really jealous of my childhood years with you and the family because he cannot own those years. Because he was not a part of them. I feel so suffocated sometimes."

I said: "Seema, Dee's really a great guy. Look what fun we have with him. He tells us stories. We rib him. He's one of the Raipur crowd. Even you felt that way. And what a fine shot he's become. The hunting is really never complete without him."

She said: "Oh, he's competing, really. But he's secretly jealous of all of you, of my past. He even resents the crucifix around my neck, says it's not 'proper' for a married Hindu woman to wear a cross especially when visiting her in-laws. He insists that I touch their feet when I greet them. He thinks I'm too 'Westernized.' Hell, I never even touched Ma's feet or even Pa's. Pa would have been horrified."

I said, sounding very adult: " These are all adjustment problems, Seema. I still think Dee's a great guy. The main thing is he loves you. And I think basically he's a good human being."

"He is a good person, I agree," Seema said. "He wears his heart on his sleeve. You know I've actually seen him crying like a baby while he was listening to the story of one of his poorer clients in his office. One winter night when we were driving home he stopped the car on the side of the road. A homeless old man was huddled under a thin sheet. He was clearly shivering. Dee got out of the car, took off his favorite jacket – a very expensive one – and as gently as a mother would, he wrapped it around the freezing man. Without a word. He once handed over his entire wallet to a beggar. And he waives professional fees for anybody who says he cannot pay. I've even seen him sign blank cheques for friends in need of money…"

"Seema, you're married to a saint. You should thank your stars. These other matters you can work out…"

"I admire him for all that, but I'm still suffocated. I guess I always liked to be protected and secure, but he smothers me. I'll tell you something. He doesn't even turn me on any more. I just go through the motions."

"You mean, you don't love him? Maybe you should see a psychiatrist."

"I don't know. I don't know what the word love means any more. I know what it means when I see the seasons change, and the first rain on dry ground, or when I feel the breeze on my face while driving in a jeep through a forest, or when I'm reading a great book. But I don't know what it means when it comes to a man. Maybe I should have had more experiences before I got married.

197

Maybe I was too young. And no shrink in the world can command me to carry out his prescription to force myself to practice his textbook interpretation of love. I don't get the butterflies any more."

"Look," I said, "I'm sure you'll see things differently in a few days. Maybe adjust better. I still believe there's a whole bunch of men out there who couldn't light a candle to Dee. And given his past, he's changed so much for you, doesn't look at another woman."

"That's what he throws at me all the time. I don't want him to blackmail me into loving him by throwing his so-called sacrifices in my face. I didn't ask him to change."

"But you were so proud of him for all that, once."

"I was a child then."

"You'll change again, Seema. Everything changes. I don't think things are all that bad. Goodnight." And I kissed her forehead and fluffed up her pillow for her. She was still wearing her crucifix. And there was a Bible by her bedside. I remembered the Christmas stockings of not so long ago.

A few months later I paid a surprise visit to Seema and Dee in Delhi. I arrived in the evening and knocked at their bedroom door. Dee opened it and gave me a big hug.

"Come on in," he said. "Seema and I are getting

dressed to go to a party. In fact, you should come with us. Should be fun. Music, dancing, good food. Good friends of ours. They won't mind you tagging along. In fact I've told them a lot about you." He called out to Seema who was in the bathroom: "Seema, look who's here."

And Seema came bouncing out wearing her make-up, her petticoat and blouse, put her arms around me, and almost lifted me off the floor. Dreamboat became silent. And I could see a frown clouding his face.

He said, his voice sounding stern and exasperated: "Seema, what have I always told you about decency? You shouldn't come into this room dressed like that."

Seema said: "Dressed like what? It's only my brother, and there's you. And this is my bedroom. And I'm not naked or anything."

Dreamboat said: "But you know, the window faces the street. And people can look in. It will just give them ideas."

Seema raised her voice: "But there are drapes on that window. And there's nobody on the street."

Dreamboat also raised his voice: "But there are always gaps in curtains, and people can still look in."

Seema argued: "But the street is so far away. You'd have to have binoculars to see anything inside here."

"I'm only trying to protect you. You don't know what people are like…" Dreamboat said.

Seema turned to me: "He's always trying to 'protect' me. He thinks the whole world has nothing better to do than look at his wife through binoculars. All the construction women working on the roads dress in petticoats and blouses. They don't even wear saris. And nobody hassles them." She looked defiantly at Dreamboat and said: "Next time I'm going to come out totally nude, open the drapes and wave to everybody who passes by. Really! why must you always start these silly arguments just before we leave for a party and spoil everybody's mood?" And she marched back into the bathroom to finish her grooming and to put on her sari for the evening.

Dreamboat looked at me, and shook his head: "She doesn't realize that this is not her American boarding school or the private environment of your Raipur home. And even there women don't come out openly in front of strangers. Now that she's married, she should wear saris as often as she can, even during the day. But she's always going out in tight jeans and a loose shirt knotted at her stomach. She doesn't realize what people here are really like. Most Indians are conservative and they'll call her a loose woman. She's very immature. Refuses to grow up. And I have to listen to all this talk about her from the elders in my family. Don't think they don't notice how she dresses, or how she refuses to cover her head in front of my parents…"

Seema shouted from inside the bathroom: "Don't go on and on about your parents and your relatives. I am married to you, not to them!"

Dreamboat shouted back: "You have to live in the real world. Grow up."

Seema emerged from the bathroom wearing a pink chiffon sari. She had changed the blouse she was wearing for a low-necked, sleeveless one. Her cleavage was just visible. She looked vibrant. And before Dreamboat could say anything Seema said:

"Dee, I don't want you to comment on what I'm wearing, whether it's too revealing or whatever. I feel beautiful in this outfit. This is how I'm going out tonight or we're not going out at all." Dreamboat just grunted. And then he poured himself a large Scotch from a nearby decanter.

Seema looked at him: "And how many times have I told you not to start drinking before you go to a party. Because you're slightly sloshed when you arrive, and then you drink more and get soppy and sentimental and argumentative and you embarrass me."

I said, softly: "Seema, just let him be. Let him finish his drink. And let's leave and have a good time."

We were among the last to arrive. The host, a garment exporter – Indian garments, Madras Cotton, tie-and-dye fabrics – were suddenly making it big in European and American markets, and those who came early into this business and were among the first entrepreneurs to benefit from government subsidies were rolling in cash, most of it undeclared income – was a rotund, curly-haired, hook-nosed dwarf with a Havana cigar sticking out of his mouth whom Papa would immediately have dismissed as a "rich loafer." He stood on his toes to give Seema a European-style kiss on both cheeks, mock-punched Dreamboat in the stomach, and then shook my hand when Dreamboat introduced me. His house was a sprawling bungalow surrounded by a couple of acres of lawn with imported turf grass, and ringed with lemon trees, silver oak, bougainvillea, clusters of guava and mango trees, beds of marigold flowers, mulberry trees, pomegranate bushes, and clay bird-baths. There was a whiff of incense in the air. There were several bars laid out on tables covered with sheets of white muslin cloth, and the whole area was lit up with Christmas-tree bulbs hanging from wires – blue, green, purple, yellow, orange, incandescent – as well as with fluorescent neon tubes. A band was playing pop music numbers, an Anglo-Indian woman crooner sang anything from Doris Day numbers to Connie Francis's *Lipstick On Your Collar* to male songs like *King of the Road* and Sinatra's *Strangers in the Night*. And waiters were serving trayfuls of mixed drinks even though Delhi was under a spell of prohibition, and silver dishes packed with mutton kababs, tandoori chicken morsels, and tandoori fish. There must have been about 200 guests, women in evening saris, men in suits and kurtas, and the place reeked of tandoori aromas, after-shave colognes, and heavy perfume. People were dancing, smoking, drinking.

I disappeared into the crowd. And a half-an-hour later Dreamboat materialized. He asked me:

"Where's Seema?"

"I don't know, maybe she's dancing with somebody."

"Can you help me look for her?"

"Why? She's probably fine."

"No, because she's got to have her first dance with me. I hope she's not dancing with somebody else." The crooner was singing *Cry Me A* River. And we saw Seema in a slow dance with a guy called Nick, a pock-marked, fleshy-lipped, broad-nosed, scar-faced, hazel-eyed, baritone-voiced fighter pilot who read books, and wrote poetry, and who was a sounding board for all women who poured their hearts out to him. He was to become Seema's first lover after her marriage. She would tell me, later, much later: "He knew how to listen. He would read to me. He hated having casual affairs. He was so different. Never made a pass. He's been in three crashes and survived. He says marriage is a prison. He's contented, often just to sit with me and listen and never judge and never ask for anything unless I want it." That he'd ditch her a month after he got what he wanted and pull the same mindgame on some other woman, was something I was to discover much, much, later. Actually, Nick read up on stuff, and memorized passages from books just before he met any sensitive, well-read woman whom he sensed was looking for adventure.

This was not the first time he had met Seema. In fact,

Dreamboat had asked him over to their house several times for advice on the legal case of an airman who had been passed over for promotion. And Nick had been so passionate in his denunciation of the British legacy of the Air Force chain of command that he won over not only Dreamboat but also Seema.

"He is a just and fair man," Dreamboat had often told Seema. "An honorable man. A man who feels deeply for his subordinates and who has the guts to take on his superiors." And Seema had applauded Dreamboat's evaluation. "Yes," she said, "and he can even quote passages out of Thomas Mann." The last name may have gone over the cognitive ability of Dreamboat's less than literary mind, but he had nodded his assent heartily.

Nick had become a regular visitor. And Seema had taken to him. Perhaps not sexually in those early days, but as a soulmate whom she seemed to admire for characteristics she found so different from the ones which had first attracted her to Dreamboat. On that night, when he saw Seema and Dreamboat dancing together, and "whispering" as he put it to me, he was livid.

"Look at them 'whispering,'" he said to me.

"But why do you say they're whispering?" I asked. "We can't even hear them from so far."

"That's it," he said. "If we could hear them, they would not be whispering. I thought Nick was a just and fair man. But this is just not done. He obviously has no

204

principles. If he had, he would have asked Seema whether she had had her first dance with me. A wife and husband should always have the first dance together. He should have known better." And Dreamboat began to take long strides towards the dancing couple.

I asked: "Hey, you're not going to punch him out are you?"

"No," he said, "we're all going home. Seema should also have known better."

He tapped her on the shoulder and said: "Come on, we're going home."

Seema looked startled. And Nick looked a little embarrassed. Nick said: "Oh, sorry, Dee I didn't see you. I was asking Seema the whole time where you were and she said you must be some place, dancing with somebody."

Dreamboat said: "I always have the first dance with my wife. You know that. And Seema, you know that too. There are certain principles. There are things that are proper. Let's leave." Nick walked away, and Seema pleaded with Dreamboat:

"Dee, please. I was having such a great time. Why is it that I have to go every time you want to go? Why can't you leave me behind once in a while? Give me some space. Give me some breathing room. I want to know and like people on my own, and not just through you and your judgements of them."

Dreamboat was in no mood for arguments. He had sensed the arrival of a serious rival. He said: "You're not going to dance with that bastard again. You're going to dance with me. One last dance, and then we're going." Dee and Seema did one stiff dance to *Smoke Gets in Your Eyes* and Dreamboat led her out of the mansion, holding her hand. And we were soon driving back. And Seema said:

"You know Dee, if you'd only said to me: 'Go ahead, enjoy yourself. Have a good time. Come back when you're ready. No curfews. Take care of yourself, and remember, I love you but I don't own you.' If you had simply uttered those words, my heart would have gushed with love for you. I may have stayed on, and maybe I would have missed you and called you at home and told you I'm coming back quickly for that first dance I missed with you and that you should wait for me and not go to sleep. Or maybe I'd simply have gone back with you immediately and put on our record player. But you kill all this in me. You kill the love only you can inspire in me by simply leaving me alone when I want to be left alone."

Dreamboat replied: "If you think I'm going to leave you alone with bastards like the one that Nick turned out to be, you're mistaken. This town is full of bastards. I know how they operate. They'll suck you out and spit you out like a pitted grape."

Seema said: "I'm no fool, Dee. Remember, my Pa taught me how to shoot even before you knew what the backside of a shotgun looked like. My family gave me the freedom of the woods. To smell, to touch, to feel, to linger, to stay in the shadows or to stand stark naked in the sun, to stamp on scorpions or to brush them aside, to stalk, to sleep, to kill, to roll in the ground and cover myself with mud…"

And Dreamboat said, softly: "That's why you don't recognize the human species. That's why I'm here to protect you. Your shikar blinded you to the human species."

Seema shouted: "And your human species blinded you to the kiss of freedom."

They remained silent until we reached home. I went to my bedroom, undressed and got into bed. But I couldn't sleep because I could hear them in the other room. I pulled my pillow over my ears because I did not want to hear their private conversation. But they were talking loudly. And they argued through the night.

Seema: "Dee, leave me alone. I don't want to. I want to sleep."

Dreamboat: "But it's been months. You used to love it. Didn't I make you come all the time ? I'm your husband."

Seema: "That's it, Dee. You're my husband! Not my lover any more. My captor. Your rights. Your view that a male and a female must be horny for each other all the time just because they went around a Hindu fire in a marriage ceremony. I'd probably have jumped into bed with you right now if you'd simply left the party and waited for me. I want a man who makes me feel free. You don't."

Dreamboat: "What have I not given you? Money? Friends? A house? Affection for your parents, your brothers?"

Seema: "Space!"

Dreamboat: "I don't know what the shit that means. That you go fucking everything in sight when you want to? That you disrespect the customs and values of our religion and country? That you take off from the kids when it suits you? That you live on the money I earn and kick me in the butt?"

Seema: "Don't talk about money. I'm your wife, not a whore. You pay a whore for what she does. You share money with me because we have a family and you don't pay me to perform, like I'm not going to perform tonight. I once loved you for what you were even though it may have been my fantasy. Now try and love me for what I am, and try and make that your fantasy. And maybe we'll last together. You're a lawyer! You don't understand!"

Dreamboat: "No, I don't. You want to go away to the hills without me. You want to go to Raipur without me. You've even been asking for your own bedroom. We'll be the laughing stock of everyone."

Seema: "Yes, I want to be alone in the hills. And I

want you to be happy about that. It has nothing to do with not being with you, but simply something to do with being with myself. And if you're happy about that, genuinely happy, or even trying, I'll start loving you a little. Stop calling me at home 10 times a day from your office! I feel like a prisoner answering a roll-call. A suspected escapee! And I'll love you more for it. If you agree to let me have my own room, it doesn't mean I'm rejecting you. It means I simply want my own privacy. The same kind of privacy you allow me in the bathroom when I'm shitting, or bathing. And don't you know that when you come to my room, at my own invitation, what fun we can have? You say you're a conservative Hindu. But this husband-wife double-bed concept is European. It kills sex. And don't lecture me on my friends, Dee. Like, 'Oh she's a bad influence on you because she sleeps around,' or 'Oh don't listen to her because she may mislead you about me…' Let me judge, Dee. Let me be myself. Maybe I'll fuck somebody else, sometime. But maybe I'll always be yours."

Dreamboat (screaming): "This is all bullshit! I don't want my wife to be a whore. These are all excuses for whoring. You're the center of my life. I love you. And I'll always love you."

Seema: "You still don't know what love is? Dammit….what a terrible thing to do to make someone the center of your entire life? What a terrible thing for yourself, and what a terrible thing for the person who has to bear that emotional burden…"

Dreamboat: "Yes, staying home together. Respecting not just your parents but mine as well. Not having a separate room for yourself. Being the center of my life. I have nobody but you. Nobody…" (and Dee starts to weep)

Seema (tough): "That's your problem. Self-pity. Possessiveness. Never challenging tradition. Playing the eternal victim. I hate that about you. I hate that about you. Your macho is all a fake. You want a woman as a shield, not as a lover. You do not know how to love…" And Dee burst into loud sobs and Seema ran into my room and shut the door, and said:

"Did you hear all that?"

I said: "Yes. But I do not judge. Seems right out of a play."

Seema said: "It's always like that. Everything is always right out of a play. Choreographed and scripted by poets and writers and maybe God himself. That's why Papa is probably an atheist. He tried to write his own script. He defied God, he defied God's biggest believer, Mama. And they both won without hurting each other."

I asked Seema: " What's the end of all this?"

Seema said: "There are no endings. For those we have to look into our scriptures. *The Vedanta. The Upanishads.* But I'll tell you something that I've learned. I was infatuated with Dee for everything he said, how he'd love me till death do us part, how he'd kill for me, how he'd destroy the guy who even dared to look at me with passion, how he'd shoot himself if I died before he did of some sickness. You know, he really believes that. Yes, those words mesmerized me at first. But I became his captive because of that. And I feel like he enslaved me with words. Today I've freed myself of those illusions of his. I hate every one of those emotions now. If he could free himself of them. And court me again, like I begged him to do before we left the party tonight, maybe I could start finding a way of loving him again. After all, he is the father of my two girls, your nieces..."

I asked Seema: "Do you love him right now?"

She replied: "No. I cannot love somebody who cannot make me love him."

I asked: "Do you love Nick?"

She said: "I have a crush on him."

I asked: "Will you make love to him and betray Dee?"

She answered: "Maybe. Maybe Dee betrayed me in the way his conventional world will never know. And boy! I may not feel happy about betraying Dee, but I'll certainly pop a champagne cork about betraying that stupid, farty, uptight family of his. I hope to God that they find out when it happens."

At this moment, Dreamboat walked into our room, silently. He stood just inside the doorway.

And he said: "Seema, will you come back to bed?"

211

Seema replied: "No. I'll sleep here. This is going to be my own room when my brother leaves."

Dreamboat said: "I only tell her what's good for her. Because I love her. She doesn't know what it's like to live in the real world. They'll use her. They'll spit her out. She'll die a lonely old woman."

Seema said: "I'll have my children."

Dreamboat replied: "And if I'm alive, probably me as well." And he walked out of the room, entered his bedroom, and shut the door, very gently.

Chapter XVIII

1

Papa was feeling the first tremor that people approaching old age first begin to feel in their knees. Beneath the quilted false ceiling, perhaps a year or so before the Shikari decided to lay down dying, there had been a tremor or two unconnected with the business of death or the paraphernalia of medical ministrations like humidifiers and sphygmomanometers. Seema, a regular child of the dining table over which the Shikari still presided, Seema now in her fifties, Seema now a grandmother, was in Raipur on some obscure political mission, but she appeared at the table neither for lunch, which was excusable because of her afternoon schedules, nor for dinner, which was inexplicable because she was an early sleeper in her family home and usually caught up with family and political matters with the Shikari over, though now infrequent, the caramel custard. She had chosen, this time to stay at the small family guest cottage from across the rambler and ask for her meals there. It was not Papa's habit to pry. But he did ask Mama

213

about Seema, pointedly, twice, and Mama mumbled something about late meetings with party workers. And the Shikari did not press the matter.

Mama was covering up. Deliberately. She knew, as Seema had told her, that she had brought a young lover to Raipur and had propped him up for the duration of her visit at the guesthouse. The man's name was Tricky, all of 30 years of age, a lanky, effusive hunk of a gigolo prototype with maniacal eyes, with a bow-shaped upper lip which always looked as if he'd rouged it and the corners of which met with the rest of his mouth in a George Wallace snarl. For the first day she bade him not to leave his room. But Tricky exploded on the next:

"What do you mean? I'm not fit to meet your parents! My intentions have always been honorable. I've sworn to you that I will never use you like all the others. I don't care if you develop wrinkles that start at your belly and drop down below your knees. This is permanent. Or why else would I introduce you to my parents? Now you've got to keep your part of the bargain." He could weep at the drop of a hat. He was a genuine poseur.

Tricky was a drifter and he preferred to drift, it was commonly known, in the company and comforts of older women. Before pledging undying allegiance to Seema's unborn wrinkles, he had taken an oath of loyalty to Seema's latest guru in Haridwar and the two had made several trips to the holy city to meditate at the hermit's little ashram on the banks of the Ganges.

"He's like a child," Seema had confided in Sara. "He's the most religious human being I've ever known. He's simple and sentimental and he protects me like an animal. He thinks of me as a guru and his horoscope says he's headed for political stardom, maybe even prime minister."

Sara said: "But he doesn't know a soul in political circles."

Seema said: "I'm introducing him to everybody important. And you should see how he impresses them. He's going to make it big. I've never felt like this about anyone in my life."

Sara said: "Seema, he's going to spit you out like a grape pit. What the hell are you doing? What are you headed for? And what if Papa finds out?" Preach to Seema and she would reach any extreme of rebellion which she might express in an argument so wild and so weird and so full of non-sequiturs for which there were no answers, or with deep, strong silence and a stubborn and studied resumption of the very behavior that was under the critical scrutiny by the opposition.

Seema answered: "He has proven himself. We are already married."

"Married!" Sara cried. "Married? You and Dee have been living apart, but you're not even divorced from him! Seema, this is bigamy. There are laws against all that. And you'll screw up your political career."

"Most of my close friends know," she said. "Raipur doesn't have to find out. We took a quiet trip to a temple before a few friends and he sprinkled my hair with red *sindoor* and we exchanged garlands. I have a companion, so what's bugging you?"

Sara retorted: "*He's* what's bugging me. The guy's a jerk. No wonder, now, that each time I call your place in Delhi he picks up the phone and asks me whether I wish to speak to his 'wife'! I don't know Seema, the guy gives me bad vibes. What does he do?"

"Oh, he's got businesses, and plays the stockmarket and he loves to stay at home."

"He does? I thought you guys were out partying every night."

"No, he thinks I'm lonely and likes to take me out and show my friends that we're a really together couple."

And now in Raipur, Their Togetherness wanted to prove to Mama and Papa that they were on to something lasting and creative. And despite Seema's earlier reticence, she decided to take the hunk to the main house to meet Mama and Papa. But she used circumspection. An earlier attempt many years ago, with an earlier beau, a "raving intellectual" as Seema had described him had ended in a farce. He had come down on his own for just the day. Papa talked books to him and the intellectual had raved about Ernest Hummingbird and how he loved his books The Moon Also Rises, and Old Man and the

Ocean, and Papa had described him as not only a loafer but also as a prize idiot and warned Seema that if he came within shooting distance of Raipur again he'd put a couple of pellets in his ass, not because Papa did not respect Seema's privacy but that he respected his own sanity more.

Seema introduced Tricky to Mama and Papa as a "political observer" from Delhi. Tricky touched their feet respectfully. But Papa lapsed into a forbidding silence. Mama served tea and biscuits – Tricky's first and last meal at the family rambler. He stayed on at the guesthouse for a couple of days and Seema washed his clothes for him. And then they departed.

The family buzzed with gossip about Seema washing somebody's clothes.

"I swear it," Sara said. "She really washed his clothes."

"And she goes to see holy men with him."

"And he's actually moved in with her in Delhi."

"No!!"

Tips, Tally, and I were in on this conversation. And Tally said:

"I've found out from my sources that he keeps her drugged. And that he's taken her to Bombay to see another guru and they're returning by the noon flight."

What would the Shikari have done? He would probably have gone to the airport with a couple of his henchmen, whacked Tricky across the gullet and kidnapped his daughter and released her only when he was sure she was safe and free of drugs. Shall we go and nab her at the airport? What if the guy pulled out a gun and threatened Seema? Or made a scene and the airport security arrested us, instead? What if Seema, in her drugged state turned against her own family? No. Too risky. The Shikari, with his stature, and self-assuredness may have pulled it off, but maybe not us. So we planned to stake them out at Seema's Delhi flat, surprise him, whisk her away.

Their car drove up at 12.30 p.m. Tricky and Seema got out. We waited. Hired bodyguards in uniform, posted along the stairs to her second floor apartment, Tally scanning the parking area with binoculars from the roof, Tips crouched behind a settee in the corridor leading to Seema's bedroom, while I sat stonefaced, with the eyes of an inquisitor at the head of the dining table. They climbed leisurely up the stairs, carrying their own hand-baggage.

None of us moved. They entered the bedroom. Then Seema came out after a few minutes. Tips was now in the dining room with me. She asked:

"What's going on? Who are those guards? You guys want some lunch?"

Tips hollered, almost savagely: "You're on drugs.

218

That guy has drugged you. We're here to rescue you. Get away while there's time. And I'll tell that guy to get out!!"

"Drugs?" said Seema. "Are you mad? Have you gone insane?"

"Look at your eyes," I said. "Look at your speech. You've got no willpower left. He's kidnapped you."

Seema was still trying to soak in the scene: "Kidnap? Me? It was I who took him to Bombay. And I'm tired. We've been busy and I haven't had much sleep and I just took a mild dose of Valium a minute ago because I aim to get some rest."

Tally said: "We hear he's taken all your jewelry from your locker."

"He's got a criminal record."

"He's just come out of Alcoholics Anonymous, dried out at an institution in Bangalore."

"You don't know about him. He got drunk at the Racing Club and pissed on top of the bar. There are witnesses."

"And besides," Tips said, "he's a rude bastard who did not even have the courtesy to say hello, when he just walked in with you."

Seema remained calm. Almost impassive. Tricky poked his head out of the bedroom door, and said:

"Look, I'll prove my credentials. I have no answers

except I love Seema and I'm warning you all, if she ever leaves me you'll find my body on a railway track," and he picked up his bags and left, and had to call for a taxi because the overzealous bodyguards had deflated the tyres of his car.

2

Seema promised she'd check him out and gave no guarantee that she would leave him. She investigated, in the way that only women can investigate. And Tricky was clean. In two cases she even established clear cases of mistaken identity. But Raipur wasn't about to give up. The townsfolk had not taken at face value the visit of this "political observer." Rumors had flown fast and furious. And the Shikari's huge, almost legendary following in the town and villages had decided that he was to be protected from the truth at any cost lest he should suffer an emotional or physical shock. "He doesn't know," they would say. And whenever we asked Mama whether he knew, she would say, "No we've kept it from him." But the townsfolk needed to know the truth. And on a cold February morning a handful of the faithful caught a bus from Raipur and arrived in Delhi.

The delegation was led by two men. Seventy-year-old Prakash, a cloth merchant with large round eyes which alternately laughed and cried no matter what he was talking about or listening to, who had migrated from Peshawar after Partition, a bulbous W.C. Fields schnozzle, who talked in sing-song burps, whose knees were giving way but who still visited the shrine of the Sufi saint at 5 a.m. every day to seek benedictions and blessing for the Shikari and his family; and his nephew, Krishan, a stout young man with a moustache that closely followed the contours of his upper lip, a chicken farmer, the corners of whose eyes were always congealed with little drops of mucous, a wealthy second generation Punjabi immigrant, a community influence peddler and part-time political aide to Seema, who also played liaison man between Papa and doctors and chemists when Papa was starting his bouts with the final ailments, and could actually decipher physicians' handwritten prescriptions and read the expiry dates on medicine bottles.

On that February evening they knocked on Seema's door, and surprised her. Luckily Tricky wasn't in, and Prakash said:

"God bless you and your family. We're only here to bless you and to pray that your family never falls apart or that anybody ever has the opportunity to say anything bad about you." Seema ordered her maidservants to make tea and cakes. The delegation ate in silence. And Seema asked:

"What can I do for you?" And Krishan, after, looking to Prakash for guidance said:

"I apologize profusely in advance for what I am

going to say. And I'm ready to accept any punishment from you for being so frank, but I must say it. There is talk that you have a second husband. We have to disprove it. The talk is killing us all. Our enemies are spreading rumors. We need to know about that 'political observer.'"

Seema said: " What nonsense! I am still married. What rubbish. How dare you."

And the old man said: "We wish you peace. But we have to know. Can we see your husband?"

Seema said: "He's not here right now. He has business to attend to so he lives in another part of town some of the time. Why can't you go and ask him?" She gave them Dreamboat's address. They departed.

Seema called Dreamboat. They had been parted for 15 years. But they saw each other at family functions or when they were ailing, at home, or in hospital, and Dreamboat had known about Tricky, "that young jackass" he called him, like he had known about all the others, become suicidal sometimes, but always forgave, and did his duty, helped her financially, looked after the grandchildren, never kept a mistress, even though we told him to forget Seema and have himself a ball, and he'd say, no, what will the children think, or what will my father-in-law-think, or what kind of example would that be for the grandchildren, and we'd say, think about yourself, stop being such a sanctimonious asshole, and he said, he's got someone on the side every now and then but that he would never do anything openly that would disgrace the family, and he always kept a room for Seema and said she would return when she knew what was good for her and we didn't know whether to cry or cuss him out or to tear our hair in irritation.

And now this delegation from Raipur comes to his home, some of whom were kids when they attended his grand wedding in the Shah of Iran tented city that Papa had created, and the music played for five days, and Papa kept spending all his money so people would remember the color and the pageantry and the smells of saffron and cinnamon and fresh *ghee* and ginger and wheat being freshly ground to make *roomali rotis* the size of elephant ears, and Prakash who had been among the honored elders when Papa gave away the bride, bows to Dreamboat and says nothing. He is tongue-tied.

Krishan is more adroit. And he asks: "We came to see sister Seema. But we believe she lives elsewhere some of the time. Is she living with you?"

Dreamboat says: "My wife is not here all the time because she needs another place for her political work which gets in my way because I need my privacy from too many people. But she'll be back tomorrow."

"My Wife" were the words the delegates wanted to hear. They went back to Raipur satisfied, and as the word went around that Seema had passed this test of fire the people of Raipur distributed sweets to celebrate the reassertion of purity. Dreamboat knew what he had accomplished. He believed that in pouring balm into

223

healing wounds miracles occur and wishes turn again into wedding horses. The very next week, Dreamboat traveled to Raipur to reassert his identity, before the entire town, as Seema's husband and to dispel any lingering doubts that the wags may have harbored, about her social legitimacy and right to inherit the Shikari's legacy. And the wags – young and old eunuchs, street barbers, dirge-singers, demented hags with halitosis, Brylcreamed pansies – came to him, touched him, scolded him for not coming often enough, nagged him about not accompanying Seema on her trips home – also became believers. And when Dreamboat left for Delhi there was a crowd that followed him to the outskirts of the city, running alongside his three-year-old Suzuki. But Dreamboat was far away.

Any hope that this act of post-adultery chivalry would be rewarded by Seema with pre-adultery noblesse oblige was shattered by none other than Papa. He saw what Dreamboat had done. He knew that Dreamboat's Great Expectations were crafted on the strategy of decency and sacrifice and that he was driven by a desire for vindication and not vindictiveness and that while the former required acts of compassion, the latter called for machinations. He had called Dreamboat – whom, he had taught how to shoot, finally, in the first few years of his daughter's married life, and Dreamboat had become a fantastic left-and-righter and a great companion to the Shikari – into his false-ceilinged chamber and said:

" I know what you've done. But with Seema you're

on a wild goose chase. She's like one of those wild geese. Ornithologists may believe this, but I don't. I don't think these wild geese ever mate forever. And unfortunately, Seema's taken on with another loafer. One day, it's a morning flight, another day, it's another flight, Dee, and you know all about that. She'll take to the one that she thinks looks the strongest in the slipstream, but she'll float out of its shelter as soon as she sees it weaken. She's an instinctive flier, not strong by herself, but seeking strength from others, but only too cognizant of the benefits she receives, she's the swimmer who goes to the mermaid, but the mermaid must not weaken, because if she does, Seema becomes a more powerful swimmer by absorbing the mermaid's strength. In most cases the swimmer drowns when the mermaid weakens, but Seema only grows stronger. And now she's latched on to another loafer, God have mercy on him."

Funny, how Papa used the word "loafer" again and again. And funny that Seema should latch on to a loafer. Because loafers were what put an end, ultimately, to the family trips to Mussoorie. Not memories of Elizabeth Seymour, as we once imagined, but the advent of loafers – whom the Shikari called "bumptious upstarts". The democratization of leisure – the most powerful demonstration of the socialistic vitality of American society (golf courses within the reach of garage mechanics, a sport still reserved for the affluent in most other countries), weekend trips to beaches, trout fishing, turkey hunts, mountaineering expeditions, five-day weeks, sandblasters and carpenters and electricians making more weekly wages than white collar schoolteachers (before the advent of computer whizkids with high school education, and by that time the Shikari was already gone, gone, gone) etcetera – was taking its toll of feudal snobbery in India. Not turkey hunts, of course, and neither golf courses for the middle class. But new money – Loafer Money – as Papa called it being able to afford Mussoorie. Greasy-haired freaks with strange accents had appeared on the Mall, fleabag motels had begun to spring up in the late fifties, the crowds had swollen near the bagpiper bandstands, where there were horses, there were now mules, and the armpits of the throngs of shoulder-to-shoulder mall-walkers reeked of sweat and cheap mall-walkers reeked of sweat and cheap perfume, and the Shropshire had closed shop and the British ladies no longer came, while alongside the deodars which were being felled, the high-rises and mountainside behemoths of macadam rose faster into the skies than the fern bushes and conifers, and the water made you sick, the streams were drying up and India was reaching into a frenzy of transistor-set music crescendo. In the *jheels* around Raipur the waters were receding, the scrub forest was thinning, the mallards had deserted their former haunts in the plains of Uttar Pradesh and preferred not to migrate any farther south than Kashmir, and the Shikari had felt the tinge of the weakening of his universe in his knees – an ailment both physical, social and sociological that would continue for the next 30 years until he decided it was time to lay dying – and now he had decided that to cure the universe he would retreat from its lowest common denominators. If it wasn't exclusive, it wasn't worth poetry. His time was over. Damn the masses. He didn't create them. They were part of his purdah system in Raipur but he'd be damned if he wanted the smell of their armpits in Mussoorie. He was like Solzhenitsyn, arch-rebel, arch-conservative, from the revolutionary archipelagos to the shades of Vermont where he trumpeted his sentimental literary yearnings for Mother Russia and the Czars.

And damn if he cared about the newer, newer, moneyed class. Le Bumptiousie. You know, sons and daughters of jewelers and cinema-hall owners, the bumptious upstarts, not like Prakash and Krishan from Raipur, who cared about their values, stifling as they might be, who journeyed to Delhi to protect one of their own, who luxuriated in being small town cloth merchants and brick-kiln owners and small time financiers, and owners of clutches of cycle rickshaws, and small town real estate lawyers with black robes and still learning to say MeLord. But the money-makers who came out of small towns and sent their children to British public schools (in India), settled in Delhi, hated their beginnings, because they had none, secretly couldn't stand their kids for speaking English, so the kids compromised by speaking non-Indian-public-school lingo, became chartered accountants and married wives above themselves, who took lovers within six months, or below them, who tried to copy *Vogue* and *Cosmo*, and couldn't do it because their mouths stank of nouveau riche Pepsodent or Monkey Brand tooth-powder, black teeth replaced with dentures, looking up what saris to wear in *Femina* catalogues, or just going to parties to see what the real people were wearing, and looking through friends and acquaintances, not because they didn't like them (which would be a genuine reason) but because they were afraid of being recognized for what they were, phoneys and frauds, disgusting creatures, feather-assed with money, coming and going not even speaking of Michaelangelo, greeting people with fake kisses on both cheeks, air-kisses so as not to smudge their cheap lipstick, pony-tailed and mascaraed, disgustingly under-educated.

Tricky may well have been the last loafer in Seema's life. At least, Papa seemed to think so. And as he was wont to cut his life off from all situations in which loafers –including those of the new moneyed variety ruled – so, apparently, did Seema. Tricky lasted maybe a year. Seema simply threw him out, not because the family thought he was a bum, not fit to be her companion, in fact the family was quite getting used to curly-lips (not Papa, but the rest of the family), but because he no longer made any sense in the jigsaw puzzle of her life. He tried what all abandoned men do, rebound affairs, heavy-breathing phone calls, women calling Seema and telling her what a great lay she was missing out on in her late fifties. O, they described his sexual prowess in lascivious detail, the ability of his mouth to hold the labia majora in a lip-like grip with only the hint of the teeth, and Seema went: "Yukkk!"

Many years after all that was over Sara and I talked about it, and I said:

"Sara, how come everybody had a lot to say to Seema, they criticized her, held her responsible for her stupidities and all that. But with all the guys and that husband pining for her, was she a slut? Was she a whore? Just like the language we use about other women and don't want to use about our sisters?"

And Sara said: "Male words but maybe there's something in these distinctions. The guys who go out and screw all the time, we just call them overgrown kids. Looking for new candy. Perhaps a double standard. But unlike men, women don't grow up into becoming kids again. Those who grow up into kids, are maybe the sluts. Those who become women, are not. And this has nothing to do with sexual behavior or frequency. And I believe Seema is more than a woman. She's a real mother for one thing. But that's neither here or nor there.

"Main thing is that Seema is a shikari. A collector of death experiences. And for her the hunt is not sexual but spiritual. An act of defying God while also playing God and totally submitting while the hunt is on. She's the huntress and the hunted. She never shied away from the consequences of the hunt and that is why people still flock to her for advice. She went into life and love fully conscious of morbidity and mortality. And people flock to her for knowledge, not because she has anything special to offer – or why would she go to gurus all the time? – but because they can imbibe from her. Her

229

laughter. Her sense of life-timing. Her ability to laugh at herself without hurting anybody.

"She was never a slut because she did not consciously use anybody for material or spiritual gain. Her husband was a spiritual inheritance of tradition. What she got she expected. Others, well, she submitted to them completely. Never asked for anything. Never wanted to dominate. Never wanted to subordinate them, never nagged, always submitted, not as a female, but as a kind person. She never needed emotional, intellectual or financial capital to sustain a relationship. Because she had them all. And most of all, she knew how to laugh, how to guffaw like a maniac, how to cry like a little baby, but after that how to guffaw, how to laugh, how to guffaw and poke fun at herself. She was able to teach others how to live and learn because while she associated with others she never sucked them dry for knowledge. She loved them and what she learned from that love she learned from herself, not from them. And did she know how and when to drop them! She never appropriated an experience. She gently entered into it. "

Part Four

Part Four

Chapter XIX

1

Seema did not know Simon Margolis whom I met at grad school in Columbia University in writing class during my first year in New York. But they seemed to be kindred souls. He was eight years younger than her and grew up in Manhattan, in a mid-town brownstone with five bedrooms owned by his real-estate business parents, Jewish immigrants from Russia, Nat and Martha, whom Simon called by their first names, and resented them for sending him to PS 148 in Brooklyn Heights instead of a fancy private school, because in school the other boys beat up on him because he refused to shoot the hoops with them inside fenced empty lots and called himself a poet. His masterpiece, until he turned 24, was penned in a small illegible cursive scrawl in red ink:

"*Hamburger Joe,*

He no mo'"

Simon, with his sparse sandy-colored hair down to

his shoulders, his male-pattern baldness making inroads from both temples into the sides of his scalp since he was a teenager. His rosebud mouth which spoke only from its center with the sides of his lips tightly compressed at both ends. Even when he smiled from its center, his lips puckered open as if he were trying to say "O" with a mischievous pout. He was sharing a loft in the lower East Side with "Turdy Dribble" Khan who had once borrowed a joint from him outside the Filmore East theatre. But Khan soon moved out. He didn't like Simon's taste in music. And he was sick to death of hearing Simon recite Hamburger Joe. And to top it all Simon wore purple-colored John Lennon glasses, even when he slept. Khan was into Basie, and Zoot Sims, and Joe Pass and Charlie Parker and Trummy Young, and Billie Holliday, and Dizzy Gillespie, and even did somersaults to Conway Twitty, while Simon blasted Lay Lady Lay, and Just Like A Woman and The Incredible String Band Quartet. And he felt badly that Simon stayed away as much as he could from Nat and Martha Margolis. "Heck, parents is parents, man," Khan admonished him. There was more. Simon hated electric lights. He lit the rooms with scented multi-colored candles with fire-proof shades invented by a gizmo dealer on Mott Street. And Khan was a sucker for 150-watt bulbs, unshaded.

As Khan told me before he moved out: "Man, those candles! They smelled of pussy-deodorant. And that Simon, I think he's a devil worshipper."

Seema and Simon were kindred souls because at

234

their particular stage in the evolution of the species – many continents apart – both had shunned or had been bypassed by the process of the journey of growth, the inheritance of the collective wisdom of the ages that transmutes tradition into common sense, faith, understanding, acceptance, doubt, questioning, reasoning, a logical embrace or rejection, loathing, rebellion and revolution. Just as Seema had once become a devout Christian without a smattering of the Law, the Prophets, and the Writings, or the covenant between God and Israel on Mount Sinai, so too was Simon a poet to whom Milton would have made sense only if he had taken lessons from Dylan in the cafeterias of the Village, just like the acid-freaked sun-scorched-eyed revolutionaries with the Shikari's Mamba piss cure had danced to the death-knell of the withered-away state.

I had liked Simon immediately. He still looked kind of beat up from his high-school days and when he didn't smile from his puckered-up mouth he wore a look of vengeful melancholia. But I liked him because he cared to listen to what Indian curry was all about. Most of my class, who suffered from gastronomic xenophobia, believed that curry was simply a hot dish, or a single spice, that made the eyeballs sweat. But Simon listened when I explained to him that curry really meant a food preparation with gravy. That spices were not synonymous with curry. That a curry dish could be fragrant, hot (depending on how much red pepper you add to it), aromatic, mild, perfumed, and could take on hundreds of different flavors, the basic ingredients being chopped onions, garlic, fresh ginger, tomatoes mixed, depending on the type of dish required, with turmeric, basil, coriander (dried or green), asafetida, cumin seeds crushed or whole, fresh mint, cinnamon, cloves, cardamom and vinegar and rosewater and much more.

And Serita, my companion – also Indian, a mathematical genius whom I met in New York and with whom I lived – and I educated Simon's palate. We weaned him from his diet of cheeses and grapes and black olives and Danish pastries and schpumpernikel and schmatzhoballs and schliverwurst and schtongue sandwiches, taught him to slobber over *dal* sauteed in whole black cumin seeds and garlic, and even cooked him, when money allowed us, Cornish Hen (a passable substitute for the Shikari's partridge) basted with honey, sherry, garlic and crushed coriander mixed with Worcestershire sauce. In fact, the Shikari had once delighted Elizabeth Seymour with this concoction.

Except for Simon, others from the class who came for dinner still called everything we cooked, "curry." Lee Thal was another person who learned the difference. Lee had replaced Khan as Simon's room-mate. A wiry, dark-complexioned, small-eyed man who Simon introduced to me as a "great sculptor." Lee spent a lot of his time carving out dildoes from leather, terracotta, shoe-heels, plastic, cement, wood, cane, and Simon's candles, using Simon's kitchen-top as his studio. He tested their smoothness, durability, safety and efficacy on Times Square whores and even hawked them in Washington

Square. But mainly he played the guitar. He banged on all the strings together with the back of a hairbrush, never using the frets, and for more mellifluous effects he stroked the strings with the bristles. His father, a wealthy pharmaceutical dealer in Hoboken, across the George Washington Bridge in New Jersey, financed Lee's band which gave free concerts outside Tavern-on-the-Green in Central Park. Lee's drummer beat upon his cymbals with a stiletto heel, and his rhythm man balanced his guitar on a wooden crate and plucked its strings in the manner of a bass player in a jazz quartet. Like Seema's early Christianity and Simon's nascent bard-ship, Lee's art was the child of muses unborn. A child who would give birth to Apollo and Calliope. An Orpheus without a lyre.

2

Serita and I had entered one another's lives, about a year after I finished grad school, without any male-part opening one-liners or female-part eye-lock routines. In fact even before I looked at Serita's teeth – perfectly white, perfectly-shaped-and-sized incisors and canines (when she smiled, it was never with pursed or compressed lips but rather with a slightly open mouth in which her smile ended at some mysterious spot just as it entered her pre-molars) – with which I fell in love and which emanated the suffused glow of moist little light bulbs when we embraced at night, my eyes were busy following the tall, brown-haired hulk who had entered the room with her. He had waist-long hair that hung down from a ponytail. He was built like a basketball player. Clint Eastwood eyes. Two chains around his neck. Butt-hugging jeans patched at the knees. Cowboy boots. A proud, bulging crotch. And while Serita's unpainted mouth was thin and, as I quickly learned, followed the shapes of her moods, the hulk had moist, thick, cherry-red lips which seemed to shape his whole persona and conjured up in my mind the weird vision of a female camel with lipstick getting ready to give her mate a blow job.

The room she walked into with the hulk's right arm wrapped lightly around her shoulders, was really a loft in the north Bronx, near Fordham University, in a muddle of red-brick row houses, tenements with prominent steel fire escapes and subway entrances that seemed to pop out of every corner. Its occupant, Javed Faridi, a twenty-something-year-old bearded artist with sunken cheeks, prominent buck teeth and moist, long-lashed bovine eyes under a pair of superbly arched jet-black eyebrows, who had moved there a couple of years ago from Bombay, painted orange and black sharply-finned fish of every imaginable variety on discarded pieces of packing crate wood. And he even sold some of them in the East Village. But mostly, he was supported by Fran, a blonde, stocky, pug-nosed, blue-eyed and massively freckled woman from Richmond, Virginia, whose bosom began right below the hollow of her neck and then curved in a neat, unified frump that ended underneath her navel. So when you hugged Fran hullo, you had to draw in your shoulders and arch yourself inwards to avoid making too hard a frontal contact with this unending mound of tit.

Fran had inherited an income from her father, a rich shipyard contractor, and from the husband she had divorced five years earlier. And she had met this "divine Hindu artist" sitting among wooden crates, and said she could smell the sea in his painted fish, and she had purchased all his paintings, and then commanded him to live with her. And Javed, though he was a religious Muslim, never corrected her when she called him a "Hindu." That, he repeatedly intoned, "is called love." And he loved her from bosom to toe for sure, for whenever she was away on a trip Javed would call his friends over the phone heaving with sobs of bereavement.

Fran's major occupation was giving parties for racially and ethnically mixed couples, mostly Indians and white Americans for she held the Indo-American synthesis to be divinely ordained. Serita and her *galoot*, that evening, were among several of her guests. It was the usual curry-and-Gallo-red-wine routine with recorded pop Hindi music, and white Americans boasting of new Hindi words they had learned from their lovers.

In the 1960s and early seventies most mixed couples I knew were Indian males and American females. Vedic genetic memory, caste consciousness dictated that the Indian line must continue in case the relationship was consummated and children were born. The male must dominate the emerging bloodline. And so, it was rare, indeed, to see an Indian female draped around a white male. The immediate explanations that emerged from a male-orientation-fogged mind was: Slut. Easy Lay. Meaning that if she could so easily junk the Indian taboo of consorting openly with a white man, then the world of taboos must surely not exist for her – especially sexual taboos. This was a powerful ethno-mental aphrodisiac. The Go-West Indian males of that era rarely dated their own countrywomen. When they did, it was usually to mate and marry. Amongst themselves they followed the sexual Puritanism of the old country. With white women, why, anything went. A white woman who went to bed with you on the first date was not an "easy lay" – she was considered simply a creature of her own culture. But an Indian woman who gave out the signals of an easy lay was a powerful sexual stimulant. She was the forbidden fruit. Something you could rarely touch before marriage back home, but here, yours for the asking. And, God! what wonderful tricks she must have learned from these white guys.

And my eyes followed Serita around the room. Decidedly a flirt, taking drags from borrowed cigarettes from several men, laughing out loud, staring with a concentration of excitement and a half-smile with whomever she conversed. She was about my medium height, wore a loose ankle-length black cotton skirt and a loose black shirt over it. Her hair, open, fell to her waist and seemed to churn there – like a black waterfall that cascaded in gentle downward streams from the sides and back of her head, gained momentum as it slid down her shoulders and then began to froth as it hit bottom just below her waist. She was fair, almost white, with large brown eyes, and she could have passed for Greek or Italian, but an Indian can usually spot an Indian no matter how far away.

Fran saw me staring at her and said: "Oh, that's Serita. She's with Ben. They're the most wonderful couple I know. I'm surprised you don't know them. Ben's either going to be, or is already a surgeon."

"Then why does he dress like that?" I asked. "I mean isn't it kind of weird for a doctor to be dressed like a porn star?"

Fran smiled: "Oh I guess they all get terribly bored with their white gowns and they've got to let their hair down."

"I just hope none of it ever falls into a patient's open abdominal cavity, Fran," I said in perfect seriousness.

And Fran said: "But you've got long hair too."

"I'm supposed to, Fran. Have you forgotten, I'm a writer, I'm a Hindu wild man. A man who grew up hunting." And when Fran introduced me to Serita, she said: "Meet the Hindu Wild Man."

And Serita said: "Hi, I'm Serita." She pronounced her name *Sereeter* as an American would rather than the real pronunciation which is *Surritah*. Another taboo gone I thought, and I also said Hi Serita, and pronounced her name the way she had chosen to pronounce it. Discreetly, I tried to figure out her figure. Couldn't make out much underneath that loose cotton shirt with two buttons open below the neck, but I decided she was small-breasted.

"What's your last name?" I asked.

She replied: "Nagraj." She pronounced that one perfectly. And I asked her if she were from the south, south India, that is, and she said I'd guessed perfectly, that she was from Tamil Nadu, and added: "No more inquisitions."

"But I've hardly even asked you a question," I protested.

"You've got a funny name, too, what does it mean?"

"Oh, you mean 'Tan'? I guess it's because of my complexion. My father used to make a joke about white racism. He used to say that while they look down on non-whites their greatest ambition is to get a tan whenever the sun shines, but instead of turning out bronzed – which is their aim – they turn all red and blotchy. I used to laugh about that here in college and tell my buddies that unless they could achieve the brilliance of my color they should Call Me Mister Bronze, or something like that, and they began calling me Tan instead. But tell me, this guy, Ben, you're with, is he with you because he thinks you're exotic or because he thinks you're white?"

Serita lowered her head, then slowly she looked at me, scanning my entire face with her eyes, her mouth set in a stern line. "No one's ever asked me a question like that before, and you have no business to. I hardly know you. I don't think it's too good an idea to get too personal."

I wasn't about to apologize. This was New York. This was the very early seventies. This was not some formal New Delhi gathering where we spoke in coded words and used polite, indirect, discreet language. We were in the land of Sensitivity Training and Esalen, and Group Therapy, and Letting It All Hang Out, and where Pigs and Motherfuckers were everyday words to condemn Vietnam-happy America.

I said: "Wait a minute. If a white American had asked you this same question you would have considered that to be part of a liberal sociological exercise and would have gotten into some great explanation. You're shy to open up with your own countryman, because you know he'll catch on to you if you're bullshitting."

Serita was angry: "I owe nobody from the old country any explanations. And I never will. India has no right over my soul or my lifestyle any more. I left that all behind. I cannot open myself up to India any more. India cannot know me any more. And you would have been better off asking me if I thought Ben loved me. A personal question, yes, but at least not a below-the-belt one. If you must know, yes he does. He's my husband. We've been married a couple of years."

Ben arrived just then. And he said to Serita:

"You haven't introduced me to your friend." He

243

pumped my hand. He had short stubby fingers, not like a surgeon's, but like a huntsman's or a shikari's. I had long, tapered hands, unlike a hunter's, and more like a surgeon's.

And Ben said: "Haven't you heard about this guy? I just found out. He's got a story just published in *Evergreen Review*. And they're all raving about it. Hey Mister Writer, your autograph pleeeeze," Ben joked. "But I really am happy to meet you. Fran and Javed just told me you've cooked the Cornish hen this evening."

Serita stared hard at me and moved away into the crowd. And I took a large swill of rum on the rocks. And people helped lay the food on the table. Olives and cheese, salami, pumpernickel bread, fresh grapes, Polish sausage, corned beef and cabbage, Fran's version of fried okra Indian style, Cornish hen cooked in sherry and Worcestershire sauce and garlic in the best tradition of Papa's Raipur partridge dish.

I raised a secret toast to Papa. His dish was a hit. There was a whiff of the Raipur dining table in the air in this apartment in the Bronx. And the Cornish hen was a hit. And the guests were asking me about recipes and I was bullshitting them about the basting techniques and marinades and the right way to defrost a Cornish hen, and Ben Galoot, looking more than ever like a satiated camel came to where I was sitting in a distant corner of the living room and complimented me on the "great curry."

"No, Ben," I said. "It was not a curry. It was an Indo-European concoction. Just because an Indian cooks something it is not a curry. Just like all Americans are not Yankees. Hasn't Serita told you that? By the way I must compliment you on your taste."

"Oh, it was not just me, everybody's raving about it," Ben said.

"I don't mean the Cornish hen, Ben, I mean Serita."

Ben's face went all soft, like it had suddenly lost all its muscles, and he said: "She's divine. She's the most wonderful person I know. I can't imagine myself married to anybody else. The last few years have just flown."

"Did your parents object? I mean, I don't know, from your accent you sound like you could be from Georgia or some such place, and these mixed marriages can be a pain, right?"

"Not bad, North Carolina, actually. Even though it would not have influenced my decision, I never consulted my parents. We were not that close because they supported Lyndon Johnson and Nixon on Viet Nam and I didn't. And I was all for the draft-dodgers. But that's not the entire reason. You know, I think I can talk to you, are you in school?"

"No I just finished grad school, Columbia. I write and edit stuff. But mostly I just hang around. And you cut people up, right?"

245

The muscles came back into Ben's face. He said: "Well, actually I'm just finishing med school at Johns Hopkins."

"So you commute from Manhattan?"

"Right. We have a small apartment on East 72nd between Madison and Park."

"Wow. That's expensive."

"Well actually Serita helps out. Right now she's making more than me. She's a mathematician. She's finishing her doctorate from NYU and she's already teaching. I think she's a genius."

"So, it was easy for you both. You both ignored your parents."

"I'll tell you, I don't know about Serita. She's never told me whether she asked them or not. She tells me it's not my business, and I respect her for that. But when we have a child it's important for the child and me to be connected to Serita's past, and her parents –the grandparents of my own child. But I don't bring that up, too often. With me, it was different. I'll tell you a secret. I was kind of pushed into an arranged marriage."

Now it was my turn to lose the muscles on my face, and I said: "What? To Serita?"

Ben laughed. He motioned me to steady up with both his palms facing my chest. He said: "No, this was a couple of years back. I'll cut a long story short. I knew this girl,

Francine, since we were kids. She was a distant cousin. We were never lovers or anything, but our parents encouraged us to date. Our parents are in big finance together. And the families had agreed even when we were teenagers that we would get married. And we were both about the same age, about our mid-twenties when they announced our engagement party. It was in Francine's home, not too far away from ours, and she'd invited quite a few of her friends from all over, and Serita was, I guess, a friend of a friend."

My mouth was still open: "You put the ring on the wrong girl?"

Ben smiled and looked a little less like a camel: "Well, not quite, but sort of. The moment Serita walked in and I saw her hair, and I couldn't make out where the hell she was from, and she was smiling all the time, I just wanted to talk to her. I don't smoke, but she insisted that I take a drag from her cigarette, and said she had a hobby of trying to turn doctors into smokers..."

"And, you took a drag?"

"Well, yeah. And another one. And we laughed and talked most of the evening. And she said things about India and Indian music. I'd never really ever talked to an Indian before, I mean for more than a few moments of saying hello. And this was just amazing. The guests and my folks were politely trying to break me away from Serita and pay attention to the other guests, and I'd say, well, just a minute and all that. And Serita looked me squarely in the eyes and asked me if I liked her. And I said, yes. And she said, Do you have the guts to leave here, with me, right now, and never come back? I waited for maybe a minute. I looked around the room, I looked at Francine, I looked at her parents, the guests, and everything was a blur and senseless. I looked at Serita and she made sense, and I said, Yes. I walked out with her to the car. We drove away. Stopped at a few motels. Drove to Manhattan where Serita bought me a few clothes. We got married in court three days later. So now you know why I didn't ask my parents. And by the way, it might be a good idea for you to come over and teach her how to cook good Indian stuff."

I thought Ben was either lying or he was completely crazy. But he wasn't even drinking much that evening. And the general buzz in the conversation that evening in Javed and Fran's apartment was that Ben was a regular guy and that Serita was devoted to him. And Serita came by to where Ben and I were sitting and perched herself on the arm of the sofa where Ben had seated himself. And she asked me:

"Can you write down the recipe for what you cooked? I mean, you've got to take a bow, Tan."

I said: "It's a secret," and I winked at Ben, who suddenly looked less like a *galoot*. He raised his eyebrows, smiled, and moved away in a gesture of a male compact that understands the need for secrecy in the passing on of recipes. Serita sunk herself into the sofa. She looked at me and said nothing.

The sexual stimulant that she had been for me the whole evening was exacerbated by mystery. I said: "So, you snatch husbands away from their wives at their wedding altars. I mean, you were just asking me to stay away from personal questions, like some Tamilian prude, and you've spent your life grabbing these guys, these white guys, away from their wedding rings. Well, hello, my little Tamilian Isadora Duncan. *Surritah*, you're something else."

She said: "I want to know your story."

I said: "You don't get it so easily. Not as easily as I got yours. You'll have to work for it. I'm here. I'm me. I'm un-arranged-not-married. I don't have a Ben blurting out the intimate details of my altar-snatching."

Serita said: " I don't mean about your life. I mean, your *story*, the one in the *Evergreen Review*. What was it all about. And you can give the recipe later. But what about your story?"

"Why don't you read it?"

"I don't read much except for scientific work. Why don't you give me a synopsis, and maybe then I'll read it."

"You want to know? Well, it's about this white American. A Connecticut Yankee. Harvard, Yale, Colgate, or whatever. He's contemporary. Father a banker. Mother a blonde. His name is Allyn – with a 'y'. He's done pot and LSD and likes Jerry Rubin and Abbie Hoffman, reads the East Village Other, and Off Our Backs, and listens to acid rock at the Fillmore East. He spells Nixon as "Nixxon," and America as "Amerikka" in his symbolic hatred of multinationals and Nazi Germany. Salutes Che Guevara and Fidel, wants American imperialism to be defeated in Vietnam. He feels that Gene McCarthy was secretly drugged by Hubert Humphry. He believes that the Third World is the path of liberation. He is against machines. He is a Luddite. He believes in Gandhi. In Buddha –heavily so. Has read Herman Hesse. In a totally pastoral existence. No technology. No want. No desire. Wonderful aspirations even if intellectually arrived at and then incorporated into the self through meditation. But Allyn decides to leave America – to jettison the Air-conditioned Nightmare – and find solace through a physical displacement in a remote part of rural India untouched by technology and comfort. The first thing, when he arrives there, is to learn how to shit in an open field. Because there were no toilet bowls and toilet seats. Also there are timings for bowel evacuation. Mostly at 5 a.m. When the peasants go out in the open fields and squat. Allyn is still asleep. When he realizes that he has to shit in American clock, in full view, and that too, sitting on his haunches he is petrified. He is constipated. His knees give way. His privacy is destroyed. He asks for a village doctor. The doctor understands. The village which has adopted this foreigner helps him by building him a wooden toilet seat even measured by the local tailor according to the size of his bum. When Allyn is presented with this he knows he has lost. He cannot even perform his most basic function in the revolution he has staged. He realizes that he is ultimately tied, no chained, to his toilet seat in his neatly-tiled Manhattan bathroom. And Allyn, defeated, goes back home to America."

Serita smiled all the time. And then she asked: "What's the title of your story?"

I answered: "No Exit."

And then Ben came around and he saw us talking, and he smiled, and asked me what I liked to do in my spare time, and I said, I liked forests, and walking the wilds, and fishing, and hunting, and reading, and that I liked walking around Riverside Drive, and taking the Staten Island Ferry, and going to Roosevelt Island near Arlington across the Potomac across Washington, D.C., near Virginia, and walking along the B&O Canal on the Maryland side. And Ben said, he'd have a surprise for me, and before he left Fran's apartment he actually gave me a hug, and he looked even less like a camel, and Serita looked into my eyes and turned away without even a goodbye. And that night I slept in a sleeping bag in Fran's living room because it was too late to take the D Train back into Manhattan and because I wanted to think about Serita because I felt her perfume lingered in the apartment even after everyone had left.

3

At 7 a.m. the next morning the phone rang. Fran told me Serita wanted to talk to me. I was groggy after too many rums and I had forgotten the names of the previous nights. I said Hello, and she said Hi. And I didn't have to be reminded of her name. I clutched the phone closer to my neck and ear and Serita with no sleep in her voice said:

"We bought the Evergreen Review at the 75th and Broadway station. Went there specially. It's the funniest story I've ever read in my life. It's like you. And yes. I did snatch him from the altar. So what? And will you give me your recipe?"

I said nothing. I grunted. But I was sexually awake. Doing my male bastard hard-to-get-routine.

"Are you there?" Serita screamed. "Well look, after Ben and I came home we talked about you. Ben's really upset about the disappearance of forests in your life. And that all you have is Riverside Drive. Look, we'll pick you up around 11 a.m. and we'll drive up to Bear Mountain near Peekskill, in the Hudson Valley. You'll love it."

"But what if I don't want to go?"

"You'll love it."

"Why?"

"Because Ben says you will. He loves you."

"And you?"

"See you at eleven. And try and get a frisbee. And we're packing a whole lot of beer and salami sandwiches."

When Ben rang the apartment bell and announced himself over the intercom from outside the lobby, Fran buzzed open the entrance door to the building and the elevator creaked itself upwards to the third floor. Ben was wearing a corduroy Stetson with a hollowed-out band at the nape of his neck from which his camel-tail dangled out and hung. Mentally, I invented words for this phenomenon, "downhung," "hungdown," "hungdownhunk," "hungdowng-alootinghunk." And I just stopped short of "well-hung" because that would force me to make a sexual evaluation of him which I was not ready to do because somehow that would relate to Serita, and the possible reality of it would destroy the satire I'd built around the camel.

Ben said: "Hey guy, you ready? Serita's downstairs in the car."

"We go, Ben," I said.

After we cross the George Washington Bridge, and make sure we don't land up in Hoboken, unless we remember to make a tricky right turn, we hit Route 9W cruising in Ben's Volkswagen Beatle along the New Jersey Side of the Hudson, and on the other side, to the right of the river we can still see the World Trade Center if we crane our necks backwards, and the Bronx, and Riverdale, and suddenly the macadam starts receding, and for a while we leave the river, and little American villages with their white steeples, and red-brick colonial facades, and maple trees and oaks, and the hills take over. And the river comes back now and again. And it's *more* again, than *now*, throughout the 50-mile drive to Bear Mountain, past where the Hudson broadens and you can still see the moth-balled WWII ships, like out of a Conrad word-painting, and deeper and deeper into the Hudson Valley in which New York city is already an hour behind, and you're entering the beginning of the Appalachian Trail.

And I know all this because Ben is talking all the time and giving me a great historical travel guide note on the whole trip. The Overlook Lodge was built in 1915 and the inn serves great burgers and sandwiches, and has a huge fireplace. He and Serita are in the front of the car. And I'm in the back, leaning forward, so Serita can pass me a can of Budweiser every now and then, and whenever Ben makes a point I say uh-huh, wow, great history, man, I lean forward and look into the rear-view mirror to see if Serita's trying to look at me, and every now and then I catch her eye and she smiles like a whore. And the smile hits me right in the groin, blood rushing in, blood rushing out, blood rushing in, blood rushing out.

Ben says: "You know, that story of yours in Evergeen. Not every American's like that. Man, I could run up to the top of Bear Mountain faster than you. There's a Bear Mountain in the Catskills not too far from here, more than 8,000-feet high, and I could run up there, too. And if Serita asked me to live in a hot Indian desert, maybe I'd do it, too. When I was growing up in North Carolina, my dad would take me to Weymouth Woods. He showed me the long-leafed pines."

I asked: "Did you ever hear the sounds of the endangered red-cockaded woodpecker?"

"Well, we were not really into birds." Ben was a great travel guide. We were nearing Bear Mountain, and he continued about North Carolina: "The Mount Jefferson State Natural area has a great overlook at a height of about four-and-a-half thousand feet –Luther's overlook. And north of Wilkesboro on the John P. Frank Parkway is Stone Mountain, a mini moonscape on this dome-shaped granite mass. I've seen things and I think I'm pretty hardy. Not like that American nut in your story."

"Oh, don't take it that seriously," Ben, I said. "It's really a parable. Tell me more about North Carolina."

"Well, actually I was born in Raleigh. There was really not that much to my life. We're Presbyterians. My dad reads the Bible. I read the Bible before breakfast every day. Went roller-skating. I still read the Bible and say my prayers. You can see I'm tall. I played basketball, and was middle line-backer in our football team. I guess I was funny because people laughed at my jokes. And I went into medicine because that's what my folks wanted." Ben said he was fascinated by Dr Helen Taussig's discovery that Blue Babies were not a freak phenomenon but simply the product of a heart valve deficiency and that she was able to cure this "idiopathic cardiomegaly" through a simple operation. He said he secretly hoped for some other such freak phenomenon to manifest itself because he was specializing in pediatric cardiology and hoped to make a surgical breakthrough some day.

I said: "Ben, to go back to what we were talking about earlier, my story is not about you. It's just a story. The Americans are still getting butt-fucked by malaria mosquitoes in Viet Nam, just as they did in Burma and Korea during the last World War and after. They've fought in deserts. In the seas. In my story I'm talking about a wonderful guy who's really a piece of shit. There are Indian shits and there are American shits. Ultimately we all cancel each other."

Serita lit up all of a sudden and said: "Enough of this crazy shit. Can't we just shut the hell up and look at what's around us?" We were climbing up Perkins Memorial Drive (which, I learned later, was built entirely by hand with stones, boulders, and timber in the nineteen-thirties by jobless Americans employed in special projects by the Depression-era Work Projects Administration) to the peak. It got its name from its resemblance to a bear lying down. And we parked the car and carried our hamper, and we all lay back on the ground, just as I had done, as part of the Papa's shikar entourage, many, many years ago near Raipur, near the *jheel*, waiting for the evening flights to arrive, and I was thinking of Gold Flake cigarettes, and the smell of the evening fires, and Ben saw me dreaming, and he picked up a beer and took a huge swallow of it and cradled himself on his elbow and dozed off. And Serita looked at me and said:

"Can we talk?"

"What about?"

"Do you think, some day I'll be able to write like you?"

"I don't know how I write. This is really my first published piece here. Maybe there'll never be another one. And in any case, the style, when I read it again I discovered is just too heavily influenced by Donleavy. And a lot of my friends told me I can't write to save my life."

"Who's Donleavy?"

"An Irish nut totally under the spell of Joyce." Before she could ask, Who's Joyce, I added hurriedly: "Do you think I could ever do calculus and all that stuff like you?"

"Well, you'd have to go back and study math, and read Leibniz and Newton."

"And you, Serita, would have to read. Period."

"But I do read a lot."

"I don't know what you read, but I know you don't read Joyce."

"Tell me where to start. You got some books you can lend me?" My mind whirled back to Papa's study and those tomes. And a feeling of giving welled up in my heart. Giving to Serita. And I knew I had to give her something. And I suddenly remembered:

"You like funny books. There's a very funny book

just out. It's called 'Fear of Flying' written by a Jewish feminist, Erica Jong. It's also about suffering and freedom. I'll give you a copy. Okay I have another favorite, D.H. Lawrence."

"Oh, I've read *Women In Love*."

"That's really pulp. Tell you what. Read a short novel by him, *The Virgin and the Gypsy*. If you like it, I'll suggest another one – not *Chatterly's Lover* but something else. About Australia. Marvelous book. And I'll suggest George Orwell, and later Henry Miller."

"He writes all that porn stuff."

"No. He's the only person that keeps me from becoming an atheist like my dad would have me become. He's a spiritual genie. A saint with a halo around his erected dick. You promise you'll read?"

Serita was looking at me with the excitement with which she had stared at all the men she had conversed with at Javed and Fran's dinner. The difference was that her nostrils were flared like those of a mare. I told her: "You're a flirt, aren't you?"

She said: "I may flirt with all but I've flipped only for one." Just then Ben stirred. Rubbed his eyes and began waking up slowly. And looking at Ben, I said:

"That's great, Serita. And you must continue to love him."

And Serita said: "These writers and authors. You

258

drop their names like you know them. I used to hear undergrads in English Literature do that and I was bored stiff with them. I hated their boasting."

I said: "They help me understand my own wilderness. Without and within. They put my childhood in perspective like no parent or friend can. They tell me not to let others choreograph my life. They help me turn away from the outer world that is so full of pain and look for the joy and me-less-ness that exists somewhere within me. They help me get an intellectual understanding of how to avoid pain."

"And you've evolved into all this?"

"No, all I understand is that when I read everything makes sense. And when I close the books I'm back into being the small-spirited shit that I am."

Evening is falling. Ben's listening to all this frippery philosophy-talk with a half-ear. And the good doctor announces that evening is at hand and we'd better get off our butts and head back across the Palisades Parkway into Manhattan, even though we haven't played Frisbee.

We listen to the FM Radio all the way back to Fran's apartment. They play some Beatles numbers, and Peter, Paul and Mary, and Judy Collins. And we hardly talk. In the Bronx Fran says Stay for dinner, and we decline, and Ben takes me home, and I say, Wait a minute, I'll be right back, and I go through my stacks of books, and I put them in a paper bag for Serita – Orwell's *"Nineteen Eighty-Four"*, Jong's *"Fear..."*, Lawrence's *"Virgin..."*, Miller's *"Black Spring"*.

Serita says Thanks, and I say Thanks to Ben, and they drive away. And I go back into my apartment, open up my sofa-bed, leaf through a boring edition of *The New Republic*, and lie around night-dreaming, and the phone rings, and I don't care who it is because I've got nothing on my mind, and I'm going to think the next day about my next story. And Serita makes no sense. And what is she about? An easy lay? But I kind of like the *galoot*. And what would I get out of laying her? She's kind of clingy. So what's this bullshit about books? Who're you trying to impress? And she's a flirt, anyway, maybe not an easy lay, she likes to make non-smokers smoke, probably does her maths in bed as well, circumcised circumferences to the power of two, erectile dysfunctions multiplied by co-efficients of cohesion, displacement of mass in cohabitation as in volume increases as pressure decreases.

4

In the morning Serita was no longer on my mind. My pornographic lust for her had mysteriously subsided. Ben called a couple of times that week and invited me to watch some surgery and I took a raincheck. Mostly, I was busy with Simon who was organizing some poetry readings, and a couple of other women I was seeing, and I had taken on a whole lot of freelance editing assignments. And I was writing long letters to Papa in Raipur. I did not send him the Evergreen story because I thought he would find it lewd and unkind. And after a week Serita called me late in the evening while I was watching the Smothers Brothers in the company of a very lovely Polish woman named Mona. We were lying in bed, leaning against the headboard and chuckling when the phone rang.

I recognized her voice immediately. "Is someone with you?" she asked, very softly. And I said, No.

"I've read Jong," she said.

"That's great. What did you think of her?"

"It's very explicit. But it's also sad. And I didn't take to that Adrian character at all. He's a phony. But I guess that's the kind of person that attracts women."

"Well, women have strange tastes when it comes to men. But Jong's a ballsy writer. Her sexuality and her fantasies are totally male, and that takes guts because even though her book is called a novel it is definitely autobiographical, I guess, as all good fiction is. But you can see the poet in her, and if you read Henry Miller, you'll see how much of Henry is in her. In fact you may have shades of her in you."

"I haven't read Miller, yet. And you know nothing about me, Tan. But I see your point about books being able to transform people. I think Jong has that power."

"Well, you've got to read her again. That's what you do with a good book. First read is for the story, and the second read is for the soul."

"I also finished *The Virgin and the Gypsy*. It's like living through a storm. It left me twisting and turning. I could actually see myself loving that gypsy myself. But isn't it terrible that people who have been so intimate should just part and never even acknowledge each other and their lives should cease forever to touch? Deep within me I guess I'll keep waiting for that gypsy to return even if I never read the book again."

I said: "Serita, that's what Lawrence does to people. In any case, why worry about what's forever, and what's not. Moments are wonderful, too. Moments can last a lifetime. Don't you ever feel that with Ben?"

"I want Ben, not his moments," she snapped. "That's why I'm with him. Well, I don't really want to get into all that. Look, tomorrow's a weekday, I know, but Ben's off, and before you say no please listen, he specially called me to ask you to come with us again to Bear Forest."

"That's 'mountain,' not 'forest'."

"Well, whatever. But it's still a forest. Ben and I call it *your* forest. Say, you'll come. It'll really make Ben happy. He seems to have fallen for you. And maybe you can just snooze and read all your books. I'll bring some good music for the way."

I wasn't doing much any way. "It's a great idea. I think it's a beautiful place. And maybe we can visit West Point Academy, I believe it's close by. What time?" She said around noon, and they'd pick me up, and I said, fine. And we hung up.

And Mona, my companion that evening asked: "Boy, who was *that* you were trying to impress?"

"No, I was just being sincere, Mona. Absolutely sincere."

"How come you never talk like that to me?"

"I will, if you like. By the way, she's Indian. Married to a white doctor. I think he's a friend of mine. We're going for a long drive tomorrow."

Serita was punctual. I was waiting for her under the awning of my apartment building. She was driving their Volkswagen. "Hop in," she said, opening the door to the passenger seat.

"Where's Ben?" I asked.

"He asked me to really apologize to you. It was his day off and we were just about to leave and he gets this call that some intern is sick and that could he please go to the hospital. He was really disappointed. I said we should call you, but he insisted that I take you with me."

I was already in the car and we were on the way to George Washington Bridge. Serita was a fast driver. Drove with narrowed eyes. And we spoke little until we hit Route 9W.

"You get bored very quickly, don't you?" she said.

"No, I said. I could come here a hundred times. I do like it here in the Hudson Valley."

"No, I mean with people. Are you sure, you don't want to go back?"

"No, I'm enjoying this."

"What kind of music do you like?"

"Oh, Jazz. Ellington, MJQ, Benny Goodman, Thelonius Monk. I like rock. I never bore of the Beatles."

"I guess you'll have to teach me about jazz. What about Indian film music?"

"Adore it."

"Good I'll play you a mix of oldies." And she slid the cassette into the player and Gita Dutt was suddenly singing to the mothballed ghost-ships in that stretch of the Hudson. And the wildlife was amazing. I told Serita I'd grown up with birds and forests and that she should stop whenever I told her to. And the region was bursting with them. At an empty picnic spot we saw a black bear grabbing at leftovers. And Serita asked me if she could feed him, and I said, No, that he'd most likely take her head off. I showed Serita, and I counted, one bald eagle soaring along the course of the river, a family of foxes, a river otter which allowed us to come within a foot of him in an inland creek, dozens of hawks, several deer, a pair of turkeys that flew across the road where it took a sudden bend, just before Perkins Drive. And several falcons. I was enjoying myself like I hadn't in a lifetime. Wait till I write to the shikaris back in India, about this. Oh I would exaggerate. I would tell them that I'd shot a wild turkey,

I'd tell them about how I was mauled by a bear and fought him off with a Bowie knife. And Serita and I walked around the park for a while. In the museum we saw mounted insects, live fish, reptiles, amphibians. I wanted to take her hand, and did briefly, as we walked and walked and followed the trail that hikers took south towards the Delaware Water Gap. We looked at elaborate pump-houses, reservoirs, sewer systems, vacation lodges, bathrooms, storage buildings, officials' quarters, all created by out-of-work workers during the Depression years under wages-for-work schemes.

And I felt terribly sentimental about America all of a sudden. I felt as deeply for Bear Mountain and this splendid valley as I felt towards Raipur and its scrub forest. To which I knew I would ultimately return. Jobless men, men without hope, inspired by Roosevelt, a man of courage and vision, had built this place. This was a cemetery of the living. A massive tombstone of joy erected in the memory of the resilience and the triumph of the human spirit. I could have walked here forever and never gone back anywhere. I wanted to look in a mirror and see my face because I knew I was smiling like a madman, a smile I had smiled when the forests of Raipur had walked with me, a smile I had never actually seen, and now I wanted to look in a mirror and see what that smile looked like, and I would preserve it in my memory, and bring it to flame, like a matchstick striking a match, whenever the world looked dark and ugly, and I wanted to write about the joy welling up inside me, I wanted to climb to the top of the mountain and dance like Zorba the Greek. Serita was talking but I couldn't hear her because amidst the chirping of crickets human voice and language are an aberration and a despicable redundancy.

I had no recollection about when we went to the inn to pick up sandwiches or how we got to Overlook Lodge and sat together on that wooden bench overlooking the most spectacular view of Hessian Lake. Serita was talking to me, and finally I was able to listen. She was saying:

"Why are you here?"

I didn't understand. I replied: "I came here with you."

"No, I mean America. Why did you come to America?"

"Because I belong in Bear Mountain."

"I mean, seriously."

"It's as serious an answer as I can give you."

She was searching my eyes. Her eyes were like the flashlight of a doctor when he looks into your pupils and examines your retina, one after another, in a darkened examination room.

I tried another answer. I said: "For one thing, I grew up on a lot of books that came from here and lot of people who wrote them – including Miller – are still alive. It's like a pilgrimage. Look, Serita, if you want to know, people make journeys and pilgrimages to figure things out in their lives. I grew up in Raipur. I loved it there. But one moves away to make sense of one's life. Not everyone does it. But I have chosen to. I'm an Indian baby-boomer. In my home, where I grew up, there are two wonderful rooms – a puja room, where my Ma's surrounded by Hindu gods and goddesses, where we chant, bow before God, perform rituals. Ma's a doggedly religious Hindu woman. But she's also gentle and liberal. Papa's a shikari, a hunter, an atheist. And he's a stoic. And when his time comes, I know he'll want his family to be by his side to watch the grand finale. And I want to see him in death, and facing death in the same way that I saw him facing life. With his shotgun. Defying God. Ma probably sees in his compulsive hunting Papa's own quest for God. Because Papa seems to believe that God is, after all, the biggest killer of all. So who is He to sit in moral judgement of the Shikari? And then there's the other wonderful room – the Shikari's room. We children used to call it the chamber of perfumes, literally because it contains the smells of the Shikari, and of the forests, and figuratively because it is here that we can sniff the past, the present, and perhaps the future.

"Maybe I am here to figure out whether I belong to Ma's puja room, or to the atheist's chamber of perfumes."

"Perhaps to both," Serita said. I did not listen. I continued:

"I need detachment from these roots for a while. I need to figure out this story from afar. Not from my own soil where I might take the answers for granted but from

267

afar. From the soil of American spiritualists like Miller and Emerson. Let's look at the plot so far, my life's plot. I'll sketch the outline for you, and perhaps, gradually I'll tell you the details some day: my grandfather exiled in his own land by the British because he chose the profanity of his own tongue – Punjabi rather than English – to castigate British corruption. After the Partition of India, my grandfather helps other victims of the Raj's politics, Punjabi refugees, to rehabilitate themselves. He pioneers a new settlement in a wasteland where his children, my father among them, are born in tents. My father, the Shikari, has weather in his blood, a quintessential Indianness that survives the onslaughts of the English language, his British boarding schools and training, creeping Americanism, an amorous British lady and nouveau riche Indians whom Papa, a patrician, a tyrant at times, and hugely humanitarian snob, loathes. But having survived these battles I want to see if the Shikari will wilt with the destruction of his beloved forests and lakes. I assume he will, Serita.

"Mama remains rooted, utterly anchored to her beliefs and coy sexuality. As longevity goes, Papa will probably lie dying in about 25 years from now. Already he probably sees a repetition of his lifecycle among his children. Will we all drift to foreign shores or remain rooted in our own civilized culture? My sister Seema, about whom I'll tell you more, is an absurd, cultural hybrid caught in the crazy rotations of an East-West grinder. Like my father went to England, I'm here in America, but Serita, unlike that guy in that story of mine,

268

and unlike a lot of Indians I know – I call them Instant Quakers – I'm trying to strengthen my psychic security. Serita, I feel something today. Here in the Hudson Valley I feel a reaffirmation of life. So many years ago, wise men preserved this forest for me. I hope that when Papa dies, I will receive signals, from wherever they may come, that ancient India will reassert herself in death-defying wisdom in the triumphant symphonies of her sages."

Then I asked Serita: "Why are you here?"

Serita said: "I cannot answer this with your oratorical flourish. Because I guess I'm not as complicated as you. To put it simply, your father would probably have sneered at my social background…"

"Now wait, Serita, he's got many sides to him…"

"Will you let me finish? I came here, I guess, to escape the puja room, as you call it. There was no chamber of perfumes in my home near Madras. It was all vegetarianism and rituals. We are Brahmins. My father is a teacher. He taught me maths. He pushed me into maths until I got so good at it that I could teach trigonometry when I was 14 years old. That was the age when all my friends and relatives were already paired off with prospective grooms they had never seen. They would be married when they reached age 18 or 19. It was the same with me. But thank God, for my father's pushing me into maths. It was my passport to America. My admission to college here. My scholarship, and now my job. I ran away. Friends lent me money for my ticket. I have no forests I can love in India. I never really saw any. I cannot hunt. My father never went to England. I am not here on any journey of discovery or introspection. I am here because I belong here and not to any arranged marriage in south India. I don't belong to my parents. I belong here.

"There is no past for me. The moment I stepped out of the plane at Kennedy Airport I lit a cigarette. I may or may not tell you more about myself. I could have lived with Ben without marrying. But I needed to see if had guts. And I had moved so rapidly away from my past, torn every mooring to shreds, that I felt I had to drop a traditional anchor somewhere, even if it meant marriage – but how different a marriage from what I would have had in India."

"Arranged marriages work out a lot of times, Serita," I said.

And she said: " I don't want any of your lectures. I've fled from persecution, like your Erica Jong."

"You're the most amazing mixture of pique and tenderness I've ever seen."

Serita smiled, the corners of her mouth coming to rest at that special spot at her pre-molars. "What have you got in that bag?"

"A few books. You said I could read, didn't you?"

"Will you read aloud to me? Please? If you have Miller..."

I pulled out some paperbacks. Inside they were dog-eared and underlined for some of my favorite passages. "This one is from 'Tropic of Cancer,' Serita. It's at the end and Miller is at peace with himself, and he's watching the Seine in Paris." And I read aloud:

"'After everything had quietly sifted through my head a great peace came over me. Here, where the river gently winds through a girdle of hills, lies a soil so saturated with the past that however far back the mind roams one can never detach it from its human background. Christ, before my eyes there simmered such a golden peace that only a neurotic could dream of turning his head away. So quietly flows the Seine that one hardly notices its presence. It is always there, quiet and unobtrusive, like a great artery running through the human body. In the wonderful peace that fell over me it seemed as if I had climbed to the top of a high mountain; for a little while I would be able to look around me, to take in the meaning of the landscape.

"'Human beings make a strange fauna and flora. From a distance they appear negligible; close up they are apt to appear ugly and malicious. More than anything they need to be surrounded by sufficient space – space even more than time.

"'The sun is setting. I feel this river flowing through me – its past, its ancient soil, the changing climate. The hills gently girdle it about; its course is fixed.'"

I glanced at Serita to see what she was doing. I'd

suspected that she would be leaning back on the bench with her eyes closed. Actually she was bent forward, her head turned in my direction and looking at me, her mouth half-open, as if she was listening to someone informing her about the death of a loved one. Her long hair had been tied in a bun with two combs holding it together at the top. She continued looking at me. Gently, almost imperceptibly she removed the combs. Her hair slipped in a U-shape onto her shoulders. She shook her head and her hair began to open out and fall to her waist. Then she bent her head towards her right shoulder, opened out the fingers of her right hand and passed them through her hair first above her right temple and her hand made an outward arc as it traveled from up to down inside her hair, her palm facing upwards. She repeated the gesture with the other side of her head. And she appeared to do it in slow motion, looking at me with the same half-frightened eyes.

"You look scared," I said.

"It's new," she said. "It's a kind of freedom that does scare me a bit."

"But you're free. You've killed your past."

"It will take me a long time to be as free as Miller sounds in that passage. It's the journey that scares me. Is there more?"

I leafed through the other paperback. "Like me to read from *Tropic of Capricorn*? Here's another passage I'd underlined. He's writing about the first woman with

272

whom he was obsessed. Lilith in the book, but in real life his wife June:

" 'Passing beneath the dance hall, thinking again of this book, I realized suddenly that our life had come to an end: I realized the book I was planning was nothing more than a tomb in which to bury her – and the me which had belonged to her. That was some time ago, and ever since I've been trying to write it. Why is it so difficult? Why? Because the idea of an "end" is intolerable to me.

"'Truth lies in the knowledge of this end which is ruthless and remorseless. We can know the truth and accept it or we can refuse the knowledge of it and neither die nor be born again. In this manner it is possible to live forever a negative life as solid and complete, or as dispersed and fragmentary, as the atom. And if we pursue this road far enough, even this atomic eternity can yield to nothingness and the universe itself fall apart...'"

Serita spoke: "Can I borrow them from you?"

"They're yours." I gave her my paper bag books. And it was evening again and the lake below was shimmering with light even as the sky darkened a shade. A sharp, almost giddying flavor arose from the lake, a flavor you could both smell and taste, a smell of sweet human breath moving over fresh saliva. Serita's nostrils had flared again. She got up, went to the railing at the edge of the deck, leaned on it, looking deep into the lake and said:

"Why don't we just drive on?"

"Yeah, I guess it's time to head back. Thanks for bringing me."

Serita turned around. "I don't mean drive back. I mean just drive on. Through the night. Into the Catskills, north, north, into Canada, with books, with a hip-flask..."

"But Ben's waiting for you. I mean won't he be worried? Sounds great, but there's work tomorrow. I mean, are you serious?"

"Never mind, it was just a thought. I guess I was trying to extend your so-called 'moment' but I guess things don't work that way. And I guess, like Miller, I'm scared of endings."

I said: "Hey, that reminds me, I've got to buy something for Ben, just to thank him for today. Maybe a stuffed animal they have in that showcase at the inn. And that special whole wheat brown bread." Serita was silent. We drove to the inn. I bought an animal and some bread. And the heavy German woman behind the counter put them in a special bag bearing the inn's insignia. Serita drove back determinedly. We sipped some beer, smoked cigarettes, and we listened to Dylan singing *Just Like a Woman*. She said she'd drop me off at my apartment first and then head home. When we stopped at my apartment I put my left arm lightly around her shoulders in the gesture of half a hug. She drew closer her face turned towards mine and placed her mouth, barely open, on my neck, just below the lobe of my left ear. Her touch may

274

have lasted no more than a few seconds, but she seemed to be in slow motion again, as she had been when she opened her hair when we sat above Lake Hessian.

I looked at her and said: "Oh don't forget your books. And the bag for Ben from the inn. And say Hi to him."

Serita said: "No. You keep that bag."

"But why?"

"Because I don't want to give away my date."

"Date?"

"He doesn't know. Ben will know I went to Bear Mountain if I give him your present. Ben doesn't know I went there with you. What I told you about Ben wanting to take you there and his not being able to make it was a lie. I wanted to go there with you, and I didn't know whether you'd go with me alone."

"But you're drawing me into a conspiracy."

"You're already in it."

"Do you always lie? I mean, you do this often? You've been with lots of guys?"

"No. Ben's the first. Can I tell you something? I think I'm dangerously close to having a crush on you."

I was still sitting in the passenger seat. And I took a deep breath and Serita smelled of baby powder. And I said:

"Don't. Sometimes it's important to keep up your defenses." I didn't know if I wanted her now. I didn't know if I wanted her to hang around for a while in my life so that I could some day live out the fantasy of banging an easy Indian lay and then call off everything. I didn't know whether I wanted to start or continue something whose ending I could control, now, this very minute, or allow this moment to continue and to unravel itself according to its allotted time span and lose my ability to control the destiny which was coming to life at this very moment.

She appeared to be reading me, and she said: "You could have said No this morning, even before we took off."

"But I didn't know…"

"That really didn't matter. You saw I was alone. I took my risk this morning. I was ready for rejection then. You're probably not even admitting to yourself that at the back of your mind you were probably thinking that we'd make quick love out there. But you chose to play the gentleman, perhaps to get my respect, perhaps to make me want you more. Like that Jong's Adrian, playing mind games."

"You mean you didn't want me to read to you?"

"Of course I did. That's the you I see that I can, right now, never be a part of. It's what makes you detached and desirable. If I ask you again, will you drive with me to the mountain again? I need to know."

I was beginning to learn, to feel, the meaning of the word 'inexorable.' Can we fight the inexorable or do we make it happen because we fail to strangle it at birth? Why is it that at the very moment that we are in the strongest position to control our fate with a simple gesture or a word we fail to do so or are simply hobbled by inaction? Is it because there are hidden forces at work – coursing through our lives like a parallel bloodstream – far more powerful, far more active, far more tenacious than our own will? I always envied the so-called hard-headed types – businessmen, team coaches, generals, prime ministers –for their quick, instant decisions. But their decisions were probably made on the basis of past battle-plans, or the wisdom contained in ledgers and numbers-books. But what experience is there in the world of emotions where something plus something has never consistently equaled anything in the past? Dale Carnegie may have had sound advice on the art of how not to piss people off. And in our lives we all learn to speak in nuances, and in suggestive tones, because words not only hurt more than sticks and stones but also break our hearts, and start wars. And so we modify language and try and control our facial expressions and the tone and tenor of our voices to avoid war and confrontation. Most of us will not cross the most fundamental codes of moral absolutism – like if someone gave me a loaded gun and told me to shoot my enemy in cold blood, I probably would give him a resounding No. But there, too, am I shaping my own destiny, or am I paving the way for hidden forces to take over; because that enemy, left alive by me, could now kill me and destroy my family's sanity. And this may later well give cause to the person handing me the gun to say that I was a fool to have turned down his offer. But what of the beginnings and crossroads in our emotional lives? Do we plunge into decisions because they free us? Are we freer because we decline, and spend the rest of our lives wondering what would have happened had we made the opposite choice? Or are we freer because we surrender, because we say Yes to an impulse, no matter where it might take us later, and spend the rest of our lives wondering whether the other decision would have made our lives richer or safer. Or perhaps this is all irrelevant. Perhaps we are all guided along, pushed by our independent muses – the parallel bloodstream – in a huge cosmological drama in which decisions don't really count except for their dramaturgical content and interest. And the only path to peace is to be able to look at our journey first as a spectator unable to influence the progress of the play, then as an intrepid actor by losing the fear of being judged, and finally, to use each experience, each sequence of every act, to plunge inwards, deeply inwards so that whether that journey takes us to the divorce court, to the gallows, or poverty, we go in peace.

I had already experienced serenity with Serita. I was already part of whatever lie she had told her husband. And she was asking me again – as directly as she could ask – whether I would continue to see her. But the journey had already begun. Even now, I could have said No, that she was a married woman, and that I had a strong moral code against adultery. Period. But she had already tested me on that. With the women I was then seeing, and they were also seeing other men, there was a routine. We went to bars, necked at concerts in Central Park, went to poetry readings, made love, and called one another at our own convenience. If they were waiting for that Someone to come along, they never told me. And my idea of romance was walking with the Shikari under the moonbeams in the Raipur scrub forests. Would I go in some other direction with Serita? I decided in my mind that I would see Serita casually, as I did Mona. What she told her husband would be her business. I could not run away from a desirable and splendidly attractive woman whose smile in a rear-view mirror had hit my groin, just because, for the first time in my life, I had begun to wonder how my relationship with her, as it unraveled, would alter the course of my life. And had I even figured out the course of my life, except for knowing that I'd try against all odds to become a serious writer of prose? And I said to Serita:

"Sure, we'll go out. And you don't have to ask me. Next time, I'll ask you."

"When?"

"Tomorrow."

"Tomorrow, Ben's taking me to the theatre."

"All right. The day after."

"Where?"

"There's a small bar. It's called The Catamaran. Owned by a Cuban guy, on Morningside Drive and 119th. I'll see you there in the evening. At 7.30."

5

Serita was wearing the same loose black skirt she had worn at Fran's dinner. She was sitting at the bar on the last stool at the right hand corner chatting with a man. Xavier, the barman, gave me a big grin:

"She's with you? What a beautiful woman. I thought she was Cuban."

I said: "She's like me Zavvy. True blue Indian. And don't let no sonofabitch get fresh with her if she comes here alone."

"Sure," Xavier said. "And how's your folks back home?"

"I just received a letter from my sister. They're just fine." I ordered a rum with a twist of lime, and Serita asked for a Vodka with coke and ice.

We clinked glasses. And I said:

"Not like this. Here's the way to do it. Let's link our elbows. Here, hold your glass in your left hand. Now put your left elbow inside my right elbow. Raise your glass to your lips. Now drink."

And we both took long gulps. And Serita said:

"I'm so glad you came."

I asked: "How much time have you got? I mean when do you have to go home?"

"Actually about an hour. Maybe more. Ben's home early tonight."

"What did you tell him?"

"Oh, the usual, that I'm going shopping, or visiting a friend, or that I have a teaching conference. But I don't want to use that last one too often. Because with that one I have more time. And I'll use it when I really need it."

"Guess what, I had a great letter from my sister, Seema. She's crazy. She wants to leave her husband. And she wants me to endorse her move and to write to Pa and say it's okay."

"I don't know what to say. I don't know her."

"I told you a little about her. And maybe some day, you'll meet her. Can I read it to you?"

"Sure, if it's not too private. Maybe I do want to get to know her. Is it upsetting you, I mean her letter?"

"Well, kind of. We were inseparable. And Dreamboat is a loveable guy. And I don't want either of them hurt."

"Who's Dreamboat?"

"Her husband. We all call him 'Dee.' Okay, I'll read to you:

" '...You've been gone three years, that makes you 27 and that makes me 31. And I've hardly even written to you. Maybe three times, because Mom keeps giving me all the news. I still can't believe YOU are in MY America. Everything we talked about in school must be so much more real over there. Gosh, how can it be that one person (Me!) dreams a dream and someone else (YOU!) make it come true. I should have been there. And I don't think I'd ever come back. I really envy your fishing trips to Vermont – Pa tells me all about them from your letters. But they all miss you terribly. Dammit why don't you visit, at least. You love it here so much and you've let shooting seasons go by without even a visit to the scrub forest, your *jheels*, your friends Gafoor and Khalifa. They pine for you. You keep asking about the shikars and when the ducks arrived. And you're not even here. You're not here for the Monsoons you loved, for the dust and grime you loved, or even to observe the changes in Raipur. And you promised me you'd be with me whenever I wanted to talk to you. Letters are not enough.

" 'Dammit, at least write more frequently than you do. I may belong in America, but you belong here. Because you're a writer and you need to be here to be honest to your writing. Besides, Mama misses you so much that she weeps when she sees the photos you send from there. She says that she goes to her puja room every day and prays for your return. Isn't that funny! Coz Pa, in the shikar room – his chamber of perfumes as we still call it – the room in which we plan the kill – still keeps a chair empty for you when the guys plan the next day's hunt. And he even keeps your gun greased. Can you believe that?!! Pa, our atheist father, doing this crazy ritual? And you were never a good shot anyway. Now it's September. Is it cold out there? The Monsoon has just about ended. It was a good one and Ma hopes it will make Pa believe in God, just for once. And there are just two months left for the ducks to start arriving again, and the shikaris are already oiling their guns. Gafoor and Khalifa are already regular visitors again telling Pa of secret corners in the *jheel* where the mallards still land, even though there's never been a mallard there in so many years. Everything you loved is still there except the forests have slowly started thinning and I have this weird feeling that Pa also thins with every thorn that is destroyed on a kikkar tree. He will disappear, one day, just like them. And he seems to sense it. But right now he's delighted that the rains came and the villagers are happy with their rice crop, and the lakes are full of rainwater because of our great Monsoon. And that's when he misses you.

" 'I know that your brothers and sisters have changed in the last few years. Let me go down the list: Tips: He's divorcing. Remember him? Crazy as a loon. Making everyone laugh. The great prankster. Lying to Pa about his graduation when he had actually failed? Shooting at peoples' feet to scare them instead of aiming at the bird when it was in the sky? Loving to shit out in the open even after our modern flush toilets were built? And how he loved his bike, and how loved to ride it, like Pa's jeep, into the villages, and arrive when the villagers were at their lunch and demand that he be allowed to dip his fingers into their community eating bowls and eat with them and they used to be horrified because he had not respected the dictates of his own caste? He's divorcing because his wife – and you've hardly known her – could simply not accept the codes of Raipur. Liberal. Strict. Orthodox hunting pattern. British. Tribal. Snobbish. Feudal (or should that be 'feudatory?') American. Me. You. Puja. Shikar. Humanitarian. He combined these in him, but was unable to express it in any kind of emotional bonding. And so his wife slipped into the first uncomplicated idiot she could find. Tips doesn't want this known. He would suffer sexually. So we all have to stick by his story. Part fantasy, part reality. And it's the kind of story that needs a suspension of disbelief. So we keep his secret and tell our version: His wife, he discovered was an alcoholic. Smoked more than she should. She wanted his child which Tips said he couldn't give her, because he didn't know how long he'd be married to her. So she went with this other guy because she wanted a baby. She got pregnant. She told Tips it was his, thought he knew otherwise. Because Tips had earlier – secretly – undergone a vasectomy. She delivered two little stillborn twin embryos. And the doctors said she should have stopped drinking when she was pregnant and should keep off the stuff in future. She didn't agree. She told Tips they were his twins. She wanted another chance. Tips now informed her that he had had a vasectomy and the still-borns therefore could not have been his. And in her insane way she turned the tables on him. It didn't bother her that Tips had virtually proved her infidelity. Rather, she said she would sue him for divorce because he had taken control over her body – her right to reproduce through him – without her permission. (An interesting phenomenon for your right-to-lifers, no?) – so it's all crazy and complicated and headed for the courts.

" 'Tally, you will probably come to know when you return. He's still shadowy, secretive, very PR-oriented, but a brilliant hunter and retriever. They say he can smell like a dog. And he's the best looking out of all of us. The only individualism he can lay a claim on is that he does not differentiate between the puja room and Pa's shikar room. He keeps a gun in the puja room, and often says his prayers, quietly, in the shikar room. He's as devoted to rituals as he is to our hunt. Which one he believes in no one knows because he's a brilliant politician. Because he believes in the synergy of both and one day will become the preserver of Raipur unlike you and Tips and me because we don't know how to choose.

" 'It's terrible isn't it. I'm already destroying the narrative drive of the book you said you always wanted to write. I'm already helping judge and describe your characters as a journalist does, rather than forcing you to put them on a stage and have them act out their roles. Maybe that's because I want you to come back here and see your land again as a shikari, a hunter, rather than become an American writer.

285

" 'But more about the family. Little Sara just got married. To an older guy. But she's so much like you. Doesn't really know you. But hears from us that you're a hippie and a writer. Unlike me, she's got business sense, and for that reason, I think she'll stick to her husband no matter what they go through. He's an OK guy, like Dee, but terribly boring, and terribly stuck on everything that goes against philosophy and freedom. The kind of guy who believes heavily in marriage and the sanctity of parenthood but is secretly a sex fiend like an American legionnaire at a convention full of whores.

" 'Dee is something like that. I know you love him. But nothing's changed. The more I know him the more I think he's like a woman. The women I've always hated. His possessiveness is driving me crazy. Even Ma has told me about this. I look at a guy and he thinks his dick is into me. I can't have friends unless he approves of them. He expects me to touch his mother's feet when I don't respect her any more. I used to, in the old days, because I did respect her, but I don't now because I think she doesn't deserve it. The trouble is that he dons macho only to attract me. It's a veneer of macho. I believed in it when we were first married. Remember that conversation we had after that party in Delhi? Just when I was getting to know Nick? But I think in real life, when his macho act peters out, he's really a woman or a child who wants to be pampered. I don't want to make love to a lesbian. And I don't want a child – or to be nurse to a sick man – I've got to mother again. After all, I've had two of my own. I want out.

" 'Who've you got? Anyone special? I saw you through you crushes. Don't go through them again. You hurt like hell. Believe in Raipur. It's a killing field but it's a pillar of strength. Remember how we forced Pa to get away from that Englishwoman from Mussoorie? Love you. Write More.'"

Serita had the same expression on her face as she did when I read her the passage from Miller as we sat above Lake Hessian at Bear Mountain. She held my hand, and said:

"You're a clan aren't you? I have no brother or sister who can write to me like that. I'd love to know Seema. Do you think I will? But I already feel rejected. This is like nothing I've known before. Your shikar, these crazy brothers and sisters. And I've never known a writer."

"Like me? I'm no writer yet. Maybe some day. Hey, maybe because of you, who knows?"

"No, probably never because of me. Mostly because of Raipur and you shikari father. Every image I see in you is from there. I saw the first one when I saw you at Fran's. Something indecipherable. Something that brought lakes and forests into my mind. Do you know that I smelled you almost as soon as I saw you? Not your after-shave. Do you use one? Something that the winds bring with them. Maybe I smell that same fragrance now. Maybe that's why my nostrils flare when I'm with you. I've seen you looking at me. Maybe I smell that *jheel*, those forests that you and Seema talk about, that crazy shikari father of yours, and I want to return to an India that's in your blood, but which I can never return to, because, India's only in my flesh and in my mind, and I left both of those behind."

"Then maybe you'll have to swim in my blood stream."

"Only if you will let me in. And for that you will have to let in a new virus. You'll have to deactivate the antibodies of Raipur. Can you do that?"

"You're talking like that doctor husband of yours."

"And you're talking like that shikari father of yours."

"Can't they meet?"

"Never."

"Can we?"

"Let's try."

Serita got off the bar stool, and stood leaning against the right-hand side of the wall where the bar top curved into it. And she gave me the whore-smile again. And I got up and faced her, standing, and I put my arms around her waist. And pulled her in till our pelvic bones made contact, and I pulled harder, and she locked her arms behind my back and pulled me in even closer, until our crotches touched, and then I moved my hands to hug her buttocks, moved my hands up to her waist, still caressing both sides of her spine, over her shoulder and my palms were on both her breasts, gently, my thumbs massaging both her nipples, left thumb, anti-clockwise, and right thumb, gently, clockwise. And with this foreplay we readied for a kiss. And I grabbed her mouth, like a shark, upper and lower incisors grabbing her lips. And she tried to move her head away, because it was painful. And I realized it and let my teeth go. And I said, Sorry, and she said Do It Again But Not So Hard. And I said Why Not You? And she opened her mouth, almost to measure mine, laid the upper incisors – which I had seen and loved when I had first seen her at Fran's party – over my upper lip, her lower ones beneath my lower lip – and gently, with the pressure of her mouth she closed my mouth, she sculpted my mouth with hers, into a gentle smile and placed the tip of her tongue against mine. Her breath smelled of jasmine. I clutched her closer to me. I was right that she had small breasts. But her nipples were as erect as small pistils emerging out of hibiscus flowers. Her breath smelled of fresh lemon. Still joined together, we straightened our arms along our sides, palms facing outwards and we held hands moving them inwards in between our thighs, and my fingers went through her fingers in the way her fingers had gone through her hair after she opened her bun when we sat on the wooden bench overlooking Lake Hessian. She pulled her face away, and asked:

"Why didn't you kiss me, when I wanted you to kiss me in the car when we came back from Bear Mountain, and I kissed you on the neck, after you hugged me goodbye?"

"Did I really hug you?"

"Still playing the asshole, aren't you?"

"I guess you've gotta go."

Serita smiled at me and said I was right. But before we left the bar, Serita gently, put her palm on my right thigh, slid her hand towards my crotch, gently, and asked:

"Is he up?"

"He?" I asked.

"And she said: "Yes, 'He.' In the future I'm going to call him my 'friend.'"

"He's up." I guided her hand into my groin, and I saw she had long, beautiful, artistic fingers, wonderfully carved, un-painted nails. And her hand rested there for a while. And while it rested there she kissed me again. I was hungry again for her. I was sitting on the bar stool, and she was standing against the corner. I hugged her waist, and I said:

"I guess we've both got to go. You better get to Ben. He's a great guy."

She said: "But my friend is still up. At least get him down before you leave the bar. Will I see you again?"

"Of course. But in a few days. I'll call you. I'm going to Vermont with a pal of mine for a few days. Writers' workshop. Maybe some fishing."

I saw Serita off to the 116th Street and Broadway subway station. I didn't know whether to kiss her goodbye or not. And we kind of half-hugged and she looked into my eyes again like an eye-doctor's searchlight. And I went back to my apartment where, I'd forgotten, Mona was waiting for me. She had my keys. And I slipped into bed with her and I kissed her and she kissed me and she asked me to suck her tongue – hard – and I fell asleep kissing Mona's tongue, and I had a dream that Mona's tongue was a bleeding artery, bleeding like a bitter waterfall into my mouth, and that Serita was stitching her tongue, bandaging it, and the waterfall had subsided into a gentle trickle of scented saliva and Serita was whispering into my ear, Drink My Darling, Drink My Beloved. From My Mouth I Created the Lakes And Ponds You have Always Loved And My Mouth Will Always Be The Source Of Your Life…

6

That whole week in Vermont I hardly thought about Serita. A couple of friends and I had booked a cottage on North Hero island in Lake Champlain whose waters divide Vermont and New York State east to west, and Canada and New York north to south. Peter S Palmer paid tribute to this great American waterway in his *History of Lake Champlain*: " …no part of the United States is more interesting from its historic incidents. Every bay and island of the lake and nearly every foot of its shore has been the scene of some warlike movement – the midnight foray of the predatory savage, the bloody scout of frontier settlers, the rendezvous of armed bands, or the conflict of contending armies."

North Hero is named after the Vermonters who fought in the Revolutionary War. Since the island is inundated for many months in the year, much of it has been reclaimed for national parkland. And it has been changing rapidly. Here, in stages, we could see old fields and pastures reverting to forests. Its passionate, clinging, iridescent moisture-laden green is as different from the dust and scrub forests of Raipur as the moonscape is different from the rings of Saturn. But the smells mingled, and I could see the Shikari and his entourage stalking the wilderness here – following the herds of white-tailed deer, watching the mallards making circles in the ponds, seeing the wood-ducks nest in the wooded wetlands, flushing ruffed grouse and American woodcock.

We fished for chain pickerel and northern pike and little sunfish, and an assortment of bottom-feeders. We talked to fishermen totally outside the pale of the American economy. Americans who were illiterate, who still carved their tobacco pipes out of briar and smoked and chewed crude tobacco and spat and burped and farted and never cared to brush their teeth. Their boats were old and tarred where they had once leaked. And they spoke with Scottish and Irish and French accents and were kind and invited us into their homes where the toilets didn't flush and where they still hadn't heard of high cholesterol and how to ward off heart attacks, but had certainly heard of preserved coons' penises in far off places like Beckley, West Virginia, and where they still cooked beans with thick-backed bacon, and fried their whole potatoes and collard greens in lard, and wiped off the drippings in their pans with home-made whole-grain brown bread and offered morsels of this delicacy to their guests. And we supped with them and we cleaned the fish together and when they asked me whether I was Sioux or Yuchi, I said, Sun-tanned, and they didn't understand the attempted humor, and so I said Yuchi, and that went down well with them and no one asked me again about my origins. That was the one time I did think about Serita, about how she'd have responded or whether she would have tried to laugh at my very American joke. Would she have liked to camp on North Hero, this small lump of earth in the middle of a lake that can probably carry ocean liners, where ferries carry cars from shore to shore, covered in green and washed by the fine spray of the green waters when the winds decide to blow?

When I returned to Manhattan there was a letter in my mailbox. From Serita. Her script was in a childish, rounded hand. The curves were clear and symmetrical when her mood showed equanimity. Ferocious, knotty and angular when she was distraught. Her writing smudged when she was crying. All this I was to decipher and confirm later, hundreds of letters later. This was her first letter to me. I did not then know her handwriting. I tore open the envelope in my apartment, reclining on my sofa, looked at the end of the letter, and I saw "Serita". She wrote:

"You've shattered my calm. I really didn't know what it was like to really miss somebody. But after you left that evening at the bar I've been haunted by your presence. I'm losing control over myself. I see you everywhere. I didn't know a week could take that long. Did you even think about me in Vermont? I know you didn't. You with your detachment and your worldview and your books and your fishing. I thought of calling you, but where? And even if I'd reached you, would you have been angry? I know about all your talk about defenses and not letting them down. But I have no defenses left any more. Don't try and analyze my feelings. I've tried to be cold, mathematical and scheming about my own feelings but it doesn't work. When I'm not with you, I'm miserable. I want to be by your side, I want to hear your voice, to smell you. Can you believe that I actually crossed the days off on a calendar waiting for your return?

"When I could bear it no longer I drove to BM (Bear Mountain) and I sat on our bench and I read. My God, I could hear your voice reading to me, I could hear you breathing with me, I could feel you turning the pages, telling me when to stop, when to read again, and then I'd read one chapter, and pretend you were reading the next one, and I could hear your voice, the gentle and intense voice when you're for real, the phony theatrical voice when you're performing, your throaty half-laugh that's polite, and the guffaw which I never know what to make of.

"But why do you give me books that always talk of rejection? Nineteen-Eighty-Four may be about tyranny, but isn't it really a love story? A great romantic novel in which Julia and Winston try and defy the rigid norms of an absolutist society. I don't mind the betrayal really – people can betray their loved ones under many circumstances – but why should the love end? How can such passion and giving and sharing turn to indifference? It's like Lawrence's Gypsy again. Or that Adrian – Jong's fraud. And I'm certain that the Miller that I'm beginning to read will betray or be betrayed by his June. I only hope this is fiction.

"You're coming back tomorrow. I can't believe it. I can't believe that I'll see you again. I don't care what your thoughts are. I'm writing to you the way I feel. And my mind and my heart have blanked out everything except you. I know you'll dismiss this as a first crush. Don't. I hurt. I don't know and I don't care where this leads. When we kissed that evening, do you know, that I still had a guard up, and I was saying to myself, Serita, Serita, You're supposed to be the wise one among your friends, always advising them against complicated entanglements, telling them to simplify their lives, oh Serita, what are you getting into? And I don't care about the answers any more. All I know is when you're not near me, I hurt. I can't think straight. Will you call me?"

My first thought was to tear the letter to shreds. The

intensity of it gave me a strange sense of power and yet I felt weak in the stomach. I wanted to throw up. In fact, I did not read it at one stretch. I wanted to avert my eyes after each sentence. I felt that I was listening to somebody passing a sentence on me, a death sentence, a life sentence, a judgement I wanted to close my ears to. But even a man being sentenced to the gallows listens against his will. I tried to block Serita's message with every mental defense I could muster. The most obvious moral one – she was somebody else's wife – had the least effect. I tried to pity Ben in this moment of betrayal and I saw him again like a camel. I tried to dismiss everything as a first crush of an Indian woman on an Indian man outside the stifling mores of her own culture and upbringing, of a schoolgirl's secret yearning for a dashing maths teacher, of a late-blooming romantic living out of a fantasy from a pulp fiction love story. And nothing worked. Serita was propelling me into something I did not know, and therefore I was scared. She was like a wild bird calling me into a forest, but asking me first to drop my hunting gun. And I could not but walk on. And I was scared because to walk into her forest would really mean walking away from everything I knew and everything that was familiar. It was a call from the wild which, in my hunting days with the Shikari—Papa—had told me to walk towards but with the instincts of a hunter still in tact. Don't drop that gun! I wanted to trap and manoeuver and kill without being trapped myself. To cast my fishing line wide and deep without being pulled into the lake by what was at the end of the line. Why was Serita making me out to be so powerful? Because she sensed that I had adapted better than her? Because she wanted to drink deeply from my experience, like a spiritual vampire, and create within herself a parallel bloodline to replenish and hold for future storage the oxygen her asphyxiated soul had been starved of for so many years? But surely, if this were the case, Serita was an accomplished gambler. For the illusion of power can lead to many things –from outright generosity, to vacillation, to hubris and stinginess. Was Serita trying to script love or the gameplan of a brilliant vampire whose intended victim, a man tutored in the art of hunting, would be an impossible adversary?

I laid my head on my pillow vowing never to call or see Serita again. And I slept in my dreams without Serita. And when the phone rang that morning and she said, Hi, it's me, I felt like hanging up, and she said:

"Did you ever think of me while I was away?"

I'd be lying if I told the truth. And I answered:

"I tried not to."

She said: "I did. You know that. It's been so long."

"But Serita, I hardly know you."

"You know that's nonsense. I'll take you to the movies. There's 'Scenes From a Marriage' playing at the Thalia. Close to you."

"Well, maybe some other time."

"Stop behaving like a middle-class hard-to-get Hindu virgin. I'm picking you up in an hour."

I had lost the capacity to say no to her. Was this what they called love? Adventure? The male sniffing a female in heat? A certain kind of female? Is being in love, ultimately very different from just fucking someone you like, because a very special female has a very special God-given odor for a very special male, for whom every other smell simply ceases to be and he – and she – remain faithful to that odor for the rest of their lives? Then, is love simply biological destiny and nothing to do with emotions? While I waited for Serita, I thought my head would burst. God, I was just a writer starting out, and she was a mathematician. Surely, she'd have the answers. Why should she lean on me? I felt weak. I tried to conjure up the sexual power I may have had over her when we kissed and fondled one another at the bar but I saw myself as a little suckling infant at her small, white breast with her pistil-nipples feeding me a milk of human humor.

When she came up to my apartment, exactly within an hour, we shook hands. She raised her face to meet mine, caught my hair above both sides of my temples, pulled my head down and brushed my lips against hers. A totally sexual animal greeting, like two dogs sniffing each other and gently rubbing noses. She said nothing. She sat down on the sofa, and I asked her if she'd like coffee, and she said, let's go. I asked her where, and she said, BM. And I was suddenly happy. There were no doubts all of a sudden. Serita was with me. By my side.

And she drove her car like someone rowing us in a gondola, and we sailed through clouds like when we had driven back from Mussoorie to Raipur in the Monsoon, when Papa had parted from Mrs Seymour, except this time I was starting something that Papa had ended because she was taking him away from his forests, and I did not know where this would end even if it meant saying goodbye to the forests forever, because Serita was driving like Khalifa had once rowed the boats and I had the breeze of the Hudson valley hitting my face and every now and then when Serita changed gears, our fingers locked, and she told me that she was now beginning to recognize birds.

7

It was mid-afternoon when we reached the overlook. The mountain was deserted. Serita pulled me on to the bench. We said nothing for a while. I closed my eyes in order to see the lake within myself. And I was still sitting to Serita's right, not touching her. I asked her:

"Why did you come here without me?"

She said: "You read my letter?"

"Yes, a little."

"You sound as if this place belongs to you. As if you resent my coming here without you. I just felt you were here… About my letter, what do you mean, 'a little?'"

"I just thought it was too intense. Too honest. I can't really bear that. It just killed me. I couldn't read on."

Serita was silent for a few minutes. She moved away a couple of inches from me. She looked at the lake and not at me and said:

"If you can't take even that much of me, how will you ever take the rest of me? Then I think we'd better stop meeting. What's the use? I'll never write to you again."

I could have walked away right then. Instead, I pulled Serita closer to me and I kissed her eyes, I licked the top of her nose, the hollow of her cheeks, bit her earlobes and then rested my head in the hollow of her right shoulder and nibbled at her neck. The lake was once again a huge breeze of sweet human saliva. The breeze was lifting a spray that rose off the lake and drenched us. And while Serita and I kissed, the evening fell, and we didn't care about time. And Serita, without guidance, held me between my legs, and she unzipped my jeans, gently, without the zipper making a rrrip sound, and she knew where to reach and lift him out, and she knew how to hold him and rub her cheeks and mouth around him, so gently, while holding him like she would her own baby, and I asked her:

"Serita, tell me, when you make love to Ben, do you think about me?"

She was silent. She raised her head from my lap, still caressing him with one hand and put one arm around my neck, looked like a searchlight into my eyes and said:

"Do you want to know the truth?"

I was excited, and I said: "Yes."

Serita said, no expression on her face: "Well the answer is, No. No I don't think about you."

Suddenly, I was down. Flaccid. I had no idea of the superiority of the ego over tumescence. The power of the ego to beat down into submission the hard-rock of creation.

"What's happened?" Serita asked, stroking me, no response.

"Nothing," I said, "nothing. I guess I thought I was very important." And again, gently, I removed her hand, held her close to me, and said:

" Let's go home." I thought it was over. What a fine ending. No defeat for anybody. And Serita said:

"Do you know why I said I don't think of you?"

I said: "Forget it. I guess it's this very male thing in me that just got shattered. I'm not used to the idea of someone wanting me so much. It's like an aphrodisiac. To be honest with you, your leading a normal sex life with your husband was something I'd accepted but I didn't realize until now that subconsciously I wanted

301

power over Ben. Forgive me. I'll learn to kill that feeling. Of course, you must enjoy Ben as Ben, and not as me. I think you must have priorities, Serita. We have two worlds and they can never meet. Your first world is your priority. Ben comes first. Then your job. And then me. You have to find a balance."

Serita had begun to cry. She took a minute to compose herself. And she said:

"It's not what you think. I was trying to tell you why I said I don't think of you. I haven't had sex with my husband in over a year. Ben's a strange person. He wanted a baby immediately. I got pregnant and had an abortion. I didn't want a baby. I don't think I'd ever wanted a baby. Before I left India I spent one of the most fascinating days of my life meeting hundreds of children, many of them orphans, who were being freed from bonded labor by a government agency. And I suddenly realized how much I loved them. And I decided I would never carry a child in my womb. For that would be so selfish, when there are so many, hundreds of thousands just waiting for love or just a warm smile, or just waiting for their grubby hands to be held, their cheeks patted.

"I sat in a field with a group of 5-6 year olds. That was their last day at work, the last time they would be plucking weeds or tending flower. These children are easy, cheap labor for the floriculture industry. They sat around me, nestling closer and closer, till all of them could touch me. They felt the fineness of my cotton shirt, tried to braid my hair, felt what they called the 'softness' of my cheeks, asked me for clothes, money, a touch, a smile. They promised to write to me when they learn to write and made me promise to visit them again. They were suddenly my family. A social worker told me these kids had never seen any beauty, anything fine. 'They touch you to see whether you're real.' And then when we got into the car to drive away, they clung on, pressing their faces, their hands to the windows, their eyes begging me to stay. It wasn't the excitement of their newly-found freedom, the thrill of having met someone new; it was just love, an uninhibited, unquestioning faith in somebody who had responded.

"I could hardly explain this to Ben. He was angry about my abortion. He stopped sleeping with me. There were tensions, of course, I don't want to go into details. He is strange in many ways. He told me that he would sleep with me only when I am ready to have his child. He's content that way. And I believe he believes in fidelity. But I do want to tell you something. I feel absolutely no guilt in being with you."

I said: "It's strange. I like Ben. But I don't feel guilty about him either." I wished Serita had not told me this story. I did not know if she was lying or telling some half-truth. But I realized that the intimacies she had begun sharing with me were bonding me to her with a force that was more powerful than I had ever experienced. Also an entirely new feeling of jealousy, of one-upmanship welled up inside me. Where I had previously never seen Ben as a rival, I now saw him as one. The equations in my relationship with Serita were suddenly going haywire. Whenever in the future Ben and Serita would decide to have sex again, would not that signal infidelity on her part – infidelity to me? But how can a woman having sex with her own husband be accused of being unfaithful to her lover? And we were not even lovers yet. And what was happening to my detachment, my philosophy of balancing things out? I showed none of my confusion to Serita. But I was suddenly driven by a desire to make love to her. Almost as if I were in a race with Ben. It was as if she might make love to him as soon as she went home tonight, and I wanted to score first. And I wanted to make love to her the way they do in porn films, crude and stark to leave an indelible sexual footprint on her body, a footprint that no subsequent lover could erase.

I asked her if she could make an excuse and come home with me that night. She told me Ben was out of town for day. And we drove back to my apartment. We undressed.

"Do you think my thighs are too fat?" she asked. "I find my body ugly, do you?"

"No," I said. "No your thighs are just fine. And so is your belly." And I began to caress her and I wanted no foreplay and wanted to go in hard and stark and I asked her if she was on the pill and she said No, and I pulled a condom out of a bedside drawer and I asked her help me wear it, and Serita said:

" No, not like this. You're behaving like a lumberjack. Gentle, gentle, make love to me differently than you have to others. I'll show you. Let's both lie on our backs. Yes, like this. Let's hold hands for a while. Yes, gently. Here, put your left arm underneath both my shoulders. Now turn me over and let me lie with my head on your chest. Let my hair cover your whole body. Now I'm going to trace your lips with tip of my tongue, starting with the edge of your upper lip, like this, across the center, to the other corner – no, don't open your mouth just yet – now along your bottom lip. Close you eyes and think that I'm painting your lips on to your face with my tongue, sometimes wet, sometimes dry. And then you do the same to me, gently, and taking your own time."

Serita talked, her voice muffled by our joined mouths. And when I drew her mouth with mine, gently, as she had asked, I felt an overpowering feeling of peace coursing through my body. It was unlike the usual desire to get on with it, to thrust and come and gush, and then ask my lover, How was it? Did you come? No, it was like being in a rowboat on a gentle lake, and Serita was softly commanding me:

"Now talk into my mouth. Open your mouth and rest it on mine. Now speak through my mouth. Say my name, say Se-ri-ta. But not from your palate. Say Se-ri-ta using your own tongue but using my palate for support. Yes like that. It doesn't come out like when you speak from your own mouth but we can taste one another's voices. Keep talking, whisper if you must."

And we talked, sometimes dirty, through one another's mouths. And Serita is saying: "Now draw the outline and then paint my face with your tongue. My eyes. My shoulders. I'll do the same to you..." We lay together until dawn. We slept and when I awoke she was still asleep with her head on my chest.

She sensed I was awake. And without moving she said:

"Just before dawn, when it was all blue outside I got out of bed and came around to your side. I wanted to see what you looked like when you sleep. I put my ear close to your nose to make out whether you were snoring. I wanted to know what you sound like when you snore, even if very softly. You were so still. And there was a smile on your face. And I had his sudden urge to breastfeed you. But you were so still, I had the panicky thought that you may be dead. I shook you and when you stirred it was as if someone had brought you back to life."

I mumbled something about sleep and death resembling each other and Serita said: "Keep talking. I love to hear the sound of your early-morning voice. It turns me on because you sound so unpretentious and the sound is totally yours, uncorrupted by theatrics and artificial modulation."

"What shall I talk about?"

"Anything. Just anything. Tell me if you think my body is ugly, tell me you think I'm beautiful. About last night. I'm still sticky on my stomach with you. I don't feel like washing. Yes, keep talking, and I'll listen. And I want to say hello to my friend again. He's like you isn't he? He's all curled up now, just as he did last evening when I told you I don't think about you and you took offense. He's like you, proud, sensitive, quick to take offense, quick to retreat. I want to see him up close. Count every vein. This is the part that's real sensitive isn't it?"

I was silent while she made love to me with her hands and with her mouth and when she sensed I was ready, as she had done that night, she guided my mouth to her breasts and we found release together and she clung on to me as if this was the climax to a last love-making before a final parting. I talked to Serita as she had asked me to. I rambled on in a low monotone saying anything that came into my head:

"Do dogs fear rejection, Serita? Probably from humans and their masters, but what I mean is, I don't think there's any war of the sexes among them. They're more civilized in this regard. No feminism needed. They only mate when in heat, and they don't give a damn who watches them. They celebrate orgiastic sex openly. No ego hassles. No possessiveness. Masters of their own inner worlds. Masters of the universe. Unlike us. Constantly horny males on the prowl. Endless mating rituals and heartbreaks. Betrayal. Indifference. Sex for power. Sex for money. Insatiability. Madness. And we call this evolution? Why should we keep evolving? And into what? Should not the real process —and a much more rational one – be devolution? To become one with the amoeba and plankton and ether and become the real lords of the beginningless-ness of the universe? Evolution is bullshit. It leads to pain, jealousy, memory, hatred, and destruction of forests."

Serita said: "But what about your Henry Millers and Whitmans? Didn't evolution for them mean their own personal war against these emotions? And were they not victorious and therefore even more highly evolved?"

"Yes but all our sages tell us that to see the light we must drop our minds, drop our egos. So where's the need for minds?"

"You're a strange conversationalist. You have your answer to every contradiction. And everybody you need or meet seems to be your own selfish creation, props against whom you can test your own philosophy. Don't you have any convictions of your own?"

"But you were the one who asked me talk."

"There you go, hurt again. All curled up again, like my friend. I'm sorry. I want to listen to you."

"If we are to drop our minds then the logic is that we should devolve from animals to vegetables. Can't you imagine this planet without us two-legged monsters – jealous, dry, turgid, destructive, full of hubris when the universe in essence is green, and fluid and ethereal? Can you imagine a jellyfish, which we consider to be a lower form of life, inventing a bomb? We forget that we are totally a part of creation, and not outside it – that the amoeba and jellyfish are *us*. Because we invent the bomb we stake our claim to humanhood and to an identity outside the connected order of the universe. In philosophical terms, our true evolution would lead us to a state of consciousness that we are not apart from these creatures of the waters. So why not devolve? What if mankind was driven into mass suicide by some strange force? What would be left? What would not survive? The answer is, everything man destroys will survive. So why have we evolved, so to speak? It's like a freak phenomenon. We're cosmodemonic freaks. It's like a sperm that splits into four and produces quadruplets. We are the quadruplet freaks of the mother tree. In order to establish our identities outside of nature we took everything out of nature and fabricated it. We are the freak four-sperm monsters deluding ourselves into believing we stand apart from the universe."

Serita said: "This is not our world."

"What do you mean?"

"I really don't belong in your world. Why can't you talk about us? About our love? About me, about Ben, about your innermost feelings and hatreds and what you think about my body and what goes on inside your head when I lie on your chest and we breathe together with our mouths locked together? When you talk philosophy, you mesmerize me. I get all confused whether my attraction, sexual and emotional is for your mind or because you hide behind your mind and I'm determined to prise it open and pull out the real you that I can sense exists there and have you all to myself. I'm going to use your own words, 'drop your mind' and come to me. I need you. I love you."

"Love is the most abused four-letter word in the language."

"Then what do you feel about me?"

"Passion. Desire. I want to swim in your blood."

"Say you love me. Say it. Why are you afraid? Say it. Say you love me."

"I love you."

Serita was crying again. I could feel her tears on my chest. Then she went to the bathroom and brushed her teeth with my toothbrush. She had to go back home. She asked me when we'd meet again, and I said, after a week.

"A week?! Why a week? You must be nuts. That's too long."

"Because I have to go some place. There's a place where we catch small-mouth near Harpers Ferry in West Virginia." I really had no particular plans in mind. I just wanted to be by myself for a while. Maybe a little distance from Serita would restore some balance that I thought I wanted at the back of my mind. Serita was burning inside of me like a fire. I wanted some respite. I even doubted her love. What was she using me for? I wanted her, yet I wanted to push her away. She said:

310

"Can't you come back sooner?"

"No. And you have Ben to be with. I told you earlier, he still comes first. Then your job, then me."

"That's nice and convenient. So Tan can evade all commitments. Yes, Ben's crazy about me. He's kind. He's gentle. And he's ready to wait until I decide to have his baby. You're not jealous of him, are you?"

"No. No. We've talked about that before. Are you jealous?"

"About you? Yes. Insanely jealous. Unlike your detachment I have had dreams about your nude body covered by the blonde hair of some bitch you're dating. It's a nightmare."

"You expect me to stop seeing other people. Serita, nobody really owns anybody in this world."

"No I cannot stop you. I just don't want to think about it. Would you like me to start sleeping with Ben, again?"

"Yes."

"And you believe I'd think about you when I'm making love to him?"

"Yes."

"You egotistical bastard. No. I'd reject you in my mind. I'd work out a balanced working relationship with him."

"And have a child?"

"Maybe."

"I'll tell you how to keep us both…"

"Why do *you* want him?"

"Because he comes first."

"No. Because you're afraid of commitment. Because you're safer that way. Because you're conservative. Because your only adventure is in the killing fields of your forests and not in the world of human beings. Ben is your convenient buffer. Your emotiotional safety net."

"Why do *you* need him? Why the deception. Why not tell him outright about us?"

"Because that's *my* adventure. And I need him because I can still escape from you if I have to."

"Then I'll tell you how to keep us both, like I was saying. Have my child and tell him it's his."

"You immoral bastard. Yes, I can even leave Ben. But I can never hurt him in that way."

"What if he found out about us?"

"He's too straight. He'd just simply walk out and never come back again."

"Then marry me."

"No. Perhaps I would have said yes, if you'd agreed to drive with me straight to Canada that day. The day I marry you will be the day that you will reject me. I still want control over myself. You are incapable of giving me the same total insane absolute commitment that I am capable of and have already given to you. To be married to me you will have to drop not just your mind, as you say, but something even more important to you – your past, as I have dropped mine. As I have dropped my history. You cannot then go back to India or to your shikar and to Raipur. Because you know I cannot ever return there with you. And you have already made your plans and I have made mine. In that sense you are already married and you must first be ready for a divorce."

I didn't understand all this at first. All I felt was rage and hurt. Why wouldn't she have my child? I had also suddenly offered Serita marriage. And she had just turned me down after pouring out her love for me. What was all this about? What the hell kind of game was she playing? Then what was wrong with my earlier suggestion about balance, and priorities and a casual, clandestine, sexual friendship? I said:

"I don't believe you. Serita. You've got to go now. I guess I'll see you in a week when I come back." I hugged her. My body was stiff. But she was soft and giving. And her face was full of love and there were tears in her eyes, and she said: "Will you write to me? Will you call? I'll miss you, because I love you." And she went down the elevator all by herself. And I thought, again, that it was all over. And I tried hard not to think of Serita, a married woman to whom I'd proposed marriage within only a few days of knowing her.

8

A scenario in which Serita would live with me as my lover and companion for 15 years, and that she would bear me a son within five years of our relationship, would require a suspension of disbelief, a galactic flight of the imagination, even if I were to attempt to script the remaining chapters of our unfolding relationship after our last parting in my Manhattan apartment. Perhaps I would have followed my last thoughts when she left and ended it there. Perhaps I would elongate it until it reached some catharsis. I left for Harper's Ferry. Alone, by myself. In a rented cabin I read that great Scandinavian Knut Hamsun's *Growth of the Soil*. I thought I would share this with Serita upon my return. I spent much longer there than I'd expected. You can't take your eyes off Hamsun as he goes about creating the universe and populating it with landscapes, wilderness, streams, people, crops, animals, emotion, and goodness. In his works, surely were contained the eternal truths before which the confused icicles of doubts I had erected in my conversation with Serita about the true nature of human evolution would melt as if pierced by a blow-torch ray from a powerful sun. I tried not to think of Serita. About her clear-headed sensuality and my confusion. They say that a change of atmosphere makes no difference when you're trying to run away from your thoughts. That no matter where you are, your mind is always with you, and that only by taking a deep plunge inwards can you rein in the wild runaway steeds whose hooves are clobbering your senses. But I believe that forests, and books in which the sages of our literature reside, can create within us senses so warm, so friendly, so forgiving, and so nourished with light that the abrasive mind is sweetened as if by nectar, and memory loses the power to corrode our beings, and every intruder is transformed into a welcome guest or loses significance in the way most of us have experienced about our own selves when we gaze long enough into a night sky when the stars are at their most luminous. It was in this frame of mind that I drove back into Manhattan after 10 days. I had not really fled to escape Serita who, after all, had shown me nothing but kindness. I had gone away, I suspect, to heal that part of my being which – even though happily and willingly vulnerable to unabashed carnal pleasure, and melodramatic episodes of love – I had previously considered impervious to trepidation born from the mixture of the fear of the ominous, the unknown, and abandonment.

It was late evening when I reached Manhattan. I was ravenously hungry. I stopped in at a streetside place and ate two thin-crust pepperoni pizzas with extra cheese, bell peppers, mushrooms and onions and I washed them down with several beers. I undressed in my apartment and saw the cockroaches scurry out of my bedroom heading for the kitchen. I decided I didn't like cockroaches because when you step on them they die with a disgusting crunch. I lay naked on my bed and thought about what I'd do the next day. Whether I'd call Simon or just browse inside some old bookstores in Brooklyn. I wondered what Serita would be doing right at that moment and what time it would be in India and whether Gafoor and Khalifa had visited Papa recently.

Were Serita and I history already? I thought that when we next met we would meet as old friends, shake hands, and make plans, along with Ben, to go to the movies, but never really keep that date, and gradually, we would just stop calling and meeting. Just ease off very naturally and not talk about anything serious. I picked up the phone and called Mona. She wasn't home. Should I call Serita? Maybe not. Maybe I'd just give it a longer break and then call her in a few days and chat casually with her, and then promise to call her again and just let time slip by and allow both of us to fall back into our routines. But after all these days, I did really owe her a call. Just to say hello, and to tell her we'd meet in a few days.

The phone rang several times before she picked it up and when I said Hello, she was silent for a few seconds, and when I said Hello again she said in a half-scream, half-whisper:

"Where the hell have you been? I can't believe you're back. How come you never called?"

The contact was immediate and intimate and more powerful than the distance I thought I had just created. Why was it that every time she spoke to me she wrapped around me layer after layer of intimacy? When I didn't answer, she asked, again:

316

"Why didn't you call? Not even one call. Just to prove you can live without me?"

I said: " I asked you to marry me. I thought it was all over."

She said: "It is over." And I felt my stomach knotting, and I gripped the telephone receiver hard as if I was squeezing Serita's wrist, and I said:

"Then what was all this about? Were you just playing games?"

She said: "No. It's not over. It will be over one day. But this is the beginning. Wait for me tomorrow at your apartment. I'll come over sometime before noon. I love you."

And she hung up. I picked up Hamsun's book and opened it in the middle and tried to read. I read several pages without comprehension and then put it aside and went to sleep.

I awoke to the sound of the doorbell. It was late morning. I wrapped a towel around myself, shuffled to the door and looked through the peep-hole. I could see Serita's face. I opened the door and looked at her. She was in black. Her hair disappeared downwards behind her shoulder blades. She was grinning. She took a step towards me and hugged me hard in the manner that male friends hug after having not met for many years. She smelled of talcum powder, shampoo and Dove soap. She said:

317

"I've missed you." And she looked into my eyes and shook her head, very imperceptibly.

"I've missed you too," I said. And I probably did not sound very convincing, because she shook her head and said:

"Liar. Probably only since last night when we talked. You are a strange person. You miss me only when you're with me, not when you're away."

"That's why I asked you to marry me."

"That's precisely why I will not marry you. Never mind. Won't you invite me in? Here, you can help me with these."

I now noticed she had two large leather suitcases with her. I had no idea what to make of this. I picked them up and brought them into the living room. Serita sat down on a green wing-chair facing the love-seat in which I sat down. And she said:

"I've left Ben."

"What do you mean? Where will you go? When did this happen?"

"I made up my mind a few days ago. Before you returned."

"But he's a great guy. Serita, You belong with him. He's been so good to you. He's done so much for you."

Her eyes flashed. She said, raising her voice: "Don't

ever throw things like that at me. Men have this horrible, self-pitying habit of saying how much they've done for their woman every time they have a quarrel. You do things because you love. Not because you want to hold that out as blackmail for some future date. I'd never throw that at Ben, and I hope I'll never throw that at you. And even Ben didn't react the way you just did. You're already putting yourself in Ben's place."

"But this was kind of sudden. What did you tell Ben? When did you tell him? Did it have anything to do with us?"

Serita was more composed than I'd ever seen her. She said: "Everything that's happening in my life is because of us. I told him this morning. Not every detail. I woke up early and said I needed to talk to him after he got dressed. I put my arms around him and said: 'Ben, I need to tell you something, and I need you to be as strong as the day when we ran away together at your engagement party. I'm leaving you. Please don't come looking all over for me. I'll always care for you, and if you need me I'll be there.' He was stronger than I thought. He didn't try to talk me out of anything. He blinked back tears and moved away from me. I asked him if he wanted a divorce, and he said, no, then he said, he'd think about it, and he said he'd wait for me if I ever decided to come back. He asked me where I was going and I said someone else had come into my life, and he asked me if you were the one, I said, yes, and he said he had guessed as much.

And he walked out of the door and left me to pack.

I asked her: "You felt no remorse? Feel none?"

She answered: "I made a decision."

I asked: "You're moving in with me?"

"Of course."

"But I asked you to marry me."

"And the answer is still, no. For the reasons you already know. Today is the first day of our few days together. You asked me to find a balance. This is my balance. Tan, ours is the start of a posthumous relationship. We're both afraid of endings. But I'm not letting that ending remain a horrible, unsolved mystery. I'm writing it together with you. In that way you can reclaim the past as your future and I can continue with the future I've made for myself in this country. When the time comes to part we will both know the reasons already. There will be no questions about who betrayed whom and why. We have a time-span allotted to us and we will live it together, not as man and wife but as man and woman and not pretend at the end that what we had was not love."

"Serita, why do I feel I've always known you?"

"We've always known each other. We cannot change what was not before. We cannot change what is going to be. But while we are together we will share much more than just moments."

She handed me an envelope, and said:

"Go out now. Go to some bar and read it. This is our obituary. I don't want to sound morbid. It's not a morbid note. But it will explain why I'll resent you in the future. Why I love you and still resent you. If you care to understand it, you will know why one day we will no longer be together. Because a lot of what I say in there will not change. Our past is not very long ago, but it is a strong past, a connected past, and in my letter you will see memories of the future."

I went to the Catamaran, and Xavier asked me where I'd been, where I'd left that girlfriend of mine, and I said I'd been traveling and that Serita was fine, and that we'd come over that evening or the next day. And I read Serita's letter, and from its varied tones I guessed she'd written it over several days, in several moods, and combined it into a single composition. I read:

"I did not script love. I did not plant characters, transpose emotions or plot meetings... it happened, without forethought or planning. I've been trying to figure things out in my mind... if I should love you for your individuality, your different-ness then why should I smother our two beings with my possessiveness? Or maybe it is because I feel you can do without me – can forget and not suffer I guess. This is always present in my mind. The consciousness of your detachment. I can come into your life only when you want it, to the point you want me to. Why do I feel so hurt and lost at your being away? Today, the second time that you've gone away and not even bothered to call, I have this inexplicable anger. Why have you robbed me of my composure, my practicality, my reasoning, how could you so selfishly rob me of myself? Okay I asked for it, I wanted you, but I didn't want to lose myself, and instead of giving yourself to me, you've taken me. Why?! I hate myself. Please, please help me. My friends tell me that love is complacency, not to question, not to ask, not to rebel. I wish I could do that. I wish I could love you from far, selflessly, without demanding. I wish I could love without hurting myself. Because today I see love in its starkness, denuded of soppy, synthetic trappings. I'm frightened for myself because the fighting the conflict is within.

"See you've slipped away. You'll never be affected by it, never feel it, never know. And you'll probably start despising me for it. You with our global world view, your cultivated sensitivity, your inherent instinct for preservation, your inability to let go... you'll remain undefiled, untouched by my brutal love. I want you to suffer with me, want your soul to be tormented just like mine. What's noble and pure and selfless? Definitely not love.

"How pretty it sounded some days back, books, little letters, walks in the mountains, bar stools, and saying the right things, the right touch, the perfect woman, the Tanned god. But somewhere I knew that that was not it. You were on guard, in control, utterly detached yet so 'passionately' involved. There, I know I've hurt you, you'll hate me for it. But I had to. Me with my pretensions

322

of total honesty, my maddening possessiveness and insecurities, my very ugly dark form under pale, clear skin. I had to make you see it.

"You know it wasn't until I had this long chat with an old friend of mine that I realized how much you've been influencing me, how much like you I've become. It was really uncanny but I was unconsciously echoing your philosophy, with such deep conviction, as if it were my own. And for me, who questions everything you say (though I may not always let you know that) who doubts words and empty philosophy for being untrue and being devoid of any real-life significance, was repeating everything you say as if it was my own philosophy, my beliefs, the truths of life I had discerned after years of experience. My friend to say the least was impressed and totally in awe of this new Serita avatar. But my love will I always live under your shadow? Turn into a hollow dispirited echo, mindless, dysfunctional, parasitically feeding on your mind, not growing, not developing? Ugh! How horrible, ugly, how utterly despicable. You won't let that happen to me will you my love? It is my dream to be your equal one day, to write as well as you, to think as finely and sharply, to devour all the books and writings that you cherish, to live in your mind so that we pick up threads of stray thoughts and converse in the same language so that some day I can speak your language. No I'm not jealous of your mind…but I'm ambitious, and competitive, and hungry.

"I'm not talking about conquering or submission or

control. I'm talking of your body which speaks its own language, which demonstrates its love without the gigantic ego and reasoning that dominate your mind

"My fear is that you love your peace of mind, your life, the life you have plotted for yourself, your returning to India to watch your father die, to enter into the pace and rhythm of life in Raipur. This is a life I have consciously barred myself from. When you re-enter it, I shall no longer be there. You want beauty and comfort all around you. You don't want pain, you want nothing that is stark, plain, and ugly by virtue of it being in the realm of practicality. You will discard me when I'm old and ugly for you my Tanned lover will never age. I can't see your passion for life fading either. At least Raipur and your life of shikar and your forests have the privilege of being the remarkable pivot of your life. I will just be reduced to a file full of fading letters, a few memories that your fertile writer's mind will immediately transpose into works – published or unpublished."

I read the letter several times. And much of what Serita had said to me in our conversations began to make sense. In this letter she had written our joint horoscope. She had taken the mystery out of endings by deciding to live with me without attachment and yet predicting the turmoil and turbulence that would continue to mold and shape and alter our lives. I decided to read it again and again so that I would remember it by heart. When I got back to my apartment, Serita was sitting on the couch leafing through an old photo album. The bed was made without an untidy ripple in the bedcover. The sofa and wing-chair had been dusted. The little kitchen had been mopped, the grease-stains had gone, and in the middle of the dining table stood a vase with some white blossoms I did not recognize. And on my writing table were textbooks on mathematics I did not recognize. Serita's books. The fruits that nourished her genius.

I sat down with Serita and we kissed silently. Then I pointed out things and people to her in the Indian album. There was little Sara making caca in the potty. That's a flight of greylag geese, not a very good shot. And that's the *jheel* in which I shot my first mallard. Papa, the shikari, wearing a crazy jungle hat full of partridge feathers and the pins from pintail ducks sticking out. Those are jhoor clumps in the scrub forests, and there's Gafoor organizing a beat to flush out black partridge. And there's Ma plucking flowers to take to her puja room. The old Willys jeep. I wondered if they'd sold it? In a few months the ducks will be flighting in, and Seema says Pa's still got my gun greased.

And Serita said: "You're already looking into your future. Can you see me anywhere in it? I'm already not there."

"But you're here. You're with me."

"This is already the past. You'll always be sniffing the shikar and the Shikari, sniffing Papa. And I guess if I were ever to become a part of Raipur I'd belong in the puja room."

That night I waited for Serita to come to bed and in our love-making she was powerful and muscular. She raised her legs high and crossed her ankles above my shoulders, and I asked her what I should look out for when she is really in heat, and she said: "They say I bite and I scratch." And I asked her: "Who do you mean by 'they'?" And she said nothing. And later she said to me:

"There's one little doubt in my mind. After I told you I hadn't slept with my husband for a year, I hope you didn't think I was throwing myself at you because I needed sex. Because men are the least of my problems…"

"No. Serita. It never crossed my mind. No, you're desirable and a flirt and men would give anything to get inside your pants. I always thought of you as strong and principled. I guess you do belong inside that puja room."

Serita said: "You know what's the best thing about moving in with you? The mornings. To see you waking up and sharing tea in bed with you without having to rush back anywhere."

"It's our world now, Serita."

She said nothing and went to sleep with her head on my chest.

CHAPTER XX

1

As I look back now I know what they mean when they say the years just "melted" away. The posthumous relationship which Serita had scripted for us, bonded us with an adhesive intensity that left little room for interests other than those which had fueled our lives when we first met. On weekends when we missed out on long drives in the countryside Serita would work late into the night correcting student papers, now that she was teaching, or on mathematical abstracts about which I was totally ignorant. And when I was writing a story, and Serita happened to be around, she would sit by my side, very silently, breaking the stillness of those moments only to ask me if I wanted to share a cigarette. She knew I was irritable when I wrote, and curt and nasty in my responses when interrupted by a question or small talk especially in the moments when I stared vacantly into space trying to chase a rapidly meandering thought. She read everything I wrote and I felt invigorated and revivified when she asked me to read aloud to her a passage or a story I had completed. In a very subtle way, she was changing me.

I remember, when I was in boarding school, about 11 years of age, my English teacher had asked me to read one of my compositions aloud to the class. It was a mawkish love story about a leper and a princess in which the princess proves her love by contracting leprosy and begins to beg on the street outside her former palace along with her lover, proudly displaying each new bleeding, suppurating lesion as proof of her devotion. It was a bubbling cauldron of fancy into which I had poured my entire heart. I had written it not as a classroom exercise but rather in the back pages of my notebook where my teacher had chanced upon it by accident. Reading it aloud was perhaps one of the more traumatic incidents of my childhood. I felt I was disemboweling myself, being stripped naked to the marrow of my bones. Because never in my life had I shared something so private so publicly. It was as if my teacher was focusing a searing spotlight at the core of my innermost being. I felt I was reading aloud to the public the most secret parts of a diary which, if I were ever to make a will, was to be cremated with me – never to be seen or read by anybody.

I felt as if my teacher was asking me to rape myself in front of the class, and as I read, a powerful sap of rage and fear coursed through my body and caused me to tremble and weep. And the boys in the class were snickering and suppressing their laughter because some of them believed that I was weeping because I was moved by my own story, while others laughed with derision because they had discovered in me – an intrepid hunter who had once regaled them with tales of the wilderness and shikar – a sissy.

After class I tore the story to shreds. And for months some of my more imaginative classmates would bandage their fingers – as lepers do – paint them with red ink for imitation blood and accost me at the corners of buildings and chant: "Princess will you marry me?"

Ever since I had a horror of reading anything I wrote aloud. Initially I was adamant in my refusal when Serita asked me to read aloud something I had written. And she said:

"I really can't understand this. You're perfectly alright when you read to me from Miller and Lawrence and Whitman and Anais Nin, but why this attitude when it comes to your own work?"

"Oh, they're supposed to be read aloud. How can you even compare those titans to me? And they're all published, and they've withstood the test of time. And none of what I consider my serious work has any takers. I'd sound too pompous."

I then told Serita the story of my experience in the English class. And she said:

"I would have taken their taunts as a tribute to your honesty. I think you're mortally scared of being judged.

If you're going to write at all – and whether you read your stuff out aloud or whether wait for others to read it after it is published – you're going to be judged all the time. It you want to write you've got to risk making a fool of yourself."

And when I started reading myself aloud to Serita, she would always judge me: "Beautifully told lies but told with imagination and honesty." "Pompous, vain, boastful." "Dishonest to the core." "Yes, Yes!!" "Imitative and contrived." " Dishonest and disingenuous." "Empty philosophy, sounds like a corporate lawyer's brief, a flourish of words designed to avoid coming to grips with emotion, your real feelings, because you're afraid to give of yourself…"

I would argue with her:

"But this is fiction. I have to make up things. I have to invent, to fantasize, to take different parts of different people and create new souls, new images. I cannot follow logic and keep fantasy as fantasy and reality as reality. The two have to meet, like air currents of different temperatures and create a fog in which everything is real and everything is unreal…"

"Cheat by all means. Lie. Embellish. Use the music of words. Create your phantoms. Dance with your rapists and demons by all means but nothing will work as true literature – even the most phantasmagorical fairy tale – the moment you're dishonest. The moment dishonesty seeps into a work, a chapter that flows because you're bleeding, the blood stops and the tale becomes bloodless.

That's the reason I like your work – because I see you have the capacity to slash, slash at your innards and to bleed in public. This has nothing to do with a work being autobiographical or true to your life, or realistic. It has something to do with creation – your ability to gouge your own eyes out in order to give them to a character you've created.

"That is what will make people feel your real pain, to hear your real voice. Or else, write science fiction or mystery novels and you'll never have to slash yourself – just, keep creating structured scenarios…"

Serita was already reading like a maniac. Anything she could lay her hands on – Kerouac, Neal Cassady, St. Simon, Guizot, Proudhon, Genet, Proust, "The Death of Ivan Ilych", "Nausea", "Lord Jim", "The Outsider", "Men Without Women". And she introduced me to Edna St Vincent Millay, Celine, John Cooper Powys.

And I was introducing her to fishing. It was the next best thing to shikar, I had told her. She came to like bottom fishing the best because that way, she said, you could really relax. No changing of spoons and plugs and deep diving lures and plastic worms and worrying about the grading of Mepps spinners. I had taught her a technique of fishing both in lakes and fast rivers, a technique with which you could cast into rapids. We fished with bloodworms in tidal basins and bay areas like the Chesapeake, with night-crawlers in fresh water lakes and rivers, and with squid in the shallow waters of the Atlantic.

She was at first revolted with the idea of sticking worms to hooks. But I told her if she wanted to be a shikari of the waters then she'd have to get used to dealing with wriggling bait. And besides, if I had a fish on the line and was bringing it in, it would be inexcusable behavior on her part to come running to me with a naked hook and a can of worms pleading for help.

Serita showed a surprising interest in fishing, studied the Friday reports, began buying Field and Stream, and though it took a while, she overcame her squeamishness about baiting books. For the most part we fished with Daiwa reels using 8 to 10-pound monofilament lines and snelled hooks sized between four and eight.

2

When she was ready to start doing things on her own we drove to a stretch of the Potomac outside Washington D.C., on a June morning, and on a forested bank I gave Serita her first lesson. And I felt as pleased as Ben would probably have been in showing an intern how to whisk an appendix out of an unsuspecting abdomen. Actually, I thought, a night-crawler does resemble an human appendix and wondered to myself what kind of bait it might make.

Serita was an avid listener, a fine learner. I was telling her:

"See, Serita, you first guide the line from your spool through these loops right along the length of your pole. Just pull on the line. It won't budge? Let me see... see you've got the drag set too tight. Loosen it – yes like this by turning that dial at the back of your reel with the numbers on it. Now pull again – it should make a *screee* sound. That means your spool's giving you line with the right tension otherwise the line can get all knotted at the bottom into a bird's nest if it gets all loose and goes haywire...."

"Got your line through that last little metal loop at the very tip? Good. Now give yourself about three feet of line past that last loop. Just pull on it. Now lay your pole across your lap. I'm teaching you to do a rig I like most for bottom fishing."

I reached into the tackle box and selected a 3-ounce triangular sinker for her. For myself a half-ounce bell-shaped one. I handed her her sinker and continued:

"See that little ring on top of your sinker? Now secure your line to that." She looked bewildered and asked:

"But you're not going to get a fish bite into this metal. It is so heavy. Don't you need a hook to catch a fish?"

I said: "Serita, do as I tell you. Most people put a hook at the end of their line but I do it differently. The hook comes later. Here, I'll teach you a strong fisherman's knot for sinker. Like this. First, you put your line through this ring and pull it out about an inch on the other side.

333

Now take the end of this between the thumb and forefinger of your right hand, press it against the main line. See how the sinker is dangling from the middle of this loop? Now to secure it, to tie it. With the thumb and forefinger of your left hand pinch together the two parts of the big loop, right at the bottom, making a tiny second loop just above the ring through which your line has been threaded. Let go the portion of the line your right hand is holding. The end of the line is now free. Now like this, starting right above your left thumb and forefinger which are making that tiny loop on which the sinker is hanging, start twirling the end of the line upwards along the main line. After you've made five or six spirals, take the end of the line and thread it through the tiny loop above the ring and pull–hard. And work the little spirals downwards. Hey this one's pretty good. It won't open up in a strong current like an ordinary knot would."

I cut loose the knot I had made with a nail clipper, and asked Serita to try on her own. She got it perfect the very first try.

"Okay," I said, "now we do the hook. For you, we take a number 6 Eagle Claw. See, it's already well tied to a nylon line, about six inches long with a ready made loop – looks like a hangman's noose – at the top. Now we take this noose and we take a distance of about a foot on your line above the sinker and this is how we attach the hook. It's easy. I'm encircling the point I've chosen on your line with the nylon leader to which the hook is attached and I'm passing the hook through the readymade noose. It makes a neat knot. But it can slip up and down your line. So we secure it like this. We take the sinker, make a loop with it just above this point where I've attached the noose and pull the sinker through this loop I've made, and pull it tight. There, this hook's sliding nowhere now.

"And now for the bait. There's about 20 night-crawlers – we used to call them earthworms in India – in that plastic container, Serita. Just put your fingers in the sod and pull out the fattest one you can find."

Serita said: "I can't do it."

I said: "But you'll have to, sooner or later. Today, I'll do it for you. And maybe the next time. But what if you want to go fishing all by yourself? And there's no one to do it for you. Hah! What then?"

"I think I'll go in for artificial lures."

"Sure some fish will go only for those, but this bottom fishing is more fun. All you've got to do is relax, have a beer, have a cigarette and watch your pole. And even with lures, you'll have to get used to disgorging them from the fish's throat or lip, and that can be messy because if a large bass or even an oversized sunfish like a pumpkinseed sucks in a small spoon too deep, you'll take half his guts out when pulling out the hook. Anyhow, this is one technique of putting a worm on that seems to work for me."

I pulled out a fat night-crawler and held him tight

just a centimeter below the fatter end of his snout between my left thumb and forefinger while the rest of him dangled trying to make loops and figures of eight. Squeezing him tight where I held him, I inserted the point and barb of the hook into his snout – at dead center – and threaded him upwards along the entire curvature of the hook, like putting a glove on the hook, until his snout reached the point where the metal was joined to the nylon leader. I guided his writhing body along a half-inch of the nylon. The sharp point of the hook was still somewhere in his belly. In this method I had to be careful not to let the barb break through the skin while guiding the worm along the hook. Only when I saw that the entire hook and part of the nylon leader had been hidden by the worm, did I feel for the sharp pint of the hook with my thumb. It was very near the tail. I pulled his tail outwards and the tip of the hook's point emerged just a little. The threaded hook looked like a fleshy, angry-red question mark.

Serita asked: "Doesn't it disgust you?"

I said: "No. Something always eats something. This is quicker than a little bird pecking at him for hours as he struggles to make an escape into the ground. You're lucky this is not a bloodworm. They squirt blood. With them it's like puncturing a human finger to take a blood sample. And they can pinch with tiny thorny teeth if you don't hold them right. But look, here's your rig. You're all ready. At the bottom – a fairly heavy sinker. A foot above it, the nylon leader at the end of which, the hook with the bait on it."

Serita asked: "But I always thought the hook came at the end."

I said: "I'll tell you how it works. This sinker is heavy because you're going to cast about 40 yards into the middle of the river, into those rapids. Why? Chances are you'll get a small-mouth bass or a bass which feed at the edge of the rapids. The rig I'm going to use is similar to yours. Except I have a light sinker. This is because I'm going to cast my line nearer the shore where the current is not so swift and I don't need anything heavier to keep my bait from floating downstream once I hit bottom. There's mostly bottom-feeders like catfish and mullet and carp where my line is going to be."

I took Serita's pole and began a new lesson on how to cast, asking her to watch and listen attentively: "This is how you hold the rod with your right hand. You hold it tight with your thumb on the back portion of the pole and your forefinger right underneath pressing the line against the underside of the rod. This big ring resting against the spool is the bale. You open it out by moving it to the left. Now the line is free, If I ease the pressure on the line I'm holding with my right forefinger, the line will just fall loose because when you open the bale the spool no longer controls the line, it simply unwinds."

I showed her how, when I loosened my grip on the line, the sinker dragged the line to the ground. I continued: "To set it up again we simply turn the retrieval handle clockwise, less than a half-turn. And see? The bale clicks back into place and the line is taut again. I'm now checking the drag setting. It should adjust easily while still keeping appropriate pressure on the fish while not breaking the line. I'll set it a little high because this will allow more line to be pulled in with each turn of the handle. And now I'm ready to cast. I open the bale again like this. Hold the line tight against the underside of the rod with the pressure of my thumb above and my forefinger below. I raise the rod a little above my left shoulder. I can raise it above my head but I have to avoid the overhanging branches. So I raise it away from my body on the left and I cast. All I've done is released the pressure of my forefinger on the line. It's the same action as if you're throwing a stone held between your thumb and forefinger. How far you want it to go depends on how hard you throw."

My cast went well over 30 yards. The line was unraveling rapidly as the sinker began to sink into the rapids, and just when the line slackened, I turned the handle to lock the bale and the line went taut again. I handed the pole to Serita, told her to hold it with the rod tip a 45-degree angle from her body. I asked her to raise the tip, gently just once and let it fall back into place because, I explained, in case the sinker had become lodged under a rock, this motion would make it shift and prevent a snag. Then I asked her to reel the line in, not too fast, not too slow until the rig came into sight just a few feet away from the shore and she reeled it out of the water, looking pleased as punch.

I told Serita: "This was just to give you a feel of things.

What is happening after you cast is that the heavy sinker is going to the bottom. When the line slackens it means you've hit bottom and if you don't close your bale the current will keep taking your line and chances are you'll snag. After you close your bale, relax. The sinker is now sitting at the bottom of the river while the hook with the bait is bobbing up and down about a foot above firmly secured to your line making a tantalizing morsel. Now's the waiting part and the fun part. Find a soft spot on the ground near you and stick the stock of your pole – this corked portion – firmly into it. Or wedge it in between rocks, or a strong forked twig if you can find one."

Serita asked: "You mean I don't have to hold it in my hand all the time. How do I know when I have a fish?"

I said again: "That's the fun part. Once you've dug your pole into the ground or wedged it firmly – and the tip should be at least at 45-degree angle from the ground – open up a can of beer and just sit by and lay yourself on the ground and watch the tip of your pole. If your line is in a strong current your pole will take rhythmic bows and straighten out every five seconds or so. Most people think this is a fish but it's only the current. What you have to watch for is when the pole really doubles over and doesn't straighten out and in that position begins to resemble the movements of a bird picking at a worm. Or when the tip of the pole starts quivering line a throbbing, ejaculating prick, like your 'friend'. That's when you grab your pole from the ground or wherever it's wedged and in response to the tug from below, yank the pole upwards, hard, in order to set the hook. If it's a big fish and your drag's set right, the line will start to unravel with that familiar *screee* sound. If you're retrieving with your handle and more line's going out than coming in, tighten the drag a little. Bring in the fish with a lifting motion, while alternately reeling in and always keep your rod tip up."

That day Serita wasn't about to put the worms on. But she was amazingly dexterous with the angling part. Within three hours she was casting by herself. She had learned that if there was no action after 10 minutes, she should reel in the bait. Examine it. If the bait was gone or tattered by the current or underwater debris, she would ask me to put a fresh worm on and she would cast again. She snagged. The line broke several times. She hooked overhanging branches while casting, pulled in twigs. But she was getting there. And as evening began to descend on the Potomac, I had drifted into a snooze. There had been no real action for me. A couple of small sunfish was about all. And the beer was feeling just right. And Serita was sitting cross-legged on a foam cushion watching the Potomac changing colors.

And just as I was entering the first stages of some dream, I felt a thumping on my chest. I opened my eyes, startled, and Serita's face was above mine. She was shaking me awake by the front of my shirt.

I asked: "What is it?"

Serita's voice, usually throaty and mellow and soft had a shrill edge to it: "The prick!" she shouted. "The

340

dick, the dick, I mean my prick...look it's throbbing, it's coming...just like you said."

At first I thought Serita had caught too much sun. Then I realized what she was trying to say. I looked in the direction of her pole, and sure enough its tip was going haywire. I jumped on to my feet and shouted:

"Serita, pick it up, pick it up! And the moment you feel the first tug again, yank it hard to set the hook like I told you."

She waited for no more instructions. She unstuck the pole from its resting place and yanked.

I asked: "Can you feel something heavy at the end of the pole? Is your line giving a little when you lift it, or do you feel it's stuck? Reel in a little and now lift the line. What does it feel like?"

"I can feel something pulling hard in the other direction. It feels heavy when I slide it, when I lift the rod and pull it inwards."

"Try reeling it in. Not too hard. Not too fast."

"I'm reeling but the line is not responding. I'm turning the handle but the line keeps going out," she shouted. "I feel like Sisyphus!"

"That mean's she's fighting you! Tighten the drag!"

"How do you know it's a she?"

"Cut out the cute stuff, Serita. Tighten your drag,

quick, or you might even loose her if she makes a run around some rock, and then your line will break."

Serita tightened the drag.

"Now bring her in, Serita, bring her in. Yes, reel in, reel in, keep your rod tip up, for godssakes! She's pulling in the other direction! Walk along the bank in the same direction. Now use your pole to guide her in. Like you guide a kite across the sky. Didn't you fly kites in India? It's the same kind of action. Yes, yes, like that. Now reel in again. If she wants a little more line, give it to her, but don't let her make too much of a run."

"How do I stop her, or him?"

"By tiring her out."

We had both broken into a small jog along the bank.

Serita asked, panting a little: "What do you think it is?"

"I have no idea. Maybe a huge channel catfish even though I've never seen them here. Maybe a big smallmouth. Could be a humongous carp."

It was all of 20 minutes before the fish tired and Serita was reeling it in gently and gradually it came into view in the shallow water a few feet away from the bank. It was a slithering black mass of something.

"God," Serita said, "God, I caught a bicycle tube. Yukk! Tubes fight like that?"

I looked closer and at first I thought it was a water snake. And then I saw it was a huge black eel. I waded out into the water with a net, scooped it out and let the eel out on the bank from where it tried to slither towards the water.

"Well," Serita asked, "what *is* it?"

"It's an eel Serita. Your first eel my fishing buddy! Wow, and it should be a record. Serita, you were just great."

I disgorged the hook, showing Serita how to hold the fish tight just below the gills. The eel measured four feet in length and had a nine-inch girth.

"What are we going to do with him?" Serita asked.

"How do you know she's a him?"

"Oh, Tan I'm serious."

"We take her home. We cook her. We eat her. We'll get some great red wine. And we'll have Simon and his girlfriend over." I taught Serita how to skin an eel. I first nailed him by his snout to a tree with the rest of his body hanging loose. Then with a precision fish-knife a made a shallow incision across the circumference of his girth right below the gills. A flap had appeared where I had made the cut. With a pair of pliers I loosened the flap all around and then I began to yank it downwards until I unsheathed the entire monster. It was like unpeeling a giant condom. The flesh was white and robust. I pulled out the nail and laid the eel on newspapers I had spread on the ground and I cleaned his gut and threw the yellowish entrails into the river. Then I chopped him into thick, steak-sized filets and packed them in ice for the journey home. I looked at Serita with a smile and a raised eyebrow.

She had been watching in absolute silence, and she said: "It´s like cleaning up after a crime."

I said: "And you're my partner in it, right up to your neck. Serita, today, you´re the real breadwinner."

CHAPTER XXI

1

I remember that particular February night because a three-day blizzard, the likes of which New Yorkers had rarely seen had kept us holed up in our apartment. Serita, like so many others, had simply refused to go to work even though the snow-removing machines had been working day and night and the roads had been salted several times over. It was late afternoon. Outside, there was now an ice-storm and a mighty gale that seemed to come in gallops. Our window-panes were covered with layer upon layer of frost and we prayed that the heating system wouldn't collapse. Serita and I had not moved out of bed except to go wash or to grab a sandwich. And Serita asked me:

"Do you like babies?"

I said: "You mean, like, to play with, and cuddle? Yeah, they can be kind of fun. I used to have a whale of a time with Sara when she was baby. And Seema's daughters were babies, too, and, yeah, I guess I like babies. Why?"

345

"Well, I was just kind of wondering what kind of a father you'd make."

"I guess I'd make a pretty good daddy."

"Would you change nappies, and wipe the puke, and bathe your baby, and help in the night feeds, and pay regular visits to the pediatrician and stay up nights when the kid has fever and is yelling his lungs out?"

"Yeah, sure. I mean, I wouldn't be alone in this task, I wouldn't be able to do it by myself. But sure, I'd pitch in."

Serita laughed: "That's what they all say. You so-called modern Indian males. But when the time comes, you want separate bedrooms until the baby starts sleeping through the night, or back in India you get the grannies to come live with you, or the wife has to quit her job."

"Would you quit your job, if you had a baby?"

Serita was adamant: "No I would not. I'd expect the father to be more flexible."

"But, Serita, that's something you've given up on. There are no babies – I mean your own babies – in your life. That's the way you've planned things."

Serita said: "I've changed my mind."

I asked, bewildered: "Are you saying you want to make a baby? With me? But I thought you said, no matter what happened between you and Ben, you would never want to hurt him in this way. Or are you telling me you're going back to Ben? Serita, I can't figure this one out."

Serita smiled, and she talked to me in a tone a mother uses in explaining something to her child: "No, I'm not going back to Ben, and no, I am not going to start making a baby with you. I have already made a baby, and it's already quite snug in my womb."

I jumped up with a start, and held her gently by her shoulders: "Whose is it? Who's the father?"

Serita laughed aloud and when her laughter subsided, she said: "You, you idiot. Who else?"

I wish I could have seen the expression on my own face, because Serita was looking at me and giggling. I said: "But we've been using precautions. You've been on the pill. It must be an accident. You want to keep the baby?"

Serita said: "Yes. I'm keeping the baby. I made it happen. I stopped the pill myself. I'm already six weeks up. Dr Hillman is a good gynecologist. I'll deliver at Beth Israel hospital."

"But what about Ben? You said you never wanted to hurt him, and he's still legally your husband."

Serita said: "I've figured something out in my mind. Something for Ben. This baby's no accident, Tan. When you asked me to have your child – how long was it? Five years ago, I think – you said it was a way in which I could keep both you and Ben. Those were the wrong reasons, Tan. In fact, the worst reason I could have given myself for violating my own belief about not bringing another baby into this world. No, I'm having this baby because I want to gift it to you. Someone – boy or girl – you will have to bring up here and then take back with you to share your forests and shikar and become part of your Papa's family. Will you accept my gift?"

I had never, in the five years I had shared with Serita, been shy of weeping in her presence. And on this frozen afternoon, I embraced her and I wept silently and she cradled my head on her breast and stroked my hair.

2

Serita's pregnancy was uneventful. She carried to full term give or take a week. Her pains started at 2 a.m. on October 10. She shook me awake.

She said: "They've started."

I called Dr Hillman. He asked:

"How far apart are they?"

I consulted with Serita and told Hillman she had had only one. And Hillman asked me to call him as soon as she had the second one. The next one came an hour-and-a-half later and in between the contractions I stroked her bulging abdomen, as Serita would love to have me do throughout her later pregnancy, with my palm. The third one came at 5 a.m. and then they stopped. Hillman opined it was false labor and that she was not due for a few days, at least, and that we should call him when the contractions were more regular and about a half-hour apart.

The following night Serita's pains started again and then vanished like before. And we kept awake through another night. On October 12, again at 2 a.m., Serita shook me again. I was like a zombie after two sleepless nights, and I told Serita to awaken me when the next one came. I awoke again when I felt Serita shaking me violently and shouting my name.

I asked, still groggy: "What is it?"

And Serita who was sitting on the edge of the bed in her maternity gown, said through clenched teeth: "I'm pregnant, remember? About to have your baby! I've been trying to wake you up for the last three hours. I thought you were in a coma."

"What time is it? How far apart are they?"

"It's 5 a.m. and they're less than a half-hour apart!"

"Why haven't you called your doctor?"

"I have! I have! That's why I've been trying to wake you up. To take me to the hospital."

"Jeesus!" I said, and jumped out of bed and began putting on my clothes. And Serita moaned loudly, and doubled up on the bed.

"Oh, God!" she said. "This is a big one. God! It's not going away. It's hurting, it's really hurting."

I shouted: "Come on! Let's go, let's go! Here, I'll help you."

Serita, still, rolling around on the bed shouted: "I don't know what's going on. I think, they're coming very rapidly now. I feel all wet. I think my water bag's about to burst. Or is bursting!"

I yelled: "You mean the baby could come any minute?"

She said: "I don't know! Maybe. Or maybe half-an-hour. God! I think my water bag has burst. I can't move now."

I grabbed the phone, and I said: "I'll call Hillman. Maybe he'll come here. He'll have to deliver the baby in bed. Or what if the baby comes now. I don't know anything about umbilical cords."

Serita was still writhing in pain. She said: "No. I don't know how long Hillman will take. Call Ben! Call Ben! Here's his number ask him to come here. He's much closer."

" Ben! Why Ben? But he's not even a baby doctor! What if does something wrong?"

"For God's sake, don't argue. Just call him. Any doctor knows how to deliver a baby. And Ben's one of the best. And he is supposed to be present at the birth of my baby."

I shouted: "What!"

Serita was turning her head from side to side on the pillow. The bedclothes had fallen off. I covered her. She said:

"Just call him, will you? I'll explain everything. Just call him."

Ben picked up after two rings. We hadn't spoken ever since Serita had moved in with me. He didn't seem surprised when I introduced myself. He asked:

"Is Serita in labor? Are you calling from the hospital? Where's Hillman?"

"No, we're in the apartment. I don't think there's time to go the hospital. I think she's going to deliver any time. The water bag seems to have burst. She asked me to call you."

Ben said: "I'll be right over."

I sat down beside Serita and stroked her hair. I said: "He seems to know everything. You've been talking to him. You've been seeing him again. You sure this is not his baby?"

Serita raised her voice: "You think I'd lie to you, you fool? What for?"

"I don't know. But women do lie. They lie, naturally, easily, effortlessly, and without guilt. You lied to Ben, when you first began to see me."

Serita was shouting both in pain and in pique: "Is this any time to throw a jealous fit? I'm delivering your baby, and you're generalizing about women. The truth is I did meet Ben. I had to. I could not have gone through this baby secretly, without saying anything to Ben and let him find out later. That would have hurt him more. I told him I was carrying your child. I told him that this could be a moment of sharing for all of us. That he should be present along with you in the delivery room and see me give birth, and to bless the child. I told Dr Hillman that while you are the natural father, Ben is still legally married to me and requested that both of you be allowed in to witness the delivery."

I still had anger in me: "But why didn't you tell me earlier?"

"Because I was afraid you wouldn´t agree. In which case this might have become a point of constant tension between you and me during the last period of my pregnancy. I believed the best thing would be to have Dr Hillman lead Ben into the delivery room in the hospital and, yes, surprise you. No matter how you felt, I knew you wouldn't create a scene there. And I sincerely believed that once you and Ben went through childbirth with me it would ease Ben's pain a little."

"But what kind of guy is he? His wife dumps him for another man, and then he agrees to come and watch her deliver the other man´s baby – a baby he so badly wanted with his own wife..."

352

"Just shut up! I feel like I'm going to die. There's too much pain. Oh God! Why can´t Ben get here?"

It seemed like hours. But Ben rang the buzzer to our apartment in less than 20 minutes after we had spoken. I let him in. He was carrying a bag of instruments. He was wearing a white gown. A nurse was with him. He went to Serita's bedside. She smiled at him. He took her hand in his and kissed it. He pulled out a white gown and surgical mask for me from his bag. The nurse was in the kitchen, boiling water in a large pan.

"Can I do anything?" I asked.

Ben said: "You can give me that chair." Ben placed the chair at the foot of the bed and asked Serita, who was lying crouched on her left side, to lie on her back to bend her knees and place both her feet flat on the mattress and to pull her gown up to her chest. And he asked me to sit by her side and to dab her brow and face with a damp towel. Serita was clutching at the bedsheet underneath her with both her hands. And she was grimacing.

"Oh God! Ben, I'm hurting. I'm hurting," she was repeating through clenched teeth.

Ben was silent. The nurse had moved to Serita's side and was tying a cuff around her arm to measure her blood pressure. The nursed pressed on the bulb of the tube and it went huff-huff-huff and then she began to release the air which made a slow hiss.

The nurse mumbled some figures to Ben and Ben

appeared to nod with satisfaction and the nurse moved to where Ben was sitting and knelt by his side. The sheet on which Serita lay was soaked with very light blood. I dabbed Serita's face and I kissed her forehead and stroked her hair.

I asked Ben: "Is she all right? Is it going to be long?"

Ben said: "It's already on the way."

I asked, my pulse racing: "Can you make out what it is?"

Ben replied: "Not from the head. I can see the head. Now Serita, you'll have to help. Take a deep breath and push. Push with all your might."

Serita was whimpering: "How, Ben, how? Push how?"

Ben said: "Like you've seen them do in the movies. Exactly like they do in the movies. You know, the last few frames before you hear the sound of the child bawling. Push like you want to get rid of a bout of constipation."

The nurse was now gently rubbing Serita's belly downwards. I was holding both her hands, which she had folded above her chest, in both my hands. Each time Serita pushed she groaned loudly through clenched teeth, her lips separated and taut at both ends in a snarl, her eyes shut so tight that the sockets of her eyes seemed to swallow up her eyelids.

Ben said: "Serita, you're doing just fine. It won't take long at all." And Ben looked at me and his eyes smiled above his mask and he motioned me to come to his side. I loosened my grip on Serita's hands and she clasped my hands even tighter, unwilling to let go.

She whispered: "Don't leave."

"I'm here," I said, "I'm here. I'm just going to where Ben is." Serita clutched the bedsheet again on both sides of her torso.

I knelt beside Ben. I looked between Serita's parted thighs. And I seemed to see an iridescent fog with glistening, ruby-red dewdrops which expanded into unknowable shapes of white light, and I could see Ben's gloved hands which seemed to be made of mist. Ben's palms facing upwards as if in supplication. A cradle of human fingers in which, ever so gently, a form had begun to materialize: a head carved out of the softest, moist, brown clay, two shoulders made out of gossamer wings, a belly into the center of which a thread of mountain water trickled ceaselessly. Serita was silent. Her eyes were now open. And she was staring at the ceiling in a fixed gaze and her breathing was gentle.

Suddenly, time came rushing back into the room. It entered with an explosion. Ben was saying, He's a fine young fella, and Serita had started to laugh aloud, tears streaming from her eyes, and I too was laughing as I watched Ben snip the infant's umbilical cord and put a clamp on it while the newborn still lay in between Serita's thighs, and the nurse began wiping him with a soft cloth, and the boy was yelling in intermittent bursts of sound that reminded me of an angry alley cat. Then Ben put drops in the boy's eyes, swabbed mucous out of his mouth and laid him on Serita's chest. Serita stroked her child's body with her eyes closed. And he was suddenly silent. Serita stroked him for about five minutes and even though the baby had begun to howl again, Serita asked:

"He hasn't got extra toes or fingers, does he?" And we assured her he did not. And Serita closed her eyes and went to sleep.

Ben picked up the baby, wrapped in a towel and handed him to me. He said:

"Take him to the other room. Put him on the couch and talk to him. Stroke his face with your fingers. I'm going to stay with Serita until the placenta comes out. Should be about 20 minutes. Sometimes less. I'll call for an ambulance to take her to the hospital. She'll be in the maternity ward for observation for most of the day and we'll register the birth and keep the little fella in the nursery for a while."

I cradled the baby in my arms, his head resting in the crook of my left elbow. I walked into the living room and put him on the sofa. I knelt by him and looked at him. He had jet black hair, lots of it, and misty brown eyes. His complexion was a beautiful bronze. He was still covered with blotches of dried blood and mucous. I inhaled his odor. He smelled of mountain ferns after a lusty rain shower. When he looked at me, as I stroked his cheeks, his eyes blazed like meteors. Then he frowned, and he knitted his brow into a question-mark and then closed his eyes. As I stared at him, he would open and close his eyes and I would see his question-mark again.

I loved him immediately. I wanted to say a prayer for him. I wanted Mama by my side teaching me how to pray. And as I tried to pray, Papa's words came rushing back to me, words I had heard when I was in my early teens. It was a conversation I'd overheard between Papa and some friend of his who had been pestering Papa about the ethics of hunting and killing and whether Papa ever felt guilty about being a shikari. And as I looked at my newborn son I heard Papa's words as clearly as I had heard them so many years ago:

"What about God, if you believe in him, that is? Is he not the biggest fisherman of all? Does he not fish you out of your mother's womb? The hook into the fetus and the fetus that emerges crying and flopping into an alien atmosphere? From the sea of the womb into the bloodless oxygen of a universe in which he is destined to die? Does a fetus have the knowledge of death? And yet the moment he is born, pulled out of his bloodsea, or flushed from the protection of his pre-natal life, he is doomed. From the very first second after birth he hangs from a noose that tightens remorselessly for 70-odd years until he is old and pale and wrinkled and sapped and ultimately strangled. Birth is death. No birth, no death. Your God gives you death as your birthday present. He is the ultimate hunter for he fishes in the mystery of wombs. What happens to his quarry after he has given it its birth-death, I do not think He really cares. I think the shikari is more sentimental than your God."

I suddenly felt sad looking at my child. Did another soul need to come into this world to suffer? Did Serita have to give me this present? Had she not been absolutely right in her reasoning when she had decided to remain childless?

I could hear Ben and the nurse washing up. And the ambulance had arrived downstairs and they would soon be bringing a stretcher or wheelchair up for Serita and we would all be on our way to the hospital. The birth had taken no more than 10 minutes after Ben's arrival at our apartment. Serita was sitting up in bed. The nurse had helped her wash, comb her hair, which was now in a bun, and she was chatting with Ben. I carried the baby to Serita and she immediately began cuddling him. I looked at Ben and he was smiling. I shook his hand and I gave him a small hug, and I thanked him. I said:

"Ben, what are we going to name this guy?"

And Ben said: "Godot."

Part Five

CHAPTER XXII

1

On Christmas eve in our West End Avenue efficiency – Serita and I had now spent about 15 Christmases together – that winter when Godot had decided to spend a few days away from home with his friends, the Arctic winds had brought down the wind chill factor to minus 20 Fahrenheit, Hal Popper came to dinner for chick-peas flavored with cinnamon and cumin and ground chuck cooked in ginger and garlic with a dash of turmeric and topped with fresh tomatoes sauteed with onions and dill. Hal had done an advanced course in international relations at Columbia, and later worked with me at the New York publishing house as an editor on books on capital formation in underdeveloped societies, thought Gunnar Myrdal was a me-too schmuck, liked Ricardo and John Stuart Mill and Jeremy Bentham and knew the difference between the Upanishads and the Puranas and Mahayana and Hinayana Buddhism. He was a tall, strapping Kentucky man with red hair which stuck out on one end like the character in Mad Magazine's Don Martin Dept. If you've never heard a drawl, then you'd learn exactly what it was the moment Hal opened his mouth. Which he didn't too often because he spoke through clenched teeth, but when he laughed his upper lip almost touched his nose. He wore polka-dotted scarves and believed most of my friends to be riff-raff, not class-wise, mind you, because they were mostly New England or fancy Orange County and Harris Tweed variety rich, and Hal was of farmer stock whose childhood sweetheart, whom he married, Becky, had run away with a Boston horse breeder a year into their marriage, but because he felt they ignored libraries and knew nothing about Ida Tarbell or Veblen.

I liked Hal because he introduced me to Rebel Yell bourbon. He looked down upon California wine drinkers. And could really put it down and spent endless hours arguing with temperance types that not all boozers were alcoholics, that alcoholism in drinkers was a despicable trait, that good bourbon, well drunk, was food for the spirit of the spirited. And he would recite verbatim from Colin Wilson:

"'The power of alcohol over mankind is unquestionably due to its power to stimulate the mystical faculties of human nature, usually crushed to earth by the cold facts and dry criticisms of the sober hour. Mystical faculties here refers to that flood tide of inner warmth and vital energy that human beings regard as the most desirable state to live in. The sober hour carries

362

continuous demands on the energy; sense-impressions, thoughts, uncertainties suck away the vital powers minute by minute. Alcohol seems to paralyze these leeches of the energies; the vital warmth is left to accumulate and form a sort of inner reservoir. This concentration of the energies is undoubtedly one of the most important conditions of the state the saints call *Innigkeit*, inwardness.'"

Simon had also joined us for that Christmas curry dinner. His idea of inwardness was to speak as little as possible. Lapse into days of silence. And to terrorize the world with poetry. He may have cowered in fear of his classfellows in PS 148 in Brooklyn, but his teachers believed there lurked within him an intellectual cannibal who would devour their brains if they didn't pander to what some considered to be incipient genius while others – the undecided – settled on describing this as intellectual lunacy. And they dared not flunk him, even in Math classes in which he filled out answers to theorems with repetitions of Hamburger Joe, and in History class, when he was asked to write an essay on "Your Reflections on Whether Custer was a Mis-guided Missile," he wrote in three pages of a red, barely legible scrawl portions of Burrough's words from "Junky" – (the first edition of which was published under the pen name of William Lee by Ace Books): " 'Morphine hits the back of the legs first, then the back of the neck, a spreading waves of relaxation slackening the muscles away from the bones so that you seem to float without outlines, like lying in warm salt water' " – a book that he always carried with him along, later, with "The Last Words of Dutch Schultz", and a half-finished work of Neal Cassady and, again, Burrough's "Cobble Stone Gardens," – ("When the world has been reduced to a dark wood to a beach I will find you filigrees of trade winds clouds white as lace circling the pepper trees an overcast morning in July a taste of ashes floats on the air a smell of wood sweating on the hearth weather...") – in a lady's handbag slung across his shoulder.

In grad school, where he had chosen to major in magazine writing, his Master's thesis, entitled "Poverty in the Alleghenies," written with a quill and ink he bought from an antique dealer, was a four-page first person fan-letter of appreciation to Nathan Rappaport, one of Manhattan's most notorious illegal abortionists who had been dodging the police for a dozen years. I was Simon's accomplice. Not because I encouraged him to conclude his last stint of formal education in what I then believed was a four-page cop-out while most of the rest of us slogged our butts reading Kennedy eggheads like Roger Hillsman, and Michael Harrington, and trying to decipher Wilhelm Reich's words in the Mass Psychology of Fascim, for the most decisive test of the final semester. Why, I was Simon's accomplice because I helped him track down Rappaport in the hope that he would do a fine interview with him.

Simon had told me that finding Rappaport would be easier for me than for him. "See," he said, "Here's being a Hindu that would really help. All of America knows you guys are overpopulated and that family planning and birth control are high on your country's agenda. All you've got to tell these guys is that you're here for a short while from India to take back modern ideas on birth control. They'll open all the doors to you."

I had no idea that Hamburger Joe's creator was also a strategist. It worked. My disguise worked wonders with Manhattan's underground abortionists who had a ready-referral system with a network of state-employed social workers who hated the Comstock Law. When I got Rappaport's unlisted phone number and introduced myself to him – in the best of Peter Sellers's exaggerated Hinglish accent and inflection – as a visiting Hindu who had traveled to New York to seek his advice, he was touched. He told me:

"The two people I admired most in the world were Mahatma Gandhi and Margaret Sanger."

He was then hiding out in a small apartment on 23rd Street and Third Avenue. Simon went with me as my American counterpart. Rappaport was in his seventies. Had forgotten to wear his dentures and spoke with a wheeze. He looked like a retired gardener. Simon took no notes as he spoke about his first abortion, his arrests, the side-effects of the birthcontrol pills, the cumbersome Lippe's Loop that caused perforations, the uncertainty of the rhythm method, the yet untested efficacy of the diaphragm and jelly.

Rappaport went on for two hours: "Like Gandhi I

believe in Civil Disobedience," he said. Simon seemed to enjoy this, because being a Trojans user but mostly an interruptus man, Simon had little use for, or understanding of, Rappaport's clinical erudition. Simon may or may not have known much about Sanger but he was moved when Rappaport (who had asked Simon to call him Nat – Simon's own father's name – in the future) broke into sobs at the end of his tale. He said, sobbing:

"I was at Margaret Sanger's funeral. And as they laid her down I saw her rise and she spoke to me. I was training to be a neurosurgeon. I dropped out of med school and have since pursued what she commanded me to do after she died. He wiped his horn-rimmed glasses with a table napkin, put on his dentures which had two fine gold teeth, and asked Simon and me to cover our heads with our handkerchiefs as he shut his eyes and muttered inaudibly for a few minutes. "I have spoken to her," he said. "If you have any referrals for me, I'll do it for half price. You'd better leave now," he said. "My next patient is on her way up. She's Catholic. Most of my patients are Catholic. It's their way of birth control. In France the most common method of birth control is still abortions."

Outside, as we walked crosstown, I told Simon: "I think this guy's a bit weird, could even be a phony. But you've got a great scoop kid, this is the first interview he's ever given. But what about notes? You didn't take a single note or even record him."

Simon did not answer. He had his story for his

366

Masters thesis. It was the fan letter to Rappaport written as a poem. And his thesis had ended:

"Nat Nat Rappapor

A Hindu brought you to my shore

Gandhi's spirit to the fore

No more poor Margaret Sangamo

One day like Hamburger Joe

You too, Nat Rappapor

You too, no mo…"

2

Simon's student advisor, Dan Goldstein, an alumnus, who had done a stint with *The New York Times* as Assistant Sunday Editor, a lean, heavily bespectacled character out of a Hank Ketcham comic strip, had a conniption when he saw the paper. He decided to flunk Simon. But before that he summoned him to a private meeting and hollered:

"Simon, this is the last straw. This stuff is shit. You're glorifying a goddamn butcher, and you've forgotten the first thing you ought to know about journalism –fairness – the duty to get the other side. And besides, as a Jew you're saying that Catholics are the most abortion-happy people in the world. You'll get slaughtered. We'll all get slaughtered. And I'm sick of your poetry. You've flunked, kiddo."

Simon argued: "Why should there be another side to the truth? There's no other side to Viet Nam. Or to Hitler."

And Goldstein screamed: "Get out."

I told Simon: "That was the wrong argument, man. Maybe there are two sides. Ho Chi Minh is no saint, and nor is Nixon or Dean Rusk or Kissinger. And if God was on Hitler's side then dammit we were the other side against both of them." Simon wasn't interested in polemics. He wanted to organize a revolt. He said America was insane. They were all insane.

He asked for a student body meeting which the Quaker types did not attend. And he read them his Ode to Rappaport. And they applauded. Just as they had applauded Hamburger Joe. And they pledged that if Goldstein flunked Simon they would all refuse their degrees. Goldstein relented and Simon won his Masters. Columbia buckled under to the same forces that had taken on Lyndon Johnson.

Simon was a silent revolutionary. He had organized the collection of pigs' blood to be thrown on draft registers inside the university President's office but had led the action from the rear. During the first semester he had – again from the rear – led a student body movement to abolish the grading system in grad school, and the Dean, an arch-Whittier conservative who probably polka-dotted his pubic hair to match his bow tie, capitulated. I rebelled.

I said at the crucial meeting: "You cannot democratize the brain. You've got to win or lose or come second or third. Education doesn't level people. It uplifts them." In Raipur, the shikar unified us, cemented us, we competed, but the best shot received the smiles and adulation at the end. "Or you guys think that Keats and Bukowski are the same."

I wasn't shouted down. They didn't shout down foreign students, then. They were simply amused by them. Little Amerikaaners couldn't often tell the difference between Nicaragua and New Foundland. India was, then, well...John Foster Dulles's appendage of the Evil Empire, still full of Maharajas who refused to join SEATO and CENTO to fight the Commies. And mainstream Amerikaaners were a little befuddled by brownskins from Asia who spoke English – phrases, conjunctions, hyphenated pauses, similes, metaphors, Farmers' Daughters' jokes. They were far more comfortable with accents, after all that's what immigrants were supposed to have – "Ling Lee No See" –rather than a Hindu intoning: "It's clear as daylight." And most first generation Indian immigrants preferred to remain anonymous, mysterious, "durn furriners" yet absolutely acceptable in white neighborhoods. Shunning the ghettos. Engineers and doctors, trained in British-legacy Indian institutions, brilliant students, who preferred to live in cohorts. Instant middle Americans, Stars-and-Stripes-flying instant suburban Quakers, never having to start from scratch like other American immigrants, Easter-egg-rolling on the lawns, trying hard to hide their Punjabi English accents, marrying German and Italian immigrant maids, or awaiting arranged marriages from India, a diaspora confined not to closed ghettos but spread across thousands of bedroom communities, celebrating Diwali together, sending money to the Old Country, buying Chevy station wagons, religiously buying the latest Hindi film music cassettes from neighborhood Indian ethnic stores; and later glued to Indian FM on local ethnic radio channels, competing like they dared not compete with each other within the confines of their villages and castes where hierarchies of family and status defined levels of competitiveness, passing each other on the streets of New York and Chicago and Michigan and Washington and Duluth, but never making eye contact because an eyelock may give you away, recognized as a lower caste, or a menial worker from the same village, in the land of mid-twentieth century egalitarianism, wanted to be recognized by a fellow compatriot, if at all, as an equal expatriate, or hoping to be perceived as a Mexican or Puerto Rican, rather than re-establish the prejudices of the past through a fleeting eye contact with Indian eyes which look thousands of years into the past.

3

It made my Ivy League classmates uncomfortable when I joined them in heavy political debate, not as a foreigner who wanted to learn but as one of them who wanted to preach, and therefore it made them uncomfortable when I predicted – much against the wisdom of home-grown Brown and Colgate-educated History and Political Science undergrads – that a Gene McCarthy win in the New Hampshire Primary would cause Johnson to call it a day and that rat-on-heat Humphry would win the Democratic primary. I say this not to seek any recognition for intuitive powers or brilliance of political analysis but only because Ivy League xenophobia combined with the arrival of Nescafe political revolution refused (but only, thankfully for a small period) to recognize anything other than indigenous campus wisdom.

Hal was my partner in that grad-school rebellion against Simon's bullying of the entire faculty. For one thing, we could talk. The head of Broadcast Journalism, for example, a man of courage, who had taken on McCarthyism, would proudly declare himself as a follower of the "Radical Center," and Hal and I would laugh at this oxymoron while most of the class applauded. Hal believed in the trickle-down theory of the embodiment of collective wisdom – not through coercive edicts to cooperate or jackbooted lobotomies – but through the gentle warmth of Rebel Yell and the kikkar forests of Raipur that walked with you and the warmth of fairy tales when Mama tucked us into bed.

I had another personal reason for opposing Simon's no-grading revolution. My first day in grad school was my second day in Manhattan. I had written to Papa a few weeks later:

371

"You worried about the color bar and racism when I left India. There's nothing of that here, at least overtly. I arrived at Penn Station which is full of black and brown and yellow faces. And they're all crooks because they took a hundred dollar bill from me, promising change to carry my baggage to the taxi and I never saw any of it again. The place simply hums and hums. Lights. Buildings so high that our mill chimneys are dwarfed. Nobody sleeps here. You see garbage one minute, the next minute it's gone. The power never fails. If you drop a candy-wrapper from your car the cops catch you and fine you. Shops list prices. You get telephone connections in a day (unlike at home where it takes a year.} You drive on highways at 80 miles an hour. Yes eighty! And they all keep to their lanes. The banks pay your utility bills. The courts decide cases within a month (not in 10 years like at home). They drench government files with pig blood as protest. In the middle of their war in Viet Nam protestors drive in their thousands to surround the Pentagon and nobody arrests them. I've never seen such tolerance of dissent. In fact the cops are tried for false arrests. Their reporters expose their own army's atrocities and that's never considered treason. They've never read the Federalist Papers but they seem to imbibe them. They're polite but not really warm. You just can't simply drop into their homes. The concept of privacy which has no value in our country but which keeps us connected is jealously guarded here. You just don't walk into people's homes or ask them intimate questions. In fact, I just broke up with a friend I considered my best buddy because he was angry that I took a banana out of his fruitbowl without his wife's permission. Crooks shoot each other on the streets and mug innocent people, but they're nabbed pretty quickly, and trials are based not on confessions obtained through torture in police lock-up but on forensic and cross-witnessed evidence. They build their homes within trees. They pull out guns in road-rage and blow each others' brains out if you honk at them or have a 'fender-bender'– a small back-to-front clash of car bumpers.

"I read they're corrupt as hell. Big time mafias controlling the vegetable and trucking and meat and waterfront and pharmaceutical and defense contract markets and punishing honest bureaucrats, banishing them into no-jobs, do-nothing Siberias, defaming them, branding them KGB agents, driving them insane. But brave journalists and honest judges can whip these fascists into shreds. Still, there's little evidence of Big Government here. Because Jefferson warned them, Don't trust your government, bind and shackle it with the chains of your Constitution. And arrested criminals have powers against the government and are given free lawyers if they can't hire their own and the big debate here is about criminals having more rights than the wronged. They argue about abortions, the war, the length of hair, they're xenophobic, with each new immigrant group more suspicious about the next one, They pursue money as a spiritual goal. As for your concern about racism... I really don't know. I've never experienced it coz I can curse worse than the lowliest midshipman on their Seventh Fleet. They support Black and Brown dictators all over the world. In the late fifties they still had segregated bathrooms. But you've heard of Kennedy and the Civil Rights Movement. Indians, especially the fair ones in saris, they did not know what to do with. They thought they were Russian tourists and let us into the whites-only toilets where we sprouted White Cloud dingleberries. But that's all over today. At least the overt part of it. They're all mad, especially my friend Simon, whom you should meet some day."

But what had thrilled the Shikari the most was one of my earliest letters about my first shikar in Manhattan. First day in grad school. Unprecedented teachers' strike in Brooklyn's Ocean-Hill Brownsville. Mayor Lindsay in a quandary. Professor Russ Carlton tells me to go write a thousand-word story on it, an interview with the out-of-school kids and how they feel about it. I know nothing about Manhattan except that when I settled in my 75th Street and River Side Drive beehive apartment and went looking for grub at night and smelled frying flounder, and grilled jumbo shrimp and honey-glazed pork ribs, which I couldn't afford, and the aromas, not as good as, but close to those of the Raipur dining table, propelled me to a cheap Mexican restaurant to eat kidney beans flavored with bacon grease, passing Gays butterfly-touched my buttocks. I tell Carlton, Sir, I don't know how to get there. He says to cut the bullshit and call him Russ, and that I should take the subway. Subway? What the fuck is that? I'd heard from Papa about the Tube in London, never seen it, and believed it was some underground pedestrian crossing. And Russ says, You don't know what a subway is? Jesus, what the hell are you doing here? You're a journalist. Go ask someone. He was not being a racist. Just a tough editor. And so I ask Simon. And he thinks I'm kidding and laughs, and then I ask Hal and he guides me to the IRT and says Just go downtown. I don't even know what a token is and the guy in the booth laughs at me until I put on an Indian accent and he takes pity on me and actually teaches me how to revolve the turnstile and get into this underground train, that's all that a goddam subway is. And I'm on the IRT train scared shitless with junkies and lushes looking at my breast pocket with its ten dollars, and I get off when I can take the scare no more and I walk left and right after I climb up the stairs out of the subway station and map my course just like the Shikari had taught me in the scrub forests of Raipur and I find these kids inside a fenced lot playing ball. And I pull the Hindu shit on them right away. Doin' what comes naturally. Hey, you guys, I've heard about his strike last week when I was in India, and the government's sent me down to interview some of you kids for the Asian press. May we talk? Great kids. Black, white, Chicano. India? They say. We've read Kipling. You read Mowgli? One even says Gunga Din. Jeez, I say to myself. Better educated than those Ivy League turds in Columbia. I say, Hey guys, do you mind if I can talk to some of your parents about this strike, I mean, how they feel all about this, and they say, Sure, why don't you wait for us at that Choc Full O'Nuts. And five of these great little punks in their baseball caps come in with their mothers, who look me up and down, and I speak in heavy King's accent, and they think I'm exotic, and I'm going to tell their story to the world, and Me, Hindu, in Brooklyn is now in an exclusive press conference, with kids and mothers, taking notes, and using a pocket camera, and the kids are talking and the mothers are cussing out the teachers, their husbands, their kids, the mayor, the school board, and an Italian breaks down in front of the others and confesses that the crisis and mental strain have forced her into her first affair – with her Haitian janitor. And her friend quips: "Well, who knows, we might even have a Baby Doc in Brownsville."

The Shikari's son tracks his way back to the subway. IRT. D Train. Broadway and 116th. Record time. Types out his story on a portable Brothers within an hour. Leads with the Brooklyn Baby Doc quip. And the next evening he gets an A Plus from Russ. And he reads out the story to the rest of the class. (God, Mama, Papa, what fun playing Hindu in New York).

And dammit! Simon, had to go and stage a revolution to abolish grades within a few days after I scored my first straight A's the traditional way.

CHAPTER XXIII

1

And on that Christmas curry dinner, years later, where Lee was also present, I'm reminding Simon about how crazy it was to abolish grades and scare off teachers, and Simon pouts into a smile and says, If I didn't I'd never be a poet. And look at Lee, he's a great musician, he's a great sculptor and if he lets the system fuck his genius he'd never be one. And Hal says, but Simon, you're not really a poet, and Lee's a Neanderthal, at which Simon bristles and says, All that formal shit destroys you, all that tradition sucks, man, you just become what you are.

Wait a minute, Simon, I say, you suck. How can you break from tradition unless you know what tradition is? How the fuck do you know what you're breaking from? How do you know you're creating something new? Even the computer guys who will soon arrive know what mathematical Ghost Quantities are. We Hindus discovered the meaning and importance of Zero, and from there we went into mathematics.

377

Simon says, We're Impressionists. We're rebels...and Hal says, But do you know what you're rebelling against? How can you break from something unless you understand it perfectly? And Simon said he had this great pal, an artist, Truman, who made these great paintings, he threw tar and kerosene on the ceilings of his loft and set them on fire and the art hung out, pulled into downward shapes by gravity in the shape of stalactites and stalagmites. And Hal said that he could do the same thing with his hemorrhoids. And Simon did not find that funny on that Christmas eve on that Indian Summer when the temperature was a freak 78 degrees Fahrenheit.

And I said, Simon you're made of poetry, just like America is, but you're still not a poet because Hamburger Joe is not Burroughs. Ginzberg learned to read and learn before he broke from tradition. Shakespeare could have learned from Burroughs. But you've only learned from Burrough's rebellion and ignored his classicism and the reasons behind, not his escape, into, but his playful entry into the world of Dada-ism . You can copycat his forays into flippancy but – yet – not his literary Odyssey. Simon, why do you ignore your own history? If you refuse to learn about your own ancient pogroms and exiles, and think you're being a rebel by lighting dildo-shaped candles on Hannukah, you're nothing more than a copycat Yid. If Chaim Potok did that, we'd laugh with reverence, but if you did it, we'd say you're not even a Jew, a man named Margolis but without the Gemara. So what makes you think you're a poet?

Lee was thumping on his guitar with the back of a

hair brush, and he said, not looking up, Well, we've always been taught that in America you forget your past, you forget everything and start from scratch. And Hal said, That's bullshit, in America you never listen to those WASP bastards who never live in the present and never will, but will preach this apostasy. In America you are always the immigrant, you love your past no matter how cruel it was, no matter how Godless, and you live to learn from it and transform it into a new God, without which you're doomed to condemn your teachers and your saints and your Gods. Condemn them by all means, but learn about them first, know them as your friends or your enemies, and then and only then break from them. And Simon, what's all this about Impressionism? Do you know what it's all about?

My curry, I said, is Impressionistic, because I defied my father's wisdom in how much turmeric and garlic to add before I made it into a new religious feast. (My guests found the metaphor a little too Indian for their intellectual taste buds, so I continued on another line). Simon, I said, remember when we visited Rappaport, and I said you had a great scoop? Well why the hell didn't you write it as a report and then end it with your poem? Past. Tradition. Rebellion. Revolution. Wisdom. What say you Simon?

And Simon says, Everything is here, today. The past, no mo. And I say, True Simon, fuck the past, but let it guide you, not imprison your mind. How do you know that without knowing the past you are simply not its prisoner over and over again? Like your artist who thinks

379

he's broken from the caveman by growing stalactites on his loft ceiling? And your Impressionism, Simon, what of it. I say, You always said you wanted to read Pound and Joyce. Did you ever? Here's Pound on Joyce in 1914: 'Freedom from sloppiness is so rare in contemporary English prose that one might well say simply that Mr Joyce's book of short stories is prose free from sloppines... he deals with subjective things but he presents them with such clarity of outline that he might be dealing with locomotives or with builders' specifications... Impressionism, however, has two meanings...or gives two different 'impressions.' There is a school of prose writers or of verse writers...whose forerunner was Stendhal and whose founder was Flaubert. The followers of Flaubert deal in exact presentation (and) often neglect intensity, selection, and concentration...They are perhaps the most clarifying... the most beneficial forces in modern writing...There is another set... of verse writers... who founded themselves on the pictures of Monet... and talked about pink pigs blossoming on a hillside,...These impressionists... are a rosy, floribund bore... Joyce's merit ...his most engaging merit is that he carefully avoids telling you a lot you don't want to know. He presents his people swiftly and vividly, he does nor sentimentalize over them, he does not weave convolutions.'"

2

Hal was into his fifth Rebel Yell. We could hear the

Santas jingling their bells on Broadway and the upstairs neighbors singing Seema's Carols. Lee's still banging his guitar and says he's playing a Christmas carol. And I argue with Lee for the first time. Lee, I say, maybe you're a great musician. But why are you not learning to be one? And he says, like Simon does about his poetry, I am an artist. Artists don't have to learn. And I say Lee, do you know what a symphony is? Do you know that the Beatles learned Elizabethan music before they got into pop? Or that your own great Jazz musicians know every movement of Brahms, and not the kind of bowel movement that comes out of your shit guitar. (I was angry, well kind of). What's a symphony, Lee? Who gives a shit, he says. And I say, maybe you should because you'll then be better than the Byrds, you'll learn about compositions in three or more movements, similar to a sonata, but with more varied elements, about overtures, harmonious combinations of elements, about symphonic poems, forms of tones scored for an orchestra, developed first by Liszt in the nineteenth century and honed by Richard Strauss who spiced the stuff with literary or pictorial plots.

Lee says that the Beatles learned from Ravi Shankar, and now I jump with joy. That last bit about symphonies, I said, I picked up from a dictionary lent to me by a teacher in my Indian high school. But I did learn to learn Brahms. But Ravi Shankar, that's all you know? There's Sarod player Ali Akbar Khan, the Sitarist Nikhil Bannerjee to whom Ravi Shankar still cannot light a candle as he cannot to Ustad Vilayat Khan, and vocalists Bhim Sen Joshi and Malik Arjun Mansur. Saints you haven't even

381

heard of. You know how old they are? Hundreds. They sing and play God. There's no other answer. No mortal dare criticize their art. They learned their music at the feet of their Gurus from different traditions of rendering the ragas that were passed down from the Rishis thousands of years ago, who claimed that the music came directly from meditations and from the basic sound of OM. They started at the age of five and practiced, starting at 4 a.m. after washing the feet of their gurus and worshipping their deities, and went without food for days while they practiced their art, a form of prayer, yoga, meditation, until they perfected the first pure sound and were told how to know whether they had resonated with the universal sounds of Creation, and then in their thirties and forties with the blessings of their Gurus, they were allowed to improvise, little by little, but never breaking from form or belief, because only by sticking to belief could they become non-believers, and those who evolved became rebels and maestros and teachers, and raaga Impressionists, and fusion and fission musicians, allowed commerce and commercialization, and the freedom of guiltless copulation and freedom from Puritannical slavery and the sexual continence they had practiced as they learned at the feet of their Gurus, to take on in their sixties and seventies and eighties multiple mistresses in Europe and India and America as part of the ritual of artistic prayer, which the West believed was Oriental sexotica, but which our musical saints recognized simply as lust to be kept far out of reach of their art because while they live and lived, their art had already passed on, the years immeasurable, the inheritors unknown, the music beyond question, yet mocking the very Gods who had sent it to earth. Wrapped in clay and mango leaves and guava scents and the fragrance of monsoon drops on the hot July baking sand-dunes, the earthy musk of cow dung, and falling sheesham leaves and morning mists and dew and the crescent moon and the religious fasts of Muslims, and the mud of the Ganges and the beauty of Flaubert's prose and Monet's pigs.

Simon says he doesn't care too much about tradition and all that stuff, but he freaks out on Indian classical music and Lee says the same and for the first time Hal agrees with the both of them. And I play a cassette of Nikhil Bannerji — the only musician whom Ravi Shankar openly admires—playing Raag Darbari on the sitar. And Christmas Eve is turning into Christmas morning, and Simon says, How come you Indians go in for so much of that tradition stuff – and this question after the whole evening's verbal outpourings – and I say, We don't, really. We try and break from it when we find a better way. And Lee says, Ya, but all this heavy stuff about your family and your old man. If I had listened to my old man, he says, I would never have been a musician. And I say, Lee, you are not, at least not yet. And Simon says, My mom would have put me into real estate, so I don't see them much, and I would not have been a poet, and Hal says, Simon, you're not one, at least not yet. And Hal says, well, I listened to my old man and he taught me how to drink bourbon and I learned to read. And I say, I still talk to my old man and my Mama and I learned how

383

to be a shikari and shove pellets up your white asses and how to be a rebel. Simon, I say, why don't you learn from them, your folks, what are you shy about, it's no longer the Jewish ghetto. You're like us late Indian immigrants who hate to look into each other's eyes in the street in shame of recognition of the past. My God, Simon, read Algren, a great para from him about the sentenced whore in Chicago: "Blinking out of the window of an Ogden Avenue Trolley at the sunlight she hadn't seen for almost a year, 'I guess I was lucky I done that time,' the girl philosophized. Chicago still looks pretty strong and America still looks mighty mighty.' Still nobody seems to be laughing."

Lee stopped thumping his guitar. Hal switched to brandy. Serita and I pulled out some Rolling Rock beer from the ice box. You guys have simply sentenced yourselves, Serita said. You can never be rebels unless you learn how to digest, imbibe and then change the past. Your parents and those immigrants from Poland and Drohobycz, and Russia knew how to do it. And they still kept in touch with relatives from the Old Country. It was the old that made America new. And people like you, the new, are who are making America old. (Serita liked to talk after a few red wines and a beer and she was not to be stopped, and Simon who had a mad crush on her and Lee who feared her because she thought his dildoes were shit, kept silent) And Serita went on, To defy God you've got to know him. Maybe you should meet your parents to learn more about the Old Testament (and Hal said, Glory Be).

Many years later, in the mid-nineties, Serita would write to me:

"That was an interesting Christmas. I wish Erica Jong had written her treatise on Henry Miller then. I could have buttressed my lecture, asking those guys, at least to try and understand their parents, or even to talk to them, by giving them the example of Jong trying to discover her ideological enemy, or someone she'd rather forget as too powerful a symbol of past oppressions, and discovering rebellion in tradition. This memorable passage: '...It is hard today to grasp how electric (Miller's) voice was in 1934. The feminist critique of the sixties came in to bury Henry under rhetoric – just as simplistic in its way as the simplistic rhetoric of male supremacy. But the feminist critique, valid as it is, neglects to address the main question Henry Miller poses: how does a writer raise a voice? How does a writer take the chaos of life and transform it into art? The raising of a voice is the red thread through chaos. The raising of a voice is the essence of freedom. It is where every writer, every person, must begin.'"

CHAPTER XXIV

1

That Christmas dinner Lee had asked me, Well, it's good that parents bring you up, but what did you really get out of them? And I said, Warmth and Spirit, and Wonderful Stories. And I learned to hate regimentation and authoritarianism unless it had something to do with acquiring the spirit and discipline of rebellion and freedom. You made a Ganesha, I told Lee. Well that's great. But would you treasure it because you copied it from somewhere and made a good likeness or because what I learned about this Hindu Elephant God from my Mom? Lee simply shakes his head and says, Go on.

And I tell him the story that Mama told me when I was about five years old. Lord Shiva was powerfully in love with his wife, Parvati. Uncontrollably libidinous when it came to her. To the extent that he reveled in watching her bathe. Parvati, wife, consort, life's companion to Shiva, however, was fiercely jealous of her privacy. When she bathed and perfumed herself with sandalwood, she insisted on keeping tightly shut the door to her private bath-house. But Shiva would remain at the door watching her through a crack in it. She remonstrated with him, gently, but when Shiva persisted, the Goddess Parvati, using the dirt that came off her body created her son, Ganesha. She instructed him to guard the door to her private bath and to let nobody come near it. On the first day that Ganesha assumed this dutiful chore for his mother, Shiva came to the door. And Ganesha blocked his path. Shiva, the God of Destruction from which all new creation emerges, was livid. He pulled out his sword and decapitated Ganesha on the spot.

When Parvati discovered what had happened she went mad with rage. She summoned from within herself, Shakti, which she herself personified – the female power before which the gods trembled. Her Shakti created an army of women warriors who vowed to kill every Brahmin in the world. It was a swift battle in which all but a few Brahmins were decimated. The sages appealed to Shiva for help. He pleaded with his wife, begged her forgiveness but she remained impassive and unrelenting. She carried Ganesha's headless corpse to Shiva and demanded that Shiva restore Ganesha to life immediately, for only Shiva could give back life to one he had himself slain. Hurriedly, Shiva, swallowing his pride, saw an elephant lying dead on the battlefield and he joined the elephant's head to Ganesha's body, and Ganesha, with his new elephant face smiled because Parvati commanded her husband to love her son as his own. Peace broke out between the warring women and the defending army of male Brahmins, the keepers of the faith and the knowledge passed on by the Gods. Parvati withdrew the army of Shakti into within herself, she bowed to her husband and he blessed her power, and she blessed him and he put a red *tilak* on her forehead.

Lee listened attentively and asked, Is this a true story? And Hal said to him, Lee it's true because like all Sanskrit literature, most of it unwritten, it is a symphony. There is no history or tragedy. And all symphonies are true. Universal harmonies that travel back and forth between earth and heaven. Sanskrit symphonies, or the song of Nelson Algren. And Hal recites from Algren:

> *"The Pottawattamies were much too square. They left*
>
> *nothing behind*
>
> *but their dirty river.*
>
> *While we shall leave, for remembrance, one rust iron heart.*
>
> *The city's rusty heart, that holds*
>
> *Both the hustler and the square.*
>
> *Takes them both and holds them there.*
>
> *For keeps and a single day."*

2

It turns into Christmas morning and there's a breeze

from across the Hudson, and Simon says to me, You're thousands of years old and you have the advantage of having grown up in India in neighborhoods that are still neighborhoods and learned your philosophy and stuff. And I tell Simon, that guys like him and Lee are themselves partly to blame for destroying their own neighborhoods instead of breaking out of them after imbibing their tradition. No, Simon, says. I'm a poet and I don't have to be part of any past. There is no past in America, man. This is a crazy country, it's insane, that's why Hemingway, and Gertrude Stein and Miller and Fitzgerald left for Europe. I reply:

You have a past that's richer than Europe and now it's even richer that these Asians, and Hindus like me are here. And there are more libraries here than anywhere else in the world. And your sense of humor, it's great. I even think Bob Hope whom you call a fascist is funny as hell. And I laugh and remind them of a joke Simon told me about New York that maybe only a New Yorker would understand – about this young couple that's fucking in the nude in Yankee stadium in the middle of a ball game, and a cop tells them to cut it out or he'd arrest them, and the young guy, still naked, tells the cop in a hurt voice, "But officer, we're married."

And Lee says, The cop was not the Puritan in this case, the young couple was. Just like I think I'm a Puritan. Do you know that I never screw a whore unless I first make her fall in love with me? And dildoes don't count. And we all say, Yeah? How? A recent episode comes to

Lee's mind. He's with this hooker in Las Vegas and he's buying her drinks. And she's beautiful and wears a huge Hedda Hopper hat. And Lee takes her up to his room and he's kissing her. And he wants to stroke her hair and she's lying on her back and she adamantly refuses to take her hat off. And while Lee's into a deep kiss, she disengages and pukes all over his face, and Lee screams in fear and she runs into the bathroom and gets a towel and cologne and gently scrubs Lee clean and Lee's a bit mad and says, What's with you, do I have bad breath or something? She's really apologizing now and when her explanations run out, she says, Well, I'll tell you something. I have cancer and I'm on chemotherapy and it makes me sick and puke all the time, and I have to do all this hustling to pay for it. And Lee says, What bullshit, you're just careless when you're drunk, and why did you not tickle your throat and get it all out in the sink before you started our petting. And the whore is really upset now, and suddenly she pulls off her enormous hat and she's bald. Now do you believe me? she asks. And Lee begins to cry and she's rocking him like a baby, and for two years, Lee writes to her and sends her money that his parents send him, and she's in love with him and when he's sure he makes love to her for the first time, and before she dies he carves out a buffalo horn dildo for her and tries to put it inside her burial casket and the undertaker throws him out and tells him he'll call the cops if he as much as even tries to attend her funeral.

And Hal says, You've been reading too much Roald Dahl. And Lee looks really hurt, and I tell Hal, it's not uncommon in India. In some of the best whorehouses in Delhi and Lucknow, you just can't throw bucks and get pussy. We have a tradition. You have to court the whore. Listen to her sing for you. Send her love letters. Arrange for secret trysts, know which perfume to use. I know. It took me one year of trying one of them to fall in love with me before I could get inside her pants.

So how should we greet Christmas morning, we wonder, and Simon says that since we've done some great curry food and listened to Ganesha stories, why not a Hindu prayer? And I say, this for all of us. Every Indian probably knows this by heart. It's from the Vedas and it goes back over 3,000 years. I say, repeat after me:

Tat Savitur Vareniam

Bhargo Devasya Dhimahi

Dhiyo Yo Nah Prachodayat

I explain, "Let our meditation be on the glorious light of Savitri. May this light banish darkness and illumine our minds." It's a mantra, and it works, I say. Repeat it thrice a day. Won't do you any harm. All you're asking is that your mind be freed of the accumulated garbage of darkness and negativity and hatred and jealousy.

Gimme more, says Simon, enthused, and I pull out Mascaro's translation from Sanskrit of one the most beautiful hymns from the Rig Veda. Simon, I say, when I was talking about tradition and all that I wanted to give you the example of Mascaro who lectured at Oxford on the Spanish mystics and learned Sanskrit and Pali before he translated Vedic hymns and the *Bhagwad Gita*. That's the kind of penance I was talking about when I was talking about the Great Masters of Indian Classical music. So here's some more music, Simon, from the Rig Veda:

"There was not then what is nor what is not. There was no sky, and no heaven beyond the sky. What power was there? Where? Who was that power? Was there an abyss of fathomless waters?

"There was neither death nor immortality then. No signs were there of night or day. The ONE was breathing by its own power, in deep peace. Only the ONE was: there was nothing beyond.

"Darkness was hidden in darkness. The all was fluid and formless. Therein, in the void, by the fire of fervor arose the ONE.

"And in the ONE arose love. Love the first seed of soul. The truth of this the sages found in their hearts: seeking in their hearts with wisdom, the sages found that bond of union between being and non-being.

"Who knows in truth? Who can tell us how and whence arose this universe? The gods are later than its beginning: who knows therefore whence comes this creation?

"Only that god who sees in highest heaven: he knows whence comes this universe, and whether it was made or uncreated. He only knows, or perhaps he knows not."

Simon said, Wow. Who wrote that? How come it's not in most anthologies of poems? I said, it was never written, Simon, it was spoken. More than 3,000 years ago before writing was even invented. It's doubt and faith. Revolutionary Indian literature to which most of you Ivy Leaguers are blinded by your instant poetry and instant music and your love for Quaker-Indians who learn to walk with dead eyes, their arms swinging diagonally across their backs with each step. And Hal had an another surprise for Simon – that Alexander Hamilton went to India in the late eighteenth century and then went to Europe and taught Sanskrit to the renowned German man of letters Friedrich von Schlegel who spread it in the rest of Europe and the *Bhagwad Gita* was even translated into Latin. We were having fun, and I told Lee, You for one, Lee, should at least start learning from Manitas de Plata. After all. Lee, you're an American gypsy. And believe me, the back of your hairbrush will really come in handy in banging out *bulerias* – when you want to mock and scoff at turgid tradition

CHAPTER XXV

1

On that Indian Summer Christmas day, in an old Chevy station wagon that belonged to Lee we traveled to the village of Seneca in Maryland, just out of Washington, many years after Hurricane Agnes had turned the whole place into a near rubble, and where the Potomac, mostly languid and unfrozen that winter stretched for a couple of miles towards the Virginia shore bordered on each shore by woods and ferns that had grown into huge trees, and Fletcher's boat house that rented out canoes and row boats that could accommodate six people easily, was still open. It was winter in Raipur, and that Christmas day I had longed to be back in the marshes and the *jheels* with the Shikari and our troupe and I convinced Hal and Simon and Lee and Serita that on this warm day we should be on water, in a boat, instead of sleeping over our Manhattan hang-overs and reciting Vedic hymns and hammering de Plata into poor Lee's dildo-headed romanticism. And they kind of thought it was a good idea, and we invited Inger to join us, which was, maybe not such a good idea because Simon and Lee both loved this tall, strong woman, with strong calves and straight Nordic blonde hair and sang better than Judy Collins and loved Simon and Lee in turns, never simultaneously, but with equal enthusiasm and sexual intensity whichever man she was with. She worked in a bookstore and each time that Lee was out of their apartment and a particular dildo was missing throughout the period of his absence, Michael would fret and stomp his feet in jealousy and refer to his room-mate as "that pervert" and woudn't talk to him after his return.

As we drove to Seneca, sexual diplomacy dictated that Hal drive with Inger and me in the front bench seat, and Serita and Lee and Simon in the back. In Seneca we got rid of the smells of the New Jersey Turnpike, particularly that acrid, pungent, skunk-like acid smell that enters your pores as you drive past Newark and the refineries and the flaring gas above the smoke-stacks, and Mid-town Manhattan's smells of steely fire-escapes and Christmas Day doggy-ick and brown paper bags with half-empty whisky pints and the stale grease of last night's french fries, and the ladies who had perfumed their faces to walk their poodles without washing or brushing their teeth, and Seneca smelled of the Potomac, not like it does when it flows under Key Bridge in Washington, but as it must have done hundreds of years ago when the steam-boats plied and horses pulled barges right to the entrance of the Chesapeake Bay.

There's not even a ripple in the water on this early Christmas afternoon and Fletcher says it's a great time to be out on a boat and there's a half-moon still out in the blue afternoon sky. And I take the oars while Serita reads and Lee holds Inger's hand while Simon glowers at him and the seagulls and swallows float in and out and other rowboats take to the Christmas waters. Inger says:

"I wish it could be like this forever. Can you feel, there's no time? And is the air breathing us, or are we breathing the air?"

Hal laughs and says: "Knut Hamsun probably answered that question many, many year ago. A good Christian answer from a good Christian man."

And Simon, who has still not taken his eyes off the Inger-Lee hand-clasp, says: "Christianity sucks. Judaism sucks. They all suck. This country sucks. They're all insane. I'll be out of here as soon as I get the chance. Jeez, I took our Hindu pal here to meet my folks, coz he insisted that good friends must always introduce their pals to their parents, and she kept stuffing us with Lox. And she even offered to darn his socks for him, and kept complaining I don't see them enough, and lectured to me when he said he writes to his mom and dad in India once a week. And she tells him, See, and Simon doesn't even call me on the phone."

I said, Simon that was a great gesture. You'll see how good you'll feel about that in the near future. You'll miss them when they're gone, and you'll never be able to learn what you refused to learn from them, and you won't even know where to look for it in the Gemara or even in the Gita."

The sun had warmed up even more and the boat rocking ever so gently and Hal was sleeping, and Lee, trying to get back for last night, said: "But you Hindus are just crystal ball gazers. I mean you guys, all you want to do is predict what's going to happen in the future."

And I said: "But Lee, what about some you guys? Most of you guys. Your entire effort is to conquer old age and death. While we in the East simply discover new symphonies in death."

Lee asks: "So what's wrong in conquering death? That's what all science should aim at. Or why not abolish hygiene, vaccines, excommunicate Pasteur, stop all research on digitalis and beta blockers and Cyclic-AMP, and catecholamines, and thyroid preparations, and insulin, and cholesteramine...."

And I say, while Inger hums, and the boat is almost at a standstill in the middle of the river: "That's hardly the point. And Lee, maybe you should be a doctor. Healing has been blessed since Biblical times. And the relief of pain is a noble pursuit, as is the relief from the hellish torture of hunger and privation. But to what extent? There is such a thing as iatrogenesis, medical overkill. The pursuit of everlasting life, freedom from death –while we are alive –would stand the logic of you and me and the universe and this boat on its head. Our

398

scriptures put it very simply. Before you are born you're not here. After you're dead, you're not here either. So if you don't miss life before you're born, how can you miss it after you're gone? It's mathematical. Zero equals zero. You only miss life when you're in it, when you're alive. In metaphysical logic this craving makes no sense, but in the logic of living it does."

Lee says: "That's all that Hindu stuff again. If your aim is not to conquer death then just let everything be. Babies perish in their cradles. Let tuberculosis spread. Pull out all the life-giving machines, abolish Aid to Families with Dependent Children, the Office of Economic Opportunity, blast the World Health Organization, give in to the Nazis."

I say: "No. And I come to this argument in this boat not because I remember my scriptures but because it makes perfect sense to fight for life and sustenance and comfort while you're alive. If I believed in God, and maybe I do, I think that's what God would command me to do in order to bring more beauty into my own existence. He is not the creator of injustice or ethics. To Him it's all the same, anyway. He simply passes on wisdom and sits back and sees what you do with it, your heaven and hell are your own. And therefore, and this may frighten you, YOU are God. And you have duties while on this earth. Lee, in simply seeking to conquer death, and knowing you may never do it, I sense despair in you, dejection, confusion. I am the same way. And the only voice that has ever made sense to me is that of Krishna in his first piece of advice to the warrior Arjuna who was weak with indecision and at having to take on the evil empire, not knowing what was wrong or right but Arjuna ultimately did what was right because, while his enemies were unable to do this, Arjuna was ultimately able to awaken and listen to and find the God within himself, the voice of Krishna, who said, and Lee I love these lines: "Whence this lifeless dejection, Arjuna, in this hour, the hour of trial? Strong men know not despair, Arjuna, for this wins neither heaven nor earth… Fall not into degrading weakness, for this becomes not a man who is a man. Throw off this ignoble discouragement, and arise like a fire that burns all before it."

Hal was on the oars now and the boat had picked up some speed and Simon was reading something. And Hal said: "I've been thinking. If you even cut out all the words of the sages and the metaphysical bullshit and even if you have never read a word of Kant or Heidegger or Hesse, look at this through plain common sense, Lee. Suppose we conquer death. We all live forever, whatever that means. Where would we start? With plankton? Fine. Then plankton, if they were to survive forever would not need water. Or let's jump to the human species. Suppose there were a billion of us still alive, and always to live. Then we would not need oxygen or minerals, or plants or animals for food, or noses to breathe with and mouths to eat with or cocks and wombs to reproduce with, for why should we need anything, including procreation if we were to survive forever? There would be no conversation, no philosophy, no disease, no medicine.

400

And where would these billion eternal earthlings have come from? Either created by parents who are still alive, and should, logically not have created us, because immortal people don't need to create other people, or created by some instant act of chemistry. And would we grow up from babies into adults? Why? Because ageing is the process towards death, and if there's no death why should there be ageing? Or knowledge. By that logic we would be a billion babies in our cradles without need of nourishment or air or water – why the need if there is no death, and life simply sustains life on its own?

"Or take another example. Suppose all human beings were granted the wish that if they ate their whole grains and beta carotene and skimmed milk, and controlled their intake of liquor and stopped smoking, they would be guaranteed a life of 200 years at which they would drop dead. But what would happen then? There would be but one aim – to live to be 200 and all philosophy and inquiry and the neurosis of human relations and poetry would come to an end. And there would be no need to debate on the existence of God because a guaranteed lifespan would eliminate any other purpose in life. And imagine what would happen if all one billion fell dead at one time when they reached their 200th birthday. Would they all shake hands the previous night and say goodbye? And why would they need children and support systems? And if they obeyed the dietary laws of guaranteed longevity, would enemies and fascists and dictators never be slain in wars? Or, in another option, suppose we are all given total immunity from freedom from any kind of disease and guaranteed a certain lifespan would not the food chain and the bacteria and viruses cease to be, and to what end? All you would know from beginning to end is that there is no beginning and there is no end. All I know is that death is the only logic, the only life-force, that gives shape and form to life."

And Lee asks: "Hal, you really believe all this stuff?"

And Hal says: "I think, belief is tougher than science. It's more hellish. In science the proof is iron-clad once its mathematical and logical parameters are defined. But you can hardly measure belief with science. You can only challenge it with doubt or ridicule. That's why death is so important. It unites all of us in mystery and fear. But death is the only scientific equation and scientific proof of life in which metaphysics and science combine to produce faith and belief."

And I clap for Hal, and I say: "I don't care about you Hal but I want to live forever on this boat on the Potomac and in the wild marshes of Raipur and be oblivious of everything. And maybe that is what the sages call pure consciousness, Me without my name, or this boat or Serita, or my face, or my thoughts, but just me floating everywhere."

And Hal says: "I think if I read the scriptures carefully that's what the mystics say is God's mischief. He creates life out of love and then lets it grow gradually into ever deepening consciousness, it's like an eternal orgasm. If the transmigration of the soul makes any sense it probably means that You as a person, with your personality and hates and desires, and names, cease to exist but the energy that inspires you and breathes "life" into you, formless and eternal simply remains an energy without a personality and ego…"

2

The boat begins to rock a little. Lee has just finished a pint of Baccardi, and he says, I see it all, I see it all, and he's rowing in the other direction, towards where the calm Potomac turns into a delta of dangerous, eddying, leaping, jumping, frothing rapids, clashing against boulders and throwing up waves, and spinning and twisting around thousands of little forested islands, until it speeds breakneck and heads towards Great Falls near Virginia's Chain Bridge where hundreds of canoeists die each year, and Lee is rowing towards the rapids, and Inger tries to snatch the oars from him to row us back into the main stream, but Lee is as strong as a horse, and he's saying, I understand it all I know it all, I have received the knowledge, When we pray to God, He's not just someone at the Altar or in the sky, He's listening and being part of every twinkling dew Drop, He speaks through me now, Like that Rig Veda stuff the Hindu read us, ONE does not mean, NOT TWO, it means ONE, and the boat is already in the rapids heading down, and we're saying Row back, Row back, Lee but he's rowing us into hell, and screaming, It means ONE – Five billion men, Hega-quatrillion ants, hooeygrassmongousmultibillion feathers, cloves, gills, butts, Mahamultibillioshitshit-trillion stars and phantoms, Biliionmega-hegabillionmanitasdapalacotrillion musicians and guitar strings, Hegahexalollyhedrillion zoospores, the ONE peeking out of every stomata, the ONE in daily sperm-counts of Fortkoxhectamegamultizillion sparrows, viaducts, Egyptian Mummies, Roman Gladiators, Cossacks, Crusades, Constantinople, the ONE in Tratratratrumpetillion Helens of Troy, the ONE and the Hexamegahooquadrillion dildoes shooting into the sky with Neil Armstrong... Lee's unstoppable...

And Simon screams, This guy's a stark raving lunatic, throw him out of the boat, you were right Hal, a guy that's got to die should die immediately, imagine if we had to live with this maniac for 200 years or forever, and strong-calved Inger snatches the oars from Lee, and Lee is still screaming, He whom the Gods want to destroy, they first drive mad, and Simon says, the guy's insane, it's because of nuts like him that I want to leave America...

And now Hal has the oars while Lee sits silently in the middle of the boat, banging his guitar with his hairbrush and sings, He to whom the Gods want to give wisdom they first drive insane... The boat is well into the rapids, banging into rocks, banging against banks of small islands and then rapidly being pulled back into one of the hundreds of fast flowing forks of water. And I scream above the rapids, We better dock at the first possible island that looks safe and within sight of the main river, and the low-hanging branches are scratching our shoulders and bodies until we spot a small body of what looks like slower and shallower water, and Serita and Inger and I dip the oar and it touches the bottom, waist-deep. And Hal and I are good swimmers, but without lifejackets, we jump into the river and because the current is weak we are able to push it to the bank of a small island overgrown with trees and thorns, and with the help of Inger and Simon we manage to heave-ho it till the boat sits partly on the bank, barely touched by the water.

We are on this island, among a thousand others dotted along this huge delta of rapids, but luckily, this island which is part beaver dam and probably no more than a hundred yards in circumference is separated by a swiftly flowing current from the main Virginia shore, thickly-forested shore about 50 yards across. We joke that we made it. We even thump Lee on the back for good measure, but he's stretched out on the small beach-like bank and gone to sleep.

Hal says: "It's an hour to sundown. Someone on the river must have spotted us. They'll be here soon. And if not old Fletcher will certainly send out a search party. We pull out chicken sandwiches and black coffee and rum and peanut butter sandwiches that Serita had prepared and some pound cake Inger has made and we eat. And we tear off a piece of cloth lying in the boat and pin it to a branch, but there's no breeze. On the Potomac, evening falls rapidly. And as the shadows begin to lengthen we begin to holler at the boats in the main stream. Simon screams: "HELP." Lee says: "AHOY." And together we all shout and wave but nobody sees us and darkness is falling and the river has turned into a grayish color and it splashes harder against the rocks.

There's no way out. We have to navigate this wretched boat across the rapids to the Virginia shore. But we've got to ensure survivors in case the boat is swept down through the rapids and into Great Falls. Probably, in the wisdom of cavemen, the women must first be protected. So it's decided that that when some of us make a dash for the opposite shore in search of help, the women must be left behind on the relative safety of the island. A man must also stay with them. Lee volunteers, but Simon, jealous of Lee spending a night with Inger, will have none of it, and Lee won't trust Simon, and uses the excuse that Simon as a guardian of two women on this island would be of no use because of his purple-colored glasses.

By default, I'm the choice to remain behind. Hal, Lee, and Simon, say a prayer and ask me to repeat the 3,000-year-old *Gayatri Mantra* of Light that we chanted as Christmas was dawning. They get into the boat, Hal pushing from behind before he jumps in as it enters the stream and we could see Lee slapping the currents with the oars on both sides as if he were in a kayak. The boat zig-zagged in all directions and disappeared at a 45 degree angle somewhere downstream.

There was silence on the island. A half-hour had passed. There were stars in the sky. To worship that

Indian summer we had not brought our sweaters along. And the temperatures were falling. And Inger and Serita and I were silent. And as I sat on the ground I listened to the water make sounds like the ones Kerouak had described when he meditated at Big Sur. And then from the other shore a voice rang out over the rapids: "Halllloooo. Serita, Inger..."

It was Hal. I screamed back: "Are you safe? Is everything okay?"

Hal shouted: "Yeah, we made it. Lee hurt his foot because we had to jump off the boat just before it was pushed to shore. We couldn't hold the boat. It's been swept down into the lower rapids. It's gone. But we found a shack with two woodsmen, and they're going to help us through the woods to the nearest Fire Department for help. But Simon doesn't want to go because he can't see he says because his purple glasses fell into the river and he's scared that these two rednecks might shoot us. He says he'll stay behind in the shack until we return."

I holler back: "Fuck Simon. Drag him along with you. He might just die of fright anyway. It's getting cold here."

And Hal says: "Light a fire. You've got matches. And you have some cheese. Don't worry, we'll be back. Good luck, Hindu."

And I say: "Good luck Kentucky Fry. And come back." And there's silence.

On the island all is black. Serita and Inger break twigs

and light a fire. Inger sings. We sit huddled together watching the black river that's getting louder all the time and the stars are brighter. And nothing moves except the water. We don't know what's behind us or on the side of us and outside the glow of the fire all is black and full of sound, and Inger dozes and Serita dozes and I'm getting scared because two hours have gone by, and we've been stoking the fire. And I see a flashlight at the other end where I had last spoken to Hal, and Hal says: "We've got help."

And the Serita and Inger whoop with delight. There's the two woodsmen, two men from the rescue department and Hal. Simon and Lee have taken off to a friend's place in Washington. The man from the rescue squad says:

"We called Andrew's Air Force base for choppers so you could climb up in ladders but it's too dark for them and they don't trust their blades with the trees at night. But we've got these ropes we can shoot across but the distance is too great. We think you're safe out there right now, and we're safe on our side. But keep that fire going for godsakes, because there are bears here."

I shout: "What if it rains?"

And he says: "Just pray that it doesn't. Good luck. We'll be back for you at the crack of dawn." His flashlight disappears

CHAPTER XXVI

I

Then there's silence. The rapids and the fire and all else is black. And I pull Serita and Inger closer to me. They try and sleep, their breasts on my chest. And I'm praying to Lord Varuna, the God of love and forgiveness: "Keep us under thy protection. Forgive our sins and give us thy love."

And my body responds with another kind of love. Serita's and Inger's hair falling over my shoulders, and they smell of water vapor and fresh leaves and Head and Shoulders shampoo, and their breasts are heavy. And there's the primeval male stirring in my loins. And the damned thing is getting so hard that it could deflect a rapid on its own. And I say, O God, not now, not now, was it Serita or Inger, or both, Jeez I hope none of them touches me there by mistake. And the worst thing about a long-duration hard-on that does not climax is the excruciating pain that begins as a throbbing in the scrotum and then begins to squeeze the testicles as if they've been caught in a vice. And I want it all to go away. All I want is the morning to come. I must deflect my thoughts. But they return in circles to the groin.

The nights in the open with the Shikari in the open *jheels* and the stars and the walking woods. And those jeep rides to flavor the first madness of the monsoon rain. I'm barely 13 or 14 and we're packed in the back of the jeep with some of the boys in front and me squeezed between Seema and her two friends Laila and Neena. And Neena is a little older and sprouting breasts. And it's dark in the back and I'm testing her thigh with mine. Will she squeeze back if I squeeze mine a little tighter against hers? And Neena, this plain conservative plain Jane with cardamom on her breath, leans forward and touches her shoulder to mine, and raises her right elbow, a little, to make just enough space for me to raise my own left elbow, which is touching hers, in order to insert my right hand from under the cover of my left armpit to fondle her right breast. A maneuver covered by our united hands. It was a technique that I learned in the Shikari's jeep, and was to repeat during my adolescent years in movie halls. And Neena wanted more and the jeep was just entering our driveway and the rain was still falling, and I disengaged but the waves and waves of sperm had wet my trousers in a huge patch. And after the climax I was in pangs of shame. I did not even look at Neena (even though in later days I would fondle her repeatedly) as I jumped out of the jeep, straight for the bathroom where I changed, and I felt I had sinned. I ran into Mama's puja room and I begged every god for forgiveness and even hoped that

410

some deity would unhinge me of this shameful appendage which, actually had been in good use for several years. Since prep school.

2

I was barely six when Papa banished me, as he did the rest of his brood, in stages, to a boarding prep school – Ridgley's – run by a six-foot tall British school-marm, Miss Herlissa, who wore her gray hair in a tight bun. Most of our teachers were women. And we moved with each year from Kindergarten to classes named Lower Transition, Upper Transition, and Lower Remove-I and Upper Remove-II and so on. Here's where Miss Cox the music teacher taught us *Green Grow the Rushes Ho,* and *Row My Nut Brown Maiden*, and we watched Queen Elizabeth's coronation in 16 mm and learned how to say Sceptre, and Orb and Elizabeth Regina.

And the first day he took me to school Papa had not informed me that he was leaving me behind to sleep in a dorm all by myself for the next four months, in a strange place. He had wept when he hugged me goodbye and lied that he would be back for me after an hour with some candy, as he got back into his Studebaker, he wept from behind sunglasses, the same way he would later weep when Seema got married, and Miss Herlissa shooed him away when she saw him crying, saying It's not good for the little boy, and she held my hand and led me to Miss

411

Whittier, my house-mistress who told me that this would now be my home for a while and that I should get to know the other boys in my dorm and that I was to practice speaking as much English as I could. I waited on the steps outside the dorm until it was dark and the dinner gong rang. And as I sat at the table with the others, put aside my soup and had to be force-fed, and I remembered Mama. And Seema and Tips at the Raipur table and I sobbed uncontrollably. My bed, in the corner of a large whitewashed room was cold. And I looked for Tips and Seema in prayer but there were only other children, and I was scared and I was sobbing because Mama had not tucked me in, and there was another child near my bed, Yogi, who was also sobbing. And I dreamed about the Studebaker coming back and Papa laden with candy, and we were crossing the Ganges in a ferry boat on to which the car used to be loaded on the way home and we would soon be able to see the two huge chimneys that spelled home, and I stood at the edge of the boat and took a pee into the river, and I awoke in the dormitory cold and wet and soaked and I sobbed loudly because I had not wet my bed since I was a year old, when Mama used to potty train me, taking me to the toilet bowl after each meal and saying "ssssss", "ssssss," until I made water. And in this cold dorm in my wet bed I slept in my urine until morning when the first wake-up gong rang, and I hated it, because it was nothing like the early morning temple bells of Raipur but like a clash of shoes on a cymbal, like the noise made by Lee's drummer. And the helper pulled me out of bed and told Miss Whittier I was a bed-wetter. And she commanded me to wash my pyjama suit. And she held me out as an example to the rest of the boys:

"See, he does wee wee in bed. He's a bad boy. We will make him stand in front of the potty every evening until he does it, or he doesn't go to bed." And for the next few nights, I was made to stand in front of the potty and I was shy of the helper looking on and even though my bladder was full, I could not do it, and I made water in bed for the next few nights. And I cursed Papa for lying to me and prayed to God each night that he and Mama would never come to visit me during term so that I would not have to miss them again, when we parted, now that I was getting used to living in the dorm and enjoying masturbating, often to induce sleep.

The act of rubbing my genitals came naturally. Probably I learned it in the womb. Yes, in a six-year-old, there is an erection, a sexual one but without concrete sexual form. And prolonged rubbing leads to sexual release, pleasurable and sleep-inducing, but without any discharge of sperm or lubrication, dry, body-stroking child-orgasms. And I was to discover that Yogi also practiced this wonderful form of self-titillation. And so did many other Kindergarteners. And we made a game out of it in our dorm. Immediately after "light-out" time at 8 p.m, Yogi would whisper, Ready, Set, Go... and little hands would rub little pee-pees into tiny erections, and the boy who would come first, would say, It's over, and there'd be a second and a third. The helper snitched on us and Miss Whittier told us we were sinners and would go blind before we entered our teens and warned us she

413

would write to our parents that we had started "Hand practice."

We were scared. The practice never stopped. It simply went underground. And fear now accompanied the end of the climax. We checked our eyes each day in the mirrors. And as we grew older we experimented with each other. And waited for the day, as we learned from the older boys, that when we were eleven or 12, the end would see a white, perfectly shaped pearl appear in the little opening in the penis and later, with every passing month, the pearls would multiply and then the milk would gush out and the pleasure would last longer and longer. And even as we grew to be nine and ten in Ridgley's we learned to use our imaginations. Our teachers' breasts and thighs, and warm hugs and secret smells, lying with them in our minds while we stroked ourselves, and writing stories in our minds, about trysts and hugs and then forming the final intense, sensual thoughts that would bring on the release. We knew nothing about intercourse, but we knew that penises had a sexual value – mechanical when boys jerked each other off for fun – but deeply erotic when in the privacy of our bathrooms or in bed we connected the exercise with women.

3

Dry masturbation liberated many of us from the

memories of homes and Mama tucking us into bed, though I would still occasionally weep early mornings, even in the senior dorms when I heard the wake-up bell, and I awoke from memories and dreams of the Shikari and Mama. I was abandoned and I feared further abandonment more than death or the curse of blindness that I had inflicted upon myself.

Sitting by the fire on that wretched island where the Potomac was still roaring, and Serita and Inger slept I tried to banish the thought of this wild river from my mind. I had walked the marshes outside Raipur and we had slept underneath the stars and I thought of this warm autumn day in Ridgely when I was recovering in the school hospital from jaundice. I was allowed to sit in the shade in the small lawn from where I could see a seasonal stream which was now a rock and boulder-strewn dry riverbed across which was a forest where they said was a witch's house. I feared that stretch of the river bed. It was white and forbidding and the forest receded into endless mountains, the Himalayan foothills full of jungle fowl and wild elephants and spotted deer. Shikar country. And on that warm afternoon, when the beetles hummed and the wasps made tiny mud-houses for themselves sticking out from the corners of ceilings, I got up and began walking across the riverbed to the forest to the witch's house, and I was already composing the letter I would write to Papa. And there were jagged tones, sharp as glass, on the riverbed, and deep pits dug for lime quarrying, and even in my weakened state I half-walked, and half-ran the entire mile, and the woods were deserted.

There were mynahs and crows and bulbuls and giant lantana bushes with yellow and purple blossoms and broad-leaved Sal trees, and the undergrowth was thick, and I followed a rabbit, and then a pack of jackals and I was getting tired and my bones ached and I called out to the witch and my screaming echoed across the foothills, and it was getting colder for afternoon clouds were gathering and I sat down under a Lantana bush and I began to dream about a huge shape, formless and forbidding that broke into faces and icons and Miss Herlissa and Miss Whittier were sitting in Mama's puja room with Papa's Holland & Holland shotgun, and Mama was lighting incense that smelled of dung and Papa took the gun from Miss Whittier and pointed it at the roof and Miss Whittier and Miss Herlissa lifted their skirts and Mama said, don't you dare pee in my puja room, and I come in naked trying to hide my wee-wee, and I'm screaming that I don't want them to see me, and Mama brings me a potty and I'm still trying to hide my nakedness and Miss Whittier and Miss Herlissa scream again and the Shikari's gun lets off a deafening blast and fire rains down in waterfalls of sparks. And I awaken under the Lantana bush and a pack of jackals is howling near me, there's thunder overhead bouncing off the lower Himalayas and droplets of rain have begun to fall and the sky is forked with lightning and it's dark.

And I'm scared but determined that I will get back to the hospital in the dark rather than sleep here and let the comfort of the morning revive me. For I was not scared of forests or rain. And as I walked to the riverbed, the woods walked with me. And streams had begun to flow through the dry riverbed, but I walked on as some of the streams became swifter and deeper – the fore-runners of a flash flood. I was weak and hungry and I thought about the Shikari, and I fell into one of the quarry hollows, and my knees and elbows were bleeding and my head hurt, and I could hardly see, because the rain was blinding me and blood dripped from my forehead, and I said to myself, I will never give up, I will keep on walking even though something inside me was telling me to die, to just sit down, or lie down and let the waters take over, to float downstream like a log of wood, and that thought comforted me, but I said I would not die, and as I walked, I stumbled again and again, and I fell and I picked myself up and the school lights shone ahead and I entered my hospital room and the staff took one look at me and the nurses were kind for they asked no questions, dried me, bandaged me and put me to bed and that night as I slept I had no dreams of Mama but I dreamed of a kindly, beautiful witch who sat beside me near a log-fire and read me fairy stories in my dream. I slept as the witch read to me.

4

Even in high school, I often wept when Papa abandoned me to the cares of the boy's hostel at the beginning of each term. And college was insane. Mostly big city boys who talked about parties and movies they had seen, and girls they would date, and my only experiences then were of Raipur and walking in the woods and flying partridge and these things bored my classmates who went to fancy tailors to order stovepipe trousers and double-breasted blazers. And they read books only when they had to cram for their exams while I chewed up the library and learned at the knees of my tutor David Hammersmith. And the most popular reading material in college at one time was Playboy Magazine. In those days, most boys and girls did not date openly, or mainly had sexual encounters like mine with Neena in the jeep. And they would preserve their memories of their dates with girls – motorbike rides where she held on to your waist, her tits pressed against your back, picnics, movie-hall kisses, groin-to-groin dancing – for night-time jerk-off fantasies. You could rent Playboy from second-hand bookshops, and the guys would pass them along and asked which of the Bunnies the other guy had jerked off on, or which story from the Playboy Advisor, had titillated his night-time orgasm. And some of the richer guys ordered Playboy directly and held on to it like a pasha hangs on to his harem. Only after he had satisfied himself with each and every one of those titties and semi-visible nether-regions, and was bored as a man gets bored with a whore he has jumped too often, would he lend it to the others. And sometimes he'd tear a nudie page out of it to keep for himself – someone he still didn't want others to share with him.

I had already been warned in prep school about

blindness, but thank God, except for reading glasses I acquired at an early age after reading *War and Peace* in bad print and Maupassant even in worse (we readers were generally referred to as "pseuds") by the hunks, the sin from my hands still hadn't traveled to my eyes. But then, a wandering Guru I met during my college days, a man of some wisdom, and firm believer in a vengeful God, put the fear of God in me. Not that you believe everything people say, but because some of those things remain glued inside your mind because they reek of ominous metaphysics: This man, Baba Rai, we called him, and he would often meet us on the banks of the Yamuna, where he meditated, once told me:

"Nothing will happen to your body if you masturbate. But it might do something to your mind. After you die, you will have to face God. And before he decides whether to free you from rebirth, you will have to recall your entire life before him, through words and images. And everyone, your parents, brothers, sisters, friends, teachers, lovers, wives will be in the audience. In the course of recalling your life, there will come a time when you will have to tell about your sexual fantasies, teachers you thought about when you jerked off, film stars, your wives' friends, your parents' friends, every perversion, every homosexual fantasy and how it brought you to a climax, lusting after maid-servants, fantasies of child pornography, fantasies of your best friends' wives and what you did with them in your sexual fantasies, and the exact last thought at the moment of climax... And all this will be acted out before every person who was

419

part of your fantasy right in front of your parents and you have to decide whether you will face this with the guilt of hell or with laughter and how you will cope with the anger, hatred, derision, scorn, loathing of those who see you sexually stripped to the marrow of your bones."

This sermon made me weak with trepidation. I did not want to believe this hocus-pocus, but what if the guy was right? This was a crazy world anyway and anybody could be right. Oh my God, would this also mean that I would be a witness when Mama and Papa and Seema were summoned to reveal their private lives and sexual fantasies? O my God, no. In our Raipur household sex was as private a matter as the hidden galaxies. O, this mad, horrible Guru. But I did make it a point to go to Mama's puja room as many times as I could to atone and ask for deliverance from standing sexually naked before my family each time I played out my karma of carnal knowledge either by myself or with a partner.

O my God, was this another comeuppance I thought, as I lay in between Serita and Inger in the woods while the Potomac gushed by? And I cursed my loins. Because on that island near Seneca, it had started to drizzle, and I was petrified that a flashflood would sweep us all away, and the closer I huddled to Serita and Inger, I thought of the cruelty of my crotch. O my God, would I so soon have to answer, on that day of sexual judgement, that as we lay close to being swept away into the rapids of Potomac death, my last thoughts, as I cuddled my dear Serita, whom I loved, were also about Inger whom I also lay cuddling, instead of prayers for their safety? And I dozed off and in my dream I went into Mama's puja room and I prayed to the framed inscription of the Rig Veda prayer to Lord Varuna:

"God made the rivers to flow. They feel no weariness, they cease not from flowing. They fly swiftly like birds in the air. May the stream of my life flow into the river of righteousness. Loose the bonds of sin that bind me. Let not the thread of my song be cut while I sing; and let not my work end before its fulfillment. Remove all fear from me, O Lord. Receive me graciously into thee, O King. Cut off the bonds of afflictions that bind me. I cannot even open mine eyes without Thy help."

In the pink morning when I opened my eyes the clouds had disappeared and the Potomac was gurgling like it was in a dying gasp – a mere shadow of the demon which had haunted me all night. And I hear turkeys gobble, and slushing sounds instead of the violent river-breakers smashing the rocks and the river rests in the silence of the dawn and the watermarks on the trees that seemed 10-feet high during the last flash flood – I had quietly inspected them with the help of match-light as Serita and Inger slept – seemed no more than knee-deep in the morning, and I yawned the yawn of the saved, like a dog yawns at its master with love, and I went back and hugged the two girls who still slept, while the embers still glowed in the fire, and the warm, freak Indian Summer was promising to return its warmth for another day and for the first time I slept, dreamless, without

Mama and Manhattan and Simon's crazy purple glasses and I thought my heart was thudding, suddenly, like horse-hooves, and I opened my eyes and Inger was waving in the pink dawn at the approaching rescue boats in which Simon and Hal were standing in stereochrome sterns while Lee hovered over both like a Redneck Alabatross. And the rescuers shook our hands and we took off for safety and waved goodbye to the embers still burning in the woods.

Part Six

CHAPTER XXVll

1

It was my last Christmas together with Serita. After some 15 years during which, through our un-married loving, we had produced a child we had named Godot, we were to go our own ways. All these years she had been predictable, strong, unrelenting, passionate, fiercely angry when provoked, private about her pregnancy, jealously protective about my freedom to move and float. In the months after we were marooned in the Potomoac, she had begun to look different and she didn't talk much and was much more passionate in our love-making, as if she was trying to say something. Even as she lay on my chest I knew she was holding back, and I said, because I knew how to breathe in her senses:

"You've got another guy. For how long?"

And Serita, my companion for 15 years, while Godot, now 10 years old slept in the second room, said: "Yes. I knew you knew. There's nothing you cannot know about me, whether you ask or not. So why ask?"

And I asked, jealous and controlling my temper: "Are you back with Ben? Do you enjoy it with him?"

Serita doesn't answer and hugs me closer. Then she says: "No. But he's also white. He's also a doctor. He's from Groton, Connecticut."

"But do you enjoy it with him? Do you suck him? Where did you meet him? You might have told me."

"You had Blacks didn't you? And Puerto Ricans and Hippies. You think I didn't know. But I kept silent because I thought writers needed experience. Every kind."

"But I couldn't even write to save my balls, Serita!"

"I saw you on your journey, and I prayed for you."

"So you're taking revenge? Your pound of flesh for every wrinkled cunt of the Muse you willed me through your self-sacrifice for my constipated pen that simply shat a blue-inked twinkie every day."

And Serita didn't think this was a time for jokes and stupid convoluted language and meaningless mixed metaphors. She said: "Look, this guy is funny. He makes me laugh. You always make me cry. You know why? Because everytime I'm with you, I miss you. I know you're going to go away. Into your books or your shikar or memories of your Shikari. And I'll never be a part of it. That's why I never married you. Why do I have to repeat this after so many years? You knew, all along. So did I. Remember our compact? The day had to come, Tan. God knows how many times you asked me. I could not. I cannot be married to a shikari, a bum, someone I'll always miss even when he's making love to me. I could put up with a lot of that, but I'm gone now, to someone who makes me laugh because, I know you're going back to India."

I ask: "Serita, how do you know?"

And she says: " I could sense it on that goddam island in the Potomac. Not because I was jealous of Inger's breasts on your breast but because I could sense your prayer."

I say: "Come back with me Serita. We'll get married Hindu style."

And she says: "You're not going there to get married to me and solemnize the birth of Godot. You're going back because you need that dirt, and filth and poverty and grime again. So you can write instead of just rotting here as an American journalist, mixing with poets and scriptwriters and traveling to Connecticut Avenue to write 300 words about the death of Martin Luther King and not being able to describe how Fourteenth Street was burning or Connecticut Avenue, right up to the Zoo didn't have a sparrow on it. But why leave? America's been good to you. You've fished the North Fork and Lake Placid and sailed on the Chesapeake, and fished off Indian Head Highway and crossed lakes that separate Upstate New York from Vermont and camped on North Hero, and driven across Canada and fished the Outer Banks in North Carolina. And Godot's a good kid, and you've taught him how to tie a fly and go for Blue Gills."

She wants me to go and she doesn't want me to leave because she's never going to leave America. She's now even a better mathematician making good money at a Think Tank. And I hate the guy who makes her laugh.

And she says: "It's difficult for me. You're still a male. Imagine me arriving back in India after more than 20 years, unmarried, living with a guy who's from the north and me from the south, and trying to tie the knot while our 11-year-old looks on. No, I'm free here. I need laughter. I love you but I don't want to cry with you any more. And you don't really need me. A woman can sense when a man, no matter how mercurial their relationship, can live without her. And then she has to protect herself. And you've got to protect yourself as a writer. You will go back to smell everything you smelled here and that reminded you of there and refresh those smells, and you will get a wife, late into your age. She will hate your creativity, she will hate your friends, she will hate your freedom, she will be jealous of your late nights of writing, she will be jealous of your phrases and sentences because they will remind her of her worst self or remind her of me, and she will create in you anger and venom and violence and she will be the one that loves you, while believing she hates you, and you will be the one that hates her, not realizing that you love her, or will love her because your hatred and violence and rebellion are what poetry is made of and you will turn away from journalism into poetry and maybe you will write not because you are full of venom but because you are full of the hatred for love and love the love for hatred."

428

Serita, I knew had already left me. We told each other that while in America her mathematician persona would look into the future to find past wisdom, I would look into my hybrid no-self to look into the past for future wisdom.

Serita said: "But the dust. The grime. The filth. The lack of privacy, I can't understand it. They give their bottom dollar to get an immigrant visa and you return to the land you left."

She had already tackled that question, but I replied: "I did not leave India to escape poverty or persecution or a culture. I do not now leave America because I hate affluence. I came to America for adventure. And because I was destined to know you. And I found you and love again. And when I looked at my watch, hell, it was 20 years past the clock, and time to get back to the Shikari and the *jheels* and have Godot meet his grandparents and his aunts and his uncles and his cousins and learn to speak Hindi."

2

Serita had gifted me Godot. He was to travel back with me to India as my son, on my passport rather than on her maiden name. On that last night after she had packed our bags, and before she was to go away to the man who made her laugh, and while Godot slept in the other room in Washington, Serita and I made love and our saliva grew into a sweet, saltless ocean that drowned both of us all night and her perfumed mouth was all over me. I asked her whether this love-making would produce another baby, and she said, probably and she'd name it Seneca, and that I should send Godot to meet her in America only after he turned 20 because she wanted to see him at about the same age that she first met me.

In the morning when she was gone, even without a last kiss, and I picked up Godot and our bags and we kissed America goodbye – I leaned forward and kissed every movement of the revolving glass door that let us out of the apartment, and we hailed a Diamond Cab that took us to Dulles Airport in which the early morning FM was blaring Cindy Crawford in between results of the WWF championships of the previous night, and I was thinking of Serita's oceans of saliva with which she'd bathed our last love-making, and hoping that her mouth would be dry forever if she ever dared to kiss that asshole who made her laugh, goddamn him. And our luggage is being weighed at the airport and the airline guy says, Too heavy. We're late already. And we've got to lighten our load, and we start throwing things out of our baggage to get to the right weight, and when we're allowed to pass the counter, there's Godot's stuff littering the ground in front of the weighing machine – Big Bird, Redskin banners, posters saying why everybody should hate the Cowboys because Jack Pardee licks the brim of his hat with spit-wet fingers, two 45-RPM Sesame Street discs including Oscar singing, "I Love Trash," a Nerf ball, an

Ocean City poster of Billy the Kid, dumb-bell weights, and 20 volumes of football-guides, and old newpaper clips of Joe Namath, and Kilmer-versus-Sonny Jurgenson, a school album and a framed portrait of his two Gay Godparents – Stan and Goodfarb –who loved him as their own, (even when the Wasps warned us that Gays fondle children – a horrible lie –) and we walked away into the passageway of the plane while Godot looked back and cried and I hugged him all the way through the bumpy flight saying he would meet the Shikari and his Grandmama and Godot slept in my lap through the bumps and grinds above the Atlantic Ocean.

CHAPTER XXVIII

1

Simon, too, had left Manhattan for London. He had not called to say goodbye. But a year later, he wrote to say he was well, working in a bookstore and married to a doctor in Kentish Town, who was supporting him while he was studying Nietzche. Simon's Muse had been faithful to him and he had rewarded her with passionate fidelity and intellectual monogamy unheard of in the Flower Children of the sixties. He had slouched, in his own fashion towards his Bethlehem. There was money to be made in America, a brownstone he would inherit in Manhattan, his classfellows had taken high-paying assignments with the *New York Times* and *Newsweek* and *Rolling Stone*, and fancy public relations firms in Chicago and Washington. Lee was actually giving private lessons on Wordsworth and learned by heart verses from Tintern Abbey – "I have felt a presence that disturbs me with the joy of elevated thoughts" – and was doing great as a stockbroker and was reading Arthur Laffer and Jude Wanniski, and

Wealth and Poverty, and in the murky years of Reaganomics, and the elevation of Jack Kemp from audibling Quarterback jargon to thumping pulpits about Jean-Baptiste Say's Supply Side convictions from the mounts of the House of Representatives' economics subcommittees – was already laying the foundation for himself to make a couple of million on his own in the Bill Clinton years a decade later when the baby boomers would become a part of those years of unparalleled prosperity and booming job markets. Hal was teaching writing at Evanston, Illinois. And by the time the nineties arrived – and Simon who would write to me often – his first letter had ended, "You broke my will, but what a thrill" – had wound up in various parts of East Europe in search of writers and poets who had written underground stuff before the fall of the Iron Curtain, and one of his finest works was an anthology edited by him of which *The European* said: "(Simon), a dedicated discoverer of hidden talents from behind the now fallen Wall, has assembled a remarkable collection of voices here..." And in the decade as it progressed Simon would help me, through letters, to discover other exciting authors like Richard Ford, Yasunari Kawabata, and the loveable literary mad-hatter Witold Gombrowicz and his hanging sparrow, 30 years after "Cosmos" was published in Polish.

Godot and I arrived in India when the New Economic policy – increasing privatization of industry, liberalized licensing policies, direct foreign investment, breaking state monopolies over service industries, the political arguments over GATT –was still being born an the endless debates were still endless and Godot understood little of anything, mindless state-controlled television before the Indian TV Glasnost of the late Eighties, and he still called America for Superbowl scores, and reacted to beggars on the streets with the same horror as do visiting tourists from the West, could not fathom why on earth, things that were his birthrights in Washington – continuous power supply, water you can drink straight from the taps without risking jaundice, neighborhood banks that paid your utility bills, roads with smooth surfaces and luminous markings and never-ending streetlights – were not a part of his new home, and why on earth he had been dragged here by me, and he resented Serita for letting him go and he missed her terribly by resolving that he would, as far as his willpower would allow him, never mention her or remain silent whenever there was talk of her. He could never know that the India I had left behind in the sixties was at that time barely making a transition from the bicycle age, and that domestic airline networks on which he traveled often in India, did not then really exist, and that there were no telephone booths and telephones did not work.

Mama and Papa and Tips and Seema and the rest had known about Godot, the love child. They believed this was common in America and since I had lived there so long they did not find my live-in relationship with Serita strange. And too, in metropolitan India, lifestyles were changing. Joint families were breaking up. And Godot's schooling – he went to the same boarding high school and college I attended –was no more Playboy's sexual Raj or the masturbators' last refuge, with the early morning wake-up gongs. The sexes were dating more freely. A new affluence had already invaded the dorms and classrooms – far cry from our near-monastic existence –weekend sneak parties, fast cars, fancy wrist-watches, Toshiba laptops, designer jeans, Dockers slacks, and the relatively less-affluent kids now had super-rich school buddies with chauffeured limos and money to blow at all-night discos, and the less privileged upper class kids made life hell for their parents at home making demands – that their parents could not meet – to live like their rich school buddies.

2

Even though we lived in Delhi where there were good day-schools all over the place, I put Godot into boarding for several reasons. First, life seemed to be repeating itself and I wanted to know whether in these repetitions, like in the raagas, and Simon's later poetry how much improvisation and thematic variations there would be. Papa had sent me to boarding because he said "it built character," something I don't understand to this day but also for the very practical reason that Raipur had no real schools, only open-air classes, attended by brilliant students whose brains were dulled into non-combustible dung by moronic government-paid teachers.

436

Also, as a single parent – and Mama's Puritanism, that I carried in my soul would not allow me to keep a mistress openly in this pseudo-Westernized town of hypocrites who screwed their tribal maidservants at night while they attended NGO meetings in the mornings to decry the sexual exploitation by the affluent Western-educated class of innocent tribal sexuality – I had no other choice. Better that Godot join the ranks of the private-school educated, and stay as far away as possible from Delhi's conspicuous consumption, than rot in one of the capital's day schools run by nouveau riche women who tried on different shades of mascara for funerals.

Papa said, he'd not send his grandchildren to those boarding schools any more, because, the old snob that he was, he argued: "They are infested with bumptious upstarts, commerce without culture, the armpit smells of Mussoorie, with cheap colognes and the sons of Loafers and cinema-hall owners, not interested in the mountains and Dostoievsky and Degas but in the stamp of instant upper class certificates, and that when they graduate they will still reek of money rather than civilization or education, and they'll never still be able to light a social or educational candle to you."

And I said: "Papa, the world has changed and it will keep on changing and you will probably never even know it. Your family has changed already. What about Seema? And do you think I could keep Godot with me in Delhi without a mother to look after him?"

And he said: "You have sisters, and brothers, and cousins. Family."

And I kept silent. We had all grown apart. When I had arrived in Delhi, I had thought I'd get a hero's welcome, the Indián Yankee back from King Arthur's Court. And I remembered that when I'd flown for America from these shores a veritable army of relatives, including distant cousins and the uncles of distant friends, had come to the airport to wish me goodbye, and Papa had carried one of my bags across the tarmac to the very door of the Boeing 707 on the runway and had hugged me and he was wearing his sunglasses. And when Godot and I arrived, we took a lonely taxi to a hotel. Papa would have come but he did not know the exact date of our arrival. And on the very next day, I had called Sara, now all married and with two children, and said:

Godot and I are back, baby. He's all yours now. And his cousins have another brother to grow up with them. And Sara, said hi, and welcome back sweetheart and she said they couldn't see us that day, and I asked why. And she said:

"Well, we all have our own lives to live, you know."

And I knew she was right, and India and its families had changed, and our Raipur household now had a diaspora with its cosmopolitan families concerned about their own survival, and after all Godot and I were not refugees from the Old Country seeking help, but strangers who had returned from the land of the free for some reason they could not understand, and were supposed to be loaded with American wealth –which we were not (O that I had become a banker in New York) – rather than

438

being a burden on them. And I knew this to be true, and I knew that Godot was to be exiled, the way I was, and abandoned, in a boarding school where he would be protected from some of the myths he had learned about Indian family life and the fabulous wealth that had once been the Shikari's inheritance.

Godot adjusted well. He learned Hindi. And I took him for his vacations to Raipur, so I could keep him as far away as possible from what Papa called "Delhi's rich loafer classes." He had learned that the family wealth was all but gone. The two towering chimneys remained but the factories had been mortgaged or parceled out to real estate developers. Papa's children were earning relatively well, and Papa had some money put aside to buy shotgun shells and Indian whiskey and fuel for the jeep rides. And Godot learned to shoot. And to kiss the Shikari.

Papa's offspring were not physically demonstrative of their affections. We hugged our parents gently and avoided cheek-pecking as much as possible. But Godot knew how to smack his grandparents with full-blooded slobbery kisses, like we did in America, and Papa kind of enjoyed that. The Shikari filled Godot's teenage years with as much hunting as he could bear. The marshes and the *jheels* and the scrub forests were to start disappearing very soon, but Godot saw the last of them, on foot, as we had done, in jeep-rides (but without furtive sex with a Neena – Godot was past that stage –) on foot, and he even talked fishing to the old man. And the villagers would tell Godot stories about the Shikari and legends they had passed on to their children about the England-returned hunter who had stalked their fields and shot at flying birds and built small schools for their children for the past 40 years.

3

Gafoor, the old tracker, a man born without teeth and which never sprouted at all even as he lived to the age of 90, had guided the Shikari through the early years. Shown him grouse country. Guided him through bandit lands. Helped him navigate the marshes on foot. Now he had insisted that he was going to die no matter that he was neither diseased nor ill, and he had parked himself in the middle of the lawn of the Raipur household and every night when he laid himself to rest on the grass, like the Old Indian in Dustin Hoffman's *Little Big Man* he would call out to Papa who was only five years younger than he, and say, Take My Body And Throw It Into That *Jheel* when I'm gone tomorrow, and the Shikari would laugh and say Gafoor is crazy and he's going to live another hundred years, and Gafoor would say, Why, the *jheels* have no water, there's brick houses everywhere, and the mallards don't come anymore and the sand dunes are being destroyed by brick kilns, and Papa would fall silent. And one morning in the lawn outside, when Gafoor still awoke alive, early one morning and Godot was looking through his binoculars at a grey hornbill, Gafoor asked him to sit by his side, and Gafoor spoke to Godot:

"Son," he said, " Do you know the ways of the Hornbill? The male, after fertilizing the female, first digs a hole on the thinner top of a mango tree trunk. The female lays her eggs inside, and the male, with his saliva seals the opening until all you can see is the female's beak poking out of that little hole, like a penis taking a pee through a half-opened zip, throughout the short period she is hatching her eggs. The male feeds her. She is well protected, and when the eggs hatch, the male pecks off the sealed material and now the female carves out a hole in the trunk through which she can feed her young. And one day, they're all gone."

The old man sat cross-legged in the dew in the grass and continued: "Son, I don't know you. But I guided your grandfather and your father through the marshes and the forests and the waters. I see something in you of them but also nothing. You've come back here and you've learned to shoot well. You inherited that from the Shikari, but you cannot inherit his spirit or his smells unless you really come back here. You never can. You never will.

"You know, recently, when Shikari Sahib was broke, and the children hadn't sent him any money, and his rents weren't coming in from his property, and it was cold and he knew I was sick with malaria and it was a one-hour drive at night across the sand dunes to my village, he awoke a money lender to buy me pain killers, and drove to my village at night to nurse me and sit by me and asked when's the next shoot! That funny man who is only a little younger than me."

Godot was learning the secrets from this ancient Muslim guide. And Gafoor went on: "I'm dying but I'm writing your grandfather's obituary. A man who cursed God and the devil at the same time if a partridge didn't fly out of a bush or if the lakes were devoid of ducks. A violent man, who kicked me with his foot when I lied to him about a scrub area being full of game. I lied and wanted to make money on tips he'd always give me whether he hated me or loved me for lying or telling the truth. He missed your father when he went away to America, you know, but he never said anything. I could see it in his eyes. I could see it in a shot he missed that he never should have. Your family is the king. You have no more of the old wealth. All of Raipur knows it. I know it. But you never let it show.

"You had ostentatious weddings. But your father fought against dowries. He built Muslim shrines when his own Punjabi Hindus wanted him to build Hindu temples after Partition. He sailed on rocky boats when the Ganges flooded our villages and the government was never to be seen and he threw food-packets to the survivors, and spent his own money on re-building their homes, built schools but made sure they did not teach religion. Built small worship houses even though he didn't believe in God and he hated pundits and sadhus and fakirs, he patted common men on their shoulders but hated any intimate-touch-back, he cursed worse than a sailor, and you know something, he loved luxury but he hated wealth. And when he fought to be elected, he was the only man we know who did not take a penny from his own political party, even as he was giving out money buying thousands of blankets for the poor who came to this house every winter, and he would scream at them and call them dirty beggars and wash his hands if they touched him and they still tell their children stories about the Shikari stalking the fields and the wilds on foot with his gun held at 45 degrees and how the birds fell out of the sky, and even the non-shikari, anti-hunting Brahmins sat at their evening gatherings and told their children about this sinner who walked through their fields like a pompous saint and fascinated them."

Godot asked Gafoor: "But what was it all about? Do you understand it? How do I get to know what my grandpa was all about? Shall I ask my own father?"

And Gafoor said: "No. Your father will tell you nothing. You must not tell him about what I just told you. Your grandfather is probably a madman and he will die a madman. And if heard me say this he would kill me. He doesn't know what he does, and he does what he doesn't know. That's what shikaris are all about. I guided you on your first shoot after you came back from America. For that I am blessed."

And Gafoor asked Godot about his mother, why she hadn't come back with us. Godot remained silent. Then Gafoor said that the Shikari had informed the

443

townspeople of Raipur that Serita was studying for a degree in America. And they believed that. Several years later, when they asked why she still wasn't back, Papa told them she had an illness that could only be treated in America. And after that there were no more questions from the folks in Raipur. They either assumed that Papa was lying to them, which they dared not question, or that it was the truth, which satisfied their social conservatism.

But we knew already from a phone call from Serita, made 10 years earlier, barely a year after Godot and I had arrived in India that Seneca had been born to us. A baby girl. Godot's sister. Mama and Papa's granddaughter. Mama had immediately ordered her horoscope made, religiously, just as she had begun to teach Godot to chant *Om Jai Jagdish Hare* on his first visit to Raipur – and which he learned by heart in her puja room never knowing a thing about Hinduism or about any other religion for that matter – and we never discussed whether Serita had been married again or not because Mama and Papa rarely questioned our private lives, and because I was certain that Seneca was my child – and not the offspring of that asshole who made her laugh and whom she's married – and because when I made the announcement to Mama, Mama looked exactly as a grandmother should look on receiving the news about the birth of her new grandchild

CHAPTER XXIX

1

Ohne day Gafoor lay quietly dead on the lawn. Godot wept. Papa who was then wasting away, as his legs were turning into spindles, and even the scrub forests that Godot knew were whispers of their former yelling and waving, heard the news, quietly, without tears. He was in his chamber of perfumes and his voice, full of phlegm, barely rising above the hissing of the humidifier, whispered that if Gafoors's family needed any money for the burial, we could sell his Winchester .22 rifle for a handsome price. And the family that had already gathered about him awaiting the final moments said, no. The Shikari had already sold his armory of exotic weapons, his beloved Holland & Holland, Remington shells, along with binoculars, jungle hats, pedometers, his prized WWII Willys jeep, not to sustain his own comforts which, in those last gasping days were more than adequate under his quilted false ceiling, but rather to keep up the dignity of the celebration of Holi, the annual festival of Spring life, in March, when the harvest of the wheat crop is celebrated, a veritable Mardi Gras, with people painted in every color and bombed out of their minds on ganja and boiled cannabis, as they spray colored water on one another come to their senses in the evening and for three days every family greets every family.

For years, our Raipur home was the great meeting ground of peasants and shopkeepers and traders and crooks and brigands and bureaucrats who, for three days after Holi, came in their thousands for the traditional post-Holi embrace, some drunk or freaked-out worse than Woodstock junkies, others, sobered up, in their thousands, for three days, and Papa had sold his weapons, and gold Rolex and Tudor Oyster watches and pedometers, in his waning years, so when Holi came, the Raipur household would look as it always had, whitewashed, the lawns manicured, the tented canopies for the guests with pitchers of tea and fresh *bidis* and fine cigarettes, and they would come in their groups and Papa and his friends would know who is who and they would embrace hugging shoulders, neck to neck, left side, right side, the very poor, the rich, the traders, the money-lenders, the Me-Lord-speaking lawyers, the town prostitutes, the eunuchs, townsfolk, village-folk who walked barefoot 15-mile distances to Holi-hug this Shikari, on that day of Mardi Gras leveling, the Shikari whose upbringing would otherwise have kept him away from their bad-breath, and who now hugs them and recognizes each of the thousands by their names and their sons' names and their parents' names, and they marvel at him, and they say, this was a bad Holi, not much celebration, a bad crop, and hooligans are misusing the festival for lewd displays of machismo, and they say that Diwali will also be bad, not too many fire-crackers, an early evening, a bad economy, bad monsoon, and they talk politics and remember the Shikari's foray into politics and the old men say, he never asked for a penny. And a still drunken man, still splashed in color mumbles, Who cares about his money, my father never did, and our Shikari is richer today than the richest man in the world because he has no money but he has IZZAT– (honor, respectability) and while you can spend 10 years making money you can be reborn a hundred times and you can never buy Izzat. The drunken man continues…This Shikari in his day was a rude evil-tempered man. A *haramzaada* (bastard) but he is my father. He walked through our field to kill birds as they flew and we hated him and we watched him and he was a wizard. He pointed his guns at those birds but never at us. And then it became a sport in our village to discuss his bag for that day and how he had done it. He walked alone. He spoke English, too, we knew that, but he poked fun of us in our own dialect, and we laughed, someone else we would have killed, but we laughed, because he was one of us, dirty, covered with thorns, finding his way on moonless nights, respecting the purdah of our women if he stayed with us for the night, O he was a true Englishman.

2

On the last Holi, the Shikari – who would sit on an

aluminum and plastic chair with the village folks for three days and embrace them as they all joined together in cursing cities and citified people and crooked politicians and talked about the insanity and hypocrisy of India and the heartlessness of the bureaucracy – was carried to that special chair of his under the tented canopy that still told of the old wealth. He sat there briefly. As they came and went they saw the recognition in his eyes but each time they hugged him and left, or simply saluted him, because he was too tired to rise and hug every well-wisher, he saw their eyes say farewell. The Indian peasant knows death. He mourns it. But he does not fear it. They looked at the dying man with living eyes. And they bade him adieu. Papa saw his own death in their eyes. The rich traders, the still wretched of the earth, the police-tortured, the cunning small-time lawyers, Khalifa the old boatman – the *mallah* – who had ferried him across miles and miles of the Ganges when it had flooded its banks, inundated villages and fields, when the Shikari had hurled thousands of food packets to villagers stranded on islands. Like Gafoor, the *mallah*, Khalifa, too was getting ready to die, and he whispers to Papa, quietly: "Who'll get there first?"

And Papa smiles back: and says: "That damned Gafoor, he beat us to it. But, Khalifa, I'll be there before you, and you'll still row me across the Ganges, like you did my car on the ferry boat, many, many years ago before our country knew what double-track bridges were. And you'll do it again, and if I see a tear in your eye, I'll come alive and I'll dunk your head in the nearest whirlpool."

And Khalifa laughed a toothless laugh and Papa wheezed a laugh and he went back to his bed of planks underneath the quilted ceiling where the humidifier was still hissing and Mama and the rest of us were waiting for him to tuck him in, and the Shikari looked at Godot and the rest of his grandchildren and he was happy and made a joke about how Mama was shy about bringing him a bed pan and why should not the youngsters find him a pretty nurse instead, and Mama blushed and in the rare moments that she chided her husband, she said: "Shhoo." While she lived and while he lived, those were her last words to him. And he had smiled at her and nodded in agreement.

CHAPTER XXX

1

In a barely legible note that lay in a crumpled heap on the floor beside his bed-pan, he had scribbled in pencil, something I was left to decipher: "Life is nothing more than a suicide note." He had still not sold off his Winchester. 22. In the early afternoon a couple days after Holi, he shot himself with the Winchester. Had he been alive he would probably have called it his last brilliant shot. Neatly executed. The Shikari in his final cosmodemonic lunge for freedom. As well planned as he would a shooting party in the wilderness. We reconstructed his last moments in detail. With whatever remaining strength he could muster, he had dressed himself in his hunting camouflage trousers and jacket over his pyjama suit. He had put on warm khaki socks and even his Hunter shoes. He put on his Australian jungle hat at a cocky angle with the strap tightly buckled under his chin. On his left wrist he wore the waterproof Guess watch I had brought for him from America. He had pulled out his Winchester from his

451

closet, oiled it, cleaned it and loaded it with a single high-velocity American Lightning shell. He knew all about trajectories and sound and the mess that killing makes. And had wanted to ensure that everything looked neat and fresh. He poured Eau de Cologne into the humidifier and splashed his face and underarms with Tabac after-shave lotion. He used several pillows and cushions. Pillows to wrap around the gun to muffle the sound. Two pillows that he must have held tightly over his jungle hat in order to prevent blood splashing all over. And then he had positioned himself, sitting, leaning a little on the head-board so that the bullet would fly out and up rather than ricocheting across the room and damaging the wall. The high velocity bullet, he knew, would make a neat hole, like a laser beam going through rather than create a small crater from where it would exit his body. The bullet, after he positioned the tip of the barrel in his mouth, holding the gun in his right hand while pressing the pillows over his hat with his left hand, when he squeezed the trigger, had ripped through his palate, passed through his brain, out of his skull, through the jungle hat and pillows and had made a neat, barely-noticeable hole in the quilted false ceiling.

No one had heard the shot. Mama and the rest of the family were snoozing. Some of the grandchildren were playing cricket on the lawn. Raju, the young servant, who had been attending to him had been sent off on some chore by Papa a half-hour earlier. When Raju returned he found the dead Shikari in a semi-reclining position, in his hunting clothes and jungle hat, his Winchester loosely

452

held at a 45 degree angle in his right hand, his left arm dangling, a pillow on his stomach, two pillows, one only slightly blood-stained lying on the floor. Raju thought he had dressed to go on a hunt and had just dozed off. He ran to tell me and Tips of this strange afternoon ritual that Papa had performed, and we went into his room out of curiosity.

I took one look at him and knew he was dead. Aggressively dead. His eyes closed as if they never ever wanted to open again from this sleep. He seemed to be smiling. His skin was taught and mostly free of wrinkles. I saw no pain. And we gently took the gun from him and after Tips ejected the empty shell we put the gun away. I kissed him and he was cold. And Tips kissed him. And the room was full of perfumes. And we put aside the pillow with the blood and we carried him to his study, still surrounded bis books, and in Hindu tradition, laid him on the ground, his feet facing in the direction of the Ganges. I told Raju to say nothing to anybody but to fetch the government doctor nearby who came immediately and examined Papa and saw the hole in his palate and removed his hat and saw another neat round one in the middle of his skull. And then he signed a death certificate calling it "death by a self-inflicted gun accident".

CHAPTER XXXI

1

We then informed the family. An accident we said. But they knew. Mama knelt at his feet and kissed them as he continued persistently and aggressively in death. She fainted for a while and then after we'd tucked her into her own bed, she went into her puja room where she remained all night. Seema shook Papa over and over again asking him to Wake Up, Please Wake Up, as he lay dead surrounded by his books and his library in his study where we had, as long as I can remember, planned the shoots on the *jheels* and drunk beer and whisky. And Seema hugged his body and kissed his jungle hat until Sara pulled her away and they went into his chamber of perfumes and pulled out his scarves and warm shirts and returned to the study and sat by his body weeping and sniffing at his garments and said he could not be dead because they smelled his life in the clothes he had worn. And they sat by the dead Shikari while the servants lit incense all around him and candles and wicker lamps and put out the lights and his body seemed to glow all night. And Tips and I asked Raju, the young servant:

"Why did you leave? Did you not hear the shot?"

And Raju said: "I was scared. Before he sent me off to the market to buy him some medicines, he had been excited. He told me there was someone at the door, and I looked and I saw nobody there. Nobody at the door. And Sahib said: 'Ask him in. Pull up a chair for him beside my bed.' I was scared. I did as he said. And then he asked about my family and about the grandchildren and about you and the family and asked me whether all were happy. And I said there was joy everywhere. And he smiled, and said: 'Ask the man in.' And I pretended to ask the 'man' in. I opened the door and asked the 'man' to be seated on the chair next to the bed. And for five minutes Sahib spoke to this man on this empty chair. Words I couldn't understand. Then he asked me to show him out. I pretended to do so, and then he smiled and sent me about my business. Until I came back and found him in his shikar clothes and I thought he was preparing to go on a shoot, and I panicked and came to you."

2

The government doctor's words and those of Raju's spread through Raipur overnight. And Raipur sent messages to the nearby villages saying the doctor was

456

wrong and that Raju was right. The word spread that there was no suicide. The Shikari, had been visited in his last moments, not by Yamdoot, the messenger of death, the Grim Reaper, who comes for ordinary people, but by Bhagwan Shankar, himself, father of Ganesha and husband of Parvati, Goddess of Shakti and wealth. Destroyer of life, life-giver, known also as Shiva, Mahesh, Parvati's consort, assuming at will, the form of half-woman-half-man, destroyer of evil when he opens that dreaded Third Eye and when *Kalyug* – Evil – reigns supreme he dances the *Tandav*, the dance of death to kill the universe and create it anew. Shankar, the sages say, takes you not into *Swarga* – heaven – which might again give you rebirth but into a highly evolved family which can learn to evolve even farther into non-being in your next life – but straight into *moksha* – freedom from form and soul that Hal had instinctively told Lee about when he was rowing us in that boat into the rapids of the Potomac. To be slain personally by Shankar was rare, and an honor befitting a select few. This was also the Shikari atheist's last practical joke on God. To defy Him by taking his life into his own hands, and then re-inforce the faith of believers by enacting a legend that would go down in collective memory as further proof of the universal veracity of the 3,000-year-old *Vedas*.

That evening, while we wept and most of the grandchildren kept away from death in the study of their grandfather because most of them had never seen death before, the pilgrims began pouring in. In many ways, even though they invaded the privacy of our grief, we thanked them. Most of us knew nothing about the Hindu way of death. We had attended Christian funerals with priests in black robes and women in black robes, and in Hindi movies we had seen funeral pyres, and seen Rajiv Gandhi mourning his mother, but we had never mourned or cremated one of our own. And as Papa lay dead on the floor we did not know what to do next, we prep-school and missionary-educated 40 and 50-year-old somethings with not a smattering of what would next happen to Papa's smiling, dead, face. And all we did was cry. We appealed to Mama but she would not leave her puja room and she said, It's now up to you kids. And suddenly, we felt we had grown up. And we had to make grown-up decisions. But the local Punjabi community leaders, who had been settled in Raipur by Papa's family after Partition made us into children again.

CHAPTER XXXII

1

It was like Holi again. The visitors multiplied. Throughout the night. And into the morning. Early morning, with the pink sun, when Godot first dared to look at his dead grandfather and to touch him and to run to Seema and Sara as they sat still huddled in a corner of the study while the incense burned and they smothered their tears with woolen socks and scarves that the Shikari had worn. Women and children rarely come to visit the dead. But the Shikari's study buzzed with them as they circumambulated his body, touched his feet, and many of them who had never before seen him, wept, and when the early morning had turned into daylight, the local Punjabi refugee immigrants –the *biradiri* – took charge. They knew about death and its rituals. They had come to claim one of their own. Dare nobody else perform any other ritual than what they had honored for thousands of years. And damn the Shikari's oft-repeated request, when he was alive, that his body be quietly disposed off without the religious ceremonies he did not believe in. And I was reminded of my conversation with Sara in which she told me how Papa had confided to her about his inability to break with the traditions he despised. His final act was his final demonstration of apostasy but even now he belonged to tradition.

The men and women who had come only a few days ago for Holi were shooed off by the Punjabi Elders. Now Krishna and Prakash who had tried Seema and Dreamboat by fire, had taken over with some others and they asked me and Tips to stay away. They were now the keepers of the Shikari's soul and damn anybody who stood in their way.

Tips and I moved into another room, and Tips said:

"Do you really think he killed himself?"

I said: "What else? The perfect last ending. The Shikari, hunting himself to find the final answer to the Great Riddle. Unafraid. Un-tormented. Ever the atheist to defy God. Taking his life, for the first time, into his own hands, fucking tradition and every ritual, including a diseased death surrounded by doctors and weeping relatives, into his own hands. Planning his last shoot undisturbed by non-Shikari nerds. His own burlesque of the last hunt with his Australian jungle hat. Killing the tradition of everything he hated but was unable to fight because he was human. No, not suicide – he would consider that cowardice – but liberation, and finally an act of Being because he found it more difficult to fight what he disbelieved in while he was still alive and human. And now they don't know whether the human is still dead. Defiance. Oh, he had so many reasons for suicide in his early years, his children breaking up with their spouses (he was a hugely sentimental man), the family business collapsing, the two factory chimneys – the architectural memories of his father's new beginnings – being pulled down into a crashing earthquake to be replaced by single-family dwellings only a few months before he died. But that would be suicide. A cop-out. And the Shikari never copped out. He was simply killed by the thorns of his beloved scrub forests and marshes which were poisoned by men with smelly armpits or by the God who took their side. And while he aimed at his palate he aimed for a straight debate with all the other atheists in the sky."

2

We knew nothing about last rites. So the Punjabi community, grandfather's proteges and Papa's protectors, took over. We were spectators. Swiftly they stripped Papa in the study. His jungle hat. His camouflaged clothes. His pyjamas. His Guess watch. And he was nude and lifeless for the first time. And they carried him into the bathroom and laid him on the bare floor as they had done to their parents and their parents had done to theirs. The body can no longer be respected but it must still be cleaned. They had no tears. And they invited me and Tips into the bathroom where Papa lay stark nude on the cement floor and they had a bucket of fresh yogurt with which he was to be cleansed. And we were to rub it on his nude carcass. And for the first time in may years Tips broke down in sobs and clung to me, and said, This is what Hinduism and religion is? This is the treatment of this grand man, lying on this cement floor, naked, his pubic hair in sight of the very people whom he would not even shake hands with unless they mattered to him? This is death? This, defilement of grandeur? Why did they have to strip him? And I said, Yes, this is what it's all about. And when we were shy of rubbing Papa's body with yogurt the Punjabi traders and shopkeepers filled cups with it from the bucket and poured the stuff all over him and began to rub his body with love and they chanted *Om, Om, Om*, and I began to rub yogurt over Papa's body, all over, on his thighs, into his groin, Tips joined me, and rubbed Papa hard on his chest and face, and we smiled, for the first time, and then we filled buckets of water and poured them on his body and the yogurt, like diluted milk, spread across the floor – Krishna, the son of cowherds had been bathed in milk – and we smelled the pastoral ages again, and heard the sounds of Krishna's flute, and dead Papa was having the bath of his life, and then we dried him, and Tips was no longer afraid of his body, and we poured all his colognes over him, all the American after-shaves, and tied him up in a fresh white shroud with his smiling face fully visible and completely undisturbed in non-life.

We tied him to a wooden bier and covered him with marigolds. And we took him past the women, who would not be allowed to see the cremation on the banks of the Ganges 10 miles away, across which Khalifa had ferried our car on his barge many, many years ago and in which I had taught Godot to fish. Out of nowhere, it seemed, the Shikari's Willys jeep, sold many years ago, had arrived bedecked with flowers. It stood in the driveway and Papa's male children, and Godot, who now cried without shame, mounted the bier on the jeep, and the cortege drove towards the Ganges. And Mama, before the jeep left, clutched to Shikari's feet and she was weak with tears and she was shaking and Seema and Sara held on to her as she tried to break free and run after the Shikari in his shroud in the shikar jeep that was leaving forever. The whole town was silent as the procession passed through it. The shops had closed. No merchant had died. No millionaire had passed away. No powerful politician who could do favors had said his last goodbye. And no socialite was on the way to a cremation ground where the fancy ladies would come with fancy eyeshades and designer funeral saris and talk of Michelangelo. But thousands of townsfolk who had seen thousands of funeral processions pass by their shops and hovels and tenements and had yawned or simply, prayerfully bowed their heads in respect, walked with the Shikari's funeral procession all the way to the Ganges.

CHAPTER XXXlll

1

Godot, with his uncles, stood on the jeep holding onto one of the wooden planks of the bier, helping hold it steady during the bumpy ride so that it wouldn't simply jump out of the jeep and have us suffer the indignity of rolling Papa back on it in the middle of the road. The Pundits, who were also in the jeep, asked us to stop midway – a half-way house – where they unloaded the bier laid it inside a small Shiva temple, which had no walls, and smashed to the ground a huge pitcher of water, the first stage of the release of the soul in a tribute to Brahma, the Creator. Godot, dressed in a plain white kurta, as we all were, after having bathed just before the body began its journey to the Ganges, looked petrified. And then the bier was remounted on the jeep.

On the cremation ground, on the banks of the Ganges, an unusual mist had arisen. Piles and piles of wood had already been ordered and the cremation Pundit was already chanting. They made a bed of wood. And

465

they laid Papa's body on it. And they rubbed his body with congealed *ghee* (clarified cow-milk butter) like a ritual in basting a barbecue hen, and they put dollops of *ghee* on his eyes, his forehead, on his mouth. And expertly, they covered his body with special logs – four by the sides, several across his body, vertically and horizontally, layer by layer, until all we could see was his head through an opening (and I said to myself in the perversion of grief, "like a nigger in the woodpile") – and the Pundits chant from the ancient Sanskit texts:

"*Om Triyambakam Yajamahe, Sugandhim, Pushtivardhanam, Urvarukamiv Bandhanan Mrityur, Mukhsiya Ma Mritat.*" (O Lord of all the Three Universes – the Mind, the Soul, and the Eternal – We adore Thee, Thou art auspicious. Help us face and overcome any difficulty with the strength of Your power, and like the skin of a melon is peeled off but the stem remains forever rooted, peel off the skin of death from our eternal souls."

And Tips as the eldest brother was handed a burning twig from a specially-blessed fire in a nearby earthenware pot and with this he gave the first flame to Papa's pyre, and as the logs exploded into flames, we circumambulated the burning pyre which smelled of *ghee* and incense and camphor, chanting *Ram Nam Satya Hai* (God is Truth), and the smoke was rising into the mists and the water in the Ganges was languid. We poured more and more *ghee* on the flaming pyre to give the fire greater intensity and every now and then, the Pundit would probe with a stick inside the woodpile to test how rapidly the body was returning to the basic elements that constitute the universe. Before the cremation had begun and the Pundit was encircling the still unlit pyre and pouring Ganges water in circles, he said to us:

"Everything that is in the Brahmanda (universe) is also in the body – fire, air, sky, water, ether, minerals. The physical. The metaphysical is unknown. The air is within you with each breath, the earth forms your nails and hair, the liquid gushes through you, ether is the sky, and eternity and fire are the energy of earthly life. You will see all becoming ONE as this fire burns."

And as the fire burned, for more than an hour, as we stood and watched, and the ashes were blowing in the wind, and the middle of the pyre was now a glowing furnace, Tips looked into it and saw a fiery reddish-white dome-shaped object and he pointed at it and said to me:

"Look. That's your father's skull burning." And as is Hindu practice, the Pundit now handed Tips a long stick with a nail hammered at the end of it. And asked him to prod through the fire and to pierce the skull with the nail. And we were horrified. We had heard of this ritual. The belief is that this finally frees the soul from the body. And we had heard that the skull explodes like a firecracker when it is touched inside the burnuing pyre. And we were afraid and aghast and repelled. But it had to be done. And with a silent prayer to Papa for forgiveness – he would have castigated this ritual as paganism had he been alive – Tips gently prodded the skull and immediately it disintegrated, without even as much as a hissing sound, into a heap of ashes, and the body, for all purposes, was no more. And my revulsion turned into wonder and the pyre no longer looked forbidding and ominous and anti-human. It was a beautiful blaze, a smaller version of the post-shikar fires which we would light with dried kikkar branches to dry our wet clothes and warm ourselves when we emerged from the duck *jheels* with the Shikari after an all-evening shoot when the greylags and pintails had swarmed in for their evening flights.

2

On the bank of the Ganges where Papa was burning we sat a little distance away from the pyre in a circle while the Pundit chanted Sankrit *slokas* for the soul and recited what every Hindu family has been taught by the ancient sages: "The body is nothing more than a rented house. The soul has no use for it after a while, and it changes bodies as you change old clothes for fresh ones. Grieve not." And he quoted from the *Upanishads*: "What cannot be spoken with words, but that whereby words are spoken, know that alone to be Brahman, the Spirit, and not what people here adore." And he quotes the dialogue from the *Upanishads* between the young Nachiketa who meets Yamadoot, the Grim Reaper, the Spirit of Death, and asks him, When a man dies some say "he is" and some say, he "is not". And the answer he receives is contained in all ancient Hindu scriptures, especially the *Bhagwad Gita*: 'The soul is never born and never dies. The Atman, the Self is never born and never dies.' Or in the words of Krishna to Arjuna on the battlefield of Kurukshetra: 'The wise grieve not for those who live, and they grieve not for those who die – for life and death shall pass away.'"

We leave the pyre burning. It must burn all night and the cremation ground attendants will stoke it and ensure that not a piece of skin or hair remains in the ashes. We go home and bathe again and change into new clothes, and one of Papa's grand-daughters is in his room trying out his hairbrushes because they still smell of him. And she sobs very silently, very quietly. And that night, we sleep the sleep of the dead, and Mama prays and weeps and sleeps and early next morning we drive back to the banks of the Ganges – without the women – and the ashes are still warm, and there is yet another small ceremony to perform that we don't quite know about. "Picking Flowers" is as good a translation as any. My brothers and I and Godot are to sift through the ashes and pick out every remaining piece of bone. The Pundit douses the ashes repeatedly with Ganges water until they are now cool. And as we begin to put our hands inside the ashes, Godot is horrified. Then he sees me doing it. And he joins in. Bone chips, pieces of knee-caps, tiny finger bones, toe bones, remnants of ribs which look like the wish-bones that Mama and Papa used to pull apart at the dining table, all tiny and splintered and warm. And we wash each piece in a bucket full of Ganges water and drop them in a *kalash* – an urn the size of a medium water pitcher. And I say to myself, as I wash my father's bone plinters: Why, these bones could belong to anything, a sparrow, a dog, a jackal. So this is all that's left? There had to be, there must be a force that put these bones together and made a skeleton, and breathed life into them, that made them think and walk and talk and make jokes. These bones were nothing. Where was that something that was once these bones? That something had gone. And we felt no fear and death seemed suddenly ordinary and mundane and so dwarfed in stature when compared to life – to which only death gave structure and form and meaning. And I wished Serita and Simon and Lee and Hal were by my side picking out bones from cold ashes. And Tips was a child again, smiling and playing pranks as he did on Diwali puja nights when we all sang *Om Jai Jagdish Hare* with Mama and he flicked hot candle wax on me, and on this day, as we fill the urn with bone chips he flicks drops of water in which we were washing the bones, on Godot's face and smiles wickedly, and Godot does not find it funny at first and then he too smiles, and splashes back some of the water.

3

The religious ceremonies were endless, starting that day on the bank of the Ganges. The Pundit had us in a circle again. And he was sculpting. From fruit, rice, wholegrain, sugar, cardamom, sandalwood-shavings, kneaded wheat dough, he made fetal shapes, first the head, second the neck, third the chest, fourth the thighs, fifth the hands and feet, sixth the ears, nose, and throat, seventh the organs, eighth the bones, ninth the blood, and tenth, hunger and thirst. He was crafting gently and we watched him in awe. He said he was re-creating Papa's body just as Creation had done it, using the earth. And we, the inheritors of his flesh and blood were to bless it and pray for his soul again. And out of peepal leaves the Pundit built a little cradle into which he put these tiny shapes and gave it to Tips and asked him to rock it like a mother rocks a cradle and say: "Papa, just as you rocked us and put us to sleep and held us to your chest and smelled us when we were babies, so too, Papa you are now a baby, and I put you to my chest and I rock you into slumber, and I pray to Brahma the Creator, Vishnu the Preserver, and Shiva the estroyer and Creator that they should either take Papa into their bosom, to send him to heaven from where he can be born again into a good and wise family, or to free him from heaven and give him *moksha* and freedom from birth and having to learn all again about life and why it should start or be painful or end." The little leaf cradle was then passed on to me and I repeated the words. And the Pundit told us a story I still don't understand:

"When the first man died, he knocked at the door of Yamdoot, the Spirit of Death, who had first come to fetch him. But after Yamdoot had done his duty he went back into his ashram. And the man who had died had to

471

request Shravana, the *dwaarpaal* (doorkeeper) for an interview with Yamdoot. To ask him to guide him to the Holy Trinity to explain what this nonsense of death was all about. Yama, as Yamdoot is popularly known, said he knew nothing about it, that he was only a messenger boy, and took him to Brahma for an answer. And Brahma, told the man: 'All I know is how to create and make things happen, why don't you ask Vishnu for the answer?' And Yama took the man to Vishnu, and Vishnu said: 'All I know is how to protect and preserve and provide, why don't you go and ask Shiva, Maharaj Shankar? He's the main man, Destroyer and then a moody Creator before whom even the *rishis* cower in fear.' And the intrepid man, accompanied by a now shaking-with-fear Yama confronted Shiva, and Shiva shrugged and said: 'Why don't you go to the real person, Sadashiva, who is even more powerful than I am, the Supreme Power, and that Supreme Power is You, you idiot, and the man asked the Supreme Power the same question and the Supreme Power, which was him replied: "I know nothing except that life is a continuous circle and not even I can interfere with it."

In America we had heard nothing of this from Maharishi Mahesh Yogi or Rajneesh or the talkathons on Indian philosophy on television. Papa's bones had filled the urn that weighed no more than a couple of pounds. And we helped sweep the pyre of the ashes, scrubbed the place cleaner than it ever was, washed it clean with Ganges water, swept it with brooms, so as never to leave a sign of the last cremation for the next one – how much

472

cleaner than the hygienic habits of urban Indians – and we collected every cinder of ash into clean white sheets and we waded knee-deep into the Ganges and we emptied them into the river and they floated into the breeze as they settled on every visible part of the river and we saw the marigold flowers bobbing up and down before they became water-heavy and sunk to the bottom. And we carried the urn with Papa's bones home.

CHAPTER XXXIV

1

The bone-carrying *kalash* was put inside a small Shiva temple for a day. At home, the prayers by non-stop Pundits who had dared not enter our home while the Shikari lived, continued by the hour, *havans*, fire ceremonies, packets of rupees being showered on them, gold rings for their fingers, all of them wishing the Shikari a holy journey to heaven, many of them having never read a verse from the *Upanishads* or the *Vedas*, and recitals every afternoon from the *Ramayana*, sometimes brilliantly explained by Pundits who knew, otherwise chanted by rote, as Mama listened.

The bones were to be immersed into the Ganges, as we had decided, a few days later as per tradition, where Papa had been cremated. But Mama was adamant. No, she said, they must be taken to Haridwar, the Himalayan foothill city of the Gods in which the Ganges, as it entered the plains of India from the Himalayas, the Holy Ganges that had first sprouted from the head of Lord Shiva, was first spotted by ordinary people before it began to wind

475

its way through the Indo-Gangentic plains in a nearly thousand- mile journey, sustaining life, during which it also passed the outskirts of Raipur where the Shikari was cremated, before it poured its power into the Bay of Bengal. The Ganges, like Jesus of the Cross is a scapegoat. Day in and day out it crucifies itself, especially in Haridwar (the Door to the Gods) where the sinners bathe, day and night and the Ganges takes on the dirt of their sins, purifies them, and carries the dirt of their sins on her ripples as she travels through India on her endless Odyssey.

Mama wanted Papa's bones to be purified even farther. Only in Haridwar. We could not refuse this last wish of hers. She accompanied us to the temple where the urn had rested and she broke down again when she realized what was in it. It was the last time she broke down. And she went back to her puja room. And Pundit Sharma and I and Tips and Tally drove to Haridwar. We spoke little. And there the Shikari, or so we like to believe now, and superstitions are more potent than reality, played another joke on us. We had done the trip to Haridwar several times, on tourist journeys. We knew every turn and village on this 200-mile drive from Raipur. And Pundit Sharma had done this journey since he was a child, learning Haridwar's religious etiquettes from his father. And at a crucial juncture on that trip, it seemed we all fell asleep. For when the road suddenly looked unfamiliar we realized we had veered 50 miles away and were on the entry to a forbidden road that led towards Haridwar through a densely wooded national forest.

Forbidden because it was potholed, and full of craters. But it was one of the last remaining rain-forests of the Shivalik mountains. The forest guards warned us against going through it. But Tips, who was driving a car that probably could not make it through our scrub forests in the old days, said, Bullshit. And we floated through the greenest, most dense, mysterious forest I had ever seen. We saw families of kalij pheasants, not seen in years, scurry across the damp mud-road. A rogue elephant, and there were not too many in those parts then, had preceded us, leaving mounds of droppings and we could see where he had rubbed his back against the thick teak and sal trees, and pulled branches down with his trunk, maybe only minutes earlier before he had escaped into the forest, and the wooden bridges over the streams were ruptured and the car skidded and slid all the way until we reached Haridwar. And it was cold and we carried the urn of bones. And when the Pundits accosted us for the last ceremonies, repetitions of rituals we had undergone endlessly, Tips said, Fuck Off, and we gently emptied Papa's bones into the swift Ganges, where they sank immediately to the bottom and we drove straight back home and reached late in the night and hugged Mama and she was happy and she slept well.

On the auspicious thirteenth day there was another ceremony which I hated. But we went through it. Hundreds and hundreds of village folk and townsfolk were invited to a feast of scrumptious vegetarian food. The Shikari would have puked at the smells and the farts and the burps as overfed people uttered their appreciation. The last day of official mourning. And then we had to feed 13 Pundits. We had to serve them ourselves as they sat on the floor outside Papa's study in his verandah where he would think thrice before letting in a holy man, most of whom he considered charlatans. But Mama had her way. And like so many pot-bellied, Brahmanical Oliver Twists, they Asked For More. And we fed them, and poured water from jugs while they washed their hands and they burped. And we were commanded to reserve a few *chappatis* for the animals – one for a dog, one for a crow. And the Brahmins left but not without demanding one final ceremony – *godaan* – the gifting of a cow to the poor.

Mama did not approve of this, but the Pundits in their cremation-contracts, had insisted on it. Of course everything came for a price. And so we found a cow. It belonged to a poor man who swept the compound of our estate. And as ceremony dictated, he brought this cow into Papa's study to be blessed, and as he led it around, the darned bovine lifted its tail and began pissing over Papa's lower bookshelves And Papa's Spinoza, and Trevelyan's Social History, and one of Churchill's tomes on World War II (*The Gathering Storm*) are still stained with cow-piss. And Sara was mad. Enough is enough, she said. She chased the cow out, the poor animal slipped, righted itself, and tail raised, raced back across the lawn leaving behind trails of frightened dung. And we paid off the Pundits, pretty huge sums. And the main Pundit, who had been at the funeral pyre on the banks of the Ganges, and from whom we had received some knowledge, he too demanded his loot, and we gave it to him, a bed, quilts, watches, flour and rice and sugar, and he was – in traditional style – lifted out through our gate sitting on his bed, while, as we were instructed by tradition – we pelted his back with little stones, a small gesture indicating that if he came back for any other relatives too soon, he might get a boulder thrown right on his bald head.

CHAPTER XXXV

1

The Raipur household continued without the Shikari. We hunted, Godot became an even better shot. But hunting was now a ritual of memory. The Monsoon came only in sporadic spurts. The summers were not that warm. And in the winters we hardly even wore sweaters. The chamber of perfumes remained as it had been for the next couple of years. But we brought down the quilted ceiling and replaced it with a brand new roof and Papa's offspring saw to it that every Diwali the house was painted and the gardens and mango trees received water. The villagers came and went. They begged for inheritors who would continue the old tradition, but as Sara had told me many years ago: "We all have our own lives to live," we lived our own lives, separately, in our own metropolitan worlds in India, and some of us were richer than others – our family, I mean – and some of us traveled abroad many times a year on lucrative business trips and I remained a reporter, traveling whenever I could, to see Mama, who had built herelf a brand new open-air temple, the proceeds of which she donated to the poor. And Mama was happy. She prayed, she slept, and secretly, she even chewed tobacco that made her groggy and forgetful. Tally was immersed in his success as a businessman. Tips, a retired engineer, into still another wife, was house-proud and distant. Sara was still producing children at age 40 and writing wonderful poetry. Coming close to divorce and then backing away at the last moment. Seema had tried to get back to Dreamboat, but Dreamboat had made the impossible demand that she share his bedroom – something she hadn't done after the first few years of their marriage – and she was looking for a new apartment and seriously thinking of moving into Papa's quarters, at least for part of the year, because none of the brothers had expressed any interest in them, and Papa had left no will and the Raipur household belonged to anybody who loved it.

Serita had written, as she always did. She wanted Godot to be part of her life again. Serita had now crossed 50. And Godot was 24, near about the same age that I had been when I had departed for America. And Seneca, if I read Serita right, had grown into a gorgeous, raven-haired 13-year-old who had started e-mailing her brother in India and now wanted to see him and be with him and kiss him and caress him. Serita never mentioned the asshole who made her laugh. Maybe they were not even together anymore. I didn't dare ask, out of jealousy. But we decided Godot would go back to America to his mother. He had degrees and experience and Clinton's America was booming with jobs.

I drove Godot to the International Airport in Delhi. He carried a cricket manual in his handbag and a hunting cap the Shikari had gifted him. I could not run with him to the tarmac and across the runway to the Boeing 747 like Papa had done with me when I had taken off for America about 30 years ago. India was in the grip of modernity and terrorism and the airport security was tighter than you find at Tel Aviv. I could only see him off at the entrance because I was not allowed to go any farther. And I asked him, Do you really want to go? And he said, I must. I must discover the Old Country again. And I hugged him, and I kissed him in the neck because he was much taller than I, and I tasted his tears as they dripped down onto his neck, and they tasted of wild marsh water and they smelled of baby milk. And Serita – had her hair turned gray? – and Seneca would be waiting for him and maybe they would take him fishing, or maybe he would teach them to hunt.

The End